"Stop talking," he ordered, and leaned over the table until his scarred, perfect mouth was far too close to hers.

"And if you bark at me again, I will tie you up and make you howl in a way you've never dreamt of, Breton lass."

They were leaning that way, each half across the table, staring at each other, angry and aroused—at least Eva was; Jamie's face revealed little—when the door of the tavern squeaked open, then slammed shut. She tore her gaze away; habit too well formed, from too many years of running and hiding.

In this case, as in so many others, it saved her life.

The squint-eyed men who'd kidnapped Father Peter had just walked into the tavern. If they saw her now, they would recognize her. Then they would take her. Mayhap kill her. And Father Peter would be lost.

She slowly shifted her gaze back to Jamie in wedged degrees, like the pointed crest of a sundial. The sound of bootheels hitting packed earth thumped inside her head with each pump of blood. Trembling rippled through her in the way of a river, with fierce currents, fear and fury mingling as they so often did, so that she could equally run or attack and not know which until she was already doing it.

But in this moment, like a hand reaching out with a gift, came a new idea: *Kiss him.*

And so she did.

Defiant is also available as an eBook

Praise for Kris Kennedy and her seductive medieval novels

The Irish Warrior

"This medieval romance has it all: tenderness, romance, danger, suspense, politics, sex and a dash of fantasy. . . . The sex is hot and the suspense is breathtaking. This one is impossible to put down."

—*Romantic Times*

"An unusual setting and a plot that comes out of the mists of legends. Kris Kennedy has penned a rare, steamy, and adventurous love story with a wild Irish warrior and a strong woman of substance. . . . Sexy and adventurous, intriguing and tender, *The Irish Warrior* is a page-turner full of high drama and hot, steamy romance!"

—Jill Barnett, *New York Times* bestselling author

"A sexy, taut medieval that'll leave you breathless and wanting more. Kris Kennedy has penned the perfect romantic adventure, overflowing with gorgeous imagery, rich characterization, and an unforgettable voice. Passionate characters caught in a page-turning adventure. . . . I devoured every delicious word."

—Roxanne St. Claire, *New York Times* bestselling author

"Medieval romance fans rejoice—Kris Kennedy captures the essence of old Ireland in this engaging, sexy adventure! The rich and imaginative story pulled me in from the start, and an irresistible hero kept me riveted till the end."

—Veronica Wolff, national bestselling author

The Conqueror

"A strong, sensual medieval romance about sworn enemies who fall in love against a tapestry of love, greed, revenge and betrayal. The characters are well written, the history accurate, and the action engaging and intense."

—*Romantic Times*

"With her debut release, Kris Kennedy has given us a stunning tale of betrayal and redemption. . . . On the surface this would seem to be just another historical romance novel, but hidden in its depths are real treasures."

—Book Binge

"If you've been looking for a strong medieval romance, *The Conqueror* is an impressive debut, indeed."

—All About Romance

"I blushed, smiled, and then happily went back and started reading *The Conqueror* again."

—Wild on Books

"If you're an old-school romance fan, especially one who adores medievals? Yeah, just stop reading my review right now, run out and buy *The Conqueror*. It has everything you'll want and more."

—The Misadventures of Super Librarian

DEFIANT

Kris Kennedy

POCKET BOOKS
New York   London   Toronto   Sydney

Pocket Books
A Division of Simon & Schuster, Inc.
1230 Avenue of the Americas
New York, NY 10020

This book is a work of fiction. Names, characters, places, and incidents either are products of the author's imagination or are used fictitiously. Any resemblance to actual events or locales or persons, living or dead, is entirely coincidental.

First Pocket Books paperback edition May 2011

POCKET and colophon are registered trademarks of Simon & Schuster, Inc.

For information about special discounts for bulk purchases, please contact Simon & Schuster Special Sales at 1-866-506-1949 or business@simonandschuster.com.

The Simon & Schuster Speakers Bureau can bring authors to your live event. For more information or to book an event contact the Simon & Schuster Speakers Bureau at 1-866-248-3049 or visit our website at www.simonspeakers.com.

Designed by Jacquelynne Hudson
Cover illustration by Craig White

Manufactured in the United States of America

10 9 8 7 6 5 4 3 2 1

ISBN 978-1-4391-9590-1
ISBN 978-1-4391-9592-5 (ebook)

To the men in my life, for letting me be mom, wife, and writer, and for being so supportive on those days when it was mostly the latter. But especially my husband, first and foremost, for everything.

To my son, for bringing me sharpened pencils with bright fresh erasers—about fifty of them—and laying them quietly beside me as I worked.

To my wonderful agent, Barbara Poelle, for knowing who's going to love what, then forcing them to read it when they're really, really busy.

To my fabulous editor, Abby Zidle, for a whole lot of patience and assistance as I trekked through this story without a muse.

To my readers, who love hot romance, hard-headed knights, headstrong women, and lots of adventure. Here's to a long journey ahead for us!

Acknowledgments

I want to especially thank V.K. and D.M. and L.C., who set aside their own work and families to do last-minute reads of this huge manuscript for one reason: to help me out. You restored my confidence. I owe you.

To my friend Rachel Grant, who always points out when I have too many moving eyebrows and too-slow-moving scenes. I thank you. So do my readers.

And a big hug to my buddies in the soon-to-be-renamed Destination Debut group, who have helped me not only feel saner but be stronger.

One

England, June 1215

t first, it appeared they both wanted the same cock.

But as Jamie watched, he realized the slender woman wasn't after the rooster at all. And neither, of course, was he.

He settled back in the shadows cast by the knobbly stone buildings along Cheap Street as clouds piled up in the twilight sky. He'd only noted the rooster because a priest had been studying it, and Jamie was on the hunt for a priest. But this was simply some poor vicar studying a fowl. Neither was his quarry.

Nor were they the woman's. Her gaze slid away with disinterest.

On opposite sides of the street, they were each tucked into dirt-packed alleyways, eyeing up the celebrations in the market square. The evening mists floated in flat ribbons around people's ankles as they rushed through the darkening streets. Jamie tilted his head to keep the woman in sight. Hood drawn forward over her head, lantern extinguished, an almost motionless stance, all bespoke hunting.

He should know.

Taking swift inventory of the busy, heedless market square, he slipped out of his alley, making for hers. Skirting the block, he came up behind her as the fair stalls closed up, leaving room for the more ferocious nighttime entertainments to come.

"Found it yet?" he murmured.

She jumped a foot in the air and tripped sideways. Quickly, with a graceful movement, she righted herself, her slim hand lightly touching the wall, fingertips trembling.

All he could see were the dark things about her. Her eyebrows slanted low in suspicion, little black ink swipes on a wide, pale forehead, framed by the dark hood.

"I beg your pardon?" she said in a cool voice. But her hand had slid beneath her cape.

She had a weapon. How . . . worthy of note.

He tipped his head in the direction of the crowd. "Have you found yours yet?"

She looked utterly nonplussed as she took a step back and hit the wall. "My what, sir?" But even in the midst of her confusion, she continued to appraise the crowd, swift, sweeping surveys of it and everyone within. Just as he did when he was on the hunt.

"Your quarry. Who are you after?"

She turned her full attention to him. "I am shopping."

He leaned his shoulder against the far wall, a state of repose. *I'm not dangerous*, it said. Because she might be. "The bargains are awful back here. You'd be better served to actually speak with a merchant."

Her eyes were dark grayish, but for all that, highly forceful. She watched him for a long moment, then seemed to come to some decision. Her hand slid out of her cape and she turned back to the crowd.

"Perhaps I am fleeing my husband and his terrible temper," she said. "You should leave now."

"How terrible would his temper be?"

She punched a small fist into the air. "This terrible."

He turned and surveyed the crowd with her. "Shall I kill him for you?"

She gave a low murmur of laughter. The dark hood she had drawn over her head swooped in small waves beside her pale face. Long black tendrils of hair drifted out around her collarbone. "How chivalrous. Would you so easily? But then, I did not say I *was* fleeing a husband. Simply that I might be."

"Ah. What else might you be doing?"

"Perhaps stealing roosters."

Ah. She was cognizant, then, that anyone watching her would have thought she was intent on the rooster. In which case, he oughtn't to be feeling the urge to smile whatsoever. A woman who knew she was being watched was a dangerous woman.

He turned and peered into the square where Father Peter was rumored to be coming for an evening meet with an old friend, a rabbi. Jamie had explicit instructions, which began with "grab the thick-skulled priest" and ended with "bring him to me." A ruthless royal summons to a skilled illuminator and agitator who had declined previous invitations. But then, a great many people declined invitations from King John these days, because so often, those who accepted were never heard from again.

Jamie scanned the market. The rooster in question was in a cage atop a cage atop a cage, all filled with bantams trying to strut. The topmost one, drawing all the attention, was a magnificent creature.

"Green tail feathers?"

She nodded. He nodded along with her, as if it were common to skulk in alleys and discuss animal thievery. "Pretty. Do you steal often?"

"Do you?"

"All the time."

She turned her pale face to him, her gray eyes cool and searching. "You lie."

"Perhaps. Much like you."

Why did he care? She was neither quarry nor obstacle,

therefore outside his realm of interest. But something about her bespoke the need to attend.

One of her graceful dark eyebrows arched up ever so slightly. "Were we to be honest with one another? I did not realize this."

"No, you would not," he rejoined, looking back to the crowd. Still no sign of the priest. "You don't often inhabit such warrens as this. I, on the other hand, regularly cavort with bandits, thieves, and the like, who inhabit such crevices of humanity as this alley, so I know such things."

From the corner of his eye, he saw one of her cheekbones rise. She was smiling. "Ah. How convenient for me. A tutor." She was quiet. "Cavort? Do thieves cavort?"

"You should see them around a fire."

She laughed, a small thing. He was vaguely surprised to find probing the intent of this stranger so enjoyable. He rarely . . . enjoyed.

They were silent for a moment, an oddly companionable condition.

In front of them passed a veritable river of humanity in the throes of madness. Or rather, jubilation, but of the mad sort. Civil war was imminent. On streets from Dorset to York, there was the feel of celebration in the air, a diffuse revelry that made men drunk. And reckless. Come midnight, it would turn to violence. It always did. The realm was like a fever, bright and hectic, flush with sickness.

"I am certain I ought to be frightened of you," she said quietly.

"You most certainly ought," he said grimly.

"Stab you with a blade, perhaps."

He shifted his shoulder against the wall and looked down at her. "We needn't go that far."

"I knew this, of course," she mused in a cool, graceful voice. "That you were dangerous. When I first saw you."

"When was that? When I crept up behind you in an alley?"

Again, the lift of her cheekbones, like alabaster curving. "When I espied you across the road." She tilted her head slightly, indicating the church on the other side of the square.

Ah. She had good eyesight. He had a way of blending in, being unseen. It was part of what made him so successful. That and the ruthlessness.

"Did you now?" he murmured. "What gave me away? The alley, the skulking?"

She glanced over. "Your eyes."

"Ah."

"Your clothes."

He looked down in surprise.

"The manner in which you move."

He looked up and crossed his arms in silence, inviting her to continue. She obliged him.

"Your smell."

His arms fell. "My smell—?"

"Your smile," she said, turning away.

"Well, that is about everything," he said, anything to keep her talking, for she was growing more intriguing with each word that fell from her lips, although he wasn't certain it was for the usual reasons. The vital ones, the sort that kept a man quick or made him dead.

"How do I smell, precisely? As if I am a hungry bear, or as if I am coated in the blood of my victims?"

"As if you get what you want."

She had a good nose as well, then. Smart and comely. And lying.

She looked back at the crowds rushing past down the streets. "And what of you, sir? Are you intent on a rooster?"

"No."

"A whore?"

He snorted.

"A head of garlic, perhaps?"

He paused, then, on impulse, told the truth. "A priest."

She started ever so slightly, a small, repressed ripple that shook the trailing black ends of her hair, which is when he had his first suspicion things were about to go downhill to such a degree he might never climb back up again.

The startle could simply have been surprise at his offhand and irreverent reference to a man of God. Or that they were speaking at all. Or that she hadn't been assaulted yet, huddled in an alley with only a blade for protection.

But Jamie had spent three-quarters of his life determining when people were hiding something, and she most certainly was.

She pushed away from the wall. "I must go retrieve my cock."

He grinned. "You will be missed."

She smiled over her shoulder, that cool, stunning smile, and he knew why he'd dallied with her. "You will not be lonely long. The Watch will come for you soon, I am sure."

He laughed. "Take care," he said, a caution that came from some heretofore unknown crevasse inside, for he hadn't seen it coming and didn't even recognize it as it emerged.

Again that little smile, which wasn't cold, he realized. It was covert. Clandestine. Beautiful.

She slipped from their narrow refuge and out into the moving tide of bodies, heading directly toward the green-feathered cock, her worn black cape swaying as she floated across the muck. Then, just before she reached the cages, she veered sharply to the left—and his downhill ride began.

By the time Jamie found the rabbi's home where the priest and his dangerous manuscripts were said to be staying, the rabbi was gone. The priest was gone. The documents were gone. And the gray-eyed woman was gone.

King John would not be pleased.

Jamie went after her.

Two

ight I intrude?"

The softly spoken words hauled him up midstride as he barreled down the street. He snapped his gaze down. It was she, the dark-eyed elf who'd stolen his quarry.

He battled off the urge to shake her, seeing as she was about to talk without such inducements. Still, it barely lessened the urge. "What?" He spit the word out. "Where is the priest?"

"Some terrible and smelly men have taken him."

This brought him up short. It must have shown. She nodded sympathetically. "Yes, indeed. I was equally shocked."

"Perhaps not to the same degree."

"No, perhaps not, because you are with two shocks, and I have only the one. But still, it is a terrible shock, is it not?"

"Terrible," he agreed grimly. "Are you saying you did not take the priest?"

"Indeed, no. But I would use your help to recover him."

How did one respond to this? "Would you?"

She looked at him sharply. "Did you think they were *your* men who have run away with Father Peter? They did not look like your men, so do not worry that you have been successful in stealing my priest."

"I was not worried," he said drily. He did not use men, in

general, but for his single friend and boon companion Ry, who was at present saddling horses for a ride they might not be taking this evening with a thick-skulled priest in hand. "Why do you say the men weren't mine?"

"Come," she said, tugging on his sleeve. "They went this way."

He followed her down the narrow alley, his senses alert, allowing she could be trusted this far, to skulk down another alley together without having her turn and bash his skull in.

"I know they are not your men," she answered as they hurried through the twisting cobbled and dirt pathways, "because these men had tiny eyes and looked mean and brutish. Your men would look dirty and dangerous."

He eyed the back of her hooded figure as it swayed down the alley. "Are you wooing me?"

"Woo? None of this 'woo.' I am telling you, these offensive men have the curé. We must retrieve him, like a sack of wheat."

"Why?"

She stopped at the edge of the alley just before it crossed over the High Street. It was busy, people everywhere, hurrying home. It wasn't so much that it was dark, but the storm clouds had brought an early end to the evening. Lanterns were lit, people heading home or out into the dark, windswept night. Awnings of shops were being lowered and locked, while abovestairs, shuttered windows flared into flickering orange strips, glowing with candlelight as families and friends gathered in warmth for food and company.

Jamie scorned this time of night.

His companion turned to him, her curving dark eyebrows now flattened in reprimand. "'Why?' What does this mean, your question 'Why?'"

Over the top of her head, Jamie spotted two men dragging an insentient priest—now wearing a cap atop his tonsured head—between their arms. Three additional men in leather armor thudded behind. The five of them turned sharply down a street that led only one place: the docks.

He tugged on his new companion's arm, stopping her forward progress, drawing her eye.

In fact, he had no intention of allowing her to remain conscious for much longer. But if he knocked her out now, people would notice. And if he let her go now, he suspected she would run after those men and trip them or bite them or something equally attention-getting, anything to stop them from escaping with "her priest." And attention was the last thing he wanted.

Three different parties were now interested in Father Peter. A street full of drunk revelers seemed an unnecessary addition.

So he would bide his time. Those men might be headed to the docks, but the way they spread out and began approaching different vessels told him they had no boat of their own. They would not gain berth on so much as a fishing wherry at this hour, not without going into the tavern nearest to the quay, the Red Cock, where the captains, oarsmen, and other waterborne flotsam congregated.

The men with Father Peter had just bypassed it. Whereas Jamie was standing right in front of it.

Eventually they would figure it out. So he would wait and, betting that all *five* of them would not come into the tavern together, priest slumped between their arms, he would use their splitting up to bring down whichever unfortunates were sent in, once they came back out again.

It was a plan. That it was also improvised and risky mattered naught: he'd spent his entire life being just that.

And he decided, looking down, he would use his bided time to learn what he could from the dark-cloaked waif before he rendered her at best not a nuisance, at worst, bound and gagged.

He tugged her back into the shadows. "It means I want an answer. Why do you want the priest? Who sent you for him?"

"Me?" She turned, her pale face angry. "Why do *those men* want him, that is the question of better asking."

"I do not care 'of better asking.' I want an answer."

She plowed forward as if he were dirt beneath her anger. "These squinty-eyes are carting him away right now. You ought to care. Why do *you* want him? Mayhap we can start there, on our want of answers. Indeed, this is the sort of question I like better."

"He has something I want."

His swift, honest reply brought her up short. She blinked, long lashes sweeping down over her eyes. He followed her glance down. The tips of battered shoes poked out from beneath the hem of her skirts. She looked up.

"Does he now?" Her pale cheeks were flushed. "That is no answer. Of course he has something you desire; why else seek him? It is why I am after him as well. He has many things I want. I am desperate for these things."

"What sorts of things?"

"Baubles. A length of scarlet. Contracts he was witness to. Trunks of coin and relics from the Holy Land."

She'd mentioned many things, none of which were the things Father Peter was being hunted for. Which was interesting, seeing as she'd named just about everything else under the sun.

"Tell yourself whatever brings you comfort," she finished, turning back to the High, "and let us be about it. Please. Or they shall escape."

A rumble of thunder rolled through the sky. He folded his fingers around the underside of her arm, just above her elbow.

"Mistress, I do not tell myself things to bring comfort." He pulled her so close she had to crane her neck to peer into his eyes. "I care naught for comfort, or for you. You may not realize this, but I've shown great restraint thus far. You lie to me, yet tell me nothing at all. That is difficult to do. I am impressed. And aggravated." Her breath came out a little shorter and faster. "So why not try a good lie, and we can 'be about it.'"

"He is my uncle," she said swiftly.

"Peter of London is your uncle," he echoed, incredulous.

"As much as."

"Which means not at all. Do you know what your 'uncle' has done?"

"Angered your king."

"Mightily."

He saw her swallow. "Everyone angers your silly, stupid king. Silly, dangerous, killing king. Perhaps those men are from the king himself," she added ominously.

"Perhaps," he said almost regretfully. "But 'ware, woman, for I am made of worse."

Color receded from her face like a tide going out. She jerked on her arm and he opened his fingers. She stumbled backward, breathing hard. The thoughts tumbling through her mind might as well have been carved on the swinging tavern sign above her head: *Danger. Run.*

Yet she'd known he was about danger when she enlisted his help. She might not have realized he was from King John— "silly, dangerous, killing king" was a grave understatement— but she knew he wasn't there to save her "uncle." She'd taken a chance and trusted him.

A regrettable error in judgment.

He placed a gloved hand on the door, just above her head, and pushed it open.

"Inside. Now."

Three

"Inside?" Eva planted her feet and glared up at the impossible man. "No. Why?"

"Because I need to speak with you," he said, turning her by the shoulders. His hands were strong. "Because I do not wish to get drenched when the skies open. Because if you do not, I shall resort to more extreme measures than simply asking."

She stilled.

"That's better. Now listen. Those men must be allowed to get through the town gates," he explained in that low, confiding tone, the sort that coated tongues of courtiers and men of power, not ruffians in black cloaks. He was changeable, then. Untrustworthy. "I cannot manage a mêlée at the city gates. Can you?"

She hesitated, then shook her head.

"Good. We are agreed. We shall allow your squinty-eyed men passage through, then run them to ground."

She eyed him suspiciously. "And who shall have Father Peter?"

He placed a gloved hand on the door above her head. "I suggest we take one assault at a time. Go. Inside. And sit."

Eva did, because her choices were fairly limited: follow the danger, or lose Father Peter.

Really, choices like this made things ever so much simpler. Danger did not frighten her. Or rather, she'd grown numb to it. Confusion frightened her. Not having a course of action frightened her. And darkness. The dark terrified.

At least this rogue had a plan, as well as a wickedly sharp sword and an arsenal of blades. Therefore, she would stick to him like pitch until they rescued Father Peter. Then she'd sidle away like so much smoke and he'd never see her again.

But this speaking commands to her as if she were a dog, that was simply unnecessary.

He pushed the tavern door open. It creaked. What in England did not creak? Damp, cold, full of rusting iron and drunkards, it was not what she desired. But here she was, with a mission darker than rescuing priests whose illuminated texts had lighted her world ten years ago and made her finally agree that there was indeed salvation in the world, even if it was never to be hers.

Her dark-eyed proteus pointed to a table by the far wall. "Over there. Sit."

Again with the commands. She wanted to growl. Instead, she looked around at the rickety wooden benches and the fat, loud Englishmen draped like linens over a counter, behind which a phalanx of whores resided. Yet, she admitted, it was not so different from France. Perhaps in the lack of wall hangings. A few would not go amiss, to cover the stains and pitted gaps and the terrible draft to which they gave encouragement.

But in truth, men hung like linens over whores in every corner of the world she'd ever seen, and the English could hardly be faulted for choosing ale to pin them up rather than, say, a fine Burgundy.

Her *routier* in his heavy boots tromped over the bulging plank floors toward the back counter that ran the length of the room. He was naught but danger, she'd known that—sooth, he'd told her so—but now the evidence was revealed more fully in the flickering shadows of torchlight.

His hair-roughened square jaw could denote either a dull blade or a rough nature, but his hair, barely tethered by a leather strip, long, dark, and uncombed, bespoke only outlawry. His cape was nondescript, calf-length. Beneath he wore a black, quilted surcoat, sleeveless, covering what she supposed was a mail shirt, although he wore a longer-sleeved tunic as well, as if to conceal what lay beneath. Both surcoat and tunic hung to midthigh, slit up the sides. Mucky knee-high boots completed the ensemble, but it was the dark hose, molded tight over his thighs, that kept Eva's attention riveted far longer than was necessary. She dragged her gaze up.

He wore no insignia on his dark surcoat, bore no identifying colors. Yet everyone either *had* a lord or *was* a lord. Even a feared, ruthless mercenary, a Brabançon, identified himself with someone. Usually the English king. By the look in this one's eye, 'twas a simple enough matter to place him there.

But somehow, she couldn't believe something so . . . beautiful could be so awful. And he was beautiful indeed, to a hard line, a masculine magnificence, all long, lean contours of hard heat and piercing eyes. A beast in his prime.

He looked over his shoulder and scowled when he saw she had not "come," was not "over there."

"Sit," he growled. "And stay."

She narrowed her eyes and, very softly, barked.

He froze.

The others in the alehouse were far too drunk or otherwise occupied to note or care that a woman was barking at a man. But her escort was neither drunk nor distracted. If the look on his face was any indication, he was startled. And perhaps a bit angry. Or more than a bit.

Eva sat, her back to the wall.

Most of the other tables were filled with men and some women, but most stood in small groups, drinking and laughing. Several torches burned in iron rings bolted to the walls, casting russet-yellow puddles of light a few paces out. On each table sat a few fat candles, stuck in swamps of tallow. A group of men in low boots and cloaks clustered at the far end of the narrow room, half-bent, shouting encouragement to a pair of bone dice that went clicking over the ground toward the wall. A roar went up; someone had won.

No one attempted to temper the revelry. A tavern open after *courve-feu* mattered naught in these days, with the country tottering on the edge of rebellion against its king.

Her escort returned to the table. A woman hurried after, carrying two tankards. Ale, Eva decided as she peered down at the grainy, brownish muck.

"Whatever this cost, you paid too much," she informed him, looking up.

The rogue stared down at her for a long moment, as if debating some course. Perhaps whether to stick a knife between her ribs. But the die was cast now, for good or for ill. One could only hope this rogue did not have sticking urges just now.

He finally sat. Unfortunately, he did so by dropping onto the short bench right beside her, his back to the wall, his hip hard against hers. Then he reached for his tankard.

She was shocked by the feel of his thigh beside hers. Unaccustomed to feeling shocked by thighs, she shifted about, angling around to consider him.

"You may not realize this, Sir Rogue, but in other parts of the world, people do not speak to other people as if they have fangs and paws."

His eyes shifted to her—how blue they were, even in this dim candlelight—then he set down his mug and wiped the back of his gloved hand over his mouth.

"Nay? Fascinating. Whereas I have found, in almost every region of the world, women do not bark." He let those blue eyes travel over her, starting at her neckline, moving boldly down. Her face grew warm. "Northumbria," he said finally, looking back at her face.

"Pardon?"

"Your tongue. Northumbria, mayhap Wales." His gaze traveled over her again. Even in the dim torchlight and candlelight, his male appraisal of her as a woman was clear. "English."

"Celt. Brittany," she countered swiftly.

"Perhaps," he murmured, clearly disbelieving her.

Her cheeks flushed hot. So inconvenient, these intelligent, cunning men with swords. She was dismayed to find her accent detectable. She'd worked hard for it not to be, to leave *everything* behind when she had fled England ten years ago. Home, family, accents: everything had been tossed overboard on the Channel crossing.

With this one, though, perhaps little would remain concealed. Or safe.

The broad hands gloved to the knuckle resting on the table looked very capable of mayhem. But then there was that vague hint of a dimple to the left of his mouth, if only he were to smile deeply. Surely it was a thing designed to make women tremble.

Which only made him more dangerous. No, the things that mattered, the things Eva must attend, were the scars, one carved across the edge of his upper lip, up over one high cheekbone, till it disappeared beneath his hair. Another, more jagged, sliced at his hair-roughened chin.

But most important, his eyes. Glittering, witching-hour blue, and, above all, perceptive.

Perhaps she had made a mistake in enlisting his assistance.

"So close, sir, your guesses about me," she rejoined, keeping her voice light and nonchalant. Her one abiding talent: feign as if nothing mattered. "Are you as skilled with chess as you are with riddling games? I shall never play with you. The heart trembles."

One side of his mouth tipped up, that faint dimple did indeed dimple, and her heart did tremble, a little bit. But it was such a great deal much more than she'd ever known before, that it felt like a miniature quake in her belly, revealing vast, heated chasms below.

"I do, in fact, play chess."

She held up her hand, palm out, into the small ring of light cast by the tiny candle stub on their table. "*Non.* I cannot bear it. Merels instead, mayhap?"

He looked surprised. "Dice?"

"Have I offended? Perhaps Whoop and Hide, then, like small children. I shall hide, and you will never find me."

He gave a low laugh. "I could find you, lass."

Shivers danced through her belly, hot, trembly things.

"Wales?" she said, taking her turn guessing land-of-origin, but her goal was to distract.

She was rather sure he knew exactly what she was doing, but he answered simply enough. "Never."

"Edinburgh?"

"Near. Upon a time."

"Ah, so I thought. I hear it in you still."

"The North has a way of doing that." One of his fingertips slid idly over the tankard of ale in front of him.

A group of men appeared at the doorway, cloaked, their wooden soles clacking hard over wooden threshold. She felt rather than saw Jamie's attention narrow in on them, like an archer taking aim. Then he subsided, but she had no way to explain how she knew this, since he hadn't moved a muscle.

It was unnerving, to have a man ignite dangerous intent like a candle flame, then extinguish it completely.

An off-tune song of ribald and lewd acts broke out in the far corner. Eva sat back, considered the tankard, then quickly lifted it and took a drink. Grimacing, she set it down at once.

"The ale here is quite bad," he said, watching her.

"All ale is bad," she agreed, leaning forward. "Why do you drink it?"

He pursed his lips, as if he'd never considered the question before.

"You should taste the wine from the duchy of Burgundy," she said firmly.

One of those dark, curved eyebrows lifted. "Ought I?"

"Assuredly." She folded her hands and leaned into them, pressing her ribs against the thick edge of the table, calling the image up in her mind. "I could tell you of a valley where the grapes grow—we could climb through the vineyards—and the air, 'tis ever hot, and the dirt cool between your toes, and at the top of the hill, the land bumps away below you as if there is something living beneath the crust of the fields. Like a pie. No, a giant stretching under his sheets, shifting his bones. Ah, and the grapes. They are a most rare thing."

He was watching her, his eyes shadowed. The candle flickered on the table between them. "Rare," he echoed. "What is your name, mistress?"

"Chivalry requires you speak first, sir."

"I am not chivalrous."

She waved her hand. "With me, you shall be. You will find it inevitable." She arched an eyebrow. "Your name, sir."

"Jamie."

"Jamie. Jamie," she whispered.

It felt like years since she'd spoken a person's name. Perhaps it had been. There had been no one but her and Father Peter and her charge, Roger, all these years.

And now this dangerous man, dangerous not only because of the blades strapped across his body, which of course made him mightily dangerous, but because of what happened to her belly when his mouth curved into a faint, lopsided smile as she repeated his name two times.

"And yours, mistress?"

She hesitated. "Eva."

"Eva, Eva," he murmured, just as she had done with his name, except there was absolutely no way she'd infused such latent sensuality into two murmured words.

The same two words.

Oh, shivers and shifting bits of land.

"Do you not," she asked, "find it most odd that here we are, wanting both the thing that is the same—that only one can have, so of course we will fight—and yet we talk of little nothings?"

His bench came tipping forward, four wooden legs onto the floor. His hand, gloved in leather midknuckle, dropped to the table near hers, by the candle, the brightest thing in the whole dingy tavern, his scarred hand beside her pale one.

"Most odd," he said. "I haven't a little nothing in my life."

"Well. Now we have this." She patted the tabletop between them, the bare inch between their fingers, the hot candle, and the cold air.

"Now, this," he agreed in a low voice. He was looking at her hands. "What have you done to your fingernails?"

"They are painted." She curled her fingertips into her fist, withdrawing them from view. "It is naught. A habit that passes the time."

"They looked like drawings."

"That is because they are."

"They looked like vines. Let me see."

She slid her fisted hand off the table entirely. "Vines. And flowers."

He looked up. "How?"

"With little brushes no wider than a grass blade."

"That is . . . remarkable."

She peered at him. "I do not wish to shock you, sir, but with your interest in little vines, you do not seem the sort to hunt priests."

He might have been crafted from marble, for all he moved or showed response. "No?"

She shook her head. "Let me be clear: to look at you, one could hardly think you did anything *but* hunt for priests." Something shifted on his face faintly. A smile. "But hardly do you *feel* like a priest ought to worry."

"That would be a foolish priest."

She nodded, absorbing. "Then I cannot let you have him, you must know this."

Again, the marble response. She did not like speaking with marble.

"You think I jest," she said sharply.

"I think nothing of the kind," he said in that low, rumbly way he had. She already knew the sort of way he had. "I think you resolute and dogged, and when you do a thing, Eva, I suspect 'tis a thing forever done."

She caught her breath as it went rushing out, disguising it as a soft laugh. The way her name had sounded on his tongue, it was not proper. "This is entirely not so. The things I do are very small and matter to no one. I am committed to nothing."

He looked at her. "What about the priest?"

Well. She would prefer to speak with marble than be *interrogated.* She narrowed her eyes. "How ever did you come to hunt priests?"

"I was given to it," he said, his voice pitched so low it almost vibrated. She'd imagine marble to have a higher range. His was more like earth and rocks and the things that lay beneath.

"Do you know you are a dreadful liar?" he inquired, sitting back, watching her.

She wiped her hand across the table, as if sweeping up crumbs. "Indeed. How could one not know such a thing? I lie so that one knows it, but that seems a less dangerous thing to give away than the truth, no?"

The smile that had been haunting his beautiful features faded. Stern again, like a wasp.

"What do you know of the *curé*?" she demanded. Did this one have the slightest notion what a great man Father Peter was, what riches would be taken from this world if anything, ever, happened to him?

"I know his use of color," Jamie replied, looking at the candle flame. "Green and red and a Hell-pit black. He introduced me to tigers, in the margins of a page. I was six. I could have stared at the creature for days. My mother said I told her I heard it roar."

She gave a small laugh, although it was more a small outbreath with sound. It was much warmer than the surrounding air. "The Everoot Psalter. So, you know of his work."

"Aye. His writings, his illuminations."

"Dangerous things, no?"

"Aye."

"England's king does not think so good of these things."

"John does not think so well of them," he agreed.

"But you do."

His eyes never left hers, answer enough. The door to the tavern swung open again, letting cold, wet air in.

"'Tis passing sad, then," she mused, "that he shall certainly be taken to your killing king to be disposed of."

He got to his feet then, unraveling, really, until she had to stare up at him. That was unnecessary. She got to her feet as well.

His eyes narrowed. So did hers.

"Sit down," he said. "Have you a blade?"

She tapped her thigh.

"I thought as much. I shall go see how things stand. You will wait here. I will be back, but should anything happen, if I do not return before that idiot falls off his chair"—he gestured to a linen-capped merchant so sopped with ale, the prediction would take but a few moments to be realized—"make your way down Fishamble—mind the gutters—to the gates. Do not wait to see our quarry, they'll have already passed through."

He shoved a handful of coins into her palm. "For the porters," he explained grimly. "They do not open the gates after dark out of kindness."

"But this is far too much—"

"If you do not spot our quarry on the road, doubtless they stopped, as I expect them to, at the Goat, a small inn on the eastern road."

"But—"

"Mention my name to the innkeep; you will be seen to."

"But—"

"Stop talking," he ordered, and leaned over the table until his scarred, perfect mouth was far too close to hers. "And if you bark at me again, I will tie you up and make you howl in a way you've never dreamt of, Breton lass."

They were leaning that way, each half across the table, staring at each other, angry and aroused—at least Eva was; Jamie's face revealed little—when the door of the tavern squeaked open, then slammed shut. She tore her gaze away; habit too well formed, from too many years of running and hiding.

In this case, as in so many others, it saved her life.

The men who'd kidnapped Father Peter had just walked into the tavern.

In other circumstances, this would have been a stroke of good fortune. As it was, lit by torchlight, Eva was clearly visible, and that was a stroke of remarkably *bad* fortune, since these men had seen her before, as she stood staring in horror when they dragged Father Peter by her, unconscious between their arms.

If they saw her now, they would recognize her. Then they would take her. Mayhap kill her. And Father Peter would be lost.

And Gog . . . her throat closed up at the thought of her all-but-brother in all this madness, Roger, barely fifteen, waiting for her in the woods outside the City. What would Gog ever do without her?

She slowly shifted her gaze back to Jamie in wedged degrees, like the pointed crest of a sundial. The sound of bootheels hitting packed earth thumped inside her head with each pump of blood. Trembling rippled through her in the way of a river, with fierce currents, fear and fury mingling as they so often did, so that she could equally run or attack and not know which until she was already doing it.

But in this moment, like a hand reaching out with a gift, came a new idea: *Kiss him.*

And so she did.

Four

They were each leaning half across the table, staring, angry and aroused—at least Jamie was; Eva simply looked murderously intent—when she put her hands on his shoulders, leaned forward, and kissed him.

He went still. Her lips skidded over his, exerting no more pressure than breath itself.

"What are you doing?" he said, but he kept his voice low, and he did not pull away.

Her lips formed whisper-words of reply against his mouth, making him acutely, infuriatingly aware of her as an object of unadulterated lust.

"They are here," she whispered. "The squinty-eyed men." Her slim hands gripped his shoulders more tightly. "I do not think they would like to see my face again." She trailed her mouth over his, delivering small, miniature kisses from one end of his lips to the other, as if his mouth were a track she was skipping along.

"What do you mean 'again'?" he demanded, but he asked it against her lips.

Their eyes met, their heads tipped back slightly, their lips barely a breath apart.

"I am of the belief that they saw me. For a moment only,

but this is something that would knock on even their silly skulls. They will say, 'Why is she here, when she was there?' and I will have no answer for them."

Jamie shifted his gaze. A thick-chested man behind the counter was speaking to the brutes, then pointed toward the door next to their table.

"I suppose you cannot do something terrible just now, such as poke out their eyes?" she asked, sounding desperate.

"No," he said in calm, measured voice. "That would draw attention."

Eva swallowed. "Indeed."

Then he moved, startling her, which was odd as they were already so close. He splayed his fingers and shoved them deep into her hair. Then he tilted her face up to his.

Leather. Night air. Cold steel. Masculine muskiness. He was all these, swirling together like smoke. Then he bent his head and kissed *her*.

It was a very definite thing, this shifting of who was kissing whom. No longer was she perpetrating the act. He had taken over, leading her down his dangerous path, and it was all hot, breathy kisses, and broad, competent hands on her hips, and . . . fire.

Burning, heated fire roiled in her groin, and so she followed him as if he were a shepherd. Let him lower their bodies back down to the bench, let him ravish her with lips that moved like dancing light over hers, so soft she had to inhale them to be sure they had occurred.

He tipped his head to the side, thumb by her jaw, long fingers brushing the hollow under her ears. He was moving breath and skillful, sinful lips, washing her through like sun into the water. Why not simply press his lips against hers, as she'd seen others do? As she wanted him to do. Why . . . this?

Oh, because of *this*.

He licked her. Slid the tip of his warm, wet tongue across her panting lips—when had she begun panting?—and sent a dizzying cord of heat through her body.

And there she was, orphaned in a tavern, bereft of anything restraining. She went *mad*. She slid her hand over the worn surface of the bench, warm from his heat, moving ever closer to him, until the tips of her fingers brushed the edge of his hard thigh.

His kiss never wandered, his devotion to her lips never faded, he simply swept up her hand and pressed it to his chest, spreading her fingers out with this thumb. She was the one who started to slide it down his chest, the one whose head started spinning, the one who, suddenly and for no earthly reason, felt like crying. Felt like crawling inside this kiss.

One hand slid a bold route south to her waist, pushing under her cloak, leather glove tugging on the worn fabric of her tunic, pulling it tight against her breasts. Hot, competent masculine hand, now making her reconsider this reckless approach to taverns and men with sunlight kisses.

Then, without warning, his hands fell away. That was all. He simply removed his hands and stopped touching her.

Eva felt as if she'd been flung backward.

She tugged on the bodice of her tunic. The laces felt highly constraining. The sleeves were far too tight—who had hemmed them? Oh, yes. She had. The collar strangulated. The thread, old and worn, scraped like teeth against her wrists.

So much for alehouses and kisses. She was done with them.

Jamie's rock-hard body shifted beside her. "They have left."

"I know that," she managed to say in a choked murmur. She'd known nothing of the sort.

The broad shoulders she'd clasped so . . . so . . . . *wantonly*, dipped forward as he got to his feet for a second time.

"You will stay here," he said grimly, his voice back to gravelly, his eyes back to hard, as if they hadn't shared . . . anything. "I will go see how things stand."

"And if I do not wish to 'stay,' like the dog you have left behind?" she inquired coldly.

He considered her with equal coldness. "Do you wish to have me tie you up like one?"

She gasped. "You would not."

He leaned in and sent his dangerous, arousing breath by her ear. "Do not tempt me to prove all the awful things I can do, Eva. Chivalry died in my heart a long time ago. Do not try me."

He straightened and strode to the door. He swung it open, creaking thing that it was, and considered the street like a man used to surveying deserted streets. He did not look at all like a man who admired churchmen's work.

He glanced back. "I shall return."

But he didn't. Because he couldn't.

He headed for the quay, his fury honed to a cold, biting edge. Eva's kiss had stopped him as effectively as a board to the skull: he'd simply gone down.

Worst of all, he'd known it. Somewhere inside, he'd known he was going down. Chosen her kiss over his quarry.

His fury dropped a few more degrees, into the realm of icebergs. Grimly he yanked his mind back to the matter at hand: Peter of London.

Retrieve the priest. Then ride away from the woman with gray eyes and stories of red, hot vineyards. Away from reckless, panting kisses that made him, for the first time in his life, choose to forget his mission.

Eva watched the draped, drunken Englishmen absently. Getting Father Peter out of London was supposed to have been a simple thing, a matter of the heart and a few blessed moments. Instead, she was balled up in waiting, colluding with a dangerous man. An absent man. She sat up straight. Absent for too long.

He wasn't coming back.

She slowed her suddenly quickened breath. "There is no time for panic," she murmured, but already her mind wanted to spin away like a top, into all the awful repercussions of failure. One needed thinking at such hours, not the panic of spinning tops. She opened her mouth and took a breath. It dried her lips. Think. *Think.*

At her last sight of the squint-eyed men, when Jamie had refused to pop out their eyes, they been speaking with two other men, both having the weathered, suspicious, capable look of seamen.

One was gone, but the other still stood there, tipping a tankard to his mouth. Upon closer inspection of his bearing and the manner in which others treated him, Eva realized he must be a captain. The squints had been purchasing passage from him.

Of course.

How could they risk dragging an insentient priest through the gates, past porters and armed soldiers? Much better to head for the quay, where the only people watching were people whose eyesight could go blind for the right amount of coin.

They were headed for the docks.

Jamie must have known.

Holding her body stiffly, her chin tilted just so, she rose and walked across the room toward the counter, fumbling for the purse under her cape, for her knife in case of need, for a reason to explain why her eyes were burning.

Fury. That was it. Sheer fury, that Jamie would think he could outfox her.

He did not know her well at all.

Five

Jamie stood in yet another alley, midpoint between the tavern and the top of the hill that led down to the waterfront, shifting his gaze between the door of the tavern and the docks. Hard darts of rain slanted down, shoving stinging prickles into collars and loose boots. A dull, chilled breeze lurched up from the river through the city streets.

The docks were coming alive; the ebb tide was nigh. Men were climbing aboard little boats. Ropes flew from ship to shore, men shouted, dogs barked, cats stalked. It might be midday on a Saturday down at the quay.

And halfway down the line, amid the scramble of sailors, soaking wet in the rain, were the five squint-eyes.

I am using the waif's terms, he thought dimly.

Two of them supported the priest between them so he looked like a drunken companion. The other three stood in a protective semicircle, dressed in thick capes that were dark with rain.

All five, plus a deckhand.

Jamie yanked his hood up and looked back to the tavern impatiently, blinking through the rain. Where the hell was the accursed captain?

Why, there he was, walking out of the tavern right now. With the gray-eyed waif at his side. He felt an oddly commingled urge: to grin in admiration and to throttle her slim, wet neck.

The captain put out a weather-roughened, almost protective hand, directing her through the door, then kicked it shut behind them. It squealed and slammed with a hollow, damp thud. Eva's pale face was tilted up as she spoke in low tones and passed him a small, bulky pouch of what looked like coin. Jamie's coin.

He drew a long breath, calming himself. Impatience had never been his weakness. It would not become so now. He was accustomed to switchbacks on a route. His entire life had been about readjusting course. Eva was an unexpected curve, a steeper climb, nothing more. He would simply crush her on the way by.

". . . as your daughter." She was murmuring some plan or instruction to the captain.

"That'll only get you so far, *bairn*," he replied in a gruff voice, gray bushy eyebrows furrowed over hard eyes that were scanning the streets ahead. "You'll be needing more of a plan than that. Especially if there's a rogue knight out here like you're saying—"

Jamie stepped out of the alley, directly in front of them, sword out.

"What a coincidence," he said, looking at Eva. "I was just thinking of you too."

Eva gasped and looked at the captain, but he was wisely keeping his gaze on Jamie. Or rather, Jamie's sword.

"I realize now I ought ne'er have left you with all that coin," Jamie went on in a scolding, affectionate tone. "What have you spent it on?"

"Jamie." The rain spit down on Eva's shocked face, making her pale cheeks gleam.

The grizzled seaman looked between them.

"My wife," Jamie explained kindly, then indicated the pouch

of money with the tip of his sword. The captain thrust it out on his upturned palm, presenting it like a platter of food, muttering out of the side of his mouth, "You made no mention of a husband."

"That is because he is a very *bad* husband," Eva snapped. Her hood, tugged up for the rain, revealed a white face, her dark brows running in a stern line above her angry eyes. "And that is not his money. His money is down here." She touched her belt.

The captain glanced down briefly before putting his gaze squarely back on the tip of Jamie's sword.

Jamie smiled. "I rarely give her the coin. She spends it so recklessly. Bolts of fabric, spices, ship captains." He nodded to the pouch still squatting damply on the man's flattened palm. "I am happy to allow you that, sir, and a good deal more, if you aid me but a piece. 'Twill take but a moment of your time."

The captain brought the sack of coins back to his chest.

Eva seemed to regard this as a discouraging development. She took a small, evasive step to the side, and Jamie snapped his hand out and closed it around her neck before she could put her foot back down. He kept looking at the captain, but he felt Eva swallow under his thumb.

The captain looked at Eva—or rather, at Jamie's hand around her throat—and cleared his own. "What were ye needing, sir?"

"Those men are abducting a priest."

"That's what the lass said."

"Did she? I wish to stop them."

"So does she."

Jamie smiled. "Then our interests are aligned."

"What do ye need me to do?"

A sudden shout at the end of the road made them all turn. There, at the top of the hill, stood three of the kidnappers, looking wet and angry. "God's bones, Cap'n, the tide's ripping out. What the 'ell is holding you—"

They stopped short at the sight of their captain with a pouch of money in his hand and Jamie blocking his way, a sword in one hand, Eva's throat in the other.

For a moment, they gaped.

It was the sort of long, stationary moment that allowed shock to translate into action. Jamie was fairly certain what the action would be. Four against one, if he put the captain in the squint-eyes' camp. He felt Eva swallow again. Make that five against one.

"Jamie," she whispered.

His mind was hurtling through options.

"I can help," she breathed.

He loosed his fingers and pushed her backward into the alley, then stepped in behind her. The men thundered down the road. The captain ducked in after them, backed up to the wall on the far side. Jamie bent his elbows out, holding his sword hilt before his chest in both hands, the blade trembling so close it almost touched his nose, ready to be swung up and to the side, the backswing to a mortal blow. He put his spine against the wall.

"There were three of them," she whispered.

"I noted that."

His heart hammered, his hands opened and closed around the hilt, minute readjustments to perfect his hold, every sinew in his body screaming for release. Fight, maim, slice, destroy. It was what he was built to do.

He kept his gaze on the empty corner. "How are you with that little blade of yours, Eva?"

"Sticking, beyond middling," she said promptly. "But I made a promise not to kill anyone today."

He absorbed this in silence. The sound of running boots came closer.

"A most solemn vow," she assured him.

"Eva, you should have something else exceedingly helpful planned, or you should run. *Now.*"

The bootsteps reached the alley. Eva crouched low as the first man rounded the corner, sword out. Jamie pushed off the wall and Eva . . . launched herself forward.

Curled in tight, she crashed into the first man's knees like a boulder. He was bowled backward and smashed into the soldier close on his heels. It knocked the two of them to the ground in a sprawling, boot-kicking mess. Jamie leapt into the fray.

It was a silent, swift fight. With deft swipes, he sliced through the chest armor of the third man as he rounded the corner and tripped over his fallen companions. Spinning, Jamie kicked him in the head just as he was clambering back to his feet. This time he went down like a rock and stayed there.

Eva fought like a mad thing, kicking her hard-soled shoes and scraping her nails and hands past hair and ears and the gripping reach of men, until she found one man's neck and pinched, just so, closing off something important. He slumped to the side, unconscious.

With similar, if more violent, efficiency, Jamie took down the last one and, before the soldier's eyes had fully rolled back in his head, was dragging the load of iron, leather, and stunned flesh over the muddy, hay-strewn cobbles, back into the alley, out of sight.

The captain stood in a forward crouch, his long dagger out but unused. He looked at the bodies strewn about, swords scattered, Eva lying entangled with the unconscious men. Jamie reached into the mess for her hand.

The captain looked at him. "Been married long?"

"Newly wed," Jamie replied curtly as he yanked Eva free. "There is a great deal more coin in this for you, Captain, if you but delay the launch until I come down."

"Agreed," he said firmly. "But if these ones awaken"—he

gestured to the downed men—"and come pelting down that hill after you, a delay will not assist you. Nor me."

"They will not be a problem," Jamie assured him.

The captain walked off, while Jamie dragged the other two back beside the first one. Eva followed, and they stood side by side, staring down.

"You knocked him clean out," Jamie observed between breaths.

She nodded, breathing heavily, and brushed a lick of dark hair pasted across her cheek away with the back of her wrist. "I have this effect on many men. They see me and go completely without sense."

He dropped to a knee and began searching the soldiers' bodies, searching for any clue of who they might be, of who else was hunting for the priest.

"Why did you not run?" he asked as he rooted through their pockets and pouches.

"Why did you not strangle me?"

He shook his head. "I suppose, deep inside, I suspected you might curl yourself up like an iron cat, roll into their ankles, and knock them down like ninepins."

"Ah. Not many men see this in their future."

"Not many men have you in their future," he said grimly, straightening. The unconscious bodies revealed nothing except that these men did not know how to fight. "Come. Help me with their pants."

She crouched down at once and started untying the laces that bound hose to braies, remarking, "I would not have suspected this of you, Jamie."

He grunted, yanking at boots. "What?"

"This, with the hose. I would have thought you the sort to make pretty women swoon, not undress insentient men in alleyways."

He paused in his work and looked over, his palm on his thigh. "Should the need arise, Eva, I can make a pretty woman swoon. And undress."

What happened next was worth the brief pause his reply had cost: she blushed, high on her cheekbones and across her forehead. On her delicate features, pale and practically glistening from the rain, it was like a pink flower turning toward the sun.

That, he thought sternly, *is ridiculous.*

The rain began falling harder. It fell in wind-gusted waves, soaking the hay-strewn streets and slick buildings and crouching humans undressing insentient men in alleys.

"And what do you want we should do with these terrible things?" Eva asked, holding a pile of hose, leather straps, and boots as far from her body as she could.

He got to his feet. "There are orphans here, as in every other town."

And indeed, even now, behind them, were the swift shiftings that heralded small heads and skinny bodies lurking in the distance.

"Look, urchin," he called out quietly. "Here." He tossed the expensive boots over. They rolled with flat, dull thunks over the packed earth and cobbles.

She did the same. "*Attendez,* pretty urchin," she called in a whisper. A head poked out, then disappeared. "*Ici. Bonne chance.*"

"In France, the boots alone would earn enough for the entire warren to eat for weeks." She turned, tucking loose strands of hair back inside her hood. Slick, knotted, and in utter disarray, it was like black gold disappearing into the billowing dark tunnel of her hood.

He looked away.

They strode swiftly back around the corner, out of the alley, back to the hill. Jamie peered down at the quay. The captain was pointing back up the hill with an angry gesture, whether feigned or real, Jamie didn't know. Nor did it matter. The two squints exchanged a suspicious glance, then one stepped forward and gave the captain a violent shove backward.

He shouted, his arms windmilling through the air, then he toppled backward into the dangerous, dark river.

The other man began climbing aboard, dragging the priest behind him, just as a head popped up from belowdecks, then another, and two deckhands came rushing up, shouting, wielding hooks and a mallet.

Jamie gave Eva one grim look. "This time, upon your life, *stay here.*"

Then he stepped out into the road and strode down the hill to the quay.

To Eva, it felt as though the world slowed down. Jamie moved with utter purpose, and the men at the boat turned to him, one by one.

He drew closer, never slowing, no hitch in his focused, relentless charge. One of the deckhands stepped forward but Jamie blew past him like the wind. One of the kidnappers fumbled at his belt and unhooked a small hatchet, but Jamie simply unsheathed his sword, still on the move, and, gripping it with two hands, smashed it flat-sided against the man's skull. It knocked him into the dark waters, where he splashed in beside the captain.

Jamie turned to stand in front of Father Peter, not only preventing anyone from grabbing him but protecting him from assault, and lifted his sword.

Loud shouts and cries exploded from everywhere along the long quay, bouncing off the stone and wet wood of the buildings fronting the river. As if from the sewers, men started pouring forth, some clamoring, some silent, all with eager, mean faces and all bearing weapons.

Jamie would be slaughtered.

Eva started running down the hill. Then she started yelling.

Slowly, as if in a dream, everyone turned to her. Then, still in that languid, otherworldly state, everyone turned back to Jamie.

She reached into her skirts for the pouch of Jamie's money and started throwing coins, wild arcs of them, all over the wet streets.

Six

ocked in mortal combat, Jamie heard her coming. Dead men could have heard her coming. She'd surely awakened the priest, who was now standing of his own volition behind Jamie, shaking his head, stumbling clumsily.

"'Ware the water, *curé*," Jamie said.

Most of the thugs who'd been coming turned like a flock of birds at the sight of coin, and chaos descended with wings. Shouting, hollering, cudgels and fists, coin and cold steel, it was mayhem on cobblestones. Jamie sliced through it, his attention narrowed and lethal. He knew the moment someone stepped up behind him.

"What took you so long?" he snapped without turning.

"My apologies, Jamie." The man he'd spoken to swung his sword, making an onrusher howl in pain and drop back. "It took me a moment to comprehend the man I saw going into a tavern half an hour back was you, seeing as we had not spoken about you *stopping for a drink.* Why are we *in* battle? I was certain we were about a job this evening."

"This is the job."

"Did you not vow to me we were done with sword fights in the streets?"

Jamie spun, sweeping his sword before him. A cutthroat

about to launch at Jamie's back went flying and slammed into a few others. They rolled into a third group, and a new miniature riot broke out to their left.

"There are a great many rank, villainous men interested in you tonight," Jamie's friend muttered as they swung their way through the crowd, backs together. "More than is usual. Is there some cause for that?"

"Aye. They asked where you lived and I wouldn't tell them. Have you seen the priest?" Jamie demanded, kicking someone out of his way. The buildings on either side hemmed the fight in, ensuring it wouldn't lessen in intensity anytime soon. They made their way to the far edge of the circle of fighting.

Jamie swept his gaze over the riot. "Where the devil is he?"

Ah, there. With Eva, at the other end of the block. Her cape rippled in the gusts of wind, her hair swept out in dark, ribbony streamers. She caught a handful and trapped it against her temple, staring across the sea of fighting until she caught sight of him.

She dipped her head forward, her eyebrows raised in silent query. *Are all your limbs still attached?*

He nodded. She smiled, which felt surprisingly warm, considering how far apart they were. Then she gave a small wave and mouthed something. It looked like, *Bonne nuit.*

Good night.

Then she disappeared around the corner and took the blessed damned priest with her.

Seven

"Have you coin?" Father Peter asked as they hurried through the city streets.

Eva shifted her arm to support him a little more as they hurried over the slick cobbles. "A bit."

"Enough to get through the gates?"

"One can hope."

"Do not flash it about."

"You should not know such things as how to bribe gate porters," she scolded. "You, a man of God."

"If I were a proper man of God, Eva, you would not be alive."

She glanced over. "Did they bash your head in?" she asked in concern.

"They tried."

She patted his arm and said briskly, "I should not worry much; it is terribly hard."

"Not so hard as yours. Why are you here in England? I do not want you here."

"In this way, we are alike, *padre*. Being in this cold, wet land is not something I enjoy like wine. It is much more like ale."

"You should not be drinking ale, Eva," he scolded in the familiar affectionate tone that would have brought tears to her eyes if she had not vowed never to allow tears to befoul her eyes again. But it was astonishing how one fell back into the old ways with an old friend.

Father Peter's brown robe swirled against his ankles as they hurried toward the town gates. "Now answer me, Eva: why have you come to England?"

"I should think that would be remarkably clear, as we creep down this street like criminals. I came for you."

"I left a message that bid you run. You and Roger."

In the moonlight reflected off the slick cobbles and squelching mud, Father Peter looked pale. She swallowed her worry like a tincture and said lightly, "It did not tell me to run, just so."

"It said, 'Fly south.' That has always meant *run.*"

"I know very well what it means."

"And yet here you stand. 'Twas a simple message, Eva, three lines long."

"I know precisely how long it was. 'They have called for me, and this time, I must go. Take Roger and fly south for the spring. Do not delay.'"

He looked over, impressed with her perfect recitation. Or perhaps irritated; it was difficult to tell, in the dark.

"And so, instead, you came north," he said curtly.

"But without delay, if that is in any way impressive." She tugged on his arm, stopping them for a moment of rest. "I came with news, Father. The French king, Philip, is in negotiations with the English rebels. He is planning a little visit, he and his army. These rebels have as much interest in this 'charter of their liberties' as I do in shearing sheep. Calling you over to assist in their negotiations was but a ruse."

"And that is why you are here? To tell me there are politics involved in this matter of kingship?"

"To tell you you were called here under false pretenses."

He eyed her. "And the brothers sent you all the way to England with this news?"

She hesitated. "I sent myself." He shook his head and she held up a hand. "*Curé*, these good friends of yours and mine, they are men of God. All the people who have helped keep us hidden all these years, the ones who would travel through danger and sea storms to assist you—and they are many—they are priests and monks. They are *helpless* in this. They fuss over sheep and write down the things other men do, but this?" She waved her hand at the dark city streets. "They are not so good at this. Whereas I am very good at it. Although not so good as you," she added in a fit of flattery.

He frowned more deeply. She took his arm and they began walking, stepping carefully over a gutter teeming with rain and small, dark floating things.

"*Mon père*, if I made a mistake in coming to England, 'tis only on the heels of yours. We have stayed away from England with great devotion for many years, yet now you come, at the height of civil war? Why is this?"

He looked ahead with great purpose. Perhaps with the great purpose of not looking at her. "I had something to do."

"This, I think, is mad. You have been knocked about the head more than is good for you."

"Regardless, I have business that has naught to do with you, Eva." His brown robes swirled as they took another corner.

"Has it aught to do with those men who stole you like a chicken?" she inquired briskly. "Having been insentient, you may not recollect this occurrence, but I do, as I watched in great heaps of horror as they dragged you down the street."

He looked over levelly. "Eva, you must get out of England."

She nodded as they began to descend the hill. "That is just why I am here. To get you out of England, you and all your pretty pictures that frighten angry men so much."

"No, Eva. *You.* They are whispering again."

"Men whisper about many things," she said lightly, but inside, she felt cold. People did not whisper about many things. People whispered about only one thing: secrets.

"They have remembered."

Fear, like a cold river, washed down her spine. "Who?"

"Everyone, Eva. Every one of them."

It ran down her legs, this cold fear. "Roger."

Father Peter looked at her, and she realized her stalwart protector for all these years could not protect her anymore.

"No, Eva. I think they've remembered you."

Eight

She had to pay dearly to get them through the gates. The cobbles in front were littered with the flotsam of human and animal traffic—spilled leeks, a lost glove, a plethora of goat droppings. The pointed crest of the gates towered above their heads, twelve feet of thick hewn oak banded with iron.

A much smaller arched door was cut within the large gates. Its bottom edge was knee-high off the ground, the opening quite narrow. One had to sidle through it. This not only was uncomfortable but prevented anyone wearing armor or swords or other dangerous killing instruments from coming rushing into the town. And after *courve-feu*, it was the only way in and out.

Tonight, the porters appeared positively gleeful as they pocketed the handful of coin Eva pressed into their dirty gloved hands. She hurried Father Peter through the opening, then wrapped her fingers around the sides of the small door and hauled herself up.

"There will be a man coming," she announced, thrusting one leg through. "Dark hair, dark blue eyes, dark everywhere. He will be in a great hurry. He must be stopped, he and his companion. The hue-and-cry has been called on them. The Watch will be close on their heels."

The guards looked up the hill. It was empty but for the

silhouette of a cat crossing at the crest, a slim, dark shape with a narrow, waving standard of a tail.

"Oh, but he will be coming," she said in a warning tone. "And he has a great deal of money. Loaded with it like a pack pony. Pennies. *Of gold.*"

They grinned and she felt a small pang for Jamie, who would be stopped, even if temporarily, while the porters tried to sort this out, with the assistance of the helmed crossbowmen on the catwalk above.

She could not worry on Jamie now. She must worry on getting her small band of loved ones out of England before they were discovered.

SILVERY moonlight shone down through the spring leaves, illuminating Father Peter and his brown robes in a glowing silvery aura. It was all very pretty, and irritating while one hurried through the woods in great danger.

"Eva," called a voice softly, from back in the trees.

Father Peter turned sharply. Roger, her fifteen-year-old charge and devoted companion for these last ten years, stepped out from the trees, lanky and tall as a young tree himself.

Father Peter turned back to her with one of the sternest looks she'd ever received, and there had been a great many stern looks over the years, so this was no small claim.

"You brought Roger," he said flatly.

"I tried to leave him behind, but he would have none of it."

Father Peter's look darkened, if that was possible. "I am familiar with the feeling."

"Pah, all your double and triple meaning, *curé*, they are lost on one such as me. I am as dull as a rusty ax. With me, you must say what you mean, or you will die a frustrated old man."

Despite all the darkness of the night and the times, Father Peter laughed. This was always the thing Eva could do for him, make him laugh. But just now, the laugh made him cough, and it became a bit hard for Eva to breathe, as if she had the cough herself, which was what happened when your heart was being pressed upon by great worry.

"We are a wagon train of peril, Eva," he said when he was done coughing.

"You are so astute, these observations of yours. Next time, I promise, I shall leave you behind."

He looked sad, and this was frightening, for Father Peter was relentlessly stalwart and forward-facing, like a shield or the sun. "All you needed to do, Eva, was allow me to leave *you* behind."

They looked at each other through a silence that had so many layers it simply could not be filled with words; then she took his arm and began leading him over the wet, crunching sticks down to where Roger and the horses stood.

A lock of blond hair fell forward over Roger's forehead as he stepped forward to greet Father Peter, smiling as he took his hand. They embraced swiftly but warmly.

"I thought you'd ne'er come, Eva," Roger murmured as he helped Father up on one of the horses.

"Indeed, and were most pleased, thinking you'd have more adventures that way," she chided, keeping her voice light, as she always had for Gog, light and airy even when they were stumbling through the woods in the dark, all those years ago.

Gog swung up behind Father Peter. Eva took a second to pat his knee. "Fortunately, I am returned and can keep you from this dangerous mischief."

He looked down. "Eva, when I am *with* you is when danger and mischief occur."

Well.

She scrambled up on the other horse. "She is quite perfect," she murmured. They did not find much opportunity to ride; horses were a luxury, and their lives did not tend that way.

Once, Roger had stolen her a pinch of scented soap from a fair stall, and now there was this beautiful, snorting, powerful, confusing animal, who had certainly cost more money than she'd given him.

She looked over sharply. "Did you steal this horse?"

"What happened?" said Gog by way of reply. He was looking at Father, but she was fairly certain the query was for her.

She pushed her bottom down farther into the seat, and they started off at a swift walk. "There was a small delay."

"A delay, as in a fight?"

"Why?" she complained, greatly put-upon. "Why do you say these things to me?"

"Eva—"

She gave a sigh of exasperation. "A small one."

"A small what?"

"Fight."

Roger shook his head. "Come." He nudged his horse off the main road onto a dim, dun-colored path. She followed, feeling slightly safer knowing Jamie's furious gaze would not alight on her back immediately if he somehow made it through the gates.

"I knew it," Gog muttered.

"It was beyond my ability to prevent. They filled Father with a terrible tincture. They were dragging him to a boat."

Roger looked over sharply. "What did you do?"

"Clearly, I stopped them."

"How?" persisted Gog, always wise to her ways. Did every mother feel this slippery hillside, the terrain between the truths you thought they could manage and the lies you could carry? Not that Eva was a mother, of course. Not the rightful sort.

"How did you stop them?" Gog pressed.

"Eva and the knight stopped them," Father Peter put in helpfully.

She passed him a discouraging look. She ensured he could see it even through the darkness enveloping the world, which she was trying desperately to ignore, as darkness frightened her.

Gog nodded, but his jaw tightened. "A knight. What sort of knight?"

"The sort who was very dangerous and not at all chivalrous," she said sharply.

"And he helped save Father Peter?"

She shifted her discouraging gaze to Gog. "Do not think pretty thoughts about this knight. He is not decent. He is the antithesis of decent. Indecent, dangerous, unseemly. He was a necessary tool along the way, that is all, like a scythe or a hammer."

Gog flicked her a glance from where he rode behind Father Peter, his arms around the aging priest to support him. "Those are very dangerous things, Eva."

"How astute of you, Roger. Now, all we need to do," she continued brightly, "is go a little ways, then a little ways more, and in these little ways, we'll soon be at an inn by a river," she said in a cheerful voice. "And in the morning, on a boat for France."

Father Peter looked over. "That will not end this, Eva."

"Nothing will end this," she rejoined briskly, looking away. But of course, one thing would end it entirely. Unfortunately, that was an impossible task.

How could one ever get close enough?

JAMIE stood before the town gates, holding his fury in check. The guards had not yet laid a hand on him or Ry, but that was only because they were wary. Wisely so, but even Jamie's unchecked fury would be ineffective against five armed porters and the additional crossbowmen on the ramparts above, their quarrels aimed at his eyes.

"Now, sir," the gate guard said, his hand out, palm facing forward, as if holding Jamie at bay, "if 'tis just as you're sayin', this won't be but a minor happenstance. We'll just turn out your pockets, easylike, and see what you've got inside. Pennies, the dark-haired lass said." Ry gave a muted curse. Jamie said a full-on nothing. "And if not all o' it is your own, why then, mayhap some of it can be mine."

The porter gave a small, coarse laugh that stuttered into silence as Jamie snapped his gaze down from the crossbowmen.

The porter cleared his throat, his hand up in a defensive way. "We'll wait for the Watch, and it'll be but a night in a cell for you both. You'll be the only ones there—all the rest were hanged or loosed last week, to join the rebels in their marching. Come morningtide, you'll be on your way, now, right? Go easy, man," he added, starting to sounding moderately frantic, although Jamie had not moved. But the crossbowmen were still above, so a frantic porter was a vulnerability Jamie could not exploit.

He moved his gaze back to the wall, saying nothing. He felt as if his rage might burn a hole through the stone.

At his side, Ry was murmuring something, but Jamie couldn't hear it over the pounding of fury in his head.

Eva was a dead lass.

Nine

Long after the fighting had ceased, a man approached the alley by the Red Cock Tavern and stared at the naked men finally coming to life in the gray predawn light.

They were giving little shakes to their heads, stumbling in circles, gaining their wits enough to realize they were neither booted nor armed nor clothed. It was difficult to know which was the most pressing issue. Then they saw him.

All three snapped straight. "Sir!"

"You never arrived with the priest." He took in their naked bodies. "Who did this?"

They looked uncomfortable. "Jamie Lost."

He gave the smallest smile. "Of course." A small crowd was starting to form. He ignored it. "I have sent the others west with the bishop. I do not like using the bishop, as he is very expensive. Get dressed and come with me."

"But, sir—," one protested. He gestured all around him. Clearly, no clothes were anywhere in sight.

"I said get dressed and join me. I do not care how you arrange to do it. Take his," the man suggested, gesturing to a gap-toothed bystander, who did not appreciate the suggestion. "I do not care how, but if you cannot figure your way out of this, I have no use for you."

He turned on his heel and walked off.

"Who the hell does he think he is anyhow?" muttered the gap-toothed bystander as soon as the object of his derision was out of earshot.

One of his men grumbled, "The Hunter."

The bystander spit derisively through his gap, a bravado to regain any masculinity that might have been compromised. "Aye? Well, there ain't no deer here in these city walls."

The naked soldier looked at him derisively. "You idiot. He don't hunt deer. He hunts heirs. Now give me your clothes."

"NOT here?"

Eva stared at the growly, wide-girthed innkeep named Roland. Equipped with three chins and two angry eyes, he glared back.

Late-afternoon sunshine poured through the grimy, salt-splattered windows in the common room behind him, making for a glaring, blaring light in the equally grimy entry vestibule.

"But he was to be here by yestereve," she said, not so much as an explanation as an attempt to reverse her current, dire reality. The man who was to sail them back to France was not here.

"Aye, well, he's not," the innkeep returned curtly. "Leastwise, not so he's announced himself to me. No fisherman named William, no fisherman's disfigured daughters. And," he added in his growly way, "you'd best have coin enough to recompense for that room you're using private, when it ought to be sleeping six."

She went back upstairs. Gog was pacing the room, Father Peter watching him, saying something in a low murmur. A miniature inkpot was on the table—Father Peter never went anywhere without the implements of his trade—but Roger was not interested in Father's letters this day.

He looked over the moment the door creaked open, but Eva shook her head, and he turned sharply away.

His boots rang hollowly on the plank floor as he paced to the window. She resisted the urge to push back the lock of blond hair that inevitably fell forward over his eye as he shoved the shutters wide, revealing a view of a winding path that led to the highway road. Pretty spring flowers grew alongside it, glowing golden and pink in the late-afternoon light.

It was a great misfortune that these pretty flowers lined a path that led to the very inn Jamie had directed her to last night, when he was lying and kissing and doing all manner of disreputable things.

But what were the chances he would come here? He would race like the wind after her, of course, but she could have taken many, many routes. He'd never think she'd be so foolish as to come to the very place he'd suggested.

Would he?

No matter. She had no choice. William the fisherman was to meet them, use his little boat to take them to a bigger boat, which would sail them to St. Malo. Then they would flee to the wilds of southern France, where no one would ever think to look for them.

"The fisherman is not coming," Gog muttered. His hands curled over the ledge, squeezing it. He would not last long cooped in this little room like a chicken.

"Perhaps this is so," she said quietly. "Gog, go to the little village, find poor William the fisherman, and inquire as to his delay."

As if she'd unleashed a small arrow, Gog shot to the other end of the room and snatched up his things: sword belt, an old, half-rusty hatchet, a pair of thick gloves. She crossed over and rested her hand lightly on his arm.

He paused in strapping on his sword belt, his head tilted up to look at her. The lock of blond hair fell forward over his eye. This time, she indulged herself and pushed it briskly back behind his ear.

"Whether poor William the fisherman keeps faith or no, we must leave England at once. If you find no sign of him, arrange passage with someone else. Use the horses as barter."

Their eyes met. No need to explain aloud; each of them could guess various reasons William the fisherman might no longer be willing to transport fugitives across the English Channel.

Or no longer be able to.

"Be careful."

He put his hand on her shoulder, as if *he* were reassuring *her,* silly boy, and left. Father Peter paused in packing his writing instruments in a soft leather bag, watching her silently.

"Think you can move your stubborn bones one last time, *mon père?*"

"I am tired, woman, not enfeebled," he retorted. She hid her smile. "And I am not getting on any boat. Although I will see to it you and Roger do."

"We shall see who will get on any boat," she replied mildly.

The room fell quiet. The silence scraped against her. She stood in the middle of it, shocked, thinking, *Years of my life have passed in constant motion. I do not know how to be still.*

There was naught to do but to stand in the abrasive silence and contemplate this unsettling fact. Then a knock rattled the door.

SHE went still. Father Peter's head shot up.

It came again, a faint rap. "I come for the priest," a whisper said through the keyhole. "I am a friend."

She turned to Father Peter. He shook his head slowly.

All the hairs on the back of her neck rose up, beelike and vibrating. She leaned toward the door, so close her lips brushed the cool wood. "You have the wrong room."

The soft voice came again, even more quiet, more coaxing. "I bid thee let me enter. I am here to help."

"Nay," she whispered back, an odd collusion of secrecy between her and the stranger outside the door. "I do not know—"

The door shuddered against its frame. The old, thin wood cracked, then the frame splintered and the door swung open. Eva leaped away, digging for a blade amid her skirts, but the sight of a churchman in the doorway made her stop. He was looking past her to the bed.

"Peter of London," the bishop said in a voice deep with satisfaction. He stepped into the room and wedged the door shut behind him. "It has been a long time."

"Ten years."

"It is most good to see you," he said, adopting an oily, coaxing tone.

Father Peter reached for his boots. "Is it?"

"Father Peter is fevered," Eva announced, backing up to stand in front of the bed with her arms stretched out, a stance that would not stop a small breeze. "Incapacitated."

The bishop looked at her. "He appears hale enough. Nevertheless." The bishop paused and smiled. Eva could only describe it as evil. Surely, he had not meant this. "We want only the papers he has with him. Documents, illustrations. He can stay in your good care."

"*Qu'est-ce que c'est*, document?" She affected to stumble over the English pronunciation of the word.

He smiled again, condescendingly. Ah, he liked a stupid woman. Then this was no place for him. "They are nothing," he assured her in a placating voice. "Triflings. Some small matters the good father saw and, unfortunately, sketched."

She scribbled with an invisible stylus in the air, her face bright and confused. "*Écrire? Il y a une . . .*" She stared into the air, then smiled. "Fire. All the poor *curé*'s favorite papers, little leaves in the flames."

The benevolence of the bishop's smile washed away, like so much grit from an onion. Then he reached out and grabbed her by her arm.

"Leave the girl go, Aumary," Father Peter said, rising from the bed, his eyes on the fat-faced bishop. "She is but a poor serving maid."

The bishop released her arm.

Father Peter sat back down on the bed, boots in hand. "Go, girl," he said without looking over, as one might speak to a serving girl.

She crept toward the door, masking her slow movements as fear, keeping to the edge of the room.

"England is not a healthful place for you, Peter," the churchman said.

Father Peter slid a boot on. "So I have been told."

"You should leave. I am telling you this as an old friend. Far too many people are interested in you. You have no friend in the king, for certes. He is displeased with this charter being bandied about. 'Twas a poor thing you and Langton did, giving the notion to the barons."

"Whereas battle is a good notion," Father Peter said drily.

"You were not brought to England for the charter or the negotiations, Peter. You must know that."

"I know very well why I was called for. And very well what I came to do."

"'Twill be so much easier this way, Peter. Just give me the papers, and I will say you were gone when I arrived. You can disappear again, as you have these past ten years. Sail for France. Give me the papers, and go. Go pray at Mont-Saint-Michel, teach in Paris; there is always an opening on the Petit Pont for a man of your caliber."

Father Peter looked up mildly from lacing his boot. "I am here on a matter of personal conscience, Aumary. If I choose to also meet with my old friend Archishop Langton while I am in England, be assured, my presence is in no way intended to serve the rebels. Nor," he added, bending back to his boot, "for that matter, the king."

The bishop's veneer of solicitude began melting away. He wiped his hands down his long robe, as if drying sweaty palms. His face was flushed.

"Give me the papers, Peter."

Ah, there was the low menace of a man who wanted something he should not have. Eva slowed down her creeping alongside the walls, making herself invisible.

"King John has had crossbow bolts aimed at your head for many years now," the bishop said, his voice stiff and cold. "He knows you are in England. If he finds you, if he procures those sketches, 'twill be to the detriment of the realm."

Father Peter leaned forward and rested his forearms on his tunic-draped thighs, his face tired and knowing, and in that moment Eva knew she was *right* to have come for him, however he scolded her for it, however much danger ensued. One paid one's debts. Father Peter had saved her life. She would now save his.

"Is that what you are about, Aumary? The welfare of the realm?"

"Indeed," he said curtly.

Father Peter considered him for a long moment. "How much?"

The bishop gave a start.

"How much did it cost, to buy you? More than a warhorse, or less? Do you serve the rebels, or someone other?" Father Peter held up his hand. "It matters naught. Your service is lacking. I would not hand you a flower from a garden. I will surely not give you what may be the most powerful bargaining chip in these negotiations. Who knows whom you might sell it to next?"

To his credit, the bishop's shiny face flushed a bright red. "So be it, Peter of London," he snapped. "Ever have you brought these things on yourself."

He reached for the door, but by then, Eva had completed her slow circling of the room and come up behind. She reached out, her blade up, and placed it against the front of his throat.

The bishop froze.

"Now hush," she murmured. "You have brought this on yourself."

"Wssst," he hissed, glaring at Father Peter. "Call the bitch off."

"Release him," Father Peter said in his quiet, never-hurried voice. "You are not killing anyone today."

She hesitated for only a second, then lowered the blade. The bishop reached around, grabbed her, and flung her headfirst across the room. She hit the wall, then the floor, and decided to stay there when two armed soldiers barreled into the room. Better to have him *think* himself successful in knocking her out, rather than giving him the opportunity to actually *be* successful by rising to her feet again.

"The priest," the bishop snapped.

The soldiers moved into the room. Eva lay on the floor, watching from beneath her hair, which had fallen in a thick curtain over her face. Good to hide what her eyes were doing.

They bundled Father Peter up. They must have drugged him or knocked him senseless, for he was slumped as they maneuvered out the door. One of them paused at the doorway. "And her?"

She stared at the pitted plank floor beneath her nose and stopped breathing. *I am dead. Do not bother,* she willed her lack of breath to say to these stupid, wily men.

There was a terrible moment of pause.

"Leave her," the bishop muttered. "She is naught but a serving maid."

They hustled out. First the clatter of their boots descending the back stairs, then their voices, already hushed, faded until they lowed like cows on a distant field. A door squealed open belowstairs, then slammed shut, and Eva was finally, terribly, alone.

She rose and bumped her way to the door, hand out. She listened. Nothing but the general din of people milling and murmuring. She started down the stairs, tiptoeing, palm on the wall for support, and peeked out.

To her left was the noisy common room. She slipped in and pinned her back against a wall, trying to look like a servant. The room was filling up with people, travelers en route to places they perhaps ought not to be going, secretive missions, just the sort of people who came and went through this unprepossessing little inn and its small cove with its very deep waters.

None of her attackers were in sight.

She turned for the door just as Roger came hurtling through it. He hurried over, staring at her face. She noted this because she was staring at *his* face, taking in a cut lip and a red, swelling cheekbone.

"What happened?" she demanded at the same moment he muttered, "Jésu, Eva, what happened?"

She touched her face briefly, feeling the rawness along her cheekbone. "Father Peter, Roger. They have taken the *curé*."

He nodded. "I know. I saw them."

She pointed to his face. "You did more than see them."

He pointed at hers. "So did you. I tried to stop them."

For the first time in this whole excursion, Eva felt fear. "That was foolish," she scolded, although what she wished to do, just for a second, was shut her eyes. Roger was fifteen years old. He had an entire life to lead. If it was spent in hiding, well, there were worse things, such as not living at all. One was given a life, not a choice about the circumstances in which it was lived. Eva did not like that Roger had so recklessly endangered the life she'd spent the last ten years safeguarding.

He took her wrist as she reached out, stopping the movement. "Did you recognize any of them, Eva?"

"Recognize? Of course not."

"I did."

"Whom could you possibly recognize, Gog?" She said it quickly, because the question caused a cold flurry in her chest, lest it be answered. "You do not know a soul in England."

"I know one."

A pang of fear nailed itself to her chest. "Oh, no. This is not possible."

"Aye," Roger said, his voice almost unrecognizable in its grim maturity. "I heard them say his name."

"No," Eva whispered.

"Aye. They are taking Father Peter to Guillaume Mouldin."

"**Is** that they?" Guillaume Mouldin murmured to his sergeant from where they sat, high on a hilltop, squinting down onto the road below.

It was a familiar position to be in, watching his men bring in someone who did not want to come.

None were better at their profession than Mouldin had been at his: safeguarding the realm's most precious resources, its heirs. It had been a highly satisfying, highly valued, highly lucrative employ.

Until the greatest of them escaped. That had signaled the end for Guillaume Mouldin.

Ten years of hunting had not turned up the missing heirs. Despite employing all the tactics that usually worked to break down informants, he had never found the dark-haired girl and the boy she'd taken with her. Even the damned priest had proven elusive.

King John had not been pleased, and Mouldin had been disgraced. Outlawed. In a fit of fury, the king had confiscated his estates and his cash, and sent hunters after the Hunter, and when Mouldin fled, the king had turned his rage on Mouldin's wife and child, starving them to death when he could not lay his hands on Mouldin.

Well, the tides had turned now, and the king would pay.

Or the rebels.

Whoever had the most coin, someone would pay and receive Peter of London. The priest and all his remarkable sketchings. The man who could bring a tottering kingdom to its knees.

Mouldin was only too happy to assist.

His stallion bobbed and pawed, restless and filled with good oats and high energy, just as Mouldin had planned for the long ride ahead. He looked at his sergeant. "Deliver the messages. Inform Lord Robert fitzWalter I found his recovery fee far too low and have taken matters into my own hands. If he wishes to make a better offer, he can join me in Gracious Hill. Let him know he will be bidding against the king." He smiled faintly. "And mention that Jamie is in on this hunt as well. I haven't the inclination or resources to stop him, but fitzWalter just might."

Mouldin galloped down the hill.

Eva put a shaky hand on Gog's shoulder. "Did you see which way they went?"

"Aye." Excitement fueled Roger's words. His eyes were bright, and he squeezed her hand.

"That is good." She took his arm, turning him toward the doorway. "They rode south? East then—no? North, then?"

Gog nodded.

"This is most fortunate," Eva said, not feeling fortunate

whatsoever. "I know those lands well. You saddle the horses, I will retrieve our packs, and away we shall go like vengeful little birds."

They turned, Gog for the stables, Eva for the stairs. Cool air rushed in as the front door pushed open.

"I still say she would be crazed to come here," Ry murmured as he shut the door to the inn behind them.

Jamie glanced around the entryway. Exit out the back, stairs straight ahead, common room to the right. "Desperate," he murmured, turning to the common room. "She's desperate. And seeking swift, secret passage back to France. This inn, and its cove, are very good for both those things."

He leaned in to scan the taproom more thoroughly.

"Jamie!" called someone from behind. Roland, the proprietor, barreled out of a back room, bellowing in happiness. "It has been years!"

Jamie turned back around.

Eva froze as the front door swung open and—would God never bless her again?—Jamie walked in.

Had there been a doubt in her mind as to the identity of the knight in the vestibule clinking with weapons—which of course there was not—the bad-tempered innkeep's bellow would have blown it away it like so much chaff.

It was Jamie and in daylight he looked more powerful, more determined, and much more dangerous than ever.

Gog's face paled, perhaps a result of the way she herself had gone white. She'd felt the blood draining away.

"Is that he?" he whispered. "The hammer-knight?"

"'Tis." She turned her back to the archway. "Go now, Roger. Swift as swift can be."

He took a step toward the door. "And if he should recognize you?"

"I worry on you, Roger. You do not worry on me. Go saddle the horses. I will slip out the back and join you." She gave an encouraging smile and slipped the rest of her coin into his hand. "In case of need. You will charter a ship and go—"

"I will not."

"—and await me at that little town with the artichokes by the river Garonne."

Gog turned away, reluctantly but obediently. Running for one's life had such an effect. They had relied on one another for many years now, and being eight years the elder had given Eva sufficient standing to make her orders law.

Then Roger turned back. With his head bent, he muttered, "If anything happens, I will follow after."

"No—" she whispered, but he was already walking away, striding boldly past Jamie and his companion and all their steely blades with great calm, never once looking over. Eva felt a rush of pride. He would be a brilliant man, if only he made it so far.

She gave him a moment to make it to the stables. This was useful in that it also gave her a moment to rebuild the ramparts of her courage. Its walls had fallen apart into thin, sticklike reeds the moment Gog disappeared from view. Bravery had always come in the form of protecting Roger. She was a wall that held up nothing without him.

But maidservants did not stand about staring at walls to gather reedy valor. They picked things up, delivered plates, shouted to cooks, and generally bustled about, drawing no more attention than a fly. Eva would be such a fly.

Keeping her back to the doorway, she reached out awkwardly for a plate on the nearest table. The three occupants of the table looked taken aback, likely because she'd taken a bowl half full of stew.

"Mold," she explained, nodding to the bread still dunked in it. "Terrible, with the rains. I'll see you've another right off."

She reached for the next bowl. The man pinched the edge of it, pulling it away, scowling at her.

People did not scowl at flies. She was drawing too much attention.

She moved on, table by table, picking up plates of food off one, setting down mugs of half-drunk ale at another, edging her way ever backward in pursuit of the smoke-grayed archway and stairway beyond.

Jamie and his companion stood with their armored backs toward the common room, conversing with the bad-tempered innkeep as she passed under the archway.

She held her breath, her arms full of dirty plates. Turning slowly, she walked by and put her foot on the bottom step. It creaked terribly, so she hurried to the second, breathing fast, inhaling the odor of garlic and fish rising off the plates. She pressed the ball of her boot onto the third step, then the fourth, and drew in a thin breath of hope. The worst was behind her. Five steps now. From the back, she would simply appear to be a maid going about her business.

She hit the sixth step, hurrying now, and—

Felt Jamie's dangerous attention turn to the stairs.

There was a small outbreath of air through his nostrils, like a soft laugh. Then, quietly, came a single rumbling word: "Eva."

She dropped the plates and took off running. The crockery crashed to the floor, spraying sharp bits of pottery and food against the wall and over the railing as she bolted up the stairs. Behind her, like a little army, thumped wood plates and mugs, bouncing down the stairs.

She lifted the hem of her skirts and hurtled up the steps two at a time, but her heart was sinking even as it was hammering, for she heard Jamie coming up behind—and he was taking them three at a time.

Ten

amie hit the landing just as Eva reached the room. She slammed the door shut behind her, no defense at all.

He kicked it open. She was clambering over an overturned bench, reaching for the bedstead, pulling herself forward. To what end, he didn't know, as the only thing ahead of her was a wall.

He grabbed her from behind, his hand on her skirts, and she fell hard, her knees and palms on the floor. He put both hands on her hips and starting reeling her in, pulling her backward into him.

Her knees skidded over linen skirts and worn wood floor. She scrabbled for a hold. It was a battle silent but for their harsh breathing. He dropped to a knee behind her and curled his body over her back.

"Cease," he said in her ear.

Instead she kicked, her hard boot making contact with the front of his bent knee and shoving it out from beneath him. He tipped forward, onto her body, but she was already scrambling forward, grabbing for the wooden bedstead to haul herself up.

He saved her the trouble. He fisted a handful of her hair and hauled her to her feet, then marched her backward to the wall and pushed her up against it, his forearm planted diagonally across her chest, her braid clenched in one gloved hand.

"Are you finished?" he demanded.

"Nay," she spat, and flung her head to the side, her mouth open to bite his hand.

He closed his other hand around her jaw and forced her cheek to the wall, pressing his body up against hers as a bulwark, a solid press of muscle from hips to chest.

"Stop," he murmured. "Or I will start breaking things. In your body."

She stilled. They stood, both of them breathing fast. Their chests pressed together each time they inhaled.

"Where is he?" he asked.

"Who?"

Jamie glanced over his shoulder at Ry. "I'm going to need a rope."

Ry nodded slowly and left.

"Jamie," she said, not quite a gasp, not yet a whisper. "You cannot do this."

He looked down. In the sunlight, she was more spritelike than she had seemed last night, all contrasts of light and dark: pale face with its graceful bone structure, clever gray eyes and the thin, ink-dark eyebrows above, and all that flowing hair, now braided and gripped in his fist. "Cannot do what?"

"This. Whatever you are intent on doing."

"Should there be any questions on what I can and cannot do, Eva, let me remove them now." He gave her braid a little shake. "Where is the priest?"

"I—I do not know."

He smiled faintly. "Surely you served up better lies than this when you spoke with the gate porters last night."

She stilled, her chest pushing against him as she breathed in swift, shallow pants. "Ah. The porters. I am pleased to hear it was effective."

"'Twas not effective."

"You were stopped."

"I am now pinning you against a wall, Eva. It was not effective. Where is he?"

"Gone."

Her lying breath came rushing out, drifting past a day's growth of beard on his jaw and neck. Her breasts, bound beneath her tunic, still pressed up in soft mounds, and he could feel her heart pounding against his chest. The narrowing of his attention made Jamie briefly, acutely, aware of her femininity.

His hand sped beneath her cloak. He splayed his fingers and ran them down her leg. Even through the skirts of her tunic, he could feel the muscular curves of a body worked hard. He felt down farther, bending his knees, making her bend hers, her neck still arched back by his hold on her braid.

He found what he expected, a dagger plunged into the top of her boot. She held perfectly rigid, jaw clenched, as he ran his hand up her inner thigh, then splayed his fingers, enclosing both the hilt of a little misericord strapped there and the bare, chilled skin of her leg.

As if she were a metal filing, he felt an almost magnetic urge to slide his hand up farther. Instead, he plucked the blade free and tossed it onto the growing pile behind him.

"You are like a little porcupine, Eva." They were still crouched, facing each other. "Are there others yet?"

She looked over his shoulder and said nothing.

"I will stake you to the wall and undress you if needs must."

Her gaze skidded back. She believed him. Smart woman. "My waist."

He found it, a short dagger lodged in a sheath lashed around her belly, tangled amid the folds of her skirt. With a twist of his wrist, he plucked it free and straightened, forcing her back up to a standing position.

"Father Peter," he said shortly.

"I tell you, he is gone."

He looked at her more closely and saw her face was scratched and her jawline had a mark that might become a bruise. She had not had such marks yesternight. His fingers tightened as he pushed her face to the side, examining. "It will heal. What happened?"

"Men. They took Father Peter." She smiled bitterly as he let her go. "There are a plethora of violent men out this day. You should be careful."

He returned an equally mirthless grin. "Indeed. Pretty women should not play with them."

"Ah, but you see how it is so much enjoyment, I cannot stop."

"You'll stop now."

He pulled her away from the wall, swung her about onto a short bench at the foot of the bed. She slid across its smooth surface a few inches, sending her braid bouncing over one slim shoulder.

"Who took Father Peter?"

She hesitated. "I cannot say for certain."

"Say it uncertainly."

She swallowed. "Some very well-armed men and a churchman."

He took her face between his palms, then dropped to a knee in front of her, so their faces were level and he could watch every shifting emotion that flickered across her beautiful, lying face.

"Eva, let me demonstrate honesty, since you struggle so to make its acquaintance. Regard how it sounds: I am come from King John."

Slowly, her jaw fell, as it dawned on her this was not an example, but a revelation. Her face, already so pale, went absolutely white.

Then, slowly again, bright spots of color flowed back onto her cheeks, so she looked like a painting being formed: white skin, gray eyes, wild coal-black hair tumbling over his hands, and the flushing red of anger and fear on her cheeks the only color to be had.

"*Mon Dieu,*" she whispered. "You are from the devil himself. I ought to have known."

"You may call me Lucifer if you wish. Kingdoms rest in the balance of what I do, and now, you. If I am not successful in my hunt for Father Peter, a great many people will be sorry. If you are the reason why, *you* shall be sorry."

From her lips came a long, low exhale. He felt it whisper over his wrists.

"Now tell me: who sent you for the priest?"

He felt her trembling, but her gray eyes met his. "He is an old friend, I owe him a great debt, and I wish only to get him away from all this trouble. The archbishop called for his aid in the negotiations, and he came, foolishly. He is like that. You would be better off asking why your terrible king wants him than I."

"I am fairly certain why the king wants him, so that mystery is solved. But you, woman, are enigmatic. Unless, of course, one assumes you seek the priest for the self-same reasons."

She went still.

"What say you, Eva?"

Her eyes narrowed into thin gray slits, but she was able to emit a great deal of enmity from between them. "I say you had best watch your back, Jamie Knight, for I may be sticking you in it one day."

He clucked his tongue. "All that will do is keep you bound, Eva, perhaps for years, perhaps in the king's Tower."

She gave a small, bitter smile. He recognized it; he'd dispensed it himself, many times. "Well, then, Jamie, I suppose I am sorry I ever met you. We are all so sorry now."

He moved his thumbs, a swift brush over her cheekbones. Someone watching might have called it a caress. They would have been in error. "I think you will be the sorriest one of all, Eva."

Ry strode back into the room, extending a coil of rope. Jamie got to his feet. "Roland the innkeep reports a party of riders left just before we arrived," Ry said. "Going fast. They had a priest."

Jamie looked at him. Then the rope, then Eva. Back to the rope.

"You are greatly troubled by your choices," she observed.

He looked up slowly.

"You ought to leave me behind," she suggested. "How do you say this? I am expendable, no? Expend me, then."

"I think you are misunderstanding the word," he said drily.

"But you should. I will be naught but a burden. I eat a great deal, and tire easily, and you've no notion of how I complain. Ask Gog. Truly, Jamie—"

He grabbed her by the elbow and lifted her to her feet. "Let's go."

Eleven

Eva felt very much like cargo, bumping down the stairs behind Jamie. This was the sort of thought that was not comforting.

But the only other thing to think about was how his arm, thrust out behind him, appeared muscular straight down through his wrist. Or how his broad hand was clamped around her wrists, his fingers encompassing her arm like an iron band. She might be able to dislodge herself if a comet exploded overhead and knocked him senseless.

They hit the bottom stair and turned for the back door. Ry put a palm on it, then glanced at Jamie, who had pinned his back to the wall and was pushing Eva likewise with arm and elbow. Jamie gave a curt nod.

Ry nudged the door open, peered out, then kicked the door wide and leaped out into the yard, sword out. He looked to his right, his left, then gestured without turning. "Come."

Jamie herded her through as if she were a sheep, he a silent watchdog.

"Are you expecting an attack?" she asked, slightly breathless.

"Always."

This was even more disquieting than all the previous unquiet thoughts. Surely, though, she could get away. She was always able to get away. Getting away was her pennant, her battle standard, her coat of arms. No one was better at escaping than she.

She looked down at Jamie's hand, locked around her wrists.

He might be better at keeping one captured, though.

"Did Roland give you any descriptions, Ry?" Jamie asked in a low voice as they crossed a stableyard raucous with an inordinate number of chickens. Eva saw no sign of Roger, and they did not seem to either. She felt a small rush of pride.

Jamie's companion, brown-haired, brown-eyed, as tall as Jamie, leaner than Jamie, but looking almost as dangerous as Jamie, shook his head as they drew near the stable doors. "Nay," he murmured. "He said he saw only their dust."

Jamie released her when they were through the stable doors, into the dusty warmth. Eva backed away, resisting the urge to rub her wrists, for she would not have been rubbing away pain, as Jamie had not hurt her. She would have been . . . touching where he had touched.

Morning light rayed in through slats between the boards. Horses and hay were illuminated by thin strips of bright light, so they glowed golden and brown and chestnut red. The horses shifted in their stalls, turning to peer at them with liquid eyes, furry ears pricked.

Jamie and his companion led their horses out, still saddled. Clearly, they had anticipated a short stop. Perhaps she should be insulted by this.

Eva's horse was standing down the row farther, a dim brown shape, her head half down, eyes lazily closed, a single spray of golden hay poking out from between her velvety muzzle lips.

Jamie patted his horse in a distracted way and tossed the reins up. He grabbed hold of a stirrup and looked at her. "Up."

She blinked. "I, I—"

"Are getting on." Then he paused and glanced down the row,

the very direction her surreptitious little glance had gone. They both looked at the sleepy brown mare. "Yours?"

She opened her mouth, then closed it, suddenly unable to determine the need for a lie.

Revealing she had a horse would betray nothing of her purposes. Jamie could easily assume she had a horse. She'd never have made it this far without. She could claim every horse in the stable and Jamie would know nothing more than he did right now.

Yet notwithstanding all these sensible notions, Eva was engulfed like a wick by the bright, burning knowledge that the more Jamie knew of her, the more her life would become . . . irrevocable.

Eva lived for revocability. Decisions were nothing but footprints in the sand; everything could be washed away. At need, Eva revoked opinions, plans, pennies, entire personal histories.

But Jamie . . . Jamie was more the edge of the cliff than the shifting sand. No going back.

That thin scar carved through the corner of his lip and up over one high cheekbone, but did not detract a whit from the beautiful masculinity of him. Hands, blades, wits: everything Jamie bore was a weapon, and a blind man would see he was a thing to avoid. Right now he was watching her, his eyes never leaving hers throughout the lengthening silence.

Never had she been unable to lie. Never had she so much as paused in the deed. Lie, always. Run forever.

Do it, the faint call came up from inside.

"Yes," she heard herself say. "She is mine."

Well.

Jamie jabbed his chin into the air. "Ry, bring her out, will you?"

Ry strode over, and while he was being so obedient and bringing her mare out, Jamie tied Eva up.

Standing a head taller and an inch away, his dark head bent to attend the ropes, she had a strange, disorienting moment of imagining him doing something helpful as he stood before her, perhaps untangling a pouch, or showing her some trinket in secret, tucked between their bodies. She watched his thick fingers tug on the ropes and the dizzy sense expanded, down from her ridiculous head into her even more ridiculous body.

"These ropes, they are hardly necessary," she announced.

"Consider me cautious."

"Other words come to mind, not so greatly *cautious*."

He tipped his head up. He had very long eyelashes. This was not right. "Such as?"

She sighed. "You seek compliments at such a time? About your eyelashes, no doubt."

His stared at her; then the small, dented curves beside his mouth deepened ever so slightly. He bent back to his tying. "Ropes make it more difficult to escape."

"But who is to say I wish to escape?"

"Fleeing and kicking me brought the notion to mind."

She made a dismissive sound. She truly had no desire to escape, not anymore. Further reflection—the sort that came while being hauled down stairs—had shown her the truth of her straits: she had no hope of regaining Father Peter.

But Jamie did.

If one had to be in captivity, it was undeniably better to be held captive by one who had the power and inclination to take down every shared enemy in your path. Then, come time, you could simply steal away. With the priest.

She gave another sigh. "But you are so daunting with your weapons and your glowering looks—"

His hands stilled. "Glowering?"

"—what can I do but succumb?"

He gave a low laugh and resumed tying. "Once, you might

have been able to make me believe that, Eva. Then I spent the night shackled in a cellar under the town walls."

"It must have been quite cold and damp."

He flipped an end of the rope overtop and gave a sharp tug. "Quite. I was kept warm by imagining just this."

She sniffed and stared patiently at the wall, for regarding his bent head, the strands of dark hair falling by his hair-roughened jaw, did not help maintain the proper sense of outrage and loathing.

"These ropes, Jamie, I am sorry to say, they make you appear . . . afraid."

He gave a final tug and yanked her so close their chests touched.

"You have been sorry to say a great many things in the short time I've known you, Eva, and not one of them has been true." His softly spoken words dropped into the hot pocket of air between their mouths. "'Tis yourself who should be afraid, for if you do not talk soon, I will make you." He bent to her ear. "It shall not take long."

Fear had nothing on the chills his words sent cascading through Eva's body. Which meant . . . this was not fear.

Oh, indeed, Jamie was peril of a most grave sort. The edge of the cliff, the tide coming in.

He put his hands on her hips and practically vaulted her into the saddle. Eva kept herself calm by reminding herself that she had only to do two things: ensure Roger stay hidden, and herself appear witless, with as much relevance to these matters as the little bits of twigs one found in uncombed wool. Which was to say, none at all.

Irrelevant. Irrevocable. Eva was determined to be a great many things that were never to be.

Twelve

omeone is following us."

The group that rode through the spring afternoon was fiercely quiet. Jamie kept his head down for most of it, attending the earth and signs of what had passed over it. He had set a fast pace, but their quarry had gone faster.

It was not surprising; there'd been many possible turnoffs, little village roads as well as more populated tracks, forcing Jamie to a slower pace, ensuring he did not gallop past any sign of a turning.

Additionally, he had the task of monitoring whoever was tracking *them*.

Eva's hands were bound, and her horse was attached by lines to both Jamie's and Ry's saddles, so the chances of her escaping, or even attempting it, were close to nil. Still, they made sure she was covered on both sides, fore and aft, like a ship that might founder, throughout their rollicking ride.

Short breaks every few miles to rest the horses were spent in silence, Eva looking directly at Jamie. Whenever he returned her look, she'd give an indifferent sniff or one of her nonchalant little shrugs and turn away. But Jamie always spent an extra moment looking, in part because in the sunlight she was a startling display of unintended, curving sensuality.

She also had bollocks. Unfortunately, he was going to have to break them.

He slowed the group to a walk and pushed back the mail coif on his head. A small breeze ruffled the damp hair stuck to the back of his neck, for it was a warm spring day, and the sun beat down hard on men in mail.

He nodded to Ry, beckoning him forward to ride alongside him. The ropes to Eva's horse stretched out behind them like those to a barge, comely, dangerous cargo.

"I thought I detected a visitor as well," murmured Ry when Jamie shared his thoughts. "What do you make of it?"

"I do not know. Why would you track us?"

Ry paused. "You mean if I were seeking Peter of London?"

"If you were seeking anything, for what reason would you track *us*? Were you a bandit and you'd foolishly selected us as your target, you would simply hit us and hit hard. We've passed enough copses to host a score of attacks. Yet, nothing. Alternately, should you be seeking Peter of London, you would not be following us at all."

Ry looked over. "And if you were after Eva?"

Jamie rested his hand on his thigh. "My thoughts exactly."

Ry nodded. "How do you think she plays in?"

"In the way that seeking Father Peter plays in."

"That is a wide net, Jamie. Upon a time, Peter of London meant high Church business, messy power struggles with the king, and illuminations on rather a grand scale."

Jamie nodded. Peter of London had been a well-known, well-respected object of royal irritation. Intelligent, self-styled, gifted, and far too subtle in thought to bend to John, even early on, when the promises were good and the follow-through not yet so befouled. The king disliked Peter of London almost as greatly as he did Archbishop Langton. Jamie's father had admired them both. Peter had fled ten years ago and had been in self-imposed exile—some said *hiding*—ever since.

Now, suddenly, the archbishop had called for his old friend to assist in the negotiations between the rebels and the king. Why?

More to the point, why had the rebels, who had as much interest as the king in reaching some unarmed agreement—which was to say, none at all—suggested bringing Peter of London over in the first place?

But suggest they had, weeks ago, just before they had renounced their fealty. That act had tarnished the goodwill of their request to a great degree, but then, surprise, surprise, the king had seconded the request.

It was the only thing the king and the rebels had agreed on in the past three years. Yes, by all means, bring over Peter of London. Aye, aye, aye.

It was an agreeable, collaborative, sensible solution and thus reeked of subterfuge and duplicity.

Jamie rubbed the back of his head. "There is more here than meets the eye, Ry. More than contracts and illuminations. And in some unfathomable way, it involves Eva."

Neither of them had so much as tipped his head in her direction. Their voices were pitched so low that Jamie strained to hear Ry, riding directly at his side. Nonetheless, he felt Eva's attention home in on him, hover against his armor like fireglow.

"And therefore, whoever is following us."

Ry nodded. "What do we want to do about him?

Jamie glanced over. "Flush him."

Ry nodded again.

They needed nothing but simple words to communicate elaborate plans. They'd been through too much together, relied on each other too heavily, knew each other's mind and responses too deeply, to require more. Sometimes they did not need to speak at all, which was occasionally unnerving to whoever was in the room—or on a battlefield—with them.

"Now?" Ry asked.

Jamie shook his head. "Let us see what Eva does. Follow my lead, and once we have him"—he looked over slowly—"leave me alone with her."

Ry had been nodding in agreement, but he looked over sharply at that. "Do not, Jamie. She's defenseless."

He snorted. "Before you lament her frail state overly much, recall she almost dislocated my knee earlier and was prickled with daggers. We do not have a ward in our keeping, Ry. We have an enemy combatant."

It was much easier to have enemy combatants in one's keeping than a soul requiring care. Jamie could not even manage a squire. There'd only been two, both failed attempts at human relations. He'd quickly set them up with other lords, less self-ruinous men, better able to give them both a future and a present. A squire, hell, Jamie could not even manage a dog. Not anymore. Not after London—

"What we have is a woman who weighs less than my saddle." Ry's voice drew him back from the streets of London, all those years ago.

Jamie tightened his leg against Dickon's side and the horse turned smoothly. He met Ry's gaze with a hard one of his own.

"What we have is a woman valuable enough to be stalked by a companion when their quarry is far on ahead. I shall discover what I must, how I must, Ry. As I ever have done. I cannot be cried off now. Kingdoms ride on the consequences."

A messenger stumbled into the great hall of the mighty Baynard Castle in London.

Robert fitzWalter, lord of Dunmow and Baynard Castle, leader of the rebel forces, glanced up in irritation, then gazed back out the slitted window he'd been looking through, brooding, for half an hour.

All around, his compatriots continued their drunken binge, celebrating their triumphant coup of the great City. FitzWalter had every reason to join them, for they'd just completed the coup no one could have forseen; his rebel army had just taken London.

London was his.

They had taken it with nary an arrowbolt fired. That was unfortunate, of course, the lack of fighting, but when the citizens opened the gates, one could hardly mow them down.

She burned now, of course, in pockets, as the men looted the Jewish ghettos. Soldiers must be paid. Plunder was easy. The Jews were the easiest yet and had the additional benefit of homes that could provide stone for the retrenchment of the City walls. Which was not to say they weren't also making use of raided monastery coffers. FitzWalter was impartial when it came to such things. This fight was hardly over.

Armies small and large were already marching, streaming like steely tributaries toward the City. The heirs of great estates were riding to fitzWalter's standard, while their fathers held the castles and kept peace with the king. The country was ripping apart like cloth along the bias. Everyone was maneuvering for position. No one knew how far this would go or where it would end.

FitzWalter looked down at the parchment in his calloused hand. On its rough surface were line after line of dark ink scrawling, detailing the charter of liberties the rebels were demanding of the king.

This time, King John would sign.

He would have no choice. The crown jewel in his array of city-stones, London, had just fallen to a rap on her gates.

All the charter wanted was John's signature and royal seal. Then it would go out to all four corners of the realm, heralded at village squares and town fairs and the castles of his greatest magnates: the barons' charter, *Magna Carta*, signed and stamped by the royal We.

FitzWalter scowled at it as the messenger ran down the stairs.

"They have the priest," he shouted as he reached the dais table. Everyone stared as he dropped to his knees, sucking in breaths, hand on his chest.

Robert fitzWalter let a slow grin lift his bearded cheeks. He turned to the earl of Essex, his cocommander. "Mouldin has brought me my priest."

A hum of excited voices broke around him, approval, anticipation. The messenger's gasped words were distinct from the murmuring.

"Nay, my lord. He has not brought the priest. He sends a message instead."

FitzWalter's grin froze. He got to his feet, as if readying himself in advance for the blow to come. "What message?"

"A . . . ransom offer."

The room fell silent. The sounds of horses and shouting men outside floated through the window of the castle walls, but inside, everyone was staring at fitzWalter.

"How much?" he said in a low, humming voice. "How much does he want?"

The messenger swallowed. "That is dependent, my lord."

FitzWalter curled his fingers around the edge of the table rather than the man's neck. Squeezing tight, he leaned forward, his words slow and deliberate. *"Upon what?"*

The messenger looked truly sick. "On how much the others bid."

FitzWalter gave a harsh bark of laughter and kicked his chair back. It squealed like an animal, then toppled off the dais with a crash. "That clever, dead man."

He stalked behind the trestle table. Men moved away, in case that got tossed next. "I will not pay. I will see him pricked with a hundred arrows in his fat arse before I surrender to him one more penny. I commissioned him. I paid him—"

He swung to the messenger. "Against whom am I bidding?"

"The king."

Fury welled up in him, thick viscous gobs of it, up his spine into his throat. "But of course. Deal you in snakes, you shall get the venom."

He turned to the far wall and stared out the window. He must go carefully here. This entire move, this taking of the City, had been predicated upon the successful retrieval of Peter of London, and was to be the last in a line of toppling royal dominoes.

FitzWalter had set the thing in motion by suggesting they invite the priest to England to assist in the parley. Once he arrived, Mouldin was to bring him in. Then, the prize: the missing heirs of England.

Everoot, d'Endshire.

Everoot was by far the greater estate, the greater risk, but both were mighty chinks in John's baronial armor. It was too many great Houses to be *in absentia*. And in these times of strife and civil unrest, the rumors were taking shape again. No one spoke of them above a whisper, but whisper they did, as if a scent had been carried on the breeze to the nostrils of the great and mighty: find the missing heirs.

Rumors swirled as to what had happened to those great lords all those years ago, but most agreed the king's temper had seen them done in.

Now the heirs were running loose in the world somewhere. Dead as well?

Mayhap. Mayhap not.

Father Peter would know.

FitzWalter knew he was closer than he'd ever been before. There could be no missteps now. First seize the priest.

Then the crown.

He plunged his hands into the nearby cistern and flung a handful of cold water over his face. Droplets stuck to his beard when he straightened.

"So be it. But I will not send an emissary. I will go to Gracious Hill and extract the poison myself. Then I will march Peter of London out on the field at Runnymede and kick the legs out from under John's throne. Essex has the City in my absence. Tell no one I am gone."

He started for the door. The members of his personal guard leaped to their feet. The messenger held up a hand.

"My lord, I was told to inform you: Jamie has been spotted. Hunting the priest."

FitzWalter stopped short. He half turned. "Jamie Lost?"

"Aye, my lord."

He stared for a moment, then threw his head back and gave a loud, coarse laugh. "Of course. Ever has Jamie been my own personal plague. Send for Chance," he ordered as he turned again for the door. "Should Jamie show up, Chance can . . . inquire if he has reconsidered his loyalties. *Again.*"

He strode out of the room.

The race was on. Whoever brought the heirs into his fold first would release the waterfall. The news would rush like a river through England and sweep up the undecided nobles. It would ripple through their pledged knights and the fat merchants who ran their rich fair towns like a dam undone.

Without the crucial support of these middling barons and their knights and merchants, the rebellion would fail.

But then, so would a kingship.

Thirteen

Eva felt as if she were riding through the middle of one of Father Peter's sketches. The trees all wore billowing green caps and stood proudly in their dark brown tunics as they marched up and down the hills of England.

Less showy but more sweet, tiny pricking flowers hurried to the edge of the track. The hedgerows hosted a profusion of flowering vines and exuberant birds, flitting their wings and chirping. Whenever the land opened up, herds of red poppies raced down the hills like ponies, all exuberance and flicking tails.

England was a most comely land. Eva had forgotten.

But then, she'd wanted to forget. She'd scrubbed at her memories with such vigor that after ten years, well, one could hardly expect little yellow flowers to survive such a cleansing.

Except they had.

She'd sketched them in a painting once. Gog had noticed. Somehow, even he recalled the little yellow flowers from when he was five, before they had fled.

It was not a comfortable knowledge, that England and its sweet flowers had stayed in both their minds.

Many other memories were pouring back now as well, including this road and its poor condition. She remembered it well; a few more miles ought to bring them near to where she and Roger had lived for a few desperate months, all those years ago.

A few scattered hamlets could be seen here and there, far-off smoke rising from their clusters, but the remote, rutted road itself was desolate and empty. For the ruts alone, no one would suspect a group of soldiers fleeing with a priestly hostage to travel this way.

But they had. When the hard and rocky ground gave the smallest clue of this fact, Jamie had followed behind. He was a consummate woodsman.

Unfortunately, Gog was less good.

His ten years of skulking in woods and the edges of towns in no way measured against the hunting skills of these two seasoned knights. There were only the two of them, but Eva felt surrounded by castle walls. An approach could come from the unprotected sides, Eva supposed gloomily, but if Gog were so foolish as to try—and he was not whatsoever foolish—he wouldn't make it so far as a yard. He'd be struck down before he made it out of the eaves.

She tried to listen for signs of him, following in the wood, but if he was doing it properly, she wouldn't notice him at all.

Jamie might, though.

"Might I have my hands unleashed?" she inquired when they next slowed the horses.

Jamie, who'd been taking the aft, came forward beside her. His gleaming chestnut horse snorted at hers, but Jamie nudged him closer yet.

"My arms ache." She shifted them to demonstrate. "My shoulders."

His gaze slid away to the wood beyond. He tipped his chin up and opened his mouth slightly, his body rock-still as he scanned the trees and the shadows beneath. She realized what he was doing: tasting the air. Seeing, hearing, smelling, using every sense to assess his proximate world, alive to any hint of a trap, an attack, a possible route of escape. He was like a wild creature.

He was magnificent.

This made Eva angry. She did not so much like magnificence. It was too often found in things such as castles and cathedrals, things of hard stone one could dash oneself against trying to get out of. Or into.

That such magnificence could come in the form of a stony person too, well, it simply beggared her for words.

His pewter-blue gaze slid back to her. "No." He turned away.

She opened her mouth to protest, then snapped it shut as he reined away, clucking to encourage her horse to follow. Her horse was lashed to his, so it hardly mattered, all this clucking and encouraging. They would all go his way in the end.

She eyed the broad expanse of his self-approving back. Yes, indeed, this was a back that approved of itself. Every easy sway of his shoulders showed it to be. Such powerful men crafted the hard truths of the hard, cold world, and she was heartfully tired of it.

"You must be very proud of yourself," she announced.

He showed no response for a moment, then shifted and looked over his shoulder, eyebrow cocked in query.

"Riding about on your very large horse, with your hard armor and your oh-so-intimidating sword."

He watched her a moment, then tipped his face up, as if catching an agreeable scent. Was he smiling? He looked back down. Yes, he was smiling, a very little bit.

"Tell me, Eva, have I intimidated you with my . . . sword?"

Shocking, the orb of heat that scorched her insides at his low-pitched innuendo, up from her belly to her cheeks and back down again. And flung out behind it, like the tail of a comet, came the searing memory: she'd dreamt of him last night. Repeatedly.

Hot, restless dreams, of slow-moving hands, of a hard-packed thigh pushing between hers, of his hands on her shoulders pulling her down to him . . .

Hot, hotter, hottest; his eyes on her just now, that little knowing smile.

She sniffed. "You are a very bad man."

Something hard flashed in his eye. "That I am, Eva." He reined in, bringing his glinting armor and hot body right up beside her, the length of his thigh bumping hers.

Then he whispered, "Who is Gog?"

Her body went cold. Just slightly, as it does the moment the air decides, *Yes, now I shall snow. No more of this driving rain; let us try the snow.* And the temperature drops, and the delicate branch tips get fat with ice, and everyone hurries into their homes. Those without huddle with the ice-fat branches and scowl at their ice-fat toes.

She looked at him coldly. It was not difficult to do; coldness emanated from both disdain and fear. How fortunate for her. "You are not only a bad man but a confusing one as well. What is this you ask? A 'frog'?"

Again, nothing, for the longest time. Blue eyes intent on you were not a restful thing, she decided.

"Gog," he said, softer now.

"I do not know of what you speak."

"I speak of what you said back at the Goat. 'You've no notion of how I complain. Ask Gog,'" he quoted her, and watched her, and the snow started falling in her heart.

"To my shame, Jamie, I did not. I said, 'Dear God.' But I shall stop committing such venial sins, as they obviously dispose you to visions."

He smiled. It was slow, small, and aimed right at her. He might as well have poked her with a stick.

"Ah."

His deep rumble vibrated inside her, and she wished very much, just now, to both crack him on the head and close her eyes, so she might feel nothing but the rumble as it moved through her body.

Some men were like roots to water for certain things. They might not seek them or even want them, but even so, they came down on them like rain. Some men sought battle; others had it thrust upon them. Some fell heedless into coin; others wanted a penny their whole lives. Some men drank to excess, some could not turn from the dice.

Eva—Eva found danger. She was like a tributary, running downhill to the great river of Trouble. And this time, she'd spilled directly into Jamie's river valley.

Fourteen

They stopped at a small crossroads where many tracks converged. Jamie and Ry convened another conference.

"The road diverges here," Jamie was saying. He shoved his fingers through his hair in an impatient, sweaty way. "Along the eastern way, in about a mile or so, is a town. West hies toward Bristol."

"They might have gone there," Ry was saying in his soft-spoken, smart voice. It was a sad thing she had met Ry in this way, with the ropes and the kidnapping, for she was certain they could have been friends.

"Aye," agreed the dark-eyed one with whom she could *never* be friends. "'Tis a major port, with ships."

"Easy to bring in a ship without being seen, sail out again."

"With a priest aboard."

"Precisely. Yet you say the signs point north," Ry murmured. He sat as straight in his saddle as Jamie, his calm brown eyes looking less dangerous than Jamie's, but she'd seen him at the docks and witnessed the calm competence when he had kicked open the back door of the inn. Surely he was as lethal as Jamie, should the need for lethality arise.

Which it would.

"Aye," Jamie said. "North. Where there are no ships, no beaches, and no borders for two hundred miles." He looked at his friend, forearm over the front of his saddle, considering this as if he were a king. "Tell me, Ry, how likely does it seem they made for a remote track that points nowhere but north for a hundred miles or more?"

Eva stifled a curt reply along the lines of *Utterly without possibility, unlike the likelihood of us being seen, sitting here like ducks.*

"More likely than heading into the remote north," Ry said, shaking his head. "I've no notion why they would head north in the first place."

Because that is where Mouldin kept his lair in days past. Eva shifted impatiently. Surely he still knew people, had contacts and connections that would allow him to conduct the negotiations he no doubt intended to host, with Father Peter as the prize.

How much would it be worth to Jamie, this news?

But there was nothing useful to her here, in this line of thought. She had nothing to bargain with. If she mentioned Mouldin, at best Jamie would release her, and she would never regain Father Peter. Worse, he would do something inconvenient, such as tie her to a tree.

Worse yet, it would get much, much worse.

Mouldin meant heirs. He could not be mentioned.

"So you counsel port?" Jamie said to Ry.

Eva tipped forward, into their conversation. "That would be most unwise."

They turned in their creaking saddles and stared. Jamie's expression was smooth and unreadable. Distant and considering.

"The port, this is a most unwise choice," she repeated. "Our quarry did not go west. Or east to a little town."

"And how do you know that?" Behind Jamie's shoulders, the

sky reddened with sunset light. His face was filled with lines of suspicion, which made him only more beautiful, which was highly distressing.

"I do not know," she retorted. "I use my reason. 'Twould be madness, would it not? To go to some busy port town with an unhappy priest and display him like new shoe leathers?"

Jamie's gaze, at once clear and impenetrable, never left hers. "I find your assessment riveting, Eva. What I do not understand is your certainty. It makes me curious."

"I do not like you curious," she said sharply. But he was not *curious* whatsoever, not unless *curiosity* and *predator* went together like garlic and butter. He was like an animal crouched in high grasses, stalking its prey.

He reined his horse beside her, facing opposite, so their eyes met.

"I do not think they went to the town," she explained with great dignity. "And you do not either. This, I know. I can see it in your face. When your Ruggart Ry suggests the thing, your eyes narrow this little bit." She held up her fingers, squeezing her thumb and forefinger almost to touching. "And you think, 'This idea is not so good.' Do not tell me otherwise. Your oh-so-good skills of tracking have held us steady to this most rutted course for miles. The dirt we see kicked up along the side, the depth of the hoofprints, the way the clouds cover the sky—I am sure all these details reveal important things to you. And I am, with great sadness, forced to agree. You are unmistaken. They did not go to this town."

He'd crossed his arms over his chest during her soliloquy, head tipped to the side. "I did not say that, Eva. But I admit, your dislike of the town makes me warm to it immeasurably."

"Ah, see? We are of no good liking. You should let me go; we do not get along like good children should."

"And what if my oh-so-good tracking skills counseled,

'What ho, bear west'?" he asked, his voice softly mimicking her tone. "What then?"

She slowly arched an eyebrow. "Then they would not be oh-so-good."

Ry nudged his horse forward. They formed a small darted triangle in the middle of the rutted road. He spoke into the chilly silence created by the dipping sun and Jamie's hard stare.

"I confess, Jamie, unfathomable as a northern route is, your tracking has ne'er led us astray before. I counsel we continue north."

Ah, see, the lines of friendships-that-could-have-been were clear. Ry was much more levelheaded and trustworthy than Jamie. He agreed with her.

But the small uprush of hope in her belly was dashed before it reached her heart as he went on, "But the horses can go no farther. We need to camp the night."

Jamie nodded in agreement. "If we branch off here," he said, pointing into the dark wood, "we can set up camp inside the treeline."

Eva followed the sweep of his muscular arm, her heart crashing entirely.

Out of all the hilltops in England, why must Jamie point to hers?

Fifteen

The wood began perhaps ten paces off the main track, heavily treed and ferned and brambled. "Atop that rise," Jamie said, "no doubt there is a view for miles down the track."

Ry was already dismounting. "Let us go, before darkness falls."

Eva made a sharp little move, wiping her hand nervously down the top of her leg. Jamie followed it with his gaze. She glanced into the trees, wiped again, then blurted out, "We cannot camp here."

Ah. He almost smiled. More secrets of Eva. Talking to her was like locating the trace line of silver in a mine.

"You're particular," he drawled. "Neither east nor west, and for certes not the wood."

Her gaze rushed over to him. "Yes, I am just that sort. Difficult to please, happy with no thing. I am the woman always wanting the new shoes, the pretty lace. I require much maintenance. I will tire you thoroughly."

Ry snorted. Jamie's gaze never left hers. She was frightened, but oddly distracted. All his senses went on high alert.

"The horses can go no farther, Eva," Jamie said, watching close.

"But—"

"No horses, no Father Peter. And I cannot track in the dark."

She stared at him, clearly caught between sense and some other, almost desperate need to move on. Ry sensed it too. He stepped forward and murmured, "Do you know something that would help us, mistress?"

Her forehead furrowed with earnestness. "I know we cannot camp in these woods."

"Why not?"

"'Tis not safe."

Jamie and Ry exchanged a glance.

"What I mean to say is, this is just the sort of wood we have in France, which is filled with surprising pockets of quicksand and thickets. That is bad. And are there not wolves?" she concluded on a faint note of triumph.

"No."

Just then, a long, low howl went up.

She smiled and spread out a hand. "We see the wolves."

Jamie gave the ghost of a smile.

"So you see, with clarity, we cannot camp here."

"I see with clarity you know a great deal about these woods."

He examined her in the pale glow, then slowly reached for the rope that connected their horses. He looped it around the pommel of his saddle over and over, drawing her closer, until her horse stood belly to belly with his and her knee bumped his, then tilted his head in Ry's direction without looking away.

"Go and check the hill, Ry, will you? The one Eva does not want us on."

SHE felt the kick of panic like little elfin boots, striking at her rib cage. She tried to breathe normally.

It was only a small hut, she thought. Ten years was a great

long time in a wet wood. Perhaps it had fallen to wreck and ruin. Perhaps it had rotted away. Perhaps all signs of its existence—and theirs—were decayed clear away.

Or perhaps not.

She'd made it their own, this abandoned little hut. Painted it, for goodness' sake, so it would be a modicum less frightening for a five-year-old boy who'd so recently witnessed terrible horrors. Laid rushes, embellished the walls with drawings like the castle rooms he'd been accustomed to, with fine red lines so they mimicked masonry bricks, flowers painted within. Painted the outer door as well, to resemble curving vines.

Just like her fingernails. Would Jamie recall such a detail?

Jamie would recall how many outbreaths she'd taken, should it serve his purpose.

They sat side by side and listened to Ruggart Ry bash through the underbrush. Eva pretended to watch. He was breaking through the brush, directly toward the old abandoned hut she'd used as a hiding spot with Roger ten years ago.

After a moment, Ry called out, "There's something here, Jamie. Just beyond the crest of the hill. A small hut."

Her heart sank as if small iron weights were attached to it, dragging it into a pit.

Jamie turned to her, his gaze, at once clear and impenetrable, aimed like an archer's arrow. "Fascinating." He did not sound fascinated. He sounded suspicious.

She nodded, not at all suspiciously. She filled it with all the nonchalance and innocence one could put into a nod. She offered a smile made of equal ingredients. One could build a tower of sweets with this nod and smile.

And then he did a terrible thing. He smiled. "I am going to do you a boon favor, Eva."

Her jaw dropped slowly, but her heart went tumbling much faster, deep into the pits of her suddenly flipping belly, which was sending the most insensible chills *up*, like rising air. She'd been stormed by a cyclone inside.

"Wha—What do you mean?"

Her stuttered, shocked reply faded into silence as Jamie kicked his foot over his horse's rump and started toward her, making everything that had been rising up inside start going entirely downward.

Off to the side, Ry stood looking . . . was that sad? Disappointed?

Worried?

Jamie clasped her by the hips and slid her unceremoniously off the horse. She hit the ground, staggering a moment as her legs adjusted to being back on solid earth. "What favor?"

Jamie gave another of his alarming smiles. "We're going to bring in your boy."

Sixteen

She hit the ground hard. Jamie closed his hands around her arms, pulling her toward him. He was not rough, but neither was he gentle. The kingdom was tottering on the brink of civil war, and she might know something that could open a door or slam it shut, to the ruination of a kingdom.

Her body ricocheted backward in swift response. He let her go. For now. She backed up and her boot trod into the feathery ferns bordering the road. Jamie tracked her slowly. No need to have her trip and bash her brains in. Yet.

"Eva," he said calmly. "I am a patient man. I have waited many years for many things, and I shall wait through many more. I have served kings and counts and dowager queens, and ne'er counted a minute wasted. But I am growing impatient with you."

An ambient reddish glow still lit the tops of the trees, but she was backing up into darkness, where thick, ancient tree limbs hung heavy with moss and cobwebs, and wild animals lived long lives, never laying eyes on a human.

"In this way, you and I are alike," she said, and it was almost a gasp. She took another step back and bumped into a tree. She stopped, her spine to the trunk. Jamie came within a stride's length and stopped.

All the bindings of her hair had pulled free, and it fell in dark, tangled streamers around her face. "I am impatient with how you keep backing me up against things," she complained breathlessly.

This was so, he realized. Three times now: in an alley, against the wall of a bedchamber, and now against a tree.

Generally, there were more dire consequences to stretching Jamie's patience, and one did not get the opportunity to do so thrice. That Eva had, required thought.

But not now. He would think tonight, while he sat sleepless around the fire. Thousands of nights it had been already, and thousands more lay ahead, filled with fires and restless half sleep. Time for many thoughts.

Now was not the time for thoughts.

Now was the time to rattle her.

He put his hand on the tree just above her head. "When you stop lying to me, Eva, I will stop backing you up against things." He rested the edge of his other hand on her shoulder, his fingers against her neck, and in the spirit of rattling, when she swallowed, he traced down the length of her throat with the pad of his thumb.

"Father Peter has itinerated with the great and mighty, Eva. How does a waif like you play in?"

"Ah, see," she said, her voice shaky, but sharp with anger, "you think these are such good questions, Jamie. You are so clever to have them. They are after me, of course. Father Peter is but a decoy."

He ignored this. "Tell me why you know about little huts in the English woods. Where are you from, Eva? Where in England?"

The telltale hesitation, the swift bump of her heart against her ribs, against his, they were standing so close.

"These woods? Did you grow up near here?"

"No, but I passed through them," she said breathlessly, "many years ago."

"Then you are from here."

She shook her head quickly. "No. But I passed through on my way to France, many years ago."

"How many?"

"Too many."

"You have a good memory of them."

She swallowed. He felt it pass under his palm. "This good memory is a requirement. Surviving oft depends on such a thing as never forgetting. This, I think, you know too."

What was that intended to mean? It was true, true as anything. He'd lived on thwarted vengeance, fed by a wellspring of hot, boiling, unforgettable memories for almost twenty years. But she couldn't know that.

Yet she knew something. Behind that pale face and those dark eyes lurked a massive, dangerous intelligence. Insightful and discerning.

"Unfortunately, Eva, you're not telling me what I want to know. Why do you not try telling me why someone is following us?"

She released a breath, a long exhalation, slow and hot against his neck. "You will never find him."

"No?"

She shook her head. "Never."

"I think he'll come, Eva. If you are in danger." She gasped as he slid his hand into the warmth under her hair at the base of her neck. "Call for him."

She opened her mouth but nothing came out.

"Call for him, Eva."

They stared at each other through an echoing silence.

Then the greenery behind him rustled ever so slightly.

His muscles bunched to push away, but before he could

move, a blade came swinging out of the bushes. It sliced through the air, arcing up to his throat, and stopped short. He froze. He heard a scream die in Eva's throat.

From the corner of his eye he could see a young man, maybe fifteen or sixteen, off to the side. His face was white but grim, one long arm extended out in a straight line, trembling slightly as he held the steely edge to Jamie's neck. His other arm was up and slightly behind him, counterbalance. He looked as if he were walking a log. The blade trembled, shivering close to Jamie's neck.

No one moved.

Then another whispered hush whirred, steel slicing through air, and Ry's sword arced down and in. It stopped half an inch from the front of the boy's throat, not trembling in the least.

Everything fell silent. Not even the birds were moving. It was an absolutely silent copse of trees. Long heartbeats hammered by.

Then the soft, rushing sound of Eva's inhale. She took a deep breath, expanding her lungs, then followed the lines of steel and human flesh down to Jamie's hard, angry eyes, and said:

"I suggest an alliance."

Seventeen

amie laughed.

A single, short bark. The movement it required bobbed the sword at his throat a bit closer.

Eva lifted her gaze over his shoulder. "Lower your blade, Roger," she said quietly.

A long, weighty pause ensued, then Roger did as she bid.

The moment the blade was a safe distance from Jamie's throat, Ry kicked it the rest of the way to the ground and hauled the boy around backward. Jamie spun from the tree, pulling Eva with him.

"Wisely done."

"Yes, I am very wise."

He turned to Ry, who had the boy's arms bent and twisted up hard against his spine, so he was bent half over. Still, he managed to keep his head up sufficiently to eye Jamie with enmity.

"Anything you want to tell me, Roger?" he inquired curtly.

The hard glare became a bit more set. No reply. Eva sighed.

"For there was a great deal you wished to communicate to me a moment ago. Care to elaborate on any of it now?"

Roger jerked fiercely, which did nothing to budge Ry's tight, twisting hold. Roger settled on fixing one eye on Jamie; the other was hidden behind a fall of dirty blond hair. "If you touch Eva, I will kill you. Sir."

"Hush, Roger," Eva murmured. "I am in negotiations here."

He did not remove his glare from Jamie, and neither did Jamie stop glaring as he asked curtly, "How old is he?"

"Fifteen," she said.

"If he wishes to see sixteen, counsel him not to issue such challenges when he is stripped of his weapons and bound."

"I am certain he is making note of that just now."

Jamie's gaze sliced to Ry. "Can you manage him?"

Ry gave a clipped nod.

"This is your last opportunity, Roger," Jamie said coldly. "Anything for me? Before I get it out of Eva?"

Roger jerked again, then said in a cold voice, "Mouldin. Guillaume Mouldin took Father Peter. Leave Eva be."

Silence. Complete silence rent the sounds of the wood, the trilling sunset birds and soft burble of the creek.

Jamie was staring. Nothing was revealed, neither in his blue eyes nor by his armored body.

Then came his harsh echo: *"Mouldin?"*

And in that single repeated word, Eva heard something that conjured a sensation she hadn't thought even a witch could magic up anymore: hope.

For what she'd heard in Jamie's echo had been disgust, perhaps to a degree as wide as her own, for the monster of Mouldin. This odd, awful affinity brought a warming glow to the perimeter of her belly. It did not warm her cold, dark core, of course, but there at the edges glowed a pale little light.

She marveled inwardly, while Jamie and Ry exchanged looks of the sort that were grim and unpleasant. But all she felt was a strange, floating sort of hope. A leaf on a stream, rushing to new lands.

Then Jamie started toward her and dashed all her hopes to hell, which was no new land at all.

———

"TAKE him to the horses," he ordered grimly, moving toward Eva. "Why is Mouldin in this matter? He deals in heirs. Rich ones."

"Mouldin deals in humans," she said breathlessly. "He was a slave trader before your king favored him."

"And why is he in this matter with the priest?"

"He is an opportunist, no? Tell me, Jamie, how much do you think Peter of London would be worth?"

"I do not know," he said slowly, eyeing her from the hem of her skirts up to her lying eyes. "Why don't you tell me: how much is he worth?"

"I do not know either, Jamie Knight. How much is a kingdom worth to the king? The rebels? Mouldin? You?"

He walked up to within an inch of her. "And there we are, come back around to the heart of the matter. Father Peter and the many people who are interested in him."

"All of the bad men," she fired back.

"For instance, me."

"For *very* instance, you. All of you, men who want nothing of his skills of negotiation."

"Except you, of course, who greatly desires peace."

She looked ready to bite him, if only she could move more than her eyelids. "What I greatly desire is that you all use your swords to push each other into the sea. I care nothing for the peace of England. Nor do they. All of you, madmen with swords."

"I agree. The likelihood of peace erupting in England is on scale with the likelihood of Cross Fell erupting."

She drew back slightly and regarded him in suspicious silence. Long trails of vines snaked down the rough bark behind her head, and the tiny white flowers within framed the dark tumble of her hair. It was surprising how regal and graceful she could look, backed up against a tree in a forest glen.

"What do you think they want instead?" he asked. "If not to negotiate, then why call for him at all?"

"I've no notion."

He slid the back of one knuckle down the side of her cheek. "Now that is a paltry lie."

Her face retained its whiteness, but her eyes fairly shot flames into him. "Upon a time, before England's interdict and the king's excommunication, Father Peter was present at a great many of your king's events. Contracts and writs and royal eyres, when the courts went out, when witnesses were needed. And, unfortunately for your king, when they were not."

"Unfortunately for you, Eva, you keep telling me things I already know. Why not try for things along the lines of, who sent you here?"

She closed her eyes, hopefully in surrender, then opened them. For a brief moment, he could see a wash of green from the branches above reflected in their gray depths.

"No one sent me. As I have said, Father Peter is a friend. I served as a nurse in a noble household for a time. The father was . . . died." She tripped slightly over the word. "Mouldin came for the heirs. My services were no longer required. Perhaps I was not so good at it. In any event, I left. Roger and I."

"And your own parents?"

This provided a full-on dam to the flow of information, for a good ten seconds. He counted them off, two beats of her heart for every one that slid by. "We have no parents. It happened when we were very young."

He showed no response, he was certain of this. A decade in the king's service required one to become skilled at revealing nothing more than a mirror would: the viewer's own self. But inside, he was thinking, *She was an orphan. Like me.*

Sunset was on them. The gloaming would not be far behind, when spring mists would slide out from the wet places of the earth.

"So," he said slowly. "You are here for a debt of the heart. And this thing with Father Peter is to do with papers and contracts. Nothing more."

She met his gaze sadly. "I know not all the things in Father Peter's head and heart. But I do know he is a friend, he once saved my life, and if 'tis within my power, I will now save his."

Which was absurd. This sparrow elf, to thwart vengeful kings and warring barons and Jamie, who had more secrets, had foisted more intrigues, and knew so many ways to kill he'd never fit through the gates of Heaven, and *she* was going to save Father Peter? Foil them all?

And yet . . . she had. Outwitted him. Aye, she was currently bound in ropes, hyperventilating against a tree, but there was something about her. Something deep set. Determined.

Resolute, he amended wryly, as he held her gaze. She was scared, but she was unwavering. With depth. Like wind or water or air. Like a storm at sea, or the pressing sun on the deserts of Palestine.

Indomitable.

Perhaps the wonder at finding such expansive elements in such a small fire explained why he did not push her any further, why he thought more of bending to run his lips down her arched neck.

Or perhaps it was the telltale crack of a stick under someone's boot. He jerked his head around. Ry stood there.

"Where the hell is Roger?" Jamie said sharply.

"Tied the hell to the tree."

He pushed away from Eva. The hilt of his sword bumped his

elbow as he shifted. He had a variety of other blades strapped across his body and wore mail that would protect against all but the most powerfully shot arrow.

Eva wore a blue skirt.

Some of the small white flowers that had framed her face had pinned themselves in her hair. They floated amid the curtain of dark tresses that swirled down to her hips, looking like little faraway candles on a river.

What would it feel like when he ran his fingers through it?

There was the smallest, oddest twinge of something in his chest. He shrugged it off and turned to Ry, who stood, arms crossed, watching him.

Miniature trails of mist started forming in the stream valley and tendriling up. Twenty years of friendship meant Ry had been subjected to twenty years of mayhem, triggered by a plethora of furious, focused choices by Jamie.

Fights of the angry sort on the London streets at eight, afterward limping to Ry's home in the Jewry, where Ry's mother would patch him up with scolding love and stinging tinctures, only one of which ever did any good. Intrigue of the precocious sort at twelve, involving barons and horses and messages gone awry; recruitment at thirteen, albeit an awful one, binding himself to King John with a larger goal, always the larger purpose in mind.

And Ry had hurled himself into the fray after Jamie each time, for some unknown and much appreciated reason. Jamie owed Ry his life a dozen times over, from the day they first met, when Ry had seen him at his weakest, his lowest, bloody and reeling down the street, half-dead, wanting to be fully so. Ry had coaxed him into his house like the wild thing he'd been. Jamie had vowed to repay him one day, a thousand times again.

At the moment, Ry was waiting for him to look over, at

which point he met Jamie's gaze impassively, arms still crossed. He lifted a brow.

"Are you finished?"

Jamie turned on his heel and started back to the clearing. "Seeing as you haven't anything useful to do, why don't you loosen the cinches on the horses? Let us go see about Eva's little hut and discover what mischief is afoot."

"I do not engage in mischief," she said primly.

"You engage in something," he muttered, reaching back to tug on her arm. He added to Ry, "Be prepared for anything."

Eighteen

Eva went ahead of them, pushing through the thick, untouched underbrush that enclosed the hill path. Twilight trickled down between the thick latticework covering of branches like water through a sieve. It was dim, but not dark.

She remembered it just like this, the haunting glossy gray glow, silvery when the moon was bright, the green leaves looking black in the shadows and moonlight.

Did Roger recall it as well? She could not risk a glance back. Who knew what it might reveal to Jamie?

Moss dripped from the tree limbs, the pale green roughness almost glowing in the twilight. Huge trees were downed right and left, their decaying bodies topped by mushrooms and baby trees, nursing on the rot. The sound of their footfalls and breath seemed to bounce back against the wall of green, rejected by all the silent growing things.

They reached the top of the hill. In the center of a large clearing was a small hut. It was utterly dilapidated.

Eva felt a small rush of relief. The south wall had collapsed entirely, and what was left of the roof had crashed in atop it. The other three walls stood, but barely, bowed in, crumbling, covered in moss and mushrooms. It was decaying, nondescript, and unremarkable in every way.

Except for the door.

Her heart sank.

Below the bowing triangulated eaves was a small, off-set door. It was a sturdy, no-nonsense sort of door, except that even now, a decade later, one could still discern it had once been painted a wild, reckless red and covered with vivid black sketchings.

She felt her captors exchange a silent glance.

"What the hell is that?" Ry muttered. "It looks like witchcraft."

Jamie shrugged. "'Tis like what Eva has done to her fingers."

Ruggart Ry turned blankly. "Her what?"

Eva curled her painted fingernails into her palms, but Jamie only tipped his head in her direction. "See, if she'll let you." He swiveled and she found herself staring into his eyes. "What of this place, Eva?"

"It is old," she said in a low voice, looking around. "Beyond that, I cannot say."

"Cannot, or will not?"

"You think I am lying?"

"I know you are lying. Just not about what."

"I do not tell lies about that hut. 'Tis as safe a place to spend the night as I have ever known."

He considered her. His boots were spread shoulder-width apart so his thighs formed a *V.* Powerful arms were crossed over his chest, and despite the faint, regarding smile playing on the edges of his mouth—he knew she lied, about almost everything—nothing about him denoted ease.

A scar cut through his right eyebrow, and she was certain the growth of beard concealed more such. His face was all hard planes, his nose ever so slightly crooked, as if broken a long time ago. His hands were absolute weapons on their own. Her throat still felt tight where he'd wrapped his mailed hand around it. God alone knew what had stayed him from squeezing the life out of her earlier, because his eyes would not reveal the reason—they were beautiful and absolutely unreadable. Sea deep, indigo blue in the fading light, filled with danger and concealed thoughts. He felt like the sort who'd lived a hard life and was dishing it back out.

"That is a good skill," he finally said, in that quiet, rumbling way he had. Jamie had many 'ways' about him. They were all dangerous. "You are not lying about this hut."

It left open an entire range of things she *might be* lying about, but neither of them ventured there.

He directed her to sit, while Roger was enlisted to help gather downed wood. Jamie swiftly dug a small, deep pit beside her, then said, "You can begin the fire, even with your hands bound." He tossed her a small flint from his pack and walked off.

Eva stared at the little gray stone glumly. This was not true. She could *not* light a fire, not to save her life, and on some winter nights it would have been exactly that. Oh, the shame of it, a five-year-old making fire for a thirteen-year-old.

She stared fiercely down into the dark pit, her jaw clamped tight, dismally doing the only thing she was capable of at present: feeding small bits of kindling—little twigs, skeletal leaves—into the cold fire pit.

They returned. Jamie looked down at the dark fire pit, at the small mountain of kindling, then at her. She sniffed and looked away. He swept up the flint, and soon a small flame caught on one of the cobwebbed leaves. He leaned forward to blow on it, the angular planes of his face lit by the sharp amber light. The flames licked higher, crackling up to catch the twigs.

Eva stifled a sigh of relief. How she hated the dark. Roger pressed close to her side.

From across the fire, Jamie glanced at them, then slid a knife from its sheath at his side, a careless, graceful move, and began slicing a wrinkled onion into thick chunks and skewering them on a stick. She swallowed.

"Eva?" Roger ventured in a whisper.

"Aye?"

"I oughtn't have got caught. I'm sorry."

She patted his knee absently. "'Tis no fault of yours, Gog."

"Aye, it was." Jamie's low voice drifted like hot silk through the flames.

This snapped her full attention to him. "Pardon?" she asked coldly.

He laid the onions beside the flames and gave a careless shrug. "I heard him banging through the brush like a bear for all of our ride."

She arched an eyebrow. "And yet you seemed most surprised, there at the end."

Roger stared at her. Jamie looked up but said nothing, just looked at her a moment, then turned to Roger. "You must be more circumspect when you are tracking."

"Aye, sir!" Roger agreed with alacrity. He appeared . . . delighted by the feedback.

"Gog," she said wearily. "Please remove your knee from my . . ." She glanced at Jamie, who seemed to be awaiting the next word out of her mouth with apparent interest. "Hip."

It was a silent meal. The fire crackled and spit little fiery twigs into the dark air. Cool drafts lifted them higher, until they burned out and became gray ashes that blew into nothing.

Within ten minutes, Ry was out on watch, and Gog was asleep, on his side, mouth open, a hand tucked beneath his cheek, looking like a child and snoring like a man. Or bear. Yet he was neither man nor boy.

But he was certainly doomed. Unless she could save him.

The tumble-down hut loomed at the edge of her vision. It looked like a swaybacked horse. Birds had made nests in what remained of the roof. Surely rodents found its sod walls quite warm. She once had. Now, it was uninhabitable. All that work, all that worrying, and running, and hiding, and now scurrying things held sway nevertheless.

And so falls the past, she thought, trying to be rueful, blowing on her hands. Rue did not ordinarily lodge in one's ribs though, just before the heart. Perhaps it was something else.

In any event, she did not pine for the past, so this was just as well. The past was a millstone of memories. She was weary of it.

But then, being weary of a thing had never signaled its end.

Across the fire, Jamie's silhouette was dark and large. He sat motionless, his head bent, staring into the flames. He was the most lethal, most capable man she'd ever known, and he'd never spoken above a rumble.

And he *was* capable. In all things. Capable, clever mind; capable, scarred hands; capable, smashed-up heart—even to one who did not care about his heart, such as her, this was clear. He'd been terribly hurt. Like knows like.

The world was full of chances. Choices and chances.

"Have we settled the matter of our alliance?" she asked, a bit too loudly for the night air.

Nineteen

Jamie gave a small laugh.

She *ought* to be seeking any sort of assistance she could just now, for somehow, this bright slip of a woman had treaded into royal swampland, a quagmire that involved King John, his chief lieutenant (that being Jamie), the rebel barons, an outlawed henchman who once dealt in ransomed heirs, and an unfolding civil war.

Could it be, as Eva suggested, a matter of signed contracts, unwanted witnesses to some unwanted thing? Or was it something other? Something more?

For now, he would keep her bound. Keep her talking. Keep her lying, and follow her straight to the truth.

"I do not know," he finally said.

She gave a faint sigh of exasperation. "That is all you have to say, after such a long wait? I thought you were deciding my fate, or perhaps what to eat, or something equally momentous."

"I shall endeavor towards more complicated replies," he said drily.

She waved her hand. "That will not suit either."

A smile tugged at his lips. "Eva, you are like yuletide: I never know what I shall find." He reached forward and picked up a stick, poked its tip into the flames. "Why should you want an alliance with me?"

"We have the same intent, we must needs travel the same path. Of a certainty, we will fight at the end like cats and dogs, but that is for later. What say you?"

He glanced up. "Who gets to be the dog?"

"But of course, you. Big and growly."

He grinned. "Am I not evil and quite impossible?"

"This is, sadly, true. But such men are good to be aligned with."

"That is also, sadly, true."

She sat up a little straighter, pushing her slim shoulders above the transparent waves of heat undulating up from the coals in the fire pit. "I think you can help me."

He laughed. "I surely can. In what manner were you thinking?"

"In not tying me to a tree and leaving me for dead in the morning."

He tilted his face and looked up at the tree limbs blowing in the darkness above them. "The notion does have a certain allure, does it not?" he mused.

"Normally, I would agree with this evil in your heart. It would make much sense to leave me and Gog behind."

Thus far, she was on the mark. But then, it would have made more sense to leave her behind at the inn. He'd brought her because, well, he had no notion why. Because she was lying, he supposed. Lying people were hiding things, and until you knew what they were lying about, everything was a potential trapdoor.

"But I would find it very helpful to not be tied to a tree and left for dead," she finished. "In this way, you would be of great assistance."

"Aye, that would be helpful. For you. What makes you think I tie women to trees?"

She pretended to ponder this, her finger at her chin. "Your general readiness to do bad things? That you serve a vile lord? I would think tying people to trees to be a discomfort, a pebble in your bed, not a true obstacle."

"I do not tie women to trees."

"Not even ones who lie to you?"

"No. I prefer to leave them behind with"—he paused as if musing—"big, angry Scotsmen."

She looked at him warily. "But this is no hardship. I am quite fond of Scotsmen."

He arched a brow. "One-eyed ones?"

She arched both hers back, and he was certain she looked better than he. "Indeed. I prefer them to some Englishmen with both their eyes."

Silence fell.

"Well, then, it seems we have ascertained how I can help you, Eva. But I am still unclear on how you can help *me*."

"Any number of ways. I can tell stories at night or fetch water for your hardworking horses."

"I find neither of those needs pressing at the moment, Eva."

"I can tell you things."

"Yes, but you lie."

"I will not."

He slid his gaze down her body, over her blue skirts, to the tips of her hard boots and back up. "I will know."

A flush rushed out on her cheekbones, a faint pink tide. Something to note: the woman prickled with blades was an innocent with an innuendo. "And so, you see? You are your own formidable protection against my terrible, pathetic lies."

He spun the tip of his stick in the fire. "And what would you have to tell me, Eva? There is a great deal I already know."

"You know a great deal in the service of a lying, deceitful king." Her words were sharp, falling out faster. "Beware of what lies *you* might have been told, Jamie, by others much more skilled than I."

Only when they spoke of John did she lose her equanimity. Another thing of note. There was so very much to note about her, one could spend a lifetime with Eva as the object of study, like trigonometry or rhetoric.

"What makes you suppose I get all my information from my lying, deceitful king?" he asked, and she looked away. "And for that matter, in what manner are you different?" he added coolly. "The lies or the deceit?"

Her gray gaze came back around. "In that I have never promised anything other than what I deliver. I have vowed neither faithfulness nor honesty, and so I do not dispense it."

"I see. You hand it out in the manner of . . . fruit."

"But of course. Oranges, I think. They are very uncommon, like the truth."

"You mean you do not get much practice eating it."

She tipped her head to the side, regarding him in silence. Strands of her hair picked up reddish glints from the fire. She must have some red amid all that ebony. "Yes. Perhaps this is why I am not so good with it."

He nodded agreeably. "Oddly, you are also quite bad at lying, yet you do that with regularity."

She waved her hand, dismissing the insight. "This is so, I am torn between worlds. I shall learn from you, Jamie, no? How to lie?"

"That would be a long apprenticeship." He turned the tip of his stick in the fire some more, watching it start to darken, then erupt into small flames.

"From the beginning of this tale, we have been adversaries, Jamie. I have had no reason to be truthful."

"And now you shall?"

She leaned forward, tipping her torso toward the fire. He

imagined the waves of heat pushing against her chest. "If you provide me a reason, Jamie Knight, indeed, I shall."

He tossed the stick into the fire and sat back. "Prove yourself."

She sat back, indecision and suspicion sweeping across her face. "In what manner?"

"Tell me something true, Eva. To a wellspring truth, through and through true."

She looked uncomprehending, as might be expected. Then she smiled in a way he'd call mischievous, or impish, if he called smiles such things, and—well, this was becoming commonplace—his heart slowed down. Everything collapsed into his male awareness of her small, crooked, seductive smile.

"Beware the hedge," she whispered conspiratorially. "'Tis filled with brambles. They bite."

He felt another grin surface. "Is that your truth, Eva? The one by which you prove yourself?"

She nodded smugly and tried to cross her arms, but as her wrists were bound, this was impossible. "Bone truth," she said proudly.

"I shall heed your warning," he replied drily.

"As do I."

He gave a snort of disbelief. "You? Heed warnings?"

"Bite. I bite."

"Ah. That is good to know."

"I also snore, complain on an oceanic scale, and find myself covered in terrible rashes when I touch certain plants."

He smiled faintly. "You are a veritable sea of problems."

"Sadly, this is so."

"Have you any talents?" he inquired. Why, he had no notion. To keep her talking? He rarely pursued that particular goal with women.

She spread her hands apart, as if presenting a feast table. "Indeed. I can sing a merry tune."

"Is that so?" he drawled, particularly and unaccountably pleased, whether by the news or her revelation of it, he did not know.

She nodded. "When I am so inspired."

"And what manner of things inspire you?"

"Being free of ropes and knots, this of a certainty has an inspiring effect."

"You will sing for me if I release you from your bindings?" he asked, halfway to incredulous. He had no intention of releasing her, so it was mere curiosity. About her reply. Not her singing.

She shifted on the ground. One knee came up, dragging the hem of her skirt up behind, so one long, white leg was momentarily exposed. She crossed her legs, the skirt fell back into place, and she looked up, the corner of her mouth curved up into one of those minute, somehow stunning smiles. "I will sing for you, Jamie, if you release me."

Madness, the way his body sped up, churned inside. He passed her a cool look. "I shall have to forgo the pleasure."

She deflated. "Oh, 'twould not have been a pleasure, Jamie. I sing terribly."

He felt yet another grin tug at his lips. "You said 'twas a talent of yours."

"I said I can sing a *merry* tune. Not a good one."

"I would like to know what else you do well, Eva."

She arched one of her little ink-swipe eyebrows. He liked when she did that across the fire. It shifted the way the light and shadows fell across her face. "Oh, yes, I am certain this is so. Men are always curious about what women *do so well.*"

It was ridiculous, how her throaty innuendo, chiding the overweening carnal desires of men, activated overweening carnal desire in him.

She sighed resignedly. "I patch clothes, carry wash, grow garlic, and poke a knife in someone, these things I do well."

He nodded thoughtfully. "You do not mention that you charm ship captains and play ninepins with your body." *And make my body ignite when you do but look at me.*

She laughed, one of those pretty, secret laughs that she'd given him in the alley. "Alas, Jamie, you have discovered all my secrets. But come, why do we speak so much of me?"

"We are ascertaining if you can be truthful." But he was not doing that, of course. Not anymore.

"Pah." She reached up to rub her head with her bound hands. It pushed her dark hair forward, over her shoulder. "My innards are as riveting as dirt. We shall speak of you, knight, while we sit by this fire, and see if you are *worth* telling the truth to."

"Shall we?" He leaned against the log behind him. "Well, *I* have a fairly good memory."

She nodded encouragingly.

"And I recall, quite clearly, you did not bite when I kissed you before."

Pale, bent at the knuckles, her fingers froze in combing through her hair. Her nails, painted with those erotic swirling lines, pushed through the tresses like barrettes, curling up out of the richness of her hair as she stared into his eyes.

"Now, Eva, listen close. For all your chatter, you have not yet given me anything of value."

She sat up straight. "I gave you Mouldin."

He smiled. "No. Roger did. And I would have figured that out soon enough, the moment I came upon him."

She looked taken aback. "Surely it helps to know what sort of evil man you are hunting?"

"I hardly expected a kind one."

She made an impatient gesture with her hand. "You hardly expected me either, yet here I am."

"Aye, there you are," he agreed, his words a slow drawl. This occasioned another blush slipping across her cheekbones.

They looked at each other for a long moment, then he slid his gaze down her body, over the long trails of hair flowing over her shoulders, down her belly to her bent knees before making the lazy trip back up again.

"In any event, I am seeking something significantly better than names, Eva."

Something happened to her then, a small quiver that shivered her hair and made her release a slow breath. He could not resist looking down at her lips as they formed her next, softly spoken words.

"I know where Father Peter's documents are."

His gaze made the slow climb back to her eyes. "You what?"

"These documents and sketches that every man with a sword in England wants? I know where they are. I can get them for you."

From across the firelight, her eyes were all reflected firelight in dark, shadowy pools. "That would indeed be a good trade, Eva," he agreed slowly. "Why would you do that?"

"Because I care naught for the politics of England."

He smiled faintly. "That is not good enough."

"It is all I have. You have your sword, I have this little truth." Silence.

"So, Jamie Knight, have we a deal?"

He smiled at her in the sudden brightness as the entire stick was engulfed in flames. "It appears so. I refrain from tying you to a tree, and you spill your innards."

Twenty

He shifted so his boots were planted on the ground, his knees bent, and slung his forearms over them, loosely linking his fingers. "Tell me a story, Eva. About Roger and you and Father Peter."

She stared into the fire for long minutes, and when she spoke again, she surprised him entirely. "I once saw a wolf at night."

He picked up another stick.

"The moon was out, I was climbing a hill. There was no color in the night, just wind and the white moon and sad brown grasses. That is when I saw him. He was gray, his fur rippled by the wind, like a sea. He looked like moon water. I knew I should be scared, but I was not." She glanced at him. "Nor was I foolish. I put Gog up on my shoulders."

"Pardon?"

She gave a ghost of a smile. "He was but six."

"And you were?"

She shrugged, as if it did not signify. "This wolf, he was so . . ." She shook her head impatiently. "His fur was so thick and lush, clearly he had eaten many fat little sheep and must have had many enemies among the villagers. But there was something about him. His eyes were"—she glanced at Jamie—"blue. Pale. Like little coins. He was significant, like a field of battle unto himself. He saw me. I assume he considered ripping out my throat." She glanced at him again. "You must know this urge."

He smiled faintly. "It passes."

She pressed her elbows onto her knees and stared into the low flames. "He put his muzzle into the air and loosed this great, howling cry. And out there, somewhere, another picked it up. There was another wolf out there, crying with him."

She shivered. "Then he looked at me again, as if to say, 'Oh, yes, I see you, little girl, and I will eat a sheep instead, this time.' Then he turned and trotted down the hill, and I knew with certainty this one would be hunted to death. They are all dead now, here in England, the wolves?"

"Nigh on."

A breeze puffed over their low fire. The coals burned in waves of hot orange and red.

"Gog and I, we have no need to howl to each other across hills."

He nodded. She held out her hand. He mimicked the move, eyebrows up.

She pointed to her palm. "Gog." She flipped her hand over and touched the back. "Eva."

He could see the long, fragile bones running from her fingers to her wrist, where they disappeared under the dark blue of her tunic sleeve. Her fingernails were painted with those swirling, vaguely erotic lines.

She closed her hand into a fist.

He looked up. "You keep Roger safe." He paused. "This is why you left England." She nodded. "You know you will not be able to keep him safe like that"—he nodded toward her white-knuckled fist—"for much longer."

The fire spat, sending a spray of tiny orange embers into the cold air.

"This I know very well, Jamie Knight. It is why we must leave England. King John is a very ambitious fisherman, and with a very big net, no? He sweeps up everyone in it, all the people he is frightened by for no very big reasons."

"Or for very big reasons indeed."

She nodded. "This is true. He is not overly discriminating."

"No, he is not." A vast, chasm-filled understatement.

"And he is easy to anger."

"Did your parents anger him?"

She stared into the air above his shoulder with a small, inscrutable smile. "My mother did."

My mother, not *our* mother, he noted silently.

The fire was burning down to a hot, orange bed of glowing coals. Drafts of wind pressed against them and blew them hotter, the bright red-orange glow undulating from one side of the fire pit to the other like a burning sea. Like her wolf pelt.

"And?" he asked, softer now, but still intent on his mission, because that was how you fished for truths with *faeries*.

"And so we left England," she finally said. "Roger and I."

They looked at each other. "Truly?" he asked softly. He was starting to feel bad, all this crushing of her pitiable lies.

But then, she said she did not care if it was obvious that she lied. What mattered was that no one ever knew the truth.

"'Twas Gog and I," she insisted.

It had the ring of truth. It likely *was* the truth. It was simply not the whole truth. "And?" he pressed. They'd been children. Who had escorted them?

She held his gaze in silence, her chin pressed into little dimpled impressions, and by this, she revealed more than all her words thus far. For in it, Jamie could hear, like a murmuring brook, a thousand words rumbling to pour forth into the quarry his *And?* had dug. She was answering him, inside her head, and her silence fairly shouted of awful things and never-mores.

He had a silence like this inside him as well. But his chin did not dimple. His eyes did not widen, his heart never broke. He revealed nothing. He was a pit.

Eva was equally broken—like knows like—but not as practiced as he. She had the feel of something grown fierce by dint of need, not nature. But then, such things could be fierce indeed.

"There is no *and* for this," she finally said. "For almost a year, 'twas just Gog and I, alone in these woods. You can see how this would have been a cold endeavor, as I cannot so much as make a fire." She lowered her eyes.

"But I do not understand—"

Abruptly, Eva turned and reached into her little satchel, awkwardly due to her bound hands, and pulled something out. "*Regardez*, Jamie Knight. These are beautiful, no? They are from the *curé* to me."

She handed him a parcel with a wooden cover, painted with a profusion of yellow flowers. Inside, it was filled with thick, scratchy parchment pages. He bent to examine them. Indeed, beautiful. If possible, more magnificent than the illuminated manuscripts for which Father Peter was renowned. Brilliantly colored drawings crowded the margins of the pages. This took time and attention. This could not be dashed off. These were not idle sketches. It appeared Peter of London had taken more effort with these miniature scenes and letters than he had with some of his greatest works, in abbeys stretching from Westminster to the Yorkminster.

For Eva.

His eyes skimmed the words briefly. Back at the inn, he'd cared only for weapons; missives were a second-run search, and they hadn't had the time.

He scanned through the spidery Latin of one of the great thinkers and artists of their time, seeing nothing of note beyond scattered mentions of the barons' charter brewing in England, and Peter's thoughts on some of the clauses and their importance. The ones mentioned had all sent King John's eyelid twitching. He suppressed a smile. Peter of London could not resist teaching. Or instigating.

Other than this, there was nothing noteworthy. Perhaps in the extravagance of using ink and paper and a messenger to tell someone of such small nothings, but elsewise, it was filled with insignificant things, the sort of words an uncle would say to a beloved niece, marking the passage of seasons, asking after the growth of Roger, scolding softly for not using some money he'd sent to buy new shoes.

And in its prosaic nothingness, it told a volume of tales.

"We are not always together now, so Father Peter writes those to me," she said. Tendrils of hair unraveled down past her shoulder, small knobbly ladders of silk as she leaned forward to look with him. He imagined the waves of heat pushing against her chest.

"I read his words, enjoy the little pictures he draws in the margins. I try to mimic his great talent." She gestured toward the hut. "I have none myself."

He disagreed. The door looked as if someone had cast a spell with ink lines. Smooth, dark, precise, burgeoning into fat, curving lines, slimming into cat's-claw precision, she'd drawn a beautiful faerie spell.

"He is special to you," he said, handing the volume back.

"He was my foster father." Mayhap it was the shimmering heat waves from the glowing coals, but her voice had an otherworldly tone. "My lifesaver. My raison d'être, after Gog. He is the only thing good in my world, and if need be, I will give my life to save his. Or Roger's."

She reached for the volume and he covered her fingers with his. He heard her take a quick, small breath. "But why, Eva? Why is this needful? Why do you do it?"

She slid her hand free, with the book. "It is what I do," she said with one of her small shrugs. "If not Roger, I would tend orphans or horses. It is nothing of note."

Her gaze flickered away, and as with all things Eva, he knew she would not speak the truth, but even so, he could not follow the lie. There were no straight lines with Eva; she was an ocean of currents, and while you might know you were not sailing south, you had no notion where you *were* being taken.

But then, he did not need her compass anymore. He knew exactly where this was headed.

His mind cast itself back in time, swept aside the bright, vivid horrors of his own childhood, to recall the tales that had passed through England ten years ago, about what became known as the Everoot Massacre. From castle to castle on the tongues of minstrels, from piss-reeking alley to alley on the tongues of commoners, the rumors had spread of how the king had murdered one of his greatest barons in a fit of foaming fury.

For the second time.

Ten years ago, England had begun a slow collapse inward when John's grand expedition to reclaim Normandy disintegrated into bickering and double-dealing. Even William the Marshal was accused of treachery. The invasion was called off. Stationed at Chinon with Hubert de Burgh, Jamie himself had watched the French king subsume Poitou and Anjou that spring.

Then the Archbishop of Canterbury died a few months after, ripping open a dispute between Church and Crown that would end, years later, in excommunication.

These were serious blows to John's power and prestige. In consequence, he had ridden forth, collecting submissions and reclaiming fealty from his lords, taking hostages from his barons, humiliating powerful men when he needed their loyalty.

The one estate that did not need to give hostages or submissions was the great Everoot earldom. Of course, that was because there was no earl *there*—he'd died ten years prior, on return from Crusade. This had placed the estate conveniently in the king's hand. King Richard had never done anything with it. Hoping the heir would be located, building castles in France; there'd been many things to occupy *Coeur de Lion's* attention.

There were not so many to occupy his brother John's. The moment he placed the crown on his head, John installed his own man at Everoot to steward the estate and the independent-minded countess left behind. He chose one of the few loyal northern barons, his trusted lieutenant, Lord d'Endshire.

And so, after the failed invasion, weary from the grueling work of antagonizing his barons, John had stopped at Everoot. He'd needed a respite. He'd desired a heartfelt welcome. He'd expected a docile estate and an obedient vassal. He got none of this.

Instead, King John saw or heard or discovered something that tipped his emotional scales into an all-out rage. And somehow—no one knew how, as all those who'd been there that night were either dead or silent for other reasons—Lord d'Endshire ended up dead, his five-year-old heir gone missing.

Rumors swirled that a nurse had taken the heir and run. That Mouldin had been sent after them, like a wolf on a hare. Some said he'd caught the children. Others claimed, no, they had escaped, never to be seen again.

Looking through the orange-blue flames, Jamie now knew the rumors were true, for he was looking at the "nurse" who had made it happen. A girl who had done what not even powerful barons fleeing into the wilds of Ireland could do: escape the wrath of King John. With a child in tow.

Roger, the d'Endshire heir, toddling through these woods. Holding Eva's hand.

"How old were you?" he asked in a low voice.

She turned her face away. "Thirteen." It sounded like surrender. It sounded like shame.

Like knows like.

He shoved to his feet, circled the fire, and dropped to a knee beside her. Silently, he slid his dagger free and sliced through her bindings. The ropes fell away, but she kept her hands thrust out, her wrists pressed together.

"You do not ask me of tricks," she said in a shaky voice.

"I do not care about tricks." Children should not run screaming through the woods. Or the London streets.

She opened her arms, and it seemed, for a moment, as if she were going to embrace him. Then she bent her elbows, hands up in the air, by her ears, and rolled her shoulders, tipping her head back. She abruptly put her arms down.

"I have no tricks, Jamie."

God's teeth, was she reassuring *him*? "That is highly unlikely," he said curtly, returning to his side of the fire.

He felt agitated, restless . . . uplifted. Hearing nightmarish stories that so closely mimicked his own usually brought on the black moods, undiluted by anything uplifting or inspiring.

Perhaps it was that, amid this ever-expanding dung heap of royal shite, there was one solid truth he could now stand upon: Roger was the heir d'Endshire. And Eva was protecting him.

There was only the briefest flicker of awareness at the next thought: *And now, I am protecting her.*

Twenty-one

Mouldin? A message from Mouldin?"

"What?"

The softly spoken word belied the rage Engelard Cigogné saw haunting the king's face. And he had seen many looks pass over the royal visage in his tenure as one of the king's most trusted captains. This was one of the less pleasant ones.

They were standing in the king's office at Windsor. The room was controlled chaos, filled with people coming and going, courtiers sharing tales, Wardrobe officials reporting income, household knights receiving instructions or delivering confirmations of payments received or deeds done. Sheriffs' men returning investigative reports. Hounds and servants and whores. It was a cacophony of humanity within the walls of Windsor as war inched closer every day.

Outside, in the corridor, was a line of penitents even yet wanting to genuflect at the royal altar of endowments.

But mostly, always, everywhere, were the messengers. They galloped along the roads of the countryside like blood through the body, bearing vital messages as the realm convulsed at the edge of civil war.

Evidence of the most recent delivery still sat on the table:

a scroll and a plate of eels, uneaten even now, hours later, after the terrible message had come in.

London had fallen to the rebels.

And now another messenger stood before the king, his hand pressed to the table, trying to catching his breath and saying things Cigogné knew were destined to end badly, such as, "I came as quickly as I could," and "I bear a message from Mouldin."

King John went still.

Bent over the long, carved table, he let the messenger's words echo off the stone walls, then straightened. His black hair hung straight down past his ears, curling up slightly above his shoulders as he pinned his gaze on the unfortunate messenger.

"That is not possible."

The messenger looked flummoxed.

"Mouldin is an outlaw. I destroyed him years ago, ran him to ground. He would not be sending me a message. And he would *never* be back in England."

The messenger paled slightly. "But he is, sire. At least, that is what the message claims. Guillaume Mouldin."

Mouldin. The name could still conjure shivers up spines. He'd had many names in the past, though: the Hunter; Keeper of the Heirs; Mouldin-head, that last name mothers used up north, a legend to frighten children into good behavior. *He'll take you and run away with you*, their parents warned. But Mouldin had never run with them. Legends always got twisted.

The messenger still had his hand on his chest, looking increasingly pale as John stared at him. "Tell me the message," the king finally snapped.

Straightening, the messenger moved his gaze just to the left of the king's face. "Mouldin has Peter of London in his keeping. His . . . possession. So the missive says."

The king stared for a long, motionless moment, then sucked in a breath so forcefully his nostrils narrowed. From outside the office chamber came the sounds of voices chattering and distant laughter, but inside, it was absolutely silent. Everyone had felt the sudden calm that so often preceded a royal storm. They'd turned as one and fallen silent, ready to bolt.

"No."

The messenger swallowed tightly at the single word. "Aye, sire."

Engelard Cigogné kept his attention squarely on the king. When you were employed by John Lackland, you learned to attend his mercurial moods with devotion. It was rather like being a military tactician, with somewhat the same results.

"No," the king said again, very slowly, as if he were explaining a complicated concept. He pushed aside the eel dish and laid his palms upon the table. "That cannot be. This message, 'tis a ruse, trickery."

The messenger fumbled in the leather pouch at his side and drew out a folded piece of parchment. He extended it. "I think not, my lord."

The king looked down at the distinctive drawings, and his jaw tightened, as did the hand clutching the pages. "Christ's bones," he muttered.

"Mouldin sends word he would be pleased for you to have Peter of London back."

The king's jaw gave a tic, a faint tightening.

"For a price."

That made John almost levitate off the floor. "A *price*?" he roared. As one, the silent occupants of the room took a step back. "Mouldin-head thinks to barter with *Us*?" He slammed his hand onto the table. "That goddamned piratical slave trader, *he* shall pay a price, with his outlawed head. All four corners of the realm shall know his flesh at once—"

"Or he will sell him to the rebels."

King John stopped short. "Repeat yourself."

The messenger looked hopeless. All there was to do was complete his mission and hope his head was still affixed to his shoulders come morn. He rallied valiantly, taking his hand off the table, straightening his spine.

"Guillaume Mouldin sends words he is selling the priest to the highest bidder. At the northern town of Gracious Hill. In five days' time."

A bright red flush spread out from beneath the king's trimmed beard across his forehead and cheeks. The faintest tremble of his silken surcoat revealed he was shaking from rage. He looked down at the table, then reached out and shifted a spoon lying atop the eel platter with precise slowness. Cig took a long, silent breath.

The king looked at the messenger. "Leave us." It was interpreted as an order for all, and people began pouring out the door like water flowing.

When everyone was gone, the king turned to Cigogné.

"Did I not take measures to manage this matter?" he said, with more of that eerie calm. "To prevent this very thing? To ensure Peter of London never reached the negotiation table? Furthermore, to prevent *anyone* from gaining access to him and his reckless, foolish, treasonous—"

The king stopped himself. "Did I not take measures to prevent this very thing?" he repeatedly softly.

"You did, sire."

"I sent Jamie for the priest."

"Aye, sire."

"In other words, I *managed the matter.*"

"Aye, sire."

"Yet now the rebels have seized London, Guillaume Mouldin is back in the game, and further to the point, he has kidnapped the one man in all of Christendom who can kick the legs out from under my God. Damned. *Throne!*"

This last was a bellow. Cigogné refrained from replying. He certainly refrained from pointing out that Mouldin's most notorious feats had been done in John's employ, in the king's name, and thus most of his riches in human trade had come as a result of not slaves but heirs.

Heirs King John had wanted watched, held, sometimes sold to the highest bidder. Occasionally destroyed. Mouldin held them all for John, heirs and wards, minor sons and heiress daughters of enemies and of friends. The Keeper of the Heirs. The Hunter. Not of deer but heirs. Because sometimes, well, they did run.

Once, they had escaped.

Thus the royal fury.

The king smashed his fist down on the table so hard it shuddered, then started picking up cups and bowls and flinging them across the room. They smashed into the far wall, one by one, tinkling explosions of pottery.

Cig tipped his shoulders back just as a platter came flying by, flinging a greasy trail of garlic sauce over the rushes. A dog under the table started to rise to taste the delicacy, then quickly went back down as John kicked his chair away. The hawk on the stand behind the seat clawed his perch restlessly, one set of talons lifting, then lowering. His hooded head bobbed in nervous agitation.

John planted his palms on the table, gripping its edges so hard his knuckles turned white.

"Bring me Jamie," he said from between gritted teeth.

Cigogné cleared his throat. "Jamie has not returned, sire."

This effected a sudden quiet. "Not returned?" The king sounded confused, almost dumbfounded. "Not returned? How could this be?"

Cig assumed the query was rhetorical and did not reply.

"No Jamie," the king murmured. "No priest. And now

Mouldin is back in the game." A moment of disquieting quiet ensued. The king looked up. "I have a job for you, Cigogné."

He bent his head. "Your Grace."

"Go to Gracious Hill and get me Peter of London. Take enough coin to ruse a ransom if need be, but above all, retrieve the priest before the rebels do. Mouldin, kill."

"Aye, sire."

"And the priest. . . . See that he does not cause problems."

A rush of cold unease slid through Cig's blood. "He is a priest, my lord."

The king's gaze sharpened. "He is a troublemaker. See that he does not cause any." The king met Cig's eye. "And bring me Jamie."

"Sire, in what manner do you mean—"

"In the manner that should Jamie emit the faintest whiff of disloyalty, you will ensure he does not cause any trouble either."

Now Cig knew fear. Cold in the pit of his chest, something that had not occurred since he'd looked down upon his first battlefield. "Sire."

The single word was so low-pitched, so clearly a countermand, so clearly a disapproval, the king stopped and stared.

"We have moved past risk here, Cigogné. We are into peril. Something is afoot that tends toward the dissolution of my realm."

Cig held his silence.

"Jamie can track a raindrop in a storm. Yet he lost my priest?" The king's tone was incredulous. "Hardly. Something is afoot. You will learn what it is. My kingdom totters upon it. Surely I can rely upon you? Or need I find another, more loyal man? One without estates?"

The threat was clear. Cig moved his gaze to the wall just

above the king's left shoulder and gave a clipped nod. "I am your man, my lord."

"Within a week, they are with me, or they are dead. Bring them to me at Everoot; I ride north."

Cig exited the room as another large, heavy object hit the ground behind him. He did not look back.

KING John waited until he left, then shifted his gaze to the darkest corner of the room, and the shadowy figure standing there.

"Follow him. Make sure 'tis done."

"DID you deliver the messages? And the sketches?"

Peter of London eyed the king's outlawed captain, who stood on the other side of the fire questioning his recently returned underling, and shook his head.

Mouldin seemed to detect the faint movement, even amid the dark shadows of the trees shrouding their campsite. He turned slightly.

"Have you something to contribute, Father?" he inquired, his gravelly voice filled with all the false solicitousness that arrogance lent it. Upon a time, Mouldin had been considered handsome. Peter recalled those days, how Mouldin's square, diffident face would lighten with a smile when the king gave him yet another hostage to hold.

"A sketch will hardly convince anyone of anything," Peter said mildly. "Least of all that you have me. You might be trying to sell them a merchant's grandfather for all they know."

Mouldin nodded to his sergeant, and he joined the others who were sitting, some half slumbering, while others were on watch. "You are too modest, Father," Mouldin said, coming closer. "Your sketchings are distinctive. No one has your talent. And although you've been gone ten years, 'tis well remembered."

"Flattery will not serve you. I still intend to recommend your excommunication"

Mouldin crossed his arms, smiling faintly. "I do not flatter, Father. 'Tis the truth."

Peter leaned back against a tree trunk; it had been a long time since he'd slept out of doors, on hard ground. It was chilly with no fire and the spring breezes pushing through the trees, and although the moonshine was bright where it shone down between the branches, it gave no warmth, just a silvery sheen of illumination.

"What a pleasure this will be, then," he said. "Two such accomplished men, telling tales in a dark wood. Ah, but then, you have only the one skill."

Mouldin laughed again. "We cannot all be as blessed in our array of talents as you, Father."

"You could attempt it."

Peter was amusing Mouldin no end, for the criminal smiled again. "Alas, I am good at only one thing."

"Auctioning slaves."

Mouldin's look hardened, but he maintained his smile. "Or priests. You should be careful of what you say, Father, and to whom."

Peter held out his hand. "We see where such care has led me. Into a cold wood with an outlawed slave trader."

"'Twasn't care that ruined you, Father. 'Twas giving it up." Mouldin stepped away from the tree and sat opposite Peter on a log, his forearms over his knees. "Why in God's name did you ever come back to England? They've been hunting you for years throughout France. Even I took a turn or two on commission. Never found you. Never would have, either. Unless you came back."

"I was called for."

Mouldin shook his head. "You were tricked. The rebels

suggested inviting you to England to assist in the negotiations. Then they hired me to abduct you."

Peter regarded him levelly. "You shall have a very uncomfortable afterlife, Guillaume Mouldin."

He gave a bark of laughter.

"You're quite high-spirited," Peter observed; then he coughed. "Have you considered mummery, or tumbling, perhaps? You could leave off auctioning human souls forevermore."

"No one is paying for souls, Father. Keep yours." Mouldin reached into his pack, drew out a wrap, and, surprisingly, handed it over.

"You will still burn in Hell," Peter said, but he reached for it. It was a wolf pelt. Warm. Mouldin watched as he wrapped it around his shoulders and leaned back against the tree again.

"You are no fool, Father. You could not have believed their purposes were benevolent. Why did you come?"

"Langton is a friend. The charter will serve England better than many kings have done."

"Why did you come?" Mouldin asked again, more slowly, more insistently. He had a nose like a rat's.

Peter shook his head. "Everyone is very interested in my purposes. I think I shall keep my own counsel."

He coughed again, and this time it lasted awhile. It was getting worse. He didn't know how much longer he had, which was why he'd come. Archbishop Stephen Langton's calling for him had been . . . a sign. It was time. He had one thing left to do, one undone thing nagging at his heart. If he could be of use in the negotiations, that would be good, no doubt, but his soul had personal reparations to make. He'd been remiss. Let things go. It was time.

Mouldin watched him with that insouciant arrogance that had always marked the Hunter. Really, the man was far too self-assured for an outlaw.

"I doubt, of course, that you shall be successful in your endeavors," Peter said blithely.

"Endeavors?" Mouldin sounded amused.

Peter nodded complacently. It never hurt to rile people up. It often helped. He'd spent much of his younger days doing just that. Kings and counts and petty princes; he'd made a few foes. Perhaps he missed it. Perhaps that was also a small part of what had drawn him back. The desire to stir the pot one last time.

He smiled inwardly, then sighed. He had never been suited to the life of a churchman. Too contrary. Too obstinate.

Of course, Mouldin did not seem to mind. This was not a flattering thought, that Peter had earned the respect of a slave trader. It made one reflect poorly on one's passage through life.

Mouldin was looking at him with a mixture of amusement and coldhearted appraisal. "How do you see my failure transpiring, Father?"

"Perhaps you will get pierced by an arrow through your chest. Perhaps someone you do not want will learn our whereabouts before it is convenient. Perhaps I will cough on you and my bad little seeds will enter you."

Mouldin leaned away almost imperceptibly. Peter smiled wanly. What he had was not the sort of thing that good air or leechings could cause or cure. It was all inside of him, he felt it, eating away at him, deep in his chest. It was all his.

His words had strummed some chord, because Mouldin turned to his soldier. "Did you encounter any problems? Anyone stop you, follow you, question you on what you were about?"

The man jerked to attention, his teeth sawing on a strip of dried meat. He removed it to say, "Nay, sir. In London and Windsor, we passed the message to street urchins and they did the work. No one ever saw us."

Mouldin nodded, but the soldier hadn't finished. "The only one who took any notice a'tall was the boy in the stables at the inn."

Peter felt his raw, shredded chest seize up, just for a second. Pain ripped down his arm in a swift, clenching bolt, then subsided.

Mouldin's head snapped around. "A boy? In the stables?"

"Aye, well, close to a man. 'Twas nothing of import. He tried to stop us, we knocked him flat."

"How old?"

The soldier glanced between Mouldin and Peter, detecting the note of sudden, lethal quiet in his commander's voice. "Fifteen, mayhap sixteen."

Peter kept his breathing steady, kept the faint, mocking smile on his face, as if this news meant nothing to him.

Mouldin turned around slowly. "What do you know of this, Father?"

"Of a stableboy in England?" Peter coughed before continuing. "Stableboys, Mouldin? Is this what we are reduced to? Your corruptions are finally decaying your mind. Rotting it away."

Mouldin stared. "Good God, the legends have come true. 'Whither goest the priest, so goeth the heirs.'" He snapped back around to the soldier. "I'm sending you back. You and the others who saw the boy. Where shall they go, Father? The inn? A port?"

"Hell?"

All traces of Mouldin's amusement had fled. His face was hard. "That day will come soon enow."

"Angels weep."

"He is at the inn?"

"What inn?"

Mouldin turned to his men. "We want a fifteen-year-old

boy." He aimed a crafty look at Peter. "And a girl? Woman, by now. Is she here as well?"

Peter crossed his arms over his chest. "What do you think?"

"I think I cannot risk losing what I already have. I will ride on with you. The others will go back."

There was no point in pretense anymore. He looked at Mouldin and said coldly, "You will never find her."

Mouldin smiled. "We need not find *her*, priest. We only need him. She will follow, will she not? She always has."

"You may not wish for that."

Mouldin paused. "What is that supposed to mean?"

Peter shrugged, the picture of unconcern. He was accomplished in the giving of nonchalant shrugs; he'd had an apt tutor. Eva dispensed them like tinctures, five or six for every tick-mark that burned away on a candle. He'd scolded her on it, and she had begun raising her eyebrows instead. Even now, in the dark and danger, he could smile, thinking of Eva. My, how he missed her. "Perhaps he is not alone."

Mouldin's gaze sharpened. "You mean the girl. The girl will be with him."

"I do not mean 'the girl.'"

They eyed each other in mutual, silent animosity; then Mouldin snapped his fingers. His men stepped forward. *All lined up, like ducks in a row,* decided Peter.

Mouldin rose to give orders. "South, then west toward the inn. Keep your eyes open. Find them, and bring them to me at Gracious Hill."

They tromped off, leaving behind Mouldin and one other soldier. Peter shook his head. "I do grow weary of seeing good men die." He brightened. "But then, your men are not good."

Mouldin was pulling a thin woolen blanket up to his chin. "No, they are not." He shifted to face the fire, lay down.

Peter coughed. He knew he was dying; it had been coming

for years now, the little cough, then the little blood, then the ever-present cough that Eva had made twenty tinctures and teas for. He was past teas. He was past terror. Now, the thought of dying was . . . visionary. A white knight on a horse, riding toward him. It was not frightening. What was frightening was the thought that Eva and Roger would be left behind, unprotected and worse, unprepared.

"You must feel the need to combust in flames of righteous indignation, Father, surrounded by all these lost souls."

"I have been surrounded by more lost souls than this, Hunter. You do not impress."

Mouldin closed his eyes. "When was that, priest?"

"John's court."

Mouldin gave a bark of laughter. "Then you must be hoping the rebels offer a better price."

"I am hoping you get an arrow through your eye and fall off your horse into a river."

Mouldin opened his eyes, then closed them again. "You may get your wish one day."

Peter stared up the English stars, which were not so different from the French stars. "'Twasn't a wish. 'Twas a prayer."

Mouldin rolled over and pulled the blanket to his chest. "God doesn't listen to the likes of us, Father. I learned that a long time ago. The evidence is all around you. Sleep now; we ride long in the coming days. When we reach Gracious Hill, I know a woman."

"Of course you do."

"A midwife. She will tend your cough."

Peter stared at the dark sky, listening to the riders gallop off. How far back would Eva and Roger be? His heart felt so tight it was as if rope were looped around it, distending it under almost unbearable pressure. And when these skilled fighters came upon them? What chance had they then?

He could only hope his veiled threats had some teeth, some power to create, that Eva—whom God had played a terrible trick upon by giving her one numinous gift, the power to bring light to any darkness, then plunged her into that darkness—had indeed found a protector, one who was not only careful with extraordinary women and brave young men but merciless and—yes, he'd name it—*deadly* to their very same enemies.

Twenty-two

Eva sat silently by the fire pit, covered in Jamie's cloak. Jamie sat on the other side with his back against a downed log, his long legs stretched out in front. He'd flicked the edge of a lighter cape over his stomach and interlaced his fingers, resting them on his lap. He'd long ago closed his eyes, but Eva knew the slightest move and he'd be awake again.

He wore the sleeveless black surcoat, which covered his mail shirt. The flat, metal, gray links of mail on his muscular arms looked like some swamp creature's skin. Rock-hard with muscle, even in repose he was a magnificent beast.

It was unfortunate, then, that she wanted to slip a hand between his thighs, like a little piece of parchment pressed between a door and a jamb, and feel his heat. But there it was, she thought bleakly.

How long could one want, not even knowing it? Eva had wanted for a long time, and now all her secret longings had taken shape in the form of a man who could, and very likely might, destroy her and everyone she loved.

But there it is, she thought bleakly. *There he is.*

Jamie. Her hidden, forbidden desire.

She angled her gaze up the smallest bit. What would he do if she walked over just now, knelt down beside him? Whip out a knife and hold it to her neck? Reel her in like a fish? Demand the answers he was allowing her to withhold?

She was not so much a fool as to think she'd fooled him with her deflections. Eva had not fooled herself either. She was not an innocent. She knew how men wanted women, and she'd seen women want men. Right now, Eva was a woman who wanted a man, and there was nothing but the tempting notion of her hand between his thighs, the question of what she wanted to do once there.

It was a little Socratic thing, this question. Like the lessons Father Peter used to engage her in, starting with some bit of knowledge you were certain of, then pushing you out onto the ledge of realization that you knew nothing whatsoever about that most familiar thing.

Who is able to do the most harm to their enemies and good to their friends in time of sickness, Eva?

A physician.

And who is able to do best good and most harm at sea in a storm?

A pilot.

But in time of wellness, then, there is no need of the physician?

But of course there is need.

And on a calm sea, the pilot?

Needful.

Eva, needful.

She wanted to kneel down in front of Jamie and unlace his leggings, those complicated things. Press her lips to his hard, flat belly, run her fingers up his chest. And mayhap he would rest his hands on her shoulders, lean down to kiss her? Cup her waist with his hands and pull her up to sit on his lap, part her lips with his and kiss her, as he had in the tavern? A rippling undulation moved through her.

She felt quite wild now, thoroughly Socratic. His neck. She wanted his neck. She wanted to open her mouth and suck in his warm, salty skin. The days' growth of hair beard would prickle her tongue, and she wanted that with a simple, sudden desperate longing.

She would coax him to slide his hand down her hip as he'd done before, in that oh-so-gentle, oh-so-skillful way, and put his hot tongue inside her mouth with all his confidence. She could hear her own breath, passing through parted lips, loud in the quiet night air. She would open for him, kiss him back . . .

She looked up farther and met his wide-open eyes.

He was watching her. He *knew*.

She drew back as if blown by a strong, steady wind. She turned away and rounded her mouth to release a hot, unsteady, silent breath.

"Come to me." His rumble shivered her from the inside out.

It was a command in word, in tone, in everything but the unspoken energy that rode across the clearing like a tiger might prowl: *Please*.

She reached for the ground blindly. Pressing her palm to the ground, she bent her knees stiffly and lowered herself down, facing away.

"Come here, Eva." His rough whisper rode up and over her body like the blowing wind.

She lay on her side, facing the trees, stiff as a spike, hardly daring to breathe. Would he ask again?

Oh, *why* did he not ask again? And again, and again, and again.

She lay with her back to the fire and felt his blue gaze burning into her all night long, making her hotter than the flames.

Twenty-three

Eva had awakened in many states throughout her life: wet, cold, hungry, afraid. But never, in ten years of running, had she awoken as she did this morn: angry and aroused.

She had dreamed of Jamie. Again. All night long.

The world was dim and utterly quiet, although a faint lightening hinted at a nearby dawn. She unrolled herself from the woolen warmth of Jamie's cloak and sat up. The campsite was empty.

Gog was gone.

A cold pang snapped through her belly. She scrambled to her feet. A tall, dark shadow separated itself from a tree on the far side of the clearing. Ry, on watch. His arms were folded over his chest, his cape pulled and tucked within the bend, warding off the chill of the misty dawn. He looked like a dark tunnel of smoke, frozen in place amid the fog.

She walked over and whispered, "Where is Roger?"

He looked down at her. "Jamie took him."

More cold pangs, this time through her heart. "And where is Jamie?" she asked, carefully calm.

Ry said quietly, "Scouting the road ahead. They will return."

She inhaled deeply, the cold pang unballing and warming, although why should these words, which could so easily be a lie, comfort her? She reached for her satchel. One small silver penny rolled out from its depths. She picked it up and considered it. It seemed like a hundred years ago that she'd sent Roger to bargain his way onto another boat for France at need. Had it only been yesterday?

Ry was watching. "Thinking of running?" he asked quietly.

She lifted the penny in the air. "It depends. How far will this English penny get me?"

She could see the faint smile on his face as he stepped closer. "That coin is clipped, mistress. It would hardly buy you a cart ride to the fields."

She considered the penny, then him. "How do you know such things? And from so far away?"

He looked over her shoulder into the wood, back on watch. "My father was a moneylender."

"Is it odd, for a Jew to be a knight like yourself?"

"I am neither of these things, mistress. I am not a knight nor a Jew. My family was. I have declaimed everything but Jamie. And he is next."

She smiled as faintly as he had done. They were amusing each other in opaque ways, she and Ry. "So. You are the most common of things, like a wardrobe or a bedstead: a simple soldier."

He smiled with another of those small smiles that made him seem so much less dangerous than Jamie. "As dense and dull as all that."

Less dangerous until he unsheathed his sword and used it with that ruthless, unemotional skill Jamie also displayed. Really, these men were the sort who could make a great deal of money hiring themselves out as judicial champions.

His gaze flicked over her shoulder, back on guard. She turned and peered into the steely green woods with him.

"Do we need water?"

"Pardon?"

She pointed down the hill behind them, to the glistening stream. "For the horses? I can fetch it."

"The horses are able to walk down, mistress."

"Ah, but so am *I* able to walk down. While there, I can also wash a bit."

He scanned the stream and far hillside, then nodded. "Aye, go, Mistress Eva. But if you run, we will find you," he cautioned in a whisper. "And Jamie will not be pleased."

"I have no intention of running. Jamie and I have made an alliance."

He smiled faintly. "Is that so?"

"Indeed. I fetch water for the horses, and he does not tie me to a tree."

He gave a soft laugh, making a puff of hot air swirl before his mouth.

"While I have no desire to displease your Jamie, you must know, sir, I fear it lies ahead. It is the *curé*, you understand. For myself, I would let your Jamie do all his masterful, angry things and would never be in his way whatsoever, for I would be living in a little cottage by a river in France, bothering not a soul. Most certainly I would not be in England."

Despite its yellow flowers and hauntingly lovely misty dawns.

She picked up her little satchel. "Have you a woman, Sir Ry, or do you stay only with Jamie, here to catch the men he destroys as they topple over?"

His smile faded. "I had a woman. And I do not catch them. I let them fall."

"Then I shall fear you both."

She slipped down the hill, through the dripping wet ferns, disrobed down to her linen shift, and waded into the stream up to her shins. She swiftly washed her face, her armpits, and everything traitorous Jamie had alit beneath her skirts. Nails, hair, skin and the clothes that covered it, all might be drab and homespun, but Eva ensured they were aggressively clean and well tended. It was one small thing left to her control, so she took it.

She was crouched low, the wet yellow tunic under the water, when she became aware of a dark shadow at the edge of her vision. She looked up.

Jamie.

She got to her feet in a slow, stunned, half-naked way. Every move she began, she halted, because everything she thought to do was insufficient to solve her problem. She started for the stream's edge, stopped, then stretched out her arm, a pointless grab for the dry tunic that was about five yards away on the riverbank, next to Jamie's boot. She settled on covering the front of her body with the wet tunic and pushed the hair back from her face.

He stood only in boots and hose and a loosely tied lin-sey-woolsey tunic and leather gauntlets he'd started to lace around one wrist, an idle if constructive act as he searched for her, she supposed. He'd stopped short, and his gaze burned down her wet skirts, as if it were a making a line of hot soldered iron.

"I inquired of Ry," she said swiftly. "He said I might."

He did not appear to be listening. It felt like ravishment, this burning path of desire, searing across her body like a brand.

"Why did you take Roger?" she asked sharply, to stop the branding.

His gaze ripped up. "To teach him how to track so he does not get killed. We ride. Now. Come."

He turned and strode up the hill, kicking through the buttery-feathered wet ferns. Again he was with the commands. Eva hurried to the grassy bank and dressed, then grabbed her satchel and hurried up the hill. Even from down here, she could see the top of the hill and the tops of their heads, hear the low murmur of male voices as they saddled the horses.

Something caught her eye off to her right. Three shadowy figures, hunched low, moving through the mists. On the other side were three more, all stealthy, all silent.

All with their swords out.

Twenty-four

She started running.

The crumbly pine needles and rich brown soil fell apart beneath her boots, sending her sliding back down, her knees crashing into the earth and rocks. She reached out and grabbed for tree roots with her hands, pulling herself up the hill, scrambling, sweating, silent but for her panting breath.

Call out? Don't call?

She must not warn the intruders. But if Roger had not yet seen them—

"Jamie!" she shouted, hurtling up the hill, not realizing she was calling for Jamie instead of Roger. "'Ware, 'ware! They come!"

She flung herself over the crest of the hill just as Jamie and Ry scraped their swords from scabbards, Jamie's gaze fixed on the woods as she ran up.

"Roger," he was saying quietly, calmly. "If you think you can resist stabbing me, we could put your sword arm to good use."

"Sword, sir," he whispered. "Put me to use. I've no love of robbers or bandits."

"Nor do I," Eva piped in.

"I have less faith you can resist urges to stab me," Jamie retorted, but was already tugging free a dagger from the belt that held his arsenal of weapons. He spun it in his hand so the hilt protruded and slapped it into her palm.

"Do not stick me," he ordered, and turned away, whispering, "Spread out." Roger scrambled to fetch the blade Ry tossed him, and they fanned out amid the dense, dark forest.

She backed up, moving to her right, whispering, "This way, Gog." There would be no spreading of her and Gog. They were blade and sheath.

She pressed her spine against a large tree trunk and peered into the small, sunny clearing. Her mouth had gone completely dry.

It was like this before every encounter. And not just the sort that had blasted down the oak doors of the monastery Father Peter had arranged for them and sent armed riders galloping through the place, searching for Eva and Gog. No, it was the simple, hail-fellow exchanges. But, of course, if you were being hunted by kings and counts, perhaps this was an understandable thing.

Six of them, she realized as the waving tree branches gave hint to the marauders moving through the wood. Six men. Bandits? Freebooters?

Heir-hunters?

She extended a hand, feeling for Gog, who was never more than a pace or two off. Blade and sheath.

Her hand swiped through empty air. She reached a little farther. More air. Gog was gone.

Shards of fear slid through her belly and arms. She turned slowly, willing her eyes to pierce dimness.

Slowly, the tall figure of Ruggart Ry emerged a few yards away, like a standing stone amid the trees. She swung her gaze farther and caught sight of Jamie, sword at the ready, his body pinned against a tree, his dusky cheek pressed to bark. His gleaming eyes caught hers. She lifted her shoulders in a little shrug, turning her hand palm up in silent question. She mouthed, *Gog?* He squinted, then briefly shook his head.

She spotted a crouched shape creeping up through the brush a dozen paces off . . . Gog.

A stream of breathy relief funneled through her lips. Fear strangled it dead in her throat the next second. A shadowy form, hunched and looming, was following behind.

She took off, a silent shadow, on the balls of her feet, knees bent, arms extended slightly. Sweat built along her arms. The shadowy figure drew nearer Gog. She started trotting.

Something closed around her neck and yanked her backward off her feet. Her blade fell to the ground. She hit the earth at full impact, then a mailed hand hauled her up and backward into an armored body, a blade at her throat.

"Scream and you die," hissed the owner of the body, the armor, and the blade.

Another bandit appeared, reaching for her legs, to lift her off the ground. She went still for half a second, then abruptly turned her head to the side at the same moment she lifted her feet off the ground. She dropped like a stone out of his grip.

Before either of her assailants could so much as curse, she flung her hand with Jamie's dagger up and back, right into Knife's thigh. He howled in pain and stumbled backward, but the other one had already grabbed her braid and yanked her to her feet. The pain was fire through her scalp. He rattled her brain with a savage shake and lifted a knife to her throat.

"Firedrake," he snarled. "I will snap your neck—"

Suddenly there was a tremendous jerk, then a sudden release. Her captor went flying backward like a stalk of wheat in the wind. Eva spun to find Jamie looking down at the man he'd just peeled off her, now writhing on the ground. The other marauder was back on his feet, knife still sticking in his thigh, moving like a runaway wagon right at her. She crouched on her knees, waiting for impact, then rammed herself upward, punching her shoulder into his armored chest. It was like shoving off a boulder. Her teeth clattered as he knocked her down, then wrapped his hands around her chest and began dragging her kicking, flailing body away into the woods.

"Drop her," commanded a deep voice.

Everything went still, then the pressure on her hair abruptly released. He shoved her viciously away. Eva stumbled to her knees, her nose practically sliding into the edge of her knife blade. She swept it into her hand and spun to face her attacker and whatever had attacked him.

Jamie was holding him, blade at his neck. Her frenzied gaze met Jamie's calm one.

"Retrieve your boy."

She spun again, crouched, scanning. Were there others? Had they gotten Gog? Was he—

There he was, swinging from one arm in the lowest branches of a tree, like some forest thing in one of Father Peter's strange and beautiful sketches. A third attacker was scrambling up after him, inching out on the branch. Gog loosed his fingers and dropped to the ground where a fourth awaited.

She started running for him. Ry came in from her side, barreling over the sticks and leaves, a few steps ahead; then Jamie appeared from nowhere. With no fanfare and silent, deadly skill, Ry and Jamie moved through the men as if they were lumps of butter, until they were scattered on the earth, melting into the dirt and decaying leaves.

Eva stared in shock, then looked at Gog. He met her eye and . . . grinned. He was panting, his hand was bleeding, and he had a gash across his face, but excitement flashed in his eyes. Eva cleared her throat several times.

"Roger." It was a croak. A terrible croaking thing, her voice. She cleared it again. "Gog, are you—"

She stopped, aghast to find her throat was unable to be cleared. Something thick was lodged there, and she could not speak.

She looked at Gog, wordless, her mouth open but no words coming out. Gog stared. She heard Jamie murmur to Ruggart Ry, who extended something. She looked down in a daze. It was a waterskin.

"Water," Jamie murmured. "From upstream."

She drank. The cool water streamed down her hot, dry throat. It ran down her chin and she kept drinking. Finally, she lowered the waterskin and handed it back with a nod.

"My thanks." She turned to Gog, who was still staring in shock. "Are you quite a'right?" she asked with great calmness, as if the last moment of speechlessness had not occurred.

The concern on his face washed away under excitement. "Fine, Eva. Fine!" His eyes shone and he patted her arm. Eva suddenly realized he was taller than she. A great deal taller. How could she not have noticed this before? How could she not have witnessed this growth taking place before her very eyes? She felt shocked in a vague, unsettled way.

Jamie and Ry looked between Eva and Roger, then began dragging bodies into the deeper woods. As if leaving them to work this out, however waifs and their charges did such things, she supposed. Unfortunately, she had absolutely no notion how they did such things.

Hunters, murderers, rageful kings, she'd dealt with many obstacles in her life. But never an argument with Roger.

Really, it was not proper that battle could so light one's inner fire. All she wished for was a cottage near a river, and sun for part of the year.

She waited until Jamie and Ry were well out of sight, then said in a low voice, "Why did you leave me?"

"I am sorry, Eva." He did not sound sorry, though, bouncing

on the balls of his feet. His blond forelock fell over one eye. "I thought we would separate, come around from behind—"

"You cannot simply leave me," she snapped, surprising herself.

Gog's buoyant bouncing stopped. He looked at her in silence. This sort of emotional river was not Eva's way. Speechlessness and now this, this upwelling of emotion that almost squeezed her throat shut.

"I would never have let them get you, Eva-Weave," he vowed in a hushed voice. "I was going to come around—"

"You think I wish you nearby to ensure I am safe?" She gave an incredulous, hurt little laugh.

"Eva," he said, his voice somehow stronger. "There were six of them. Six. The same six from the stables. The ones who took Father Peter.

"That means they were sent back, Eva. He knows we are here. And I am not going to hide behind your skirts and let *anyone* take us, Eva. Either of us. On my life."

They stared at each other, a thousand unsaid things roiling below their silence. Jamie and Ry came into the clearing, shoving out of the trees. Roger straightened, raised his voice, loud enough for them to hear. "I was going to circle around, Eva. Come at them from the back. Protect you."

"*You* do not protect *me*," she said in a fierce, concluding tone.

"But he did," Jamie's low voice broke in. "If he'd have stayed with you, he'd have been captured. Both of you. Two of them holding you, the other four concentrated against Ry and me. He did well to circle around. It forced them to separate."

She looked over coldly. Jamie was watching her, paused with his sword half-plunged back into his sheath. "I think it showed a good bit of warrior craft," he concluded.

"Do you?" she said in a slow, low tone. It was intended as a caution. He did not heed it.

"Aye. Roger had a choice. He made one." Jamie's eyes held hers. "It only gave us a few minutes, but that's all we needed."

She stared sightless, seeing not Jamie but the past. All the men who had hunted them, all the things that had almost been. Sooth, all the things that *had* been. The murderous rage, the blood, the screaming, the running. And after, the innocent monks who'd tried to help them cast out like bloody jetsam whenever the hunters came on their big black horses, forcing Eva and Gog into the woods, running again.

What did Jamie know of it? Of the years spent protecting Gog, of running? From men like Jamie. Barren fury welled up in her.

If Gog died, she didn't know what she'd do. Die herself, she supposed. If he was captured, though, oh, the thought of the horror of King John inflicting itself on Gog as it had his father . . . She knew precisely what she'd do: eat her way through the world, up to and including King John, who had started this madness.

Of course, if she was captured . . . . whatever was in store for Gog, 'twould be doubly, trebly, innumerably worse for her.

Best not to think of that.

"That is all we needed, is it?' she said in a low, barely controlled voice. "A few moments, and all is well again? What would you know of it?"

JAMIE watched her closely, in part because she looked like a mine about to explode. Her hands tightened so her painted fingernails bit into her palms. Her jaw worked once or twice, then stilled with great effort. Her gaze bored into his, then ripped away with an almost physical force.

Whatever he had done to her before—and it could be argued that was much—she was tenfold more angry now than anytime before, not for something done, but for something said.

What had he said?

His gaze slide from her rigid, fisted stance to Gog's animated, boyish bobbing. Something was niggling at the edge of his attention. Something disquieting.

They finished removing signs of a fight while he ticked off events in his mind, and his awareness coalesced around a single irrefutable fact: these men had not been about random attacks or petty robbery. They'd been hunting.

They'd gone directly for Eva and her Gog.

Which meant Mouldin knew Roger was back here and had sent his men back, yet continued on with the priest. Which meant however valuable Roger was, the priest was more valuable yet. As all his value lay in knowledge, Peter of London must know something even more valuable than where the missing heir of d'Endshire was.

Twenty~five

They rode hard through the rest of the day, as hard as the horses could handle, moving over to ride inside the treeline whenever they heard hooves or voices drawing near. By Jamie's estimation, their quarry was no farther on ahead. They were keeping pace. Apparently, this was fast as Mouldin could go as well.

Else he was holding up, waiting for soldiers who would never return.

Or perhaps biding his time for a rendezvous. Or a confrontation.

But that seemed unlikely. These were empty lands, except for the wild things, and the only tracks visible went straight on north, so Jamie rode them onward, ever wary.

As the day wore on, Jamie allowed Eva and Gog to move on ahead a few paces, while he and Ry lagged behind.

Jamie said nothing for a few moments, and finally Ry looked over. "You suspect she knows more than she is saying."

"I *know* she knows more than she is saying."

"Why do you not push her, then? You have a long and illustrious history of pushing people into saying and doing things they do not wish to say or do."

"I have been pushing her." Although not as much as he could have.

Eva's upright, slender back swayed as she pointed out something to Roger off to their right. The faded, tight-fitting tunic was cornflower blue, so she looked a bit like a flower herself, which again, he reminded himself, was ridiculous. She'd attempted a taming braid and enclosure in the morn, but strong breezes and hot spring sun had rendered her hair defiant. Now, by midday, she had the bindings off, her hair knotted in a complicated concoction atop her head, held in place by a few peeled sticks, allowing only wisps to fall down. They stuck to the sheen of her sun-heated neck.

He greatly appreciated the view.

"And our plan?" Ry broke into his reverie. "Are you going to be a 'very bad man'?"

"I am."

"How?"

Jamie gathered the reins more tightly as a hare bounded out from the ferns, making Dickon startle. The horse reared up slightly, and Jamie put his hand on the horse's neck, calming him. "If Mouldin keeps on thusly, we will come very close to the town of Gracious Hill."

He felt Ry examining his profile. "I don't think she believed you about leaving her with a one-eyed Scotsman."

"Angus owes me."

Ry looked skeptical. "What will you tell him?"

Angus, compatriot in years past, had been the most loyal, the most ruthless, the most angry, of Jamie's former companions. And he owed Jamie a blood debt. He also weighed in at over fifteen stone. He would be an excellent, if frightening, watchdog.

"I shall tell him what I need him to do," Jamie said.

And then he'd never see her again. He'd leave her captivating, clever, butterfly self behind and never see her again.

———

THEY rode through the springtime sun for two days. Roger spent a great deal of his time talking with Ry and Jamie, discussing blade edges and hilts and the correct wood for bows and other questions that would help him kill someone. Or, she admitted, prevent someone from killing him.

Gog looked quite pleased to be standing with two such strong knights, with their bright swords and clinky mail. She had not been able to breed this out of him. Despite being raised around monks who chanted and prayed, and woodland creatures who ate and mated, Roger was a boy fast becoming a man, and showed fervent devotion to such things as swords and the men who wielded them. This, sadly, had proven beyond her ability to prevent.

In the mornings, the sun would burn through the mists, giving the mornings a fresh, amber ambience. The light came from no single place; the wood simply glowed with gold. Wet green branches and dark brown trunks glistened with dew. The air was fresh and clean and cool. Small birds trilled morning songs. It was a glorious spring.

At night, she would hunker close to the fire. The men would polish their swords and talk in low voices, including Roger in their discussions, while the horses crunched grass and nickered in the background and the fire burned bright in the little pits Jamie dug.

These were comforting sounds, these quiet friends who worked so seamlessly together. She and Roger were this way as well, except there was more chatter, she admitted. But this quiet, this was nice as well. It did not shiver with the fearful quality she often felt in the night.

But of course Jamie and Ry *were* what she'd been fearing. The fear, having been founded, and thus satisfied, must have left to haunt others who had not yet had their nightmares realized in the form of dark-eyed knights and their closest friends.

Occasionally, they would burst out in quiet laughter. It was a good sound. A good scene, Roger sitting with men who smiled at him.

The problem lay in what was to come. The problem lay in Jamie. The problem lay in Eva and her nighttime dreams.

He'd sit cross-legged by the fire, sword balanced across his knees, wiping it down with the devotion of a master with his tools. He would listen to Ry, or Roger, mayhap smile or offer some notion; then his gaze would slide to hers and hold.

Then something hot and shivery would move through her, like a fiery, burning icicle. Being watched by Jamie was a dangerous proposition. He was a beast in his prime, his body honed to a taut cord of musculature that practically vibrated masculinity. Controlled, predatory, intent. On her.

Unfortunately, there was no room for passion, for caring, and most positively no room for a dangerous knight with pretty eyes and a shredded heart that made her desire to reach out and stitch it back up again.

JAMIE knew she watched him at night. He lay on his back staring up at the dark sky between the tree branches, waiting for the moment to be right. To probe her true intent. Perhaps to lay her curving body out beneath his and turn those little, unsteady pants he heard across the fire each night into long, breathless howls shaped around his name.

He stared up at the pinprick stars and let the fire die down, but he rarely slept.

"ALL of them?" Mouldin snapped. "All *six* of them? My best men, and not one of them has returned?"

Mouldin and his sergeant sat on horseback at the bank of a rushing river swollen by the recent storms and stared back across the bridge they'd just crossed. The wooden bridge creaked as the river rushed under it, and the sun burned hot, making the water glisten and burn the eye.

Father Peter leaned his head back, enjoying the coolness, the cessation of riding. He enjoyed a horse as much as the next man; donkeys were his usual mode of travel. But he had not ridden this much in years, not since he was irritating kings and counts, itinerating from one baronial hornets' nest to another. Proof he was back in the business.

Mouldin turned to him. "What do you know, old man?"

"In total, a great deal more than you. Of the disappearance of your ninny-headed soldiers, naught."

Mouldin stared across the river, up the hill on the far side. "A fifteen-year-old could not take down *six* of my men," he muttered. "No one could."

"Jamie could, sir," his sergeant said.

The only thing to be seen were bright green spring grasses and a dirt road winding away in jagged, whipping curves down the hillside, like a mangy pup's wagging tail. The air smelled of fresh grass and sun-hot pine needles. The wind rode by on the back of silence, rustling the reeds along the banks of the river. Otherwise, it was quiet.

Mouldin reined around. "We ride. Fast now." He spurred his horse up the hill. "Burn the bridge behind us."

Twenty-six

They stood at the crest of the ravine late on the fourth day and stared down at the river below.

"We'll have to use the ferry," Ry observed unnecessarily.

It was unnecessary because they all could clearly see the wreckage of a little wooden bridge that used to cross a stream that so obviously wanted to be a river. Eva nudged her horse closer. His muzzle drew level with the others', and they all peered down at the rushing currents below.

"The recent storms must have been too much for it and washed it clean away."

Eva sympathized with the little bridge.

"Some of it is burned," Jamie said. They stared glumly at the charred black edges of the support beams, poking out of the earth like dark, broken fingers.

"They know we're following."

Jamie shoved his hands through his hair, impatiently tugging it free of its leather binding. It framed his face so that, despite three days' growth of beard on his jaws, which would make anyone look like a vagrant at best, Jamie only looked more striking.

Eva scowled.

"Nothing for it," he said, a touch of impatience sharpening his words. "The ferry it is." They reined around to follow the bank of the river south. "We and every other soul in these parts."

They began encountering people almost immediately. Until now, it had only been the occasional villager or fairgoer or pilgrim, riding or walking, or small groups. But now, as they crested the hill that led down to what was now the only river crossing for twenty miles in either direction, the numbers rapidly grew.

The river widened here, from where the burned upland bridge crossed over. The current was thus calmer, perfect for a ferry crossing. Afternoon sunlight made it glow.

A small village had grown up around it, mostly shops, the sorts of crafts and trades people on the move required. A blacksmith for wheel and weapons repair, a buckle maker, a candlemaker, a leather shop, someone selling hot pasties, and of course an alehouse.

No, two, Eva amended crossly. One could never be enough for the men of England.

And the mud. It was everywhere. A swampland of hoofprints and cart tracks and bootheels. Mud and tracks and . . .

"We might never find them again," Jamie said. He wiped his chin with the heel of his hand, his jaw tight. "All these tracks, then a five-mile ride north to the burned bridge to pick up their trail again."

A moment of silence ensued as the horses walked on, wherein they all contemplated the consequences of this outcome.

They rounded a small bend in the path and were finally able to see just beyond the copse of trees on the far side, to find a huge, pulsing line of people swarming there.

The flat, rectangular ferry was just docking on the near side. The ferryman had his pole shoved into the water, preventing the ferry from hitting the muddy shoreline too hard. The men and horses on the barge braced their feet and swayed with the movement. They were all dressed in armor.

"Jamie," Ry said in a low voice.

The human and hoofed traffic now off-loading chugged up the hill toward them on the narrow, rutted path.

"That is an army," Ry said.

"I took note of that."

Another beat of silence. "'Tis the rebels. They bear fitzWalter's insignia."

"I see."

"I thought they were occupied besieging Northampton," Ry muttered.

"I heard they moved to Bedford Castle and took it instead."

"So why are they marching south?"

Jamie blew out a breath. "The only reason to leave a giving stream is to find a bigger fish."

Ry looked over. "London is a goodly bit bigger."

"You think they've taken London?"

If the rebels had taken London, things were going to deteriorate rapidly. But it was unlikely they could ever take it by force. Sooth, they had been unable to take even the relatively undefended Northampton Castle. London, even with its tumbledown walls, could resist until the Rapture.

If she wanted to.

But London was fickle, and the castellan of the once-mighty Baynard Castle within belonged to the leader of the rebel army, Lord Robert fitzWater. Should London *choose* to open her gates, well, that would be a different matter entirely. A bloodless coup.

It was not inconceivable that fitzWalter might try to assail the City. Neither was it assured, though. It was a bold move, a great risk.

Why now?

For the past five months, fitzWalter's army had feinted, harried, poked, and prodded the king, but it had hardly been decisive. After weeks of besieging low-level castles and failing to gain entry unless the gates were opened from within, why had the rebels *now* moved to such a precious target? Why *now* test the king, why now show their hand?

The reins felt heavy in Jamie's hands. Ry looked over and they said together, "Father Peter."

"Son of a bitch," Ry muttered.

Then they did as anyone did when in the path of an army on the move: they got out of the way.

"Keep your face down," Ry muttered, but Jamie already had his head bent and turned to the side.

Both he and Ry swung off their horses as the gang of soldiers jangled and clomped off the ferry and through the small string of shops on opposite sides of the street, flowing up toward them.

Eva sat like a plank of wood in the saddle, for once without a flexible response. For ten years, the sight of a single helmed rider had meant danger. To be now confronted with an entire army froze her like January.

Gog, riding on Ry's opposite side, sat up straight, practically vibrating with tension. Ry tipped his head, gesturing the boy off. Eva felt Jamie's hands close around her hips. He pulled her to the ground, his hand immediately locking around her wrist.

Ry stepped up beside and put his arm around Jamie's side, supporting him as if Jamie were injured. Not enough to draw focused attention, just explanation enough for why a man's head would be down, his face obscured by long dark hair tugged from its binding and three days' growth of beard.

They executed the move within seconds, too fast for Eva to be fully aware it was happening before it was complete. Then they limped down the bumpy, rutted path as they were overrun by soldiers flowing around them. Ry kept his arm around Jamie, looking grimly ahead, while Jamie held one arm bent in front of his stomach. The other hand stayed locked around her wrist.

"These men," she asked quietly, "they would not like to know who you are, would they?"

Ruggart Ry lifted his gaze over Jamie's bent head and stared. Gog, walking beside Ry, jerked his gaze over as well, his face locked and tense.

Jamie's words came low and clear, like pebbles being rolled by river water.

"To the contrary, Eva, they would like it very much. Ry, we need to know what is afoot at the ferry, and how we shall get across. Roger, we could use your help with the horses. And," Jamie added, noting the exchange of looks between Roger and Eva, "should you think to do anything rash, consider this first: whatever you worry I might do to your lady, 'tis but a pale shadow of what they would do." Jamie tipped his head toward the soldiers.

Gog gave a strained nod and avoided Eva's eye.

Ry said in a low voice, "I will go on ahead with Roger. Find some way to occupy your face in an alley or doorway. I will return."

"Aye. I shall follow along more slowly. With Eva."

Ry and Roger walked on ahead, down the long slope to the riverside, the horses reined behind. They were figures of men, then they were dark caped blobs leading larger blobs, then they were almost undetectable amid all the masses of other human bodies scurrying around the ferry landing.

Jamie tugged on Eva's wrist. She tripped toward him and he slung his arm over her shoulders, so it looked as if she were supporting him. But in truth he was controlling her. He might as well have had a rope around her hips and a bit in her mouth. Like a tidal force, irresistible and inexorable, even in restraint, he propelled them to the side of the path and they moved slowly along, as more soldiers clambered up the hill, their murmuring like a tide of foul mouths and loud boots.

Up ahead, far down the hill, the dark spots of Roger and Ry had merged into all the others massing down at the landing, trying to get passage across. Clearly this was being forbidden. The sergeant stood holding back the tide of people who wished to go from south to north. On the other bank, the army stretched back up to the hills.

In fact, they were building a few boats of their own, sawing and hammering like Roman soldiers. Soon they would overrun this riverbank, and everyone in their path.

Twenty~seven

amie propelled her down the path, off on the side, affecting a limp, ensuring they looked like beggars, anything to be inconspicuous, for Eva had no idea how truly she'd spoken.

Jamie was known far and wide as King John's favorite lieutenant. Capturing him would be a significant coup in the slow dance of supremacy and demise the king and rebels had been locked in for months now. But it was more than that. For Jamie was more than that.

An encounter with the rebels would prove highly painful, possibly fatal. Robert fitzWalter, commander of the rebels' Army of God, lord of Dunmow and of Baynard Castle, was a powerful man with a short temper and a long memory, and he did not like Jamie a'tall.

But then, that was because he did not like being betrayed.

The list of all the people whom Jamie had infuriated was as long and twisted as a vine. The great irony being Jamie had never forsworn an oath, never breached a confidence, ne'er so much as bald-faced lied to anyone but the king. And still he had amassed a long list of people who absolutely hated him.

Robert fitzWalter was at the top of that scroll.

If he or his men got hold of Jamie, nothing would stay his fury. The soldiers would grab Jamie easily, outnumbered as he was a thousand to one. Then they would take him apart, limb by limb. Literally.

To the good, a great many travel-stained, hair-roughened men were traveling the roads these days. As long as no one knew him on sight, Jamie would appear to be one of legion. Nameless, immaterial.

Then he spotted Chance.

Chance, one of fitzWalter's inner circle, his woman and his harbinger, had been in fitzWalter's employ as long as Jamie. She would know him *before* sight. And beneath that feminine tunic was a thick leather gambeson, and beneath those dull red skirts were any number of blades.

Anger surged through him, hot and fast. He reined it in at once, but after came a sudden weariness. It was so common a thing, to be so furious. To be so thwarted. To curb the strong emotions pounding through him, so that he felt as if he were sawing on a bit that yanked in hard.

He kept his head down, his gaze up, his hand on Eva's hip, propelling her forward, heading toward the recessed doorway. She stumbled. Black hair swept in a tangle across her face as she looked over at him.

"Are these bad men hunting you?"

Of a sort, he thought. Bad women.

"Shall I save you?"

Clever Eva had detected something beyond the normal concerns of being in the path of an onrushing army.

"I am beyond saving," he murmured, listening for any signs of being recognized.

"And then, of course, *you* are a very bad man."

"That is most certainly so."

"A shame."

"I suppose there is nothing you can do."

"I could call out."

His attention came roaring back. Her voice had taken on a musing tone, so he did not know if she was thinking out loud, or speaking to him. "Cry for help." Her gray eyes slid his way. "Call out your name."

His eyes gleamed at her from within the hood. "Oh, Eva, you could, but that would be a very bad mistake."

Twenty-eight

He pushed his hip against her hard, propelling her toward the narrow, recessed doorway, and when Eva took her next natural, stumbling step forward, he stepped behind her and pulled her backward against his chest. Then he stepped them sideways into the alcove.

His arm was already slung over her shoulder, so she felt like a shield before him. They were practically invisible, capes slung over them. In the shadows under the eaves on side of the road, they must look like unaccomplished beggars.

One arm curled low around her abdomen, his hand locked on the far hip. He kept his other arm draped over her shoulder but dropped it low, so his forearm rested between her breasts. He cupped her ribs just below her breast, tipped his hooded head to the side, and put his lips by her ear.

"Do you see what I mean, about the error?"

His breath warmed her ear, but the dark rumble coming so close made her shiver. Sadly, it was not in fear. "Tell me, Eva, if you think the soldiers are eager for me, how much do you think they would pay for Roger?"

A chill sliced through her belly like a frozen dagger. "What?"

"How did you do it?" He pushed her forward again, until they were tucked far back in the doorway.

Her knees were made of water. "Do what?"

"How did you get Roger out of England, all those years ago?"

He might as well have punched her in the belly. She could not draw breath. Her knees did as they'd been threatening and washed clean away. Reflexively, she felt for something to support her, but of course there was nothing, only the arms of the man holding her hostage. She curled her fingers over the forearm he had clamped across her belly like a bar of steel.

"How did you know?" she whispered.

"How could I not?" He shifted the hand below her breast for additional support, and his thumb brushed over her breast.

She exhaled slowly. It was wrong to notice that, to be aware of his lean, powerful body behind hers, his hips pressing up against her buttocks and the small of her back.

"I will do it," she vowed, her voice shaking. "I will call out."

"You will not."

She shoved back against him, hoping to throw him off-balance. All that happened was that she felt the hard length of him more fully for a moment. "Release us, Jamie, and I shall keep my silence."

He gave a low laugh and bent closer. He hung low over her like wings now. The hand below her breast slid up, a startling move, utterly without seductive intent, but it awakened something fiery and insistent, then he closed it around her throat.

"Open your mouth, Eva, and you will die."

"By their hand or yours?" she asked tautly.

"Do you wish to attempt it and find out?" he whispered, his lips against her neck.

She shoved her hips into him again, twisting. He flexed his arm, stilling her. "Eva, have you a brain in your head, you will not do that again," he warned in a low, steel-edged voice.

She did it again, bucked her hips while pushing down on the forearm wrapped around her belly, but he clamped down harder and lifted her off her feet, yanking her up against him and what she now realized was an erection.

She froze, his arm like a steel band around her belly, the other hand still encircling her throat. For long seconds they were motionless, Eva's toes barely scraping the earth. Then slowly, he lowered her back down.

She loosed a long, hot breath.

She did not move—couldn't—so their bodies kept touching, and she knew the moment he stopped using his hand as threat and began using it as seduction. He slid it down her neck, his thumb making small strokes as he went, down to the collar of her dress, slowly, as if testing her resolve. He kept moving down, past her collarbone to her breast without stopping, and slid up the swell and brushed the tip of his fingers gently over her nipple.

The breath shuddered out of her.

This was the stuff of her dreams, to have Jamie touching her. He'd hauled her out of the saddle and backed her up against things numerous times, but he'd never set his hands on her body in this slow, lingering, *devoted* way, and it was like being torched. Set aflame.

Then, because everything was in peril, and all the safe choices she'd made up to now had resulted in only more peril, and because Jamie's danger was the safest thing she'd ever known, and because she was burning and her dreams were coming true, she tipped her head back the small inch required and rested it on his shoulder.

His heart beat strong against her back, then he pressed his mouth to her ear. "Eva."

Was it a warning? A survey? A request?

"Aye," she whispered in reply. It should serve for them all.

"I want you more than breath," he rasped.

Hot shivers came like rain down her belly and legs. "I know," she whispered. She pressed her thighs together involuntarily, pressing on the tempting shiver-ache, then shifted infinitesimally, moving her hips back, into his body and his erection.

His heart beat strong against her back; then he ordered in her ear, low and heated, "Do that again," and followed his words with his hot tongue. "Again, Eva."

She did; her head on his shoulder, she arched her back and pressed her hips into him, hard against his arousal.

So this is the feel of Jamie's hands on a woman's body, she thought, and knew a sudden, inexplicable, steaming jealousy for all the other women who had known such touches.

"Do you know how much I want you?" He slid his hands down and closed them around her hips, more of his holding power. One booted foot came forward, so his knee pushed between hers, nudging them apart.

"Aye," she said breathlessly. These rough-edged questions being spoken from behind, his hands on her body, not knowing what he would do next, it was the most arousing thing she'd ever known. Her body was throbbing, her head spinning.

There was an assessing pause, then he reached around, took one of her hands, and brought it slowly behind her, down between their bodies. He curled her fingers against the rock-hard length of his erection. "Do you feel?" he demanded in a low voice.

Another broken sob escaped her. This was what she wanted. This. Her fingers tightened around him, and his laid his hand over hers. Together, they stroked him, a long, hard pull. Eva's head was spinning; she was panting, dizzy, wet.

He leaned low and ran his tongue down her neck, murmuring, "And you, Eva? How great is your desire?"

"Ever so much," she whispered. "I burn."

He set both his hands on her belly. "Show me." One calloused palm slid up to her breasts, the other went down, and as he ranged like a mountain over her body, she arched into him with a single hot, gasping breath.

Ry's head poked around the corner of the alley.

Eva flung herself away so fast her nose knocked the far wall. Jamie's hands dropped like rocks.

Ry looked at him grimly. "There's no getting across the river this day." Roger stood just behind him, looking just as tall, just as worried. The line of soldiers had dwindled to naught, but the next ferry would bring more.

Jamie shook his head, his face tilted toward the building. "That is not what I want to hear. The entire rebel army is about to encamp here."

"Aye, well, the soldier at the platform is on orders from fitzWalter himself. He's commandeered the ferry."

"Give him coin."

"He does not want coin. He prefers his head. We need something more convincing than coin. And he doesn't look a persuadable sort."

"How far to the southland bridge?"

"Same as it was before, Jamie. Ten, twelve miles. And we'll not make it through those soldiers a second time. We sleep the night here in town, out of sight in a stable somewhere, and come morn, when the army has passed, we move on."

"And in the wait, lose days on Mouldin. No. I will not," Jamie said in a low voice, then added, "Chance is here."

Ry started. "What?"

"I saw her. She does not usually travel with the rabble. She must be coming for Mouldin." Jamie moved to the doorway and peered out. "If we wait the night out, she will get to him before us."

Ry put his hand on the wall, considering Jamie hard. "And to correct this, you will . . . ?"

"Stop her."

"Of course. Why did I not think of that?"

"Ry, if she has been sent for Mouldin, then she surely knows where he is headed. Information that could take *days* off our travel. If I am right, we need not backtrack to the bridge to pick up the trail."

Ry nodded. "And if you are wrong?"

"Have you another plan?"

"As usual, my plans go no further than keeping you alive a few hours more."

"Whatever for?" Jamie peeked around the corner of the doorway again.

She saw the resignation, perhaps mingled with anger, enter Ry's face as Jamie looked back. "Wait here. Watch out for them." He tipped his head in Eva's direction.

"Here?" Ry gestured to the recessed doorway. His voice was full of tension.

Jamie tipped his head up. The shapeless hood framed his face in darkness, so his eyes glinted within. Ry met them. Then without warning, Ry stepped back, lifted his boot, and kicked open the door to the shop.

Jamie gave a small smile and they all hurried inside.

The dim little lower chamber was empty, but they could hear the sound of footsteps above, hurrying down the stairs. Jamie unsheathed his sword just as a round, sweaty face poked out from the the stairs and stared in amazement.

Jamie extended the blade, forming a line from his muscular shoulder to the sword's steely tip, and said in a low, lethal voice, "Upstairs. Lock the door behind you."

The husky command did not need to be repeated. The shopkeeper flung himself backward, sat down hard on the steps behind, rose again, and slammed the door shut. The sound of fumbling with an iron lock, then hurrying footsteps back up the stairs.

Ry was already reaching for the angled crossbar that held the front shutter of the shop window up. He yanked the bar out. The shutter fell like a hammer. Jamie picked up an iron poker and shoved it between the latch and the corner of the wall, wedging it shut. A murmured word to Roger had him hurrying to the back door to repeat the same.

When all the doors were locked, the window shuttered, they stood for half a moment in the close silence. Then Jamie strode through the brazier-lit darkness to the door, his boots echoing off the worn plank floors.

"I will be back, Ry. Keep them here. Keep them occupied."

Ry gave a clipped nod. "Shall I put them to work mixing lard, or perhaps laying the rushes?"

Jamie inched the door open and peered out. "Ry, this is important—"

"This is you about to get killed. *Again*. While I play nursemaid."

"Ry—"

"How do you know you'll even find her?"

Jamie's body stilled. Without looking over, he clapped Ry on the shoulder. "Because I just saw her walk inside the tavern down the road."

Jamie stepped off the small stoop and disappeared.

Twenty-nine

Eva looked at Ry, who returned her glance briefly, then strode to the door.

"I have known many tavernkeepers in my time," she said.

Ry put his hand on the latch, depressed it slowly, and pulled the door open a narrow crack. He peered through.

"And I have found they are quite unlike your reluctant ferryman."

Ry barely glanced over.

"In that they very greatly desire money and will do almost anything for it."

He looked over more fully.

"Such as allow people in their back doorways unseen, so they may be on hand in case of need."

He shut the door and turned. "And you will wait here?" he said with something like hope in his voice. Hope being such a precious commodity, like pepper or saffron, she hated to dash it, but there was nothing for it.

"No, we will not wait. But neither will we run. I think, for the moment, we will stay as Jamie's cargo."

Roger's hand was on his hilt, his face already taking on the edges of hardness she'd tried to keep at bay for so long. "I will not wait, sir. I can help."

Eva ignored the painful pang in her heart. "He is not a sir, Roger," she said quietly. "And I think none of us, least of all Master Bucklemaker, is pleased to have us waiting here in his shop, Ry. Let us all go."

Ry looked between them, obviously in inner debate, then nodded and started for the back door. "We go around the back," he murmured as he yanked the iron poker out. "Eva, you stay close, and we will find a place for you out of sight."

She followed him without complaint, but Eva knew no one could find a better place for her to be out of sight than she, and she had often found the best place to become invisible was in plain sight.

Thirty

Jamie stepped inside the tavern. Men in boots and cloaks clustered around the high tables or leaned against the walls, mugs in hand. Most appeared to be merchants and travelers, not soldiers.

He was surprised. It appeared the little river port would be spared—there was no evidence of an intent to loot—and apparently drunkenness was going to be confined to the army camp.

Even so, the inhabitants had reason to be uneasy. People drank when they were uneasy. The tavern was crowded.

Alert with every sense, Jamie moved through the crowd to the last empty stool at the end of the counter, ordered a drink, and waited.

It did not take long.

Chance appeared at the far end of the room and looked directly at him. Two other figures emerged and spread out on either side like dark wings, her ever-present henchmen.

She strolled closer, as if the tavern were a hall strewn with rushes and herbs. Her hair was long, so blond it was almost white, and a narrow, embroidered band around her head was shot through with silk threads. She wore a dark cape, thrown back. and looked quite impressive.

She certainly had been to Jamie when he had come under fitzWalter's tutelage fifteen years ago, as a boy of fourteen to her seductive eighteen. As she was now, to the men in the tavern who turned to watch her pass. When they spied her bulky escorts, they quickly looked away.

Jamie glanced over, then took another sip of his ale. It was not good. He set it down.

"Jamie," she murmured as she drew near.

He passed a glance over her without fully turning his head. "Chance."

She rested her hand on the sticky trestle counter, her back against the wall, and smiled at him. "I am surprised."

"You do not appear it."

"I was looking for you."

"I am not surprised."

"We had word you were in on this little hunt."

"What hunt?"

She smiled slowly and glanced over his shoulder. "Where is your Ry?"

"Napping."

She gave her feline smile. "You are never without him."

"I am now."

"He will be missed. Lucia pines for him."

"We left Baynard's service years ago."

"So did she."

"I see you've brought an army. What are you going to do with it?"

Her smile expanded. "You have not heard?" She tipped forward a little, and the silvery embroidery at the collar of her gown shivered in the torchlight. "We have taken London."

He felt deep winter coldness rush through his chest. "Ah."

"Armies are marching from every corner of the realm to join the rebels at London. FitzWalter is seeking allies. He is willing to show great mercy to those who seek his goodwill now."

"How unlike him. Do you mean me?"

"That depends on your reply." She smiled her cat's smile. "I have a proposition for you."

Eva sidled along the wall in the tavern making no attempt to look like a servant this time. This time, she would be invisible.

It was quite crowded, making it simple to disappear. She inched her way along toward the back where a small divider wall separated the room into two sections. On one side was Eva and all the smelly, armed men, and on the other was Jamie and that woman, the one from his past whom he must oh-so-desperately see.

He was half resting his hips against a stool, one boot on the ground, the heel of the other hooked over the low rung. His cape hung, deceptively casually, around his shoulders, flowing down over the stool, hiding what Eva knew was a battery of blades.

So why was she here, being invisible in this grimy little tavern? In truth, she did not know. She only knew why she was *not* doing it.

She could have been doing it to save Father Peter's life, for she had no chance of regaining him without Jamie. But that was not it.

She might have been doing it because of the smallest shred of curiosity—so minute it was barely detectable, really—about the willowy woman from Jamie's past. But that was not the reason either.

She might have been doing it because she'd heard in Ry's voice a thing she recognized: the sound of someone caring desperately for a person they could not protect.

Perhaps she was doing it, in part, because of the confused

wash of deeper emotions she felt with Jamie, which went far beyond being propped against walls by his capable male hands.

One thing was certain; she was *not* doing this because Jamie might need her help. The enemy who had abducted her, tied her up, and held her captive was now intent on accomplishing the very thing that would destroy her and everyone she loved?

That would be a ridiculous reason to risk one's life.

She sat down on one of the wall benches, as close as she could, and aimed her hearing the way the one might aim a fishline, reeling in their words.

Thirty-one

"I have a proposition for you."

Jamie finished his visual inspection of the tavern and looked at Chance. "I have one for you as well."

The woman's smile went brittle. "Now, no biting, Jamie. We are not speaking of me. Baynard wants you back."

"Why?"

A glint of rushlights shimmered on her hair band. "Who can say what moves him at times? Coin, cunts, power."

That did bring a harsh laugh. "None of those reasons are compelling to me. The answer is nay."

"You are always so impulsive, Jamie." Eva was fairly certain Jamie was the opposite of impulsive, but Jamie didn't bother to point that out, so neither did she. "Wait until you hear what Lord Robert has planned. Mayhap I can get an aye out of you yet. For this"—Chance reached out and touched his forearm—"is an alluring offer."

He glanced down at her fingertips. Eva edged half out of her seat to do the same. "Nay."

"Why not?" Chance asked.

"Because Fitz would have me tied and splayed with picks under my fingernails before I made it through his outer gates."

"Not so, Jamie." Chance pitched her voice low and persuasive.

She'd learned the concoction at Baynard's feet. Jamie knew the tone; it generally preceded beatings. "Lord Robert is . . . repentant. For the way things went. For the way he treated you."

Jamie shook his head. "He has not the inner coffers for such a sentiment. He is all acquisition. I am done with him, with them."

Eva sat up a little straighter. Done with the rebels? He could not mean that. She must be misunderstanding.

"You have not even heard the offer. It concerns retribution, Jamie. Or, if you please, reparations."

"It does not please."

The woman's hair was like a sheet of white-gold in the torchlight, shimmering as she leaned closer to Jamie, a tone of glee in her voice. "We have taken London, Jamie."

Jamie's face remained unreadable, hard and implacable.

"Come join us," she urged in a voice at once coaxing and steely. "'Tis time to force the king's hand, as he has repeatedly refused to extend it. We shall parley no more. Archbishop Langton was useful, but the time for peacemakers has passed."

"I am sure it has," Jamie agreed coldly. "Seeing as you are en route to barter for Peter of London."

Her face extended into a delighted grin. She touched his arm again. "We are close, Jamie. Much closer than your lord. Do not think Mouldin will ever sell Peter of London to the king, not after what John did to him. He would sooner slit his own throat. All these maneuverings, they are playacting for coin. Mouldin will sell to us, then we will have the priest, and everything inside his head."

"Which is . . . ?"

"The heirs," she whispered, almost sounding gleeful. Eva felt her stomach turn. She swallowed the thick spit filling her mouth. "Peter of London is the only one who knows where the missing heirs of England are."

Not the only one. Jamie knew too. Eva's heart slowed. Jamie knew precisely where Roger was.

"And whoever has the heirs, has the crown," the woman concluded.

Jamie pursed his lips. "Is that what fitzWalter is planning? No more charters, big or small? He wants the throne?"

Chance shook her head. The silver and gold threads woven in the narrow band around her head glinted in the torch- and candlelight. "If you wish to concern yourself with the travails of the rebels again, Jamie, you will have to come with me."

Eva's head was spinning, her heart falling, her belly churning. She was in a maelstrom. *Again?* What was this *again*?

Jamie burst into low laughter. "To London?" He tipped his head toward the guards. "It will take more than four of them to ever get me through the gates of London again."

"Come, Jamie. I can assure you, fitzWalter can make it worth your trouble. Should you recall your loyalties, he knows you can be of use again."

"My loyalties?"

Eva saw the edge of what she could only describe as a cat's smile. "And in return for such a pledge, he promises to rectify the situation that has plagued you so long and ensure you are invested with lands. Many lands."

"My pledge? Of fealty?"

The woman nodded.

"My pledge, to a man who has renounced his oath? My fealty to a man who tried to commit regicide?"

The woman's fingers tightened around his forearm, like a cat's claws. "You misremember, Jamie Lost," she hissed, but Eva heard the wet syllables as clear as a stab. "*He* did not try to assassinate the king. *You* did."

Eva sat back as if struck.

Jamie? *Regicide?*

Thirty-two

The tavern air chilled around Jamie, colder with each beat of his heart.

It was not that he was surprised to hear the truth; he knew his past well enough, as did Chance. It was a splinter of something deeper than shock or even fear, a small dart, barely visible, sharply painful, a small dark shadow untouchable without peeling back the skin of his heart.

After years of surviving on the streets of London as a child, with the occasional visit to Ry's home for patching up his head and heart, Jamie had found himself a mentor in the aggressive, ambitious Robert fitzWalter, powerful lord of Dunmow and, moreover, Baynard Castle in London.

Perceiving the urchin's ruthlessness and skill with weapons on the streets, Baynard took Jamie in and shaped his proclivities into fearsome proportions, for a precise purpose: to be his royal assassin.

FitzWalter ensured Jamie gained employ as part of John's personal guard, but Jamie himself ensured he rose quickly through the king's ranks, a junior among the likes of men such as Engelard Cigogné and Faulkes de Bréauté, Brian de Lisle, and John Russell. Eventually he became favored even among the favorites, until the king trusted Jamie with everything. He was sent on missions of utmost secrecy and gravity, reporting back only to the king. Paymaster, diplomat, counselor, captain of his men—come a time, Jamie knew everything that passed in King John's realm. Every court case involving high justice, every baronial wife John lusted after, every invasion planned, every expense recorded: Jamie knew it all.

Then, three years ago, the fruit had ripened. King John planned an incursion into Wales, and his murder was plotted to the smallest detail. Jamie had been ready, prepared to execute his destiny—even now he recalled the dull throbbing that had filled his ears—until, at the last moment, he learned whom Robert fitzWalter and his ilk planned to put on the throne instead: the brutal, canting butcher of the holy war against the Albigensians in southern France, Simon de Montfort. This crossed some line Jamie had not understood and could not, even now, put into words. But he did not need to name it to know it.

So he turned. He revealed the assassination plot to the king, betrayed his mentor, aligned with the king he'd sworn to murder.

John had turned almost rabid with fury and fear. Heads rolled, estates were seized, the rebel leaders fled into exile, and an escort of crossbowmen with quarrels cocked and ready had surrounded the king ever since.

Jamie's role was never discovered. Once the king's assassin, he was now John's reluctant protector, the only one who stood between him and a legion of nobles who would like nothing better than to draw and quarter their anointed king and bury his innards in a pile of manure, then place his crown on their own heads.

Chance's feline eyes glittered at him.

"And yet Lord Robert spoke no word of it, did he? He took you in off the streets as an orphan, raised you up, found you service in the king's employ, and you had to do but *one errand* in repayment. Instead, you betrayed him. He left the realm, left his lands, fled in ignomy. *You owe*, Jamie."

Something happened to Jamie's eyes, something not so much of hardness but recoil, and his reply was twisted in its low-pitched fury. "I have paid, Chance."

"Not yet you haven't. Tell me, do your illustrious, *loyal* companions know of your role in the plot? Archbishop Langton, William the Marshal—do they know you are an *assassin*?" She hissed the word. "Shall we tell them? I do not think the king would be happy to learn of your past. I think he would be positively murderous."

She leaned forward. "'Tis is a well-deep debt, Jamie. FitzWalter is giving you a chance to repay, before you are made to recall exactly who created you. Do you understand?"

Jamie leaned forward suddenly and she jerked back, banging into the wall.

"I understand you, Chance. Now understand me: should Fitz wish to speak with me on matters of loyalty, let him come and find me himself. If he dares."

In her corner, Eva felt like cheering, an odd and utterly inappropriate response, surely.

Chance tipped her head to the side and a thoughtful tone entered her words, but beneath it was fury. "Who is she, Jamie? She was comely. In a rare way. And yet, so petite and . . . windblown. Earthy. I am surprised. You always went for the rarefied sort." Eva heard the snake-smile in Chance's voice. "Oh, not that you wouldn't taste the rest of us, but I saw you, I watched. And your eye always tracked the nobles."

Eva felt a tiny pinch at the corner of her heart, as if something heavy had been dropped upon its edge.

She must have moved in response, for Jamie's gaze snapped away from Chance's like a whip and locked on hers.

It was a physical thing, this look. It grabbed hold. Jamie saw her, knew her, then let her go, released her the way a hawk drops its prey, snapped his gaze back to the woman who so clearly wished Jamie were hunting her instead.

"You have had a great many chances to crawl out of the muck, Chance, but you will die there," Jamie said coldly. "And you are foolish to have your men stand so far off when you are delivering threats to *me*."

She lifted her pale brows. "Surely you would not lay a hand on me, Jamie?" On the surface, her voice was filled with disdain and threat, but clearly, underneath that lay hope.

Jamie pushed up off his stool. "My fealty is a defiled commodity, Chance, as you have pointed out. In any event, I have none to give. Let us bypass it for what truly matters: how much is fitzWalter offering for the priest?"

A sickening feeling began in Eva's belly, as if she were on a boat crossing the Channel.

The woman angled her head to the side, considering him. "A great deal. Why? Do you know something?"

"I know Mouldin will not be bartering the priest to the rebels. I know I have something better, for the right price. Where were you told to meet Mouldin?"

She hesitated, then said, "Gracious Hill. Why?"

Jamie shook his head. "Already you've been crossed. The king was told Misselthwaite. Mouldin, I expect, will not be at either location."

An even longer moment of hesitation, suspicion, ensued. "Why have you have changed your mind so suddenly?" Chance asked.

Jamie gave the woman a look Eva had also received and did not much like: hard intent. "My mind has ne'er changed. I am as I have always intended to be: self-serving and rich."

Eva felt frozen in an unconscionable way. This news should not freeze her like ice. Jamie had never been her ally. She was not bound to him, nor he to her. But this . . . this felt like something breaking inside her chest, like kicking out the stained-glass windows of a church.

Chance was breathing through her mouth. It was choppy, as if she'd been running. "What do you have?"

Jamie glanced around the room. His gaze did not avoid Eva so much as slide over her as if she no longer existed. "Not here."

He kicked his stool back, the woman straightened, and Eva got to her feet. The soldiers pushed off the wall. Another two moved in from a more distant position at the front of the tavern. The woman put her hand on Jamie's arm. She looked . . . happy.

Jamie gestured to the back door. "Come, this way, and— What the hell is that?"

Eva's hand went, shaking, to the little blade always tucked within her skirts, before she remembered that Jamie had long ago disarmed her.

Thirty-three

Jamie tempered his shout of surprise just enough to furrow Chance's brow, to make her glance toward her men, but in the end, to hurry to his side, just outside the back door.

In a single swift move, he clamped his hand over her mouth, which muffled the sound of his other hand coming up and hammering into the back of her skull, knocking her senseless against the wall.

Her goons were already on the move, pushing through the crowds, shouting, but no one else seemed to care, except that now they were all looking at the goons. And standing, jostling, getting in their way.

Jamie dragged Chance out the back door, into the small, shadowed courtyard, thinking, *What the hell is Eva doing here? And where the hell is Ry?*

He didn't stop to reflect on possible answers, just pinned his spine against the wall as the two closest guards came rushing through the doorway.

Jamie turned to the side and kicked out, smashing his boot into the first man's kneecap. He went down with a shout of pain, clutching his leg.

The second man, running up behind, flung his arms out reflexively. Jamie grabbed hold of one and yanked so hard the shoulder snapped as it popped out of joint. The man howled in pain as he swung around entirely until his face smashed into the wall. He rebounded backward and fell across the downed man, who was writhing in pain, trying to stand on his broken knee.

Jamie crouched beside him. Making a fist and cupping it with his other hand, he slammed his elbow into the back of Broken Knee's skull, just as the one with the dislocated arm staggered back to his feet, swinging his sword in an indiscriminate, rage-fueled arc. Jamie ducked as it swooped overhead, then leaped to his feet and launched himself shoulder-first into the man's stomach. They went flying, scuffling as they rolled.

Jamie was staggering back to his feet when he heard a soft call. "Dick?" It was one of the two guards who'd been stationed in the front. "Dickon? You a'right?"

"I have to change my horse's name," Jamie muttered as he drew his sword, keeping his attention on his current target, uncertain if he'd have time to select a second before they came rushing up behind him.

Then he heard the low crunch of boots on pebbles. He froze and slowly turned his head.

Ry and Roger stood there, swords drawn. In a swift glance, Ry took in the unconscious man on the ground, his leg bent at an unnatural angle, and the bloody soldier, facing off against Jamie, one arm hanging helplessly. Then he looked at Jamie.

"You didn't save me even one?"

"Oh, they're coming," he replied grimly as the first beefy soldier barreled through the doorway. Another lumbered through behind. Both had their swords out.

They took them down quickly. He and Ry had been doing this sort of thing for over a dozen years; it was almost ridiculously simple. Skill and cunning always won over brute idiocy, but it was gratifying to have Roger's sword arm in the mix. It took hardly a minute to sprawl them senseless on the ground, then another couple to lash them together like hogs for the fire.

Ry had his boot on one man's shoulder while Jamie gave a final yank to the rope that bound him to his mate. "I owe you, friend," Jamie said roughly.

Ry nodded, tossing his head back to get hair out of his face. "You had best hope I never start collecting, friend, or I will bankrupt you."

Jamie gave a laugh as he dropped the rope. "You would know. You handle the money."

"Only because you have fooled yourself into thinking I have some talent for it."

Jamie clasped his shoulder. "Only because you do," he said, then turned to Roger, who was standing a few paces off, breathing hard. "Roger?"

"My lord," he croaked, holding his left hand to his right upper sword arm, as if in pain.

"Do not call me that," Jamie muttered as he prised Roger's hand up to inspect the arm. "Are you injured?"

"It is naught," the boy scoffed, but Jamie walked him backward, out from under the shadow of the willow, and examined the wound in the wash of late afternoon sunlight. "'Tis but a flesh wound," Jamie said, releasing him. "You fought well. Now we must retrieve Eva. She was inside—"

"I am here," came her soft voice.

Jamie spun. She stood in the doorway of the tavern draped in her dull-blue overtunic and hard brown boots, her hair flowing down over her slender shoulders. She examined each of them in turn, their gashed cheeks and bleeding chins and Ry, who was limping slightly. Then she looked at Jamie. "Did you make them all sorry to have met you?" she asked quietly.

"Aye," he said, rather fiercely, because he could neither describe nor understand the feeling of rightness at seeing her there, waiting for him, her gaze calm on his after the fighting.

"That is good," she said. "I did not like her, with the long hair."

Jamie gave a soft half-laugh, Roger laughed outright, then the scowling, barrel-chested innkeep came rushing through the doorway. He stopped at Eva's heels.

"Now, lass, what's this about—"

Everyone froze. Jamie, Ry, Roger, even the innkeep. The only one who moved was Eva, who pointed gracefully to the bound and bloody collection of unconscious men and one woman sprawled across the innkeep's courtyard.

"There they are," she explained calmly, as if she were indicating buckets of water. "They were causing problems, you see."

He stared at the downed men, then at Chance. "They Baynard's?" he asked shortly.

Jamie readjusted his grip on the sword. "Aye."

The innkeep's gaze came back up. "You the king's man?"

He hesitated slightly. "Aye."

The man wiped his hands on his apron as two burly guards he clearly employed for the purpose of bouncing unruly guests out the door appeared. The innkeep nodded. "Men who can't keep to their word do more damage than pestilence. That's what I've always said."

Jamie gave a small laugh. "I agree entirely."

He turned to his men and hooked his thumb. "Take them into the reeds, down by the river. They'll awaken come morn. Or not." He turned to Jamie. "You'll want away, sir. The ferry's offloading again."

Jamie sheathed his sword. "We could greatly benefit by having a place to pass those moments, Master Innkeep."

The innkeep examined their battered crew somewhat doubtfully, ending on Eva. She smiled. He nodded and said, "My root cellar's around the back."

Thirty-four

It took only a moment for them all to be ensconced in the vaguely musty earthen pit that was the innkeep's root cellar.

Twice as wide as a plough and again that long, it housed few vegetables this time of year, but a great many roots. They nudged out of the fertile earth as twining brown fingers and indignant elbows. A wide swath of russet sunset light spilled down the steps into the room before the innkeep shut the door above them with a sudden, shocking slam.

Eva stared into the flesh of darkness around her. She was in the belly of dark. She could see nothing. The only sounds were the others' breathing, the dim, distant thud of boots on pebbles on the road above, and the unrelenting absence of breeze. Around them, as if in vapors, rose the peaty scent of earth, ensuring things aboveground could grow, while down here in the dark, it was . . . dark.

"It is dark," she announced quietly.

Her words could not even bounce back against the enclosing earth; they were sucked into it and disappeared. Silence. Someone shifted, the creak of leather and a miniature clang of metal against metal. Eva's heart beat faster, and faster yet. She could hear it deep in her ears, feel the whipcords of coldness ripping through her. If anything had ever counseled *"Run!"* this dark tomb did.

"Eva?" Roger murmured.

She could not answer. The ridiculousness of this fear, of dark and dirt, when the dangerous things all lurked aboveground. The mind had no power over this panic, though. She opened her mouth to breathe.

Suddenly, there was movement, boots thudding on hard-packed earth. A dull bump, then light, glorious red-gold light, came pouring in as Jamie threw back one of the two doors that lay flat atop this lifesaving grave.

"'Tis naught," he said curtly, sitting on the step. "It lies flat to the ground; they will neither think to look, nor notice if they do."

Eva stared up at the entrance, glowing with light, Jamie's dark silhouette in the foreground, and breathed. The sun, the fresh air, Jamie, and that he had known what she needed; she inhaled all the things that made her feel alive.

He leaned back, looked up, then got to his feet, bent at the waist, and peeked out. He turned.

"They have passed."

"Roger," Eva murmured, getting to her feet. "Pull down your hood and look scrofulous."

Thirty-five

oger looked at her, startled, but he did so a second later, almost as quickly as Jamie had at the top of the hill. Ah, there was a lesson in that. If she kept them on this way, he would turn out as lethal and lost as Jamie.

"All of you," she said briskly, "pull down your hoods, put on your gloves, tend leeward on the path. Yes, most certainly, you too, Ry, for all you are nothing but a very common bedstead." Jamie's leather creaked as he turned to look at Ry. "And you," she said, turning sternly to Jamie, "for once you will keep your good mouth shut and your wolf eyes down."

Jamie slid his hand down off the wall. "My what?"

She turned away. "Your everything."

Ry grinned. Gog gave a small laugh, and these things helped to pass the tense moments wherein they pulled their hoods far down over their faces, then trod down to the ferry.

They waited for the next group of soldiers, with all their clanking steel and iron, to off-load. Eva felt the ground shudder beneath her feet as they passed. But more than that, she felt Jamie's strong body an inch behind her own, felt his intent appraisal of every man passing by, and knew at the least the first man would die before he could strike.

It was the hundreds following that so terrified.

They hurried down the rutted track as soon as the last man passed. The tall, long-faced ferryman glanced up in surprise as Eva and her hooded little group approached. The sergeant stood on the bank above, grim-faced and potbellied, a subordinate wearing the livery of Robert fitzWalter.

Eva stepped forward.

"Nothing for ya," the sergeant said before she'd even opened her mouth. "Get back." He turned to the oarsman. "Push off."

The ferryman, tall and pale, had his pole in the water when Eva caught his eye, a finger lifted slightly. It was not a command, not by any measure a commanding action, but he stopped. She turned to the sergeant.

"Sir, I am sorry to trouble you, but we must needs cross the river this eve."

It took a moment for his leathery, glittery bulk to turn fully. He was easily a head taller than she, which must all be filled with empty air, for he cast a squinted, suspicious glance at her and said, "What?"

She nodded as if this were a wise thing to say. "Indeed, you are correct, we must pass tonight, sir."

Setting him up to think agreeable thoughts did not seem to be effective, but the repetition helped her words penetrate the depths of his skull. It also made him scowl.

"Not t'night, you don't. The lot o' you can spend the night enjoyin' the pleasures of the soldiers' hospitality. Or lettin' them enjoy the pleasures o' you." He gave a bark of laughter. "In the morning, mayhap, you can pass. If you make it worth my while," he added with a smirk.

Eva gestured behind her, to the men whose lives were in her keeping at this moment. "You will not wish these ones here near your soldiers' camp, sir. Lord Robert would be most displeased. I would rather not have this worrisome chance taken with all his honorable men."

He scowled. "What chance?"

She gave a helpless shrug. "'Twas a most *virulent* case."

His eyes narrowed, marked between suspicion and utter confusion. He looked at Ry and Jamie and Roger again, all with their hoods drawn down to their noses, all slightly hunched over, all gloved, and all holding reins of horses.

"Case? Case o' what?"

She sighed. "A passing sad one. Now, 'tis true that they're *all* remarkably scrofulous." She gave a general hand-waving to include the three of them, then extended one finger to indicate Jamie more directly. "But on him, it has spread everywhere. I do not exaggerate a whit: *everywhere.*"

She aimed in the direction of his groin and spun her finger a few times, drawing an invisible circle in the air around this most private of places.

The guard took an involuntary step back.

"'Twas most was awful to see, sir. Or not see, as the case was. It simply shriveled up and . . . fell off."

This time the guard took such a large and decided step back he almost tumbled off the embankment. Pressing her advantage, Eva took that step with him, lowering her voice.

"Even the monks were uneasy, which is why I am hurrying them to the leper colony by the priory, where they tend only the most *virulent* cases."

She neglected to mention which priory, but he did not seem to be bothered by the omission.

"Christ's teeth, go." He snapped at the ferryman, whose face had gone pale. "Take 'em, you. Go on," he ordered again, keeping his distance, willing to risk the edge of the muddy bank rather than come close to the lepers. He kept a careful eye on Eva and Roger and Ry as they passed, but he did not so much as glance at Jamie.

Eva nodded her thanks with a calm, dignified nod, letting

her patients board first. The ferryman, too, kept his distance from the hooded lepers as much as the small craft would allow, and thus they began their river crossing, four men rowing, the horses swimming behind in the high, gently burbling waters.

STANDING as far to the rear of the flat-bottomed ferry as possible, Jamie murmured to Ry, "We cannot walk into that nest of soldiers. The horses alone will draw their eye. It appears fitzWalter has given no looting orders, but one cannot trust an army on the move."

"At the least, we shall not."

"So, we bribe him."

Eva, standing a foot away, shifted with the bobbing flow of the river beneath their feet. Roger, standing at her side, looked slightly pale from the bobbing.

"Let me manage the negotiations," she suggested in a low voice. Her and Jamie's eyes met and she put out her hand. "I understand your reluctance to share with me your coin, but he might rather deal with me than a tall, angry leper whose . . ."—she lifted her brows delicately and tipped her head to the side—"fell off."

"*Shriveled up* and fell off," Jamie corrected.

She smiled the faintest bit. "So sad. Such potential wasted."

Ry snorted quietly. The winds blew with brisk efficiency down the channel of the river valley, bobbing the boat, as Eva moved with light, weaving steps to the ferryman's side.

"Good sir, might we inquire about a small detour?"

She might have asked if they could please carve out his eyes. His jaw fell, then snapped shut. "A *de*tour? Are ye bleeding *mad*? Lord Robert has this ferry now, and if I don't get his men across . . ." His voice faded at the sight of silver coins in Eva's flattened palm.

"Just a few dozen yards downriver is all we require. I do not like to think what those soldiers might do to a woman and three lepers."

"I know what they'll do to me. They'll have me head," he said with feeling. But he was looking at the coin.

She looked at it too. "But these currents can be swift and shifting, can they not? They must trust you in this, no? And then, of course, you will be removing a terrible threat from his men, keeping the lepers away. Even the brave sergeant at the dock agreed. How can Lord Robert argue with this?"

Before twilight came, they were downstream at the head of a small footpath, armed with directions on how to get through the darkening woods toward the road north, to their new target, the town of Gracious Hill.

Thirty-six

Silently they climbed the path, then stopped to let the horses dry off before resaddling them. Jamie stood beside Dickon, rubbing him down with a rough cloth. Roger stood with Ry, practicing feints with a sword as sunset light came down in thick streams of yellow glow through openings in the branches. Where the bands of light hit the earth, the soil glowed a rich brown.

Eva sat in the middle of one such shaft, on a mossy log, an ankle resting atop her opposite knee. She had closed her eyes and was rubbing her calf with two thumbs, making slow, circular motions. Jamie watched a moment, then tore his eyes away and went back to brushing Dickon.

"Do you not find this all rather tiresome some days?" she inquired of his back. "All this hunting and capturing and running from soldiers?"

"Most," he said drily. He made a long sweep with the rag down Dickon's glossy back. The horse swept his chestnut tail. "I would much rather be sitting by a fire with a mug of ale."

She made an impatient sound. "You Englishmen and your ales. I would sit by a river with a little cup of wine and have the sun shine on my shins."

He was nonplussed and paused. "Your . . . shins?"

"They so rarely see sun. They are jealous of the top of my head."

He smiled faintly and looked over. "Not of the inside?"

She gave him an arch smile. In the single thick cord of sunlight, it looked positively sultry. "You mean my brain? My very smart thoughts?" She switched ankles and began rubbing the new one.

He looked away, back to Dickon. "My shins are surely not envious of *your* head. Taking us to that ferry was a most bad plan."

Ry and Roger paused in their mock battle and Ry chimed in helpfully, "I agree with Eva."

Jamie rested his arm on Dickon's back and shook his head. "I should have pushed you into the Thames twenty years ago. What other course of action could we have taken?"

Roger at least remained a staunch supporter. Sweating lightly from his exertions, he said, "There were none, sir. None a'tall. And you mustn't mind Eva. She likes to . . . instigate."

She looked over with all the solemn wisdom of an elder sister. "This is a shameful lie, Roger. I do no such thing. I simply point things out. Such as the fact that your hose are unlaced, there in the front."

He jerked his head down to where she pointed and immediately began making repairs to the little leather thongs that kept his hose bound to his belt. Eva smiled at Jamie over the top of Roger's bent head. Slowly, he smiled back.

She not only had a fiercely sharp, insightful mind but a body he'd known was made of lush curves. Now he'd ranged over them and wanted her more than ever.

But it was more than that. Like the ray of sunshine she was sitting in right now, she kept shining up pathways of thought he'd never encountered before. Enough so that, amid their dark business, she made him want to smile and even laugh, and the wanting was even more rare a thing than the act itself.

But then, Eva made him wish to do many things he'd never done before, and not all of them involved hiking her up against a buckle maker's wall and stepping between her thighs. The remnants of that adventure still pounded between his legs. Looking at her body, her face into the sunset light, did little to reduce it. The opposite in fact.

"You were speaking about your river wine," he prompted, which proved she was a *faerie*.

"Ah, see?" She smiled happily. "Already I am turning you from the ale. Let me think . . . where was I?"

"Standing by the river getting snockered," Roger piped up, his head still bent as he fumbled with his ties. He must be well accustomed to Eva telling such fanciful tales. Perhaps she had told them as bedtime tales when Roger was a boy and she was laying him down to sleep.

Jamie felt a sharp, dusty tug inside his chest.

"Ah, yes, Roger, thank you for reminding me," she said in that voice Jamie could only describe as graceful, which boded no good for him, to find grace in her, not with what was to come. "We would be snockered," she began again, and Roger grinned, "and as I sipped my wine, I would look over my shoulder and see my little home, with its red roof and garden. I would make supper, and before covering the fires, just about this time of night, I would go out and sit by the river and . . ." Her voice faded away.

Jamie was utterly captivated by the potency of the simple images, the red roof, Eva cooking supper, Eva sipping wine, Eva sitting by the sunset river. Eva.

"And maybe there are some little children," she finished, so softly he could hardly hear.

Everything kept this last far away. Her volume, her words; everything was sent away on the breath leaving her body. She owned none of this. There were no *my*'s or *I*'s or *One day I shall*'s. It was all indefinites and passives and things that might have been.

Eva knew as much about standing apart as he.

Thirty-seven

They set up camp quickly. Ry took the first watch. At Jamie's murmured request, he took Roger with him.

Eva stood beside the fire, toeing little pebbles out of dirt pockets and shredding sticks in uncharacteristic restlessness. Jamie sat cross-legged and thrust a fat branch into the low flames. A few spindly twigs still clinging to it spat into angry flame, but the branch itself was a huge dark center in the midst of the glowing hot coals.

Eva broke the silence.

"Assassin?"

He countered this by looking up with his dark eyes and saying, as if picking up an interrupted conversation, "I believe the most surprising thing of all is that you were telling the truth all along. Just not about what."

She let out a long breath. "Jamie, you lie. You have not once seemed surprised."

He looked at the fire.

"You do not understand," she said quietly.

"And you do not explain."

"Jamie," she said with a helpless, laughing gasp, "what is this you ask of me? How could this be, this 'explaining'? We are on the top and bottom of a map, you and I. Mountains and seas divide us. How can it be that I would explain myself to you? And in the end, it would not matter."

He did look up at that. "It matters."

His eyes had darkened to that deeper blue, something she now knew happened when day fell to night. It felt a very intimate thing to know about someone.

"Oh, Jamie," she said softly, "you have done poorly, to bind yourself to King John."

"And you have done poorly to bind yourself to no one."

She took a swift, quiet breath and gave a sad smile. "We are a poorly matched team, then, you and I. The naught and the darkness, one of us bound to nothing, the other to the devil."

His eyes slid back to the fire. "I am what I am, Eva. You know what that is, or you do not."

As he looked at her with his hard, dark, dangerous eyes, Eva saw it all, stretched out before her like a road, the truth of what would be with Jamie. It had already begun. Her heart turned toward him like a flower to the sun.

To her horror, tears of impotent fury pricked at her eyes. This was the dangerous thing she'd seen in him from the first: this connection. But all of it was a lie. A dirty lie. She'd never known it before; what on earth had made her think it was a true thing now?

This was the truth of her life: everything was exactly as it seemed.

Patterns repeated and people were just as they appeared. Jamie was not decent, no matter how desperately she wished him to be. Given sufficient cause, everyone bent. Even she.

That was what she feared the most.

"Tell me what happened."

She looked away. "We hid, and then we ran."

He rolled the tip of his stick in the fire and said quietly, "Some said 'twas a massacre, that night at Everoot."

She nodded. She did not see the memories anymore, a small gift from God. She recalled what had happened only as dim, rote collections of images, such as one might collect plate or silver.

"I had been living at Everoot for years. I was sent there . . ." She took a breath. "When my mother displeased the king."

"When was that?"

"When he took the throne."

"So you lived there for . . ." He did swift computations. "Six years?"

"Approximately." She bent over, picked up a twig, and dropped it in the fire. "I know what you must think."

"What must I think?"

"You suspect I am the Everoot heir."

His shook his head, his gaze never leaving hers. It was a hard, penetrating look from his night-dark eyes. "Never. You could never have run and left your mother behind."

Accursed Jamie. Her nose pinched tight and she swallowed hard once, twice, a third time. How did he do this, home in like an archer on the things of the heart, when he was so clearly lacking one himself?

"I did not run," she said with rigid precision. "She made me promise to take Roger and flee, the moment we saw the king ride up. I ne'er would have left her, you must know that. Someone must know that," Eva repeated, suddenly harsh. But knowing did not matter. Roger knew, and Father Peter knew, and still the awful guilt remained. No one could give absolution for it. "But the countess Everoot made me swear . . . and there was Roger . . ." Her voice broke and she stopped until she could see Jamie clearly, and not through a shimmering veil of tears. "Yes, Jamie, *massacre* fits. The king would have killed us all if he could that night."

"What pricked the king's rage?" Jamie asked.

She shook her head, although he was not looking at her, but into the flames. "I cannot say," she murmured.

But of course, she could. She simply would not. One did not tell such tales. They were not hers to tell. Tales of how a beloved widowed Countess Everoot and the equally widowed Lord d'Endshire had not only developed *la liaison amoureuse* but had also been trying to spirit away treasures hidden in the vaults of Everoot's castle before the king thought to confiscate them himself.

But everything else . . . Eva knew everything else was going to be unleashed tonight. She felt it in some strange and inexplicable way. It was as if the words had been herded in her throat for ten years now, and once she opened her mouth, they all came galloping out.

"We hid in the wall, Roger and I. We watched him. He murdered Roger's father, Lord d'Endshire. The king knows we have seen this; he is not happy with knowing it. I hid Roger in a hidey-hole behind me." She broke off. "Then Mouldin came. I took Roger and ran."

"You fled with the babe," Jamie said. It was a low-pitched, smoldering summary.

"He was not a babe. He was five."

"That is a babe. And no one ever saw either of you again?"

"Father Peter did. He came for us, much later, in the woods. I think he must have known something bad would come. He used to travel north as a judge, on the royal eyres. The countess would invite him to stay. He first showed me how to draw when I was very young. We"—she shrugged—"were kindred."

"And the attack back in the woods, Eva?"

She gave up on the gully; there was simply no way to kick out enough dirt to match all the truths coming out of her this night. She released a sigh and tipped her head back and peered between the shifting tree branches.

"Mouldin's men," she admitted. Whyfor not? She could barely discern which truths were yet untold. "Gog saw them. To Roger's detriment, they also saw him. And do you know what good and foolish thing he did? He jumped them and tried to stop them from taking Father Peter."

"All six of them?"

She nodded glumly. "This is another of his so-good reckless decisions. We are a mess, our little family, are we not? They slapped him down like a mosquito. But they did not forget him. They must have told Mouldin of the little bug who tried to sting them, and he sent them back."

"How could a description of a fifteen-year-old harken to him a five-year-old boy?"

She stared into the flames. "You do not know Mouldin. He is like a wolf trap, all claws and cold steel. He knows when heirs are due him."

Nighttime breezes brushed like a soft hand through the new leaves, humming little lullabies. The fire crackled and flared up as it licked its way over a pocket of air. In front of the suddenly flaring flames, Jamie was a solid black silhouette.

"Do you know what a good man Roger will become?" she asked in a shaky voice.

Jamie rolled the tip of his stick in the fire, a slow, highly controlled move. "I do. You have raised him well. You made a man decent and good, who would have otherwise been lost."

"And if you take him to your king?" she said bitterly. "Then of what good is goodness?"

The fire hissed and hummed as he watched her.

"You do not even know how easy it would be to ruin him. This goodness of his, it is like a grass blade. It will be trampled."

He said nothing.

"And yet, you will do what you will do, will you not? You will say you have no choice. That you are bound by vows and oaths, and this will hold you to terrible things." To his credit, he did not look away. "But, Jamie, how could you? Do you not know . . . ?"

Her voice faded off. He knew. He was a mythic warrior-king, sitting cross-legged before the fire. He looked every inch of it, with his flashing sword and dark eyes, his hands that had done so much, waiting to take whatever he wished. And yet, and yet . . .

He looked down into the fire. "Eva, do you know what state this realm is in?"

"Dying."

"No. Exploding. Erupting. It will not last long."

"And so men do terrible things while they can."

"And in their madness, would put on the throne a man worse than the known evil."

"There is no worse thing," she protested, then pressed the back of her hand to her lips to hide that her voice had cracked, like a wall pressed upon too hard.

He looked up then with a smile overflowing with bitterness. "Eva, there is always something worse."

The heart hangs over a pit. Strung up like a sacrifice, it swings in the winds of the world, of things done and things that might have been. Sometimes it is in terrible sway, those hopeless moments of *How did it ever come to this?* Other days are calm, and it is easy to forget what lies below.

Then there are Jamie days. Hurricane days. Days where the worst winds are nothing but pale zephyrs beside the sweeping hurricane force of one other lost, swinging soul.

"Eva." Rough came his words, quiet and hoarse. He reached up and touched the end of her half-spun braid, where it hung in front of her belly. He might have stroked her with a lightning bolt, for the shock it sent through her. "If I could do a thing of my choosing tonight, it would be to walk in your vineyards, holding your hand. But I am not bound that way. I am shriven for something other."

Oh, loose the hurricane, she was lost in him.

Tears pushed at her eyes with their little wet elbows. It hurt a great deal.

She was bereft. Beggared. Without resources to meet this unexpected truth that it had come to this: her heart was seen by the man who would be her destruction.

So she did the only thing left: she reached for him.

Thirty-eight

Jamie saw her extend her hand. Her slim, pale arm, her fingers, reaching for him. Trusting him to do no harm.

He had a moment of knowing he could turn away. Do the decent thing, and not reach back.

But Jamie wasn't decent.

Her body ached to unfold for him, and he wanted to make her do it. As he was not capable of anything more than this, the weight of needing of this one thing from her was almost crushing.

And she wanted him. It carried her toward him in waves, and he would not resist swimming in her any longer, not if she gave the least encouragement. Not tonight, when the past and future were so close to hand. Not when she was so close to hand.

Wry, perceptive, cynical, hurt, desperate Eva, right there.

So he swept down on her like the wind, hoping to blow her over and move on, as he had been doing ever since his father had been murdered before his eyes on a London street.

He reached up and touched the curling ends of her half-spun braid, where it hung in front of her belly. He could hardly feel the silk of her, against his rough touch.

"Loose your hair."

"No," she whispered, but the word rode out on a trembling

breath, and she bent her arms and pulled the pins from her hair.

His heart started a sluggish, hard beat.

Dark hair tumbled all around her shoulders. "You are exquisite," he said, his voice hoarse.

"You are dangerous."

His eyes slid to hers. "You should run away."

"I am trying." Her voice broke.

No quarter given tonight. He touched her fingertips and tugged her down to her knees. Eva had a way of moving such that even in dropping to kneel before his warrior's body, she looked like a princess. With the back of a hand, he brushed the hair away from her ear and curled his fingers against the base of her head, coaxing her forward.

A long, hot breath slid out of her. She felt as if the freshest wind were blowing past her, making her dizzy.

Then he leaned in and touched his tongue to her earlobe, whispering, "Lift your skirts for me."

Whoosh. "I will not let you," she said, but her voice shook. Everything shook. He was the wind, blowing her over.

"Yes, you will."

Hand light on the back of her head, holding her steady, he leaned forward from where he sat and trailed a line of soft kisses down her neck to the soft dip at the base of her throat. No more breathing slow and steady. Her breaths came in sharp little pants now, pushing past her lips.

He slid his hand down to the curve of her back, under the warm curtain of her hair, drawing her closer, until her knees were pressed up against him. Not stopping, he reached up and tugged down the collar of her bodice, then together unlaced the ties of the bodice of her gown. Then he looked at her, and her body started trembling.

He took her nipple, cool and hard, into his hot mouth and

sucked. She threw back her head as he sucked harder, and she cried out and threaded her fingers through his hair. And so, hard and commanding, but ever slowly, to torment her, he lapped from one breast to the other, nibbling and sucking, until her body kneeling before him began to tremble. He closed his hands around her waist, holding her to him.

He ripped his mouth away and looked at her. Eva cupped his face, never having felt as weak as she did just now. The way he looked up at her, with potent masculine lust and something almost affectionate, made her tremble from the inside of her heart to her hot, flushing skin.

He reached out and slid his thumb over one of her nipples, slippery from his suckling. Wetness throbbed inside her. His hard, dark, dangerous eyes locked on hers.

"Now, you will let me."

She would. She did.

He wrapped a handful of hair around his palm and slowly, irresistibly, pulled her head back as he rose on his knees in front of her, then bent his head and kissed her. Hot and hard, he took possession with a ferocious kiss that never ended. He mined deeper with each plunge. Her arms were around his shoulders, and he slid one hand down between their bodies. A flick of his wrist flipped the hems of her skirts up, and with slow, devilish intent he put his hot, calloused palm on the inner side of her knee and stilled. She exhaled a shuddering gasp. His eyes held hers as he slowly, achingly, slid his broad hand up the shiveringly sensitive inside of her thigh, higher and higher, until he reached the hot juncture between her legs. He stopped. She held her breath, whimpered, and pushed against him.

"Jamie."

"How far shall I go, Eva?"

"Oh, much, much further," she pleaded.

He gave her that small half smile and slid a thick finger into her heat, a single thrust, deep inside.

She flung her head back, crying out. Immediately his mouth was over hers, covering the dangerous sound, sucking her tongue into his mouth, his finger still inside her, sliding almost out, then in again, hard and fast.

He pressed his forearm against her inner thigh, coaxing her knees apart even farther, and she spread her legs for him. He slid a second finger in, and his thumb began circling against her slippery folds, perfect little pushes of sensual torment. She threw her head back and rocked her hips forward, and they made a slow rhythm of his capable hand and her tossing head, and his lips in her ear, his low voice urging her on. He bent with her as she arched back, his body tight against hers, one broad hand behind her shoulder blades as she clung to him, the other inside her, thrusting, harder and faster, so she could do nothing but toss her head on each rhythmic push.

"I want more." Dark and full of promise and threat, he spoke against her lips.

She didn't even realize that he'd sat back, bringing her forward with him, until he sat on the ground and she knelt over him.

"Lean into me," he coaxed in his low warrior voice, his hand still doing wicked, wonderful things, and she was unable to do anything but his bidding. She put her palms on his shoulders and leaned forward, her mouth by his ear. His arm stretched out under her belly as he slid his fingers in deeper, pressing for more.

"Will you lift your skirts for me now?" he asked in his sinfulness.

"Dear God, Jamie," she gasped, shocked and so fiercely aroused her body was humming.

"Rise up on your knees," he ordered, and when she did, when she was up on her knees for him, shivering with desire, he tore her skirts up and forced her to hold them, and he watched her as he plunged his fingers into her deep and slow, over and over.

"Jésu, you are beautiful," he rasped, and leaned to kiss her belly.

She hung on to his shoulders as his sinfully capable hand worked her, rocking two fingers inside her, and his thumb wicked in its slippery little strokes, his tongue hot, lapping, moving lower, his teeth making little shivery nips down her belly and abdomen, going lower, so that her thighs shuddered as she leaned on his shoulders, and her head dropped back so she was looking up at the blowing tree limbs, sobbing his name.

"Come for me," he ordered ruthlessly, his voice a harsh rasp. "I want to watch."

A stick cracked in the woods.

They flung themselves apart. Danger had been too long a part of their lives for anything, even mad passion, to curb its bite.

Eva practically bounded to the opposite end of the clearing. Jamie got to his feet and stared into the fire, trying to calm his breathing, just as Ry's armored body appeared at the edge of the clearing, Roger beside him.

Ry stopped short. He looked at Jamie, then at Eva, then back to Jaime. Roger did the exact opposite: looked at Eva, then Jamie, then strode to Eva's side. She stood with her back to the clearing, to the fire. To Jamie. Gog stepped close, murmured something to her.

"What happened?" Ry asked, drawing near.

"I got in," Jamie replied in a low voice.

Ry examined him closely. "Aye? And?"

"Roger is the d'Endshire heir."

Ry let out a low whistle. "Jamie, you could smash open a rock. Why on earth did she tell you that?"

Jamie shook his head at the glowing bed of orange coals in the fire pit. Why had she told him that? Because he'd practically manhandled it out of her. Pushed on her when she was already tipping. Stomped on her where she showed the slightest weakness. Waded in where she was most transparent and dragged her through the shallows.

This was not generally the sort of behavior that elicited reflection, and certainly not remorse.

"That is what I do," he said flatly.

Ry eyed him. "Now what?"

Jamie finally looked up. "Your query means what?"

Ry swept his arm in a semicircle, to indicate . . . whatever had happened here. As if whatever happened here would change his plans. Affection never changed his plans.

"Now we find the priest," Jamie said.

Ry glanced at Roger and Eva, a few paces off. "When we have one of the heirs right here?"

"We have not made it this far, you and I, my friend, by relying on the king for our intelligence. I do not see why we would start now."

Ry glanced across the clearing. "And Roger? Do we tell him?"

"Tell him what?"

"That a barony is waiting for him, I suppose."

"Ah." Jamie gave a small, humorless smile. "Not that I am Satan's minion, come to take him to hell."

"I do not think that."

"You are alone in your good opinion of me."

"I did not say I have a good opinion of you," Ry retorted. They looked at Eva and Roger, murmuring together. Roger had his hand on her shoulder and his head was tipped down, nodding, as if confirming something. Or encouraging her.

Eva's hair tumbled over her shoulders. Her bodice was laced, but barely. She was speaking in low tones, her face pale, her hands animated, moving in the air between her and Roger's bent head. The light cast by the glowing embers brightened the front of her slim, tousled silhouette. Then she wrapped her arms around herself and bent her head.

"If I have the stick to measure Eva by," Jamie said slowly. "Roger knows very well who he is and exactly what awaits." He turned away. "I have the watch till morn."

He climbed the hill and stood peering into the valley below. The narrow dirt road was visible crossing a distant hill, looking like a skinny belt on a fat man. Moonlight shone, making it shimmer here and there in puddles. The wind whispered through the trees, shivering the leaves. It was crisp from trees and salty from the far-off sea. Chilly.

Then, far in the distance, he heard a wolf loose a great, howling cry. They were not all dead, then, not yet. He closed his hand into a fist, clenching it around the strange, fierce . . . joy that moved through him.

He waited, but no answering cry came.

He slowly unclenched his hand and raked his fingers through his hair. She was strength and courage, an erotic nymph with a glowing vulnerability at her core, and Jamie could carry no one's vulnerabilities. Not his own, not anyone else's. No vulnerable things in his life. Not anymore.

Hopefully he'd proven his worth tonight, which was naught. For his sake and hers, he hoped he'd warned her off.

He had a mission, and it did not involve butterflies or smart, sultry women who could be hurt by a look and wanted much more than whatever he had inside.

Enough of women. It was time for war.

EVA felt him leave the clearing, felt his absence the whole time he was gone in an ambient, echoing way, as you might know you were in a room without any furniture, even in the dark.

Everything had come true, just as she'd foreseen. She'd given Jamie everything, her body, her secrets, her heart.

All he'd had to do was look at her with those dangerous eyes, kiss her with his scarred mouth, show her a piece of his shredded heart, and she'd given him all. She'd unleashed the river and told him everything.

Almost.

Thirty-nine

Her shame knew no bounds.

She washed briefly, but no amount of scrubbing could remove the evidence of last night. Her debauchery. It throbbed between her legs. Pounding, scorching memories of Jamie and his body. His confident, sensual assault of her body. His hands, his powerful legs, his lips on her—

Worst, he was ignoring her. He had reverted to some cold, gruff, efficient being, with a demeanor more steely than the sword hanging at his side. There were no little half smiles that made her heart sway, no dry rejoinders that made her want to keep talking because he so clearly wanted to listen. No making her feel *seen*.

They rode swiftly through yet another bright spring day, slowing only to rest the horses.

"I hear you tried to wrestle six men to the ground when they rode off with the *curé*," Jamie said to Roger as they went. Jamie's arms hung deceptively easy and loose, one bent to lightly hold the reins, the other to rest his gloved hand on his thigh. High boots and his cloak covered but did not conceal the truth of his muscular body, nor did the linked mail of his armor.

Gog beamed at him. "Aye, sir."

Jamie smiled faintly. "Did you not consider you might have been killed?"

"No, sir!"

Eva sniffed. Jamie glanced over briefly. "If you had been hurt, Roger, what would your lady have done?"

Roger looked confused. He followed Jamie's glance. "Eva?" Roger laughed. "Why, she'd have hunted them down until they were hanging from gibbets she hammered herself."

Ry joined in Roger's laughter, and even Jamie smiled. Eva lifted her eyebrows. "You all think this is so funny? Your chivalry, Roger, it is blinding."

He turned to her, baffled. "I wasn't being chivalrous, Eva-Weave."

"This I know."

Jamie ignored her and said to Roger, "And you are certain the six who attacked us were the same men who took Father Peter?"

"Most assuredly. I know, because one of them said, 'Oh, Christ's mercy, he's only a boy. Can't a couple of us knock him down?'" Roger grinned. "Then they did."

Eva shook her head. "This helps not even a little bit, such foolishness."

"Bravery." Jamie said it quietly, but Roger seemed to sit straighter in the saddle. He did not, though, openly counter Eva.

"Yes, yes, this matters so much to you men, I know. You all must be so wonderfully brave, in the foolish things you do."

"Better than not being brave," Gog said, his smile undampened. "Eva, truth, you are sorely mad to complain suchly. What are we doing in England in the first place?"

She pushed back a few sprays of hair that had pulled free and were tickling around her face. "To secure Father Peter before evil men like Jamie do."

Jamie showed no response to this impolite observation.

"Just so," Roger agreed. "We are in England, running dangerous men to ground to rescue the *curé*. We chase him. *You* chase him, Eva. What do you call that?"

"Foolish?" she suggested, to please him.

He smiled. "And brave. Sooth, Eva, if I learned it, I learned it from you."

She sniffed. "You are foolish to say that."

"And you are brave."

"We are a lot of fools."

"Better than being a lot of cowards" was all Gog said, still grinning.

Eva stared at his familiar profile. He was moving away from her, like a ship from a dock. It was visible in everything, his actions, the way he disagreed so impolitely with her sensible thoughts, and . . . in the bright sunlight . . . was that, was that . . . blond stubble on his face?

She felt shocked. He was becoming a man, and Jamie . . . *Jamie was his teacher.*

Anger built to unsustainable degrees. She turned to the object of her enmity with a most noxious glare. "Certainly *you* know a great deal about such things, and yet you do not tire of them." Her voice was so low-pitched it was almost a hiss.

Jamie's head inched around. "Of what?"

"Foolishness."

He reined abruptly to a halt. "Ry, ride on ahead with Roger, would you?"

The two took measure of the look Eva was giving Jamie, and the look Jamie was decidedly not giving Eva, and happily cantered off. When they were a dozen yards away, Jamie turned.

"Now, Eva, what were you saying?"

The mocking politeness of his tone was almost more infuriating than that Gog admired him. Than that she had bent for him. That his hand had been . . .

Her glare turned glowerlike. Her entire face, in fact, heated up. "Would you not say *you* occasionally indulge in foolishness, Jamie?"

"Let me consider a moment . . . Aye. When I first laid eyes on you and did not bind you hand *and* foot. And tie you to that tree."

She nodded coldly. "And I ought to have stuck you with my little blade when I first had a chance."

His eyes went hard. "Aye, Eva, if you could have, you should have."

"*You,*" she snapped, "who would kidnap a priest. *You,* who are in league with the devil, *you* should beware." She was close to snarling, she was so incensed. It was impotence, she realized with a sinking heart. She could not make him care the way she knew she cared. "For if I ever find less than a yard separating us and have a blade in my hand—"

"Consider very carefully what you say next, Eva." His voice was lethally quiet. "For if I do not like it, you will be sorry."

"You have been threatening me since the moment I met you," she snapped.

"And delivered on them last night."

There it was, out in the open, like a dead bird fallen onto the path between them. She practically reeled backward, stricken speechless.

His eyes were merciless. "And I shall deliver again and again, if you give me cause."

Oh, dear Lord, she deserved to die, the way her body turned wanton at the mere suggestion he might touch her again. Again and again.

He reined his horse around in a spirited pirouette. "You've had my mark from the start, Eva: I am no good. Believe it. Do not tempt me again."

Her jaw dropped. She yanked it shut. "*Tempt you?*"

He skimmed her body with a level glance before returning to her eyes. Level, yes, and worst of all, dispassionate, neutral. Untouched.

"Aye. For I will take you, Eva; then I will toss you aside. I vow it. That is all I am made of."

Forty

Ragged lines of people and merchants and carts were pushing up to the gates of Gracious Hill, an ambitious little village that had sprawled into a fair town.

The spring fair began on the morrow, and the town bustled. It was filled to overflowing, and the meadows outside its walls were filled with tents and cook fires, a camping arena for merchants and shoppers from miles around.

Despite the general atmosphere of celebration, though, something dark and watchful was in the air as they rode through the tents. In these restless times, butting up against civil war, trouble came in many forms. Freebooters and bandits haunted the dark woods, because outlawry was a much safer bet than trusting your fate to a hot iron in hand or the ability to float in cold water, but there were other threats as well. Trouble came more often from renegade lords who preyed upon their own subjects. And now, armies were on the move.

All in all, it was safer to be inside walls come nightfall.

Jamie was ambivalent about town. Gratified at the prospect of drinking freshly brewed ale and sleeping in a bed. Eager to get a good wash.

On edge, at being within walls. Trapped.

And towns stank to the high heavens. Out riding, away from

large groups of people and their accumulated filth, it was easy to grow accustomed to only the faint musky odor of one's own body and fresh air. But in town, the wastes of the world converged. Sewers running down the edges of the cobbled streets. Tanner cast-offs. Entrails. Unwashed bodies packed close together. Fires burning. Dog shit, cow shit, human shit. An unmitigated, malodorous mess.

They drew near the gates.

"Ready?" Jamie murmured, turning to Ry; then his eye fell on Eva. He went still for a few beats of his heart.

She was tossing her hair, running her fingers through it, fluffing it. Despite all the rigors of the last few days, it fell like a silky, dark curtain around her fine-cut face and proud shoulders. She pushed her cape over one shoulder and, with a twist of her fingers, slightly loosened the ties of the bodice of her gown.

His heart tightened. He'd had the privilege of unlacing her last night, but had he taken full advantage of the ability to run his fingers through her hair, to make it do . . . that? Hardly. Hair had been a low priority when his hands were on her.

Given another opportunity though, he vowed to attend it with devotion, to make it do . . . whatever she'd just made it do. Be like a flowing black river.

She hooked her arm through his and tipped her face up.

"I am full of readiness. And lest you think to 'make me so sorry,'" she added, "do not regard this as temptation. You've no need to prove anything to me. I am well acquainted with what a bad man you are."

They stepped to the gate, next in line.

The porter surveyed their faces while his counterpart began a search of horses, weapons, and packs. He took in Jamie's weather-beaten cape, dirt-caked boots, and soiled tunic, and his face took on a suspicious slant. The hint of gray mail showing at Jamie's wrists, added to the gleaming swords hanging from his belt and Ry's and Roger's, kept his tongue in his mouth, but he looked disposed to refuse entry to the small group of well-armed men who looked the part of troublemakers.

"State yer business," he snapped.

Then his gaze moved to Eva and her river hair and her loosened ties and the softness that lay beneath. For a second, he froze. Then he sniffed, like a rabbit. He jerked straight and his eyes lost their skeptical, suspicious regard. They became positively warm.

Jamie said, "Our business is the fair."

Eva nodded and smiled. Jamie was fairly certain what occurred next was more due to that crooked smile than anything he did or did not say.

"It's a right fine fair, sir, and you can't do better here in the west. But you'll not find lodgings easy like," the porter went on, returning Eva's smile. He was missing two teeth, top and bottom, right side. It formed a narrow doorway into his mouth. "The town is nigh on full up. You might try up north end, near Chandler's Way. Under the arch, on the left. There's a woman that takes in lodgers, but she's up the hill, and somes don't want the extra walk, or even know she's there. Clean and honest she is, and right good board to boot."

He nodded and his smile broadened, pleased with his own information and, no doubt, the way Eva's smile grew in response.

The porter looked back at Jamie, then Ry and Gog, who were lashing up bags and packs that had been searched. They all looked dirty, dangerous. Even blond Roger, with his puppylike enthusiasm and gangly limbs, had a hardness to him, come from years of living on the run, which was now translated into a hard gaze aimed at the gate porter as each moment of inspection continued.

The porter's gaze narrowed back to suspicion and mistrust, a much wiser state for a gate porter to be in than wide-eyed and informative with lust. "And where are you all from?"

"What is your name?" Jamie asked sharply.

The porter's face turned more sullen yet, but the commanding tone fetched a dour "Richard."

Jamie bent close, so no one behind them heard, but ensuring Richard the gate porter, who also bent slightly forward, heard every nuanced syllable. "I am from the king, Richard Porter, and I am on a mission. If you detain me a moment longer, I may recall your name. To the king."

The porter stayed bent at the waist a moment after Jamie had straightened, a stunned look on his face. Then he jerked upright.

"Pass on, then. Halfpenny each," he announced, but he did not look into Jamie's face again.

Jamie tightened his elbow on Eva's arm and practically swung her like a dancer under the archway, dumping out the coins for the toll as he passed. Ry and Gog followed a moment later, bags searched, nothing but a hoard of weapons found. In other words, no contraband goods to be sold at fair, snuck in and therefore untaxed.

There they stood, just inside the stone walls of Gracious Hill, their first target met. It was a breathing moment, and they all used it as such.

The town bustled as people moved from shops to homes to taverns in one last burst of energy before the evening slowdown. The westering afternoon light hit the three- and four-story-tall buildings high up, but little made it as far down as the cobbles and dirt. The tops of the buildings shone glory-bright, amber light pulsing on the dark brown of crisscrossed timber frames and thatched roofs. Down on the cobbles, it was all cool purple afternoon shadows and murmuring voices and the smell of hay and iron from the blacksmith and hot suppers being cooked by the bakeshops.

Eva stood beside him, looking around, her arm still tucked in his. It seemed unconscious. But Jamie was highly conscious of the way her slim fingers curved over his mailed forearm, featherlight and firm.

"It has been years for me, Jamie," Ry murmured, looking around. "I recall this main thoroughfare, but beyond that, I do not recollect Gracious Hill enough to say where to start."

Jamie nodded absently, peering up the High. He too knew the town from a few visits on various tasks, but that was years gone. The king kept a house here, with a tavern belowstairs, cover for the lodgings it provided his mercenaries when on mission or the hunt. But all that ensured tonight was a place to stay. It gave no directional for locating an outlaw ransoming off a priest.

"Once, I knew this town," Eva said blithely.

"Why do I find myself unsurprised?" Jamie murmured, looking down.

"Because you are by nature a wise and suspicious man. Now, *attendez*, for here is where you shall see our little alliance paying fruit."

"Bearing fruit," Roger muttered. He stood rigid but ready. Alert, gaze scanning between the faces and the shoes of the people passing. Orphan watch.

Roger would prove useful, if Jamie could ensure his alliance. Which he probably could. Roger was ready to come together. A few moments alone, some truths, an offer, and Gog was his. No ropes, no threats, no problems.

Eva, though . . . Eva was a different matter. Entirely. In every way. From her broken-down shoes to her fine eyes and the honed, beautiful edge of her mind. A different flavor, a different kingdom, a different matter entirely. She was a flower amid their weeds.

All around, people were hurrying, busy about their business of buying and selling and cooking and carrying well water in great buckets. Eva stood still amid the bustle, her eyes half-closed, face tipped slightly up to the golden blue sky. Then, without warning, she snapped her eyes open and started off down the street of shops.

Jamie grabbed for her arm.

She stopped and sighed. "You worry a great deal, Jamie."

"You give me so much to worry *on*, Eva."

She made a little sound of impatience "Come if you wish. But stay back," she added, "if you have any desire to discover where our quarry has gone."

He let her arm slide free.

Ry stepped to his side. "I suppose we should be prepared to be struck repeatedly on the backs of our heads at any moment?"

"Let's," Jamie agreed grimly. "It might prove useful to know if there is a back entryway to where she has gone."

"I'll reconnoiter." In a trice, Ry had ducked into the back alley.

Jamie turned to Roger. "Have you a need for ribbons?"

Gog threw him a startled look. "Not a'tall, sir."

"Let's go see."

Forty-one

They crossed to the far side of the street just as Eva tipped her head through the open doorway of a shop, then slipped her slip of a body inside as well.

Many goods hung at the doorway of the shop across the way, where Jamie stopped to keep watch. Ribbons and needles and silk bits were piled high. Jamie positioned himself just to the side of the counter, affecting to examine the goods, while Roger stood beside him, an inch shorter and still years to grow, peering with undisguised interest at the ribbons and other bright things.

"Do girls truly desire such things?" Roger said, his voice incredulous.

Jamie smiled faintly. "Indeed. Do you not regard them?"

All around, women and girls trotted through the streets, sternly pointing or flirtatiously smiling or happily laughing, but they *all* had ribbons in their hair. On their dresses. No matter how poorly attired they were, there was always enough for a bright ribbon.

"I see them," said Roger in a low voice, his gaze trained on the girls from beneath his errant lock of hair, and Jamie heard the longing in his voice.

"Does your mistress not wear ribbons?" But Jamie knew well Eva did not have a ribbon anywhere on her body.

"Nay, sir. She hasn't . . . the time. We didn't spend much time in towns."

As Roger spoke, his head swiveled to follow the passing of a pair of young women in capes and hoods and long, glossy hair, who returned his look over their shoulders. They turned away and giggled, heads together, their curving backs to Gog, but their footsteps slowed by half. Jamie could almost feel the tension and desire rising out of Gog.

"You may go speak with them, " Jamie said quietly.

The boy whipped his head around, bright red spots on his cheeks.

"Nay, sir," he croaked.

An older matron came hurrying up the street, scolding the girls in fond tones, and the small group passed on, down the cobbled street, into the deeper shadows of encroaching evening. One peeked back, green eyes bright, then she turned the corner and disappeared.

Roger turned back to the silks, and Jamie returned to watching Eva. "Do you know what she's doing?"

The boy briefly glanced at the spill of golden light coming out of the jeweler's. "Finding out where Father Peter is, sir."

"How?"

Roger looked confused. "However it must be done."

"Do you know the man?"

Roger peered hard this time, eyeing up the burly man inside, then shook his head. "Nay." He looked at Jamie. "If Eva wished away from you, away she would be. Sir."

Jamie took measure of Gog's guileless but savvy eyes. He'd seen as much brutality and had as little security as Eva, and from a younger age. As Eva said, he was indeed of a good and generous spirit, but that was only because of her tutelage. Jamie was certain of this, for Roger carried an edge of hardness like a tempered blade. He could not be pushed, or he would turn and slash. Eva, for all her light-handed officiousness, did not push him. She *owned* him.

"Aye," Jamie replied lightly. "I suspect Eva could slip through a mousehole, should the need arise. But, then, you are with me. So she will not go anywhere, will she?"

They were speaking plainly now, the beginning of the alliance, and Roger considered him for a long moment.

"I am with you now, sir, for I think 'tis the right place to be."

"So you could slip away too?"

The boy nodded. "Aye, sir. In a heartbeat." No arrogance, not even pride. A simple statement of a truth. "But Eva and I cannot do this thing alone. Father Peter is worth some risk, for what he's done for us. And, I believe"—Roger fumbled for a moment—"I think you are an honorable man."

A side of Jamie's mouth curved up in a faint, weary smile. "Your mistress would carve out my heart if she heard you say that."

Gog grinned. "Assuredly."

Jamie could see Eva now, stepping around the tall wooden workbench, her curving back to the road, her hands moving in that animated chatter of hers. The jeweler seemed entranced. "But my thanks for your trust, Roger."

"'Tisn't trust, sir."

Jamie touched the end of a swaying green ribbon, his gaze on Eva.

"You've done nothing to make me trust you."

That brought Jamie's gaze around.

"Sooth, sir, you're hunting Father Peter. You've bound Eva and me in ropes, and even now, I do not know what you are truly about. You know Eva and me to a much greater depth, yet I've no idea how you will make use of that knowledge. 'Tisn't trust; how could it be? You've done nothing to make me trust you. 'Tis faith. I have faith you one day will. Sir."

Jamie laughed, but it was short-lived and tempered by a kind of grimness. "Roger, I am indebted. Plain-speaking men are hard to find, and most are horses' asses. But in this, I would counsel you suchly: Follow Eva's lead. 'Tisn't wise to put your faith in men like me. I have not earned it."

Nor do I wish to, Jamie thought grimly. Vulnerable creatures had faith. Fools believed in honor. Such people were masticated in the jaws of the world, for God was hardly better than a romance, King John but a scrape on the battered knee of the world going down.

Better to leave off hope and faith and other useless things. Stick to missions and vengeance and hard, simple things, elsewise, people grew to need you, and should you one day be taken away, murdered on the streets of London so the cobbles were rimmed in red, the ones left behind might feel as though their hearts had been ripped out by nails and shredded beneath a plough.

Jamie was not fertilizer. Not anymore.

Roger looked at him, brow wrinkled, as if Jamie were misunderstanding something simple, such as how to drink water. "'Tis faith, sir. You don't *earn* it."

"No, Roger, you do not," Jamie agreed grimly, and met the boy's gaze square on. "You are aware we are about danger here? There is not a safe step to be taken from here on out."

Roger straightened. "I know, my lord."

"Do not call me that. You additionally know Eva cannot so much as spit an arrow from a bow?"

"True, sir, she cannot fire an arrow. But even so, she is hardly without defense."

Jamie met Roger's eye. "Has she ever been hurt? In an attack? In the way of an injury."

Roger looked uneasy. "Indeed, sir, she has. Once in the neck." He touched his own. "Almost bled to death, she did. I stitched it up, but rather clumsily. You can see the scars still, by her ear." Yes, he'd seen them. He'd seen them last night, touched the edge with his tongue as he licked down her neck. "And once, here," Gog went on, pressing the side of a fist against his abdomen. Their eyes met.

Jamie hadn't known he had this sort of reservoir inside him. He'd thought himself nothing more than shallow earth, a hard, mineral, impervious layer of dark intent and waiting vengeance. You couldn't have grown weeds in him.

And now came Eva, so that the thought of her being hurt made his breath stop.

"Ah," he said, and kept it short like that.

The proprietress came up, smiling. "How good to see you, sir. We are just about to close up, my lord, but if you've something you see for your mistress, sir, you've only to let me know."

Jamie nodded absently, barely noticing the urge to warn her off calling him "my lord." He was staring into the shop with renewed focus. Eva had taken a step closer to the jeweler inside.

"Is she for the fair on the morrow?" the shopkeep inquired.

Jamie gave some monosyllabic reply. Gog said something slightly more informative, something about "aye," and "a wedding."

The woman beamed. "Well, ye'll have to send her here, for we've the best silks around, and that's not a whit of exaggeration. Has she a preference for shade?"

Even from this distance, Jamie saw Eva begin to smile at the jeweler. It expanded to fairly expansive proportions, the sort of smile he'd never received from her. Which made perfect sense.

". . . blue, then?"

Jamie looked down. "My apologies, madam. What were you saying?"

The proprietress clucked her tongue in tolerant way. "I see

she likes blue, but I think a fine red would contrast quite finely now, don't you, my lord?"

"Blue?" Jamie looked at the woman blankly. "Red?"

"Her tunic." She gestured toward Eva, where she was visible through the doorway. The firelight in the darkened shop backlit Eva and the burly man she was smiling at. Her hair flowed down her back like that damned river.

"And red, for the ribbons," the proprietress went on. "Nay. Perhaps the darker crimson."

She squinted critically at the bright red one, then tossed it aside and slid her fat fingers under an entire row of rainbowed ribbons suspended from a nail and lifted the strands of silk into the air so they looked like toy ponies, tails lifted in the breeze.

"The dusky one, perhaps," she said triumphantly. "For her dark hair."

Yes, he thought vaguely. *Yes. The dusky red, for her dark hair.*

He dragged his eyes away from the ribbons and back to Eva, where she now stood, much closer to the burly jeweler with the appreciative eyes. She was very near him, smiling up at him . . . laughing. She was laughing with him. She touched his arm.

Jamie heard Gog say dimly, as if from a distance, "Eva doesn't wear ribbons, sir," and heard himself say, "I'll take five."

Forty-two

Eva smiled at Pauly, the one person in the town she recalled from years past whom she also trusted. Or had trusted, years ago. He'd been apprenticed here in his father's shop, barely five years older than she. She wasn't so certain she ought to trust him now, but one had to take chances.

"Aye, I saw the man you're describing, with a priest. Came in not a bell ring ago," he said, and so Eva knew it had been mayhap an hour. Not so long.

"They passed by here. Everyone does," Pauly said proudly, gesturing to the main thoroughfare leading in from the gates, but of course Eva already knew this. It was partly why she'd cultivated his friendship when she was fourteen, and why she'd come back now. Far too often, fortune was simply a matter of being in the right place, not at all being the right person.

But she'd also loved the small, cloudy gems and vinelike wires he and his father had worked with, making jewelry for those who could afford it.

"He was coming for the midwife, aye?" Pauly said, setting down a fine steel strip he'd been working on. It was thin as a thread, the same used for armor, only not ringed and linked, so instead of staving off swords, it was like a twisted nest for dusky gems. A hot fire burned in a covered pit, for heating the metal he hammered into thin, precise settings for the jewels someone else could afford.

"The midwife? Why do you say that?"

"I recognized the man riding in with your priest. Used to come into town fast regular to visit the mad midwife, Magda. Swiving her, he was."

"I see."

"But I'd say they went for the physic," he mused.

"The physic? Why?" Eva said, affecting mild interest. She ran her fingertips along the graveyard of skeletal-like wires scattered across the high table, like a graveyard in the moonlight, bones unearthed.

Pauly's gaze was riveted on her hand for a moment. "Why, for we've the best physic west of London and south of Chester," he said, once again with pride in his voice for things he had neither made nor owned. "And not a moment too soon, for the priest looked right sickly."

"But, yes, that is just so, he was ill," she agreed, her calm voice belying no tension. But her fingers tightened around the trestle table in front of her.

Pauly's eye fell to her hand again. She let it drop, but that only drew his eye to her skirts.

"Are you here alone, Eva?" he asked, a certain depth to his tone alerting her to potential trouble. She did not wish for Jamie to come charging through the doorway like a bull and frighten Pauly out of talking.

Although why he would, over some silly jealousy, eluded her.

"But, no, I am here with my partners."

"Partners?"

"Shippers."

His gaze moved to the dark doorway, outside of which stood Jamie, armored and silent, somewhere in the nighttime, watching, waiting for her.

She stepped around the table, closer, distracting him. "And you, Pauly, over the years, have you done so well with all these things?" She gestured to the bits of metal across the tabletops, the tiny links for affixing gemstones. Some were woven together like iron wickerwork.

"Well enough. But no wife, no family. You, Eva?"

"Oh, aye, I am wed to an old dog," she said, laughing. "He barks and I jump."

"That is too bad."

"Indeed, it is most terrible."

"I do not recall you that way. Jumping for a man."

"Oh, Pauly, we all change. And which physic were they going to, do you think?"

"The only the one who's worth his salt. As I said, the best west of London and south of Chester, and the whole town goes to him." His gaze fell to her chest, and she saw a ripple of tension move through his jaw. "Where is your husband, Eva?"

She took a deep breath, stepped closer, and opened her mouth.

"He is here," said a rumbling voice behind her.

She closed her eyes, aghast at the relief rushing through her body from the sound of Jamie's voice. She turned.

He stood in the doorway, wide-shouldered, lean-hipped, caped and dark, his eyes fixed on Pauly's burly figure. With Jamie's dark hair banded at the base of his neck, with his unmarked tunic, dark gauntlets, tight hose, and muddy boots, the only thing that shone about him was his sword hilt, etched with those curling silver vines, and his eyes, deep blue, glittering and unmoving on Pauly.

Pauly backed up three steps and bumped the edge of another trestle table.

"Pauly was just going to tell us where to find the best physic in the west country," she announced brightly.

"Good."

Pauly cleared his throat. "Eva and I are friends from times past."

"How friendly?"

Pauly's face fell, and he said in a slightly high-pitched voice, "Jakob Doctor is the one you want, up the High, past the goldsmith's."

"Thank you," she murmured, patting his arm. Jamie's eyes snapped to the movement. Pauly swallowed and took a step away from Eva.

"He's got one of them right *tall* buildings," he said quickly, eager to add to his store of information. He lifted a flattened hand above his head. "Slate on his roof, if ye can countenance the cost. But then, he's a fycking Jew," he spat the last words out.

Jamie, who had been still the entire time, went motionless. Everyone else stilled as well, including Pauly, who looked ready to do something drastic, such as urinate on himself.

Jamie's head tipped slightly to the side. "Is this where you live, jeweler?" he asked, his voice low.

Pauly's face went white. Absolutely white, like a wall that has had a bucket of wash thrown on its face. Like a lamb in spring. Like a man who's just realized he has made a terrible mistake.

Eva went into motion. She turned for the doorway, sweeping up Jamie as she went, calling over her shoulder, "Pauly, I will be back tomorrow—"

"No," he seemed to call out weakly.

"—and we can talk again of old times. It was most good to see you." She waved, smiled, then yanked the door shut and moved out into the street, her hand on Jamie's arm, practically pulling him after her.

The four of them met in the middle of the slowly emptying streets.

Jamie looked at her. Ry looked at Jamie. Gog looked between her and Jamie. Eva looked at everyone but Jamie.

"So, we have found out Father Peter may be at the doctor's," she said in what even she considered a chirpy tone. "Or a midwife. An old hearthmate."

Ry said, "Very good," but he said it slowly, his eyes not leaving Jamie's face, which Eva had no intention of looking at herself. Watching Ry and Gog would be a sufficient indicator of what was passing over Jamie's face. One did not always need to see such things firsthand.

She began, "So, we ought to go up the hill—"

"Are you *mad?*" Jamie's question was dangerously low-pitched.

She did turn to him then, slowly and with great dignity. "Indeed. I am past mad. I am standing here with you."

They all heard the deep breath he took through his nostrils, sucking them in with the force of it. A steadying breath, if Eva's experience with deep breaths was any measure of how it went for others. She saw Ry's eyes close momentarily, his lips move as if in silent prayer.

"Eva," Gog said uneasily, glancing at Jamie before he took a step her way. "Evening comes. Perhaps we ought find lodg—"

"Aye."

They turned warily at the sound of Jamie's clipped agreement. "Ry, take Roger and stable the horses, will you?"

It was a question in everything but intent. Ry nodded. Roger nodded just as speedily. Eva scowled.

Jamie stepped to Ry's side, cloak hem swirling about his boots, spoke quietly into his ear, more of their secrets, then backed up and clapped Gog on the shoulder in an approving way.

Gog glanced at her. "Shall I, Eva?" he said, even though really everyone knew this was not a question to be asked. Or, at least, answered.

Yet Jamie shifted, stepped out from between her and Gog. "Aye, Eva, shall he go now?"

She frowned at the faint undercurrent to his question, but as one could do little with undercurrents but swim along, she settled on a nod and a smile.

"Indeed, Gog. It would not be so good to have four of us dirty people show up on Jakob Doctor's doorstep. We will frighten him, and he will slam the door upon us. If 'tis just Jamie and I, then I can kick in his knee at some point along the way, and, *voilà*, we shall have our injury for the doctor to inspect, and our way in his door."

Jamie gave a minuscule, humorless smile. Well-nigh undetectable. Neither Gog or Ry seemed inclined even that far.

Eva touched the hand Gog extended to her, gave it a squeeze, and said a few cautionary words about not drinking *anything* alelike that Ry might put in front of him. Gog rolled his eyes and squeezed her back.

Jamie murmured another few words to Ry, then sent them on their way, into the shadowed streets.

"Let's go," Jamie said grimly, and grabbed her hand.

Forty-three

"We're for the midwife's," he announced.

"But—"

"She is his woman."

Eva felt a little fluttering at that notion of *his woman* rolling off Jamie's tongue. At the belief that this was the first place a man would go. It was nothing to take notice of, just a little shivering deep in her belly.

As it happened, there was no need for flutterings or anything that harkened to excitement. The midwife was willing to share very little.

She peered at them sullenly for a long minute after they rapped at her door, then glanced over their shoulders into the encroaching darkness and tried to slam the door shut in their faces.

Jamie wedged his boot in just in time, then pressed a palm on the door and pushed it open, which was ridiculously easy, as Magda had given up her resistance and stepped back into the room.

They stepped inside.

She stood in front of a huge cauldron suspended above a roaring fire. Her face looked as if it had once been beautiful, but was now sunken and grayed by poor harvests and long late nights and scraping for coin from people who had none. Her hair hung down her back in a thick braid, but a great deal was frizzed around her face, framing her suspicious scowl in brown fuzz.

In the back room, they could hear the sounds of women moving softly, whispering and occasionally laughing.

"And why do you want to know who was here?" Magda said curtly in response to Jamie's query.

"We have business with your man."

She gave a clipped bark of laughter. "Do you now? Does he know it?"

Jamie looked at the door that led to the far room. "Who is in there?" he asked, moving toward the door, pulling out his sword silently.

"That is not your concern," Magda said, turning slowly, watching him with her sharp eyes, making no move to stop him.

He put his hand on the latch. "Who?"

The midwife's lips were pursed tight enough to deepen the little lines that ran up and away from her lips. "A poor village girl. Someone rich decided to plow her fields, but her parents did not wish to reap them."

Jamie's hand stilled. Another round of soft laughter drifted out. He inched open the door, looked inside, then shut it again.

"He didn't mention anyone like you coming around for him," Magda said, eyeing Jamie with a look part suspicion, part curiosity.

"So he was here."

"Aye, he was here." She reached for a pile of clean, folded linens on the table. "And he'll not be back."

"Did he have anyone with him? Was he traveling with anyone?"

A sudden gasping cry from the back room drew everyone's attention. Magda's face compressed even further. "I've got to be about my business now."

"Mistress midwife, I shall not bore you with the whys and

wherefores, but I must know where he is. I am not leaving until I do."

"You can stay all night if you've a mind. I do not know where he is."

"But you can find out."

The midwife regarded him with a look equal parts disdain and respect and a deep, desperate kind of longing. "I dunno who you are, sir, and I don't want to know. No one who wants Guillaume is going to find him tonight."

He kept the midwife in his locked gaze, measuring how to proceed. Then, like a flittering of wings at the edge of his attention, he felt Eva's touch, light on his arm.

He shrugged it off. "I think he will be back. And I suspect you think so as well." He laid a few coins on the table. The midwife looked at them, showing no response.

Jamie felt a rising anger within him. Deeper than that. Fury. "You know who he was, in the past, midwife?"

She gave a short snap of laughter. "To my misfortune, I know everything about the old dog." She started folding the clean rags on the tables, slowly, tugging to get tight, clean lines on the folds. "They come to God the same way they come into this world, one at a time, a little at a time. Some simply take longer than others."

"Some never come through at all."

She set down the towel and met his eye. "When they're my patients, they do."

He drew out a much larger handful of pennies and dumped them on the table. Everyone looked down at the sprawling mound of dirty silver disks.

In the hot, dim room, dust motes spiraled up from the musty rushes like dancing amber bugs; then Eva stepped forward. She seemed to glow in the grimy brilliance of the room. "He was my foster father."

Magda looked up from the coins.

"This man who was with your Guillaume, he is ailing, as you no doubt saw. I must see to him. You understand this, no?"

A look passed over the midwife's face. She quickly turned aside, but just as Jamie considered he might need to find other measures of inducement, and what they might be, she muttered, "Aye, the priest was here. He was ill."

Cold relief rolled through Jamie's chest. "And now?"

She shook her head. "With Mouldin."

"Where?" he demanded at the same moment Eva asked quietly, "How ill was he?"

Magda's gaze dropped to Eva's hand, still resting carelessly on Jamie's forearm. A look passed over her face then, perhaps relief, or hope. A decisive look. "I told them of a doctor, but I do not know if they will make use of him. The meeting is to take place in the morning, when the gates open. In the old vintner's hall, by the market square."

The coldness of this relief raced down through Jamie's limbs. "My thanks, midwife," he said, but she'd already turned to Eva. She reached out and touched Eva's hand.

"I gave him a poultice. That was all I could do."

Jamie allowed Eva to squeeze the midwife's hand before taking her by the elbow and backing them toward the door. Magda turned for the birthing room.

"Others may come," he said. "I suggest you inform them you have not seen Mouldin for years."

She glanced over her shoulder. "Until this morning, that was true." She wore a smile that was bitter but not quite sad. "That is the way of it. They come at need."

Jamie swung the door open. "Aye, mistress. We're a wretched lot, and that is all we know."

He shut the door behind them.

All around were the sounds of the town closing down for

the night. The crier was calling out that the gates were about to close, earlier than dark in these dark times. Everyone who wished to be inside the walls already was and would no doubt be lolling in piss-reeking alleys come morn. The shouts and laughter were already ringing forth from the plethora of taverns that would no doubt stay open illegally long during this fair night.

"Now, Jakob Doctor," Eva said firmly.

"Why?"

She looked over. "Magda is a caretaker. And that is what caretakers do."

"Send them to doctors."

"Make sure the people they care for are where they need to be. He is with Jakob Doctor."

They strode up the street. The peal of five churches' bells rolled over the rooftops and into the open plain beyond, chiming out Vespers. "Do not cry me off when I am in the midst of questioning someone, Eva," Jamie said as they walked up the darkening street. A ridiculous caution, seeing as she would not be beside him during any future questionings.

"You were going to frighten her straight into silence," Eva replied placidly. "You may not have noticed this, but when you frighten people, they cease talking. And then you must part with even more coin to induce them to talk again. If you smiled more at people, the way you every now and again smile at me, you would be a much richer man."

He stared at the roofs of the buildings, most thatched, a few slate, absorbing the dark blue sky light. After a moment, he said warily, "Is that so?"

She nodded. Her hard boots hammered on the cobbles and her worn blue skirts blew around her legs.

"In what manner do I smile at you?" he inquired flatly, although he did not want to hear her reply. So why pose the query?

"In this way." She stopped. He drew to a halt beside her, and people swirled down the street around them like water around a boulder. She stared reflectively into the near distance, composing herself, then shifted her gaze to him and did something he'd never seen a person do before: she transformed. Went dead-down seductive.

Her whole body shifted in subtle, undisguisable ways. Her head tipped to the side, her eyes took on a knowing languidness. She smiled, her lips curving up just slightly, deeper on one side than the other. Her eyelids became heavy. One looked as if it were about to drop into a wink, and there was the exquisite, senseless tension of wondering, *Will she do it, to me?*

Her hair fell over her shoulders in a dark cascade, and her bodice, ties still loosened, parted, hinting at the tempting valley of her cleavage below. One slim shoulder dipped a little, the other pushed slightly forward, her hips cocked ever so slightly. And then, God save him, she rested her palms on the small of her back and with confident sultriness deepened one side of her smile until her cheek dimpled.

She had a dimple.

A low, white roar filled his head. With nothing more than intent, she'd transformed into a creature of fluttering wings and sultry color. And he went hard as a rock.

"I have never in my life looked at anyone in such a way," he announced through gritted teeth.

She peered at him, the sultry Eva fading but not quite gone. "Perhaps not quite so much with the hips and hands, but in every other regard." She squinted at him. "Nothing whatsoever like this look you are giving me now. This is worse than the other ones. I shall certainly require money to do anything you ask of me while you are looking at me in a such a manner."

"Let's go," he practically growled.

"Two pence." She held out her palm.

Your body, he thought dimly, staring at her hand. If he offered her money, would she give him a few minutes with her generous body? The erotic images of last night were so potent he could almost feel her body pushing against his right now.

He turned on his heel and started walking, grabbing the palm she'd extended, but he should have known he was not out of the woods, for even when she was beside him and he could have let go, he didn't.

Forty-four

As they strode up the street, Jamie practically dragging Eva behind him, his eye fell on someone standing up ahead. The man was leaning back against a wall, one leg angled out, boot planted, the other bent, toe planted in the dirt.

An easeful pose, completely at odds with how ready one was in such a stance. He could twist either way at a moment's notice, nothing could come up behind, and the hand tucked in his belt was certes closed around the hilt of a blade. His watchful eyes scanned the crowd. He looked just like Jamie.

Perhaps that was because he *was* just like Jamie, one of the inner core of King John's lieutenants.

Their eyes met and the man pushed off the wall. Joining the river of people moving through the street, he started making his way toward Jamie.

Jamie turned to Eva. "Wait here," he instructed, pointing down.

"More bad men?" she asked coldly.

"Exceedingly."

She scowled, which was not a very daunting thing, because on her pale, graceful face, it looked like a flower crumpling.

"Trust in me, Eva, staying here is better."

"Oh, yes, to avoid meeting more of your ilk, I am happy to wait here."

He turned and walked down the street and met up with the weather-beaten man who looked a lot like him. They stepped to the edge of the stream of evensong traffic.

Jamie shifted around to keep Eva in view. She might try to bolt. Not that it would matter. She'd make it two steps, maybe three. Then she'd have not only Jamie on her tail but Engelard Cigogné as well, and while Cigogné would have no notion why Jamie was chasing her, he would join the hunt, run her to ground, then eat her up like the wolf he was.

"I've been looking for you," Cigogné said without preamble.

"You found me."

"You are wanted."

Jamie shook his head. "I'm on a task."

Cigogné's eyes slid to Eva.

Jamie stepped in front of him. "For him. Hunting someone down."

Cigogné's gaze came back. "I am aware of your mission. We need to talk."

"So talk."

Cigogné paused, an ingrained response in these dark times. But this was more than a wise caution for secrecy. The king was renowned for his paranoia, and he'd instilled it in his men. He sent coded messages all the time now, codes he himself ofttimes forgot and then needed revealed to him, which defeated the purpose entirely.

But lest anyone think John a fool, he had henchmen and bankrupt baronies and hostages swinging from gibbets to remind people he was not a fool in every way. He knew how to lance fear and terror straight through the hearts of his followers, both those willing and those unwilling.

Cig's eyes flickered back. "People don't often get away from you. How did the priest?"

"An error."

"Whose?"

"Yours, if you keep questioning me. "

A faint tenseness ripped along Cigogné's jaw. "You err if you think this is me questioning you, Jamie. The king wants to know. He's pissing royal fury. The war is about to burst open."

"I am well aware of that."

"What you perhaps do *not* know is that 'twas Mouldin who took the priest from under your nose."

The proper thing to do here, Jamie reflected, was to inform Cig he had just visited Mouldin's mistress, and was now on his way to a doctor, who might be able to lead them to the priest, thus negating the need to engage in the negotiations he'd just learned were to take place in Old Vintner's Hall come morn.

He said nothing.

"Mouldin has the priest," Cigogné said. "And he's selling him to the highest bidder. FitzWalter will be sending someone, no doubt."

Yes, now was certainly the time to speak up.

Cig went on. "I am here to help you get the priest before that auction takes place."

Jamie nodded, using the movement to gain a few seconds. He ought to be rejoicing at the assistance. He ought to feel relieved to have the help.

What he knew was a strong and sudden resistance to the notion that Cigogné would have keeping of Father Peter, for even a moment.

Perhaps it was the look deep in Cig's eye, the undertone in every syllable uttered thus far, that bespoke suspicion and double-dealing. Jamie had marched too long to this beat; he could hear it coming a mile off. And each hammer of Jamie's heart told him it was so: deception, lies, duplicity.

So Jamie returned Cig's appraising look in cold silence, keeping telltale flickers of any emotion but disdain off his face. One did best around men such as Cig, whom one *did* disdain, to show nothing but the truth.

Cig glanced at the people hurrying by. "The king thinks the heirs might be close by as well. 'Whither goest the priest, so goeth the heirs.'"

Twenty years of experience in hiding all emotions came into play as Cig watched him. Jamie watched Cig back, and no one said anything. Cig finally gave a twisted grin. "Or did you not know about the heirs?"

Jamie let the silence extend, taking the opportunity to shift slightly to examine the alley Cig had emerged from. No lurking shadows could be detected; his men weren't hiding down that warren. Cig must have put them back farther, out of sight. Perhaps stabling horses, as Jamie's were. The dull bronze of the pin affixing Cig's cape slowly brightened, until it gleamed as the rays of the setting sun hit it on its way down.

Cig's eyes hardened as the silence extended. "And the king has called for *you*, Jamie. When we're done here, he wants you. At Everoot."

Jamie controlled his start. "Everoot? The king is at Windsor."

Cig shook his head. "This matter was important enough to bring him riding north. Where are you staying?"

"Ry is securing our lodgings," Jamie said evenly. "I am to meet up with him."

"Where?"

Jamie hesitated, for perhaps a second too long, he reflected later. The mercenary's eyes slid back to Eva. "That good? She's a pretty piece." He gave a crude grin. "I shall not tell the king you were distracted."

"I do not care if you do or if you don't," Jamie said coldly.

"As you will, Jamie. You are lead. As always."

"Where is the auction to take place?"

Cig smiled shrewdly. "Where are you staying?"

They stared at each other. Cig's eyes drifted back to Eva. "Mayhap we can share her."

The sounds of the busy street faded to a low drone. Jamie thrust out his arm, indicating the alley. "There are but two more things." They stepped into the narrow passage.

Cig turned to him. "Aye?"

"You have a foul mouth," Jamie said, and punched him in the face. "And I do not share."

The mercenary staggered backward, his feet slipping out from beneath him on the rounded cobbles. Jamie swung again, and there was a crack of bone. It felt good to swing and punch. No wonder Ry grew weary of the fights; they were Jamie's way of making the blood surge through his body, of releasing pent-up energy so it was not all pooled inside him, dammed by reason and good cause. For twenty years, the answer to *when?* was always *Later.*

A slight to Eva meant this answer became *now.*

Cig hit the cobbles with a thud. Blood poured out of his nose and perhaps his mouth too; it was hard to tell where it was all coming from. Vagrants and stray dogs in the alley scurried away. Gushing blood and cursing, Cig scrabbled for his sword.

Jamie kicked the blade away, catching Cig on the underside of his chin, making the back of his head smash against the ground. He dropped to a knee and hauled Cig's shoulders up. His head was lolling and his eyes kept shutting; then they rolled back in his head entirely and he went limp.

Jamie bent close and listened; Cig was still breathing. Glancing up, he saw a boy scurrying by. The urchin looked at him, then Cig, and turned to bolt. Just before he spun, Jamie pinched a coin between his thumb and forefinger and held it up in the air. It glinted in the sunset light, the way Cig's surcoat had. The boy froze, midturn.

"Bring the constable," Jamie said quietly. "This man was wild. Too much drink."

The boy hesitated, pitched his shoulders forward, and sniffed the air in an exaggerated way. "He don't smell like it."

"He will," Jamie said grimly, getting to his feet.

The boy squinted one eye suspiciously. "Is he a bad sort?"

"The worst," Jamie replied gravely. "He claims for the king."

The edge of the boy's lips curled in derision. Jamie extended the coin. "Is your word good?"

Something warred in his dirty, pinched face. Then he nodded, snatched the coin, and dashed off. "I'll bring 'em, milord!" he shouted over his shoulder. "The 'ole Watch. It's the blacksmythe's night, milord!" he added in what could only be considered a tone of glee.

"Do not call me that," Jamie muttered. He purchased a small beaker of ale from a tavern, poured it all over Cig, then turned out of the alley and walked back to Eva.

It was two hours before Cig's men found him and unlashed him. He was seething with anger, battered, and missing all the coin he'd had on him for negotiations.

"Send word to the king," he snarled when his men freed him. He clambered to his feet, rubbing his wrists, and glared up the street. "Jamie has turned."

Forty-five

Jamie strode back to Eva's side as the world of the living raced home around her. She stood like only a hunted thing could, somehow managing to blend in with rock and wicker, and looking as if she were about to bolt.

But for her pale face and dark hair, she was brightness. She might be tromping through this shit field as deeply as he, but she did not stink of it. She was clean and clear and better than all this.

Jamie had not met many people who were better than the things they were doing. People's sunken lives generally reflected sunken hearts. But Eva was bright and clear, like a little star.

"I was not sure if you would try to run," he said as he drew near. They started walking.

She sniffed. "You may yet prove passing helpful in retrieving Father Peter."

He snorted. "You vastly underestimate your use of the word *may*. And *passing*. And *helpful*."

"If we must indeed assail people with swords and other sharp things," she explained stiffly, "you shall prove passing useful. If, however, we must sidle up like stealthy things, perhaps your big and bold arrogance will bedevil us all, Jamie."

He was walking half a step behind her and bent by her ear as he steered her toward a doorway on the right.

"You forget, Eva, I sidled up on you in an alley in London." She inhaled slowly. "I sidled up on the last man I killed, as I will likely do the next. Shall we compare our sidling skills? Stealth is how I live my life, woman, and I do it in the cities, under the king's eye, not hiding in the woods like you and the last wolves."

He straightened and saw Ry coming out of the shadows, as agreed. Ry stepped up behind Eva as Jamie rapped sharply on the door. She started slightly at Ry's unexpected appearance, and how closely he crowded in behind her.

"Roger?" Jamie murmured to Ry. Eva looked between them sharply.

"Stabling the horses at an inn, the White Heart."

"Good. I had a visitor."

Ry glanced over. "Who?"

"Cig."

Ry's brows went up. Heavy footsteps thudded inside, and the door swung open.

Eva's face paled as she looked up a foot into the eyes of the huge, one-eyed Scotsman standing in the doorway. She took a reflexive step back and hit the wall of Ry. His arms went up, cupping her sides. Jamie stood to her right.

Realization swept over her features like a rainstorm, transforming them from confusion to fear to fury. She turned to glare at Jamie. For what seemed like the hundredth time, he closed his hand around her elbow to keep her from running away.

The Scotsman took swift appraisal of them, starting with Jamie, then ending on him as well. "Jamie Lost," he muttered. "What the hell are you doing here?"

"I need something."

The Scotsman gave a bark of unfriendly laughter. "Ye need a whole mess o' things, far as I can see, boyo."

"You've never seen far, Angus. Let us in."

He glanced at Ry, barely registering Eva, then back to Jamie. "Why?"

"Because I will make you sorry, once again, that you ever crossed me."

He scowled, but swung the door wide. "I do it for the debt. Quick, now."

Jamie didn't say anything, just pushed Eva past him into the small apartment. Ry followed.

"I have changed my mind," she spat, pushing dark hair out of her face as they bustled inside.

Her mind?

Jamie maneuvered her by the elbow to the center of the room just as Angus swung the door shut. For a moment, they were plunged into silence and darkness. Slowly their eyes adjusted, and the pale glow from a window on the far north side of the hut illuminated the room enough so they were all shadowy figures standing in a jagged semicircle in the center of the room.

"I can never be your friend," she announced, looking straight at Ry.

Jamie looked at Ry too. Ry looked at him. Angus looked confused.

"Never," she repeated firmly.

Ry? Never be Ry's friend? When had she considered being his friend? And not Jamie's?

He turned to Angus. "We need to talk."

Angus gave a twisted grin. "Ye've confused me with yer confessor. The rebels have renounced their fealty. I hear they've even taken the City. What is your bloody king going ta do now?"

"Dismember you, should you not cooperate."

Angus turned and strode to a back room. Jamie dropped Eva's elbow. He hesitated, made as if to speak.

Her hand shot up, warding off the words. "I care not what

you have to say. You are leaving me here, with him? And what will you tell Gog? A lie. You *are* a lie. I wish for nothing more from you. Not even—"

She stopped. Simply stopped talking, her words falling like pebbles off a cliff, into silence, leaving a quietly burning fire and far too many ways to finish the sentence.

She stared at the wall, her slim, curving figure in a tattered blue gown. Her profile was all pale lines of sculpted jaw and those sensuous, crooked lips. Around her shoulders, thick dark hair streamed down to the perfect curve that was the small of her back. He needed more time with her, more touching, more of her pale skin and dark hair and devoted attention and—

"Jamie," Ry said quietly. "I'll stay with her."

Eva didn't move. Jamie jerked away and without a word followed Angus into the back room.

"I need you to keep her here."

"Her?" Angus glanced at the door. "The girl?"

"Aye."

Angus hesitated, then gave a clipped nod. "How long?"

"Not long a'tall. Ry and I have some business this night. Keep her a few days, until"—Jamie hesitated—"things calm down. After that, she can leave."

"Simple enough."

"Don't let her fool you."

"Fool me?"

Jamie looked at him coldly. "Trick you."

"That was a long time ago, Jamie."

"Seems like yesterday. She is . . . clever." An understatement akin to *it is cold in winter.*

"Clever how?"

"She might ask for a drink, and when you return with it, she'll be gone. Clever like that."

Angus shrugged. "I'll not offer her so much as a drop of water."

Jamie's face hardened. "Give her water. Food. Wine. Do not touch her."

Angus's face flooded red, his fists clenched at his sides. "I will no' *touch* her. You know that."

Jamie pushed to his feet. "And do not let her escape, at least before the morrow."

Angus's voice dropped into an octave heard usually from chanters, low and reverberating. "I owe a debt, Lost. If holding her is the repayment, I'll hold her till Michaelmas. But this is me, paying it, right now. I'm squared after this. Do ye hear me?"

"I hear you. Now you hear me: do not be fooled."

He looked outraged. "She'll no' escape! Why do ye keep sayin' she'll escape?"

"Because she will. Just not before tomorrow night, when we're far gone." He turned for the door, then paused at its threshold. "And, Angus?"

"Aye?" he snarled.

Jamie looked over his shoulder. "The debt is paid when I say 'tis. If anything so much as scars her little finger, I will hunt you down for the rest of your days. Then I will end them."

He shut the door behind him.

Forty-six

Eva listened to Jamie's boots tromp away, without so much as a good-bye. Not the boots, the man.

So this is what she'd been reduced to. She ought to be thinking about what would happen next, how she would get away. She ought to be angry, planning how to find Roger, how to make Jamie pay.

Instead, at the realization he was leaving her behind, it felt as if her heart started breaking into translucent bits, like crystallized honey, thrown to the ground and stomped upon. Far more force than required. Smashed, when all it had needed was to be melted down.

"You did not take your leave of her," Ry said as they strode down the mostly uncobbled streets.

"My *leave*?" Jamie ducked below a low-hanging sign thrust above the doorway of a home-cum-alehouse. "You cannot mean say good-bye?"

Ry shrugged. "These are words you know, concepts familiar to many. 'Tis a courtesy."

"I am not chivalrous, I am not courteous. Nor is she." Jamie scowled at a woman closing up a shop of sewing needles. "She is a hellion. Mayhap you recall she tried to stick me with a blade? And she started a quayside brawl, and—"

"I know what she did to you, Jamie," Ry interrupted in the quiet voice that harkened to unnecessary things, such as conversations about what Eva did to Jamie. Which, he reminded himself, was naught.

"So why did you take her to Angus?"

Jamie looked up at the windows above. A few shutters were pushed wide for the evening spring air, candlelight reflecting off the walls inside. From a distant church, the sound of monks singing evensong floated through the streets. "Is there a reason we are speaking about this?"

"Since you just left her imprisoned with someone who despises you, aye, I thought it warranted a bit of attention."

"You'd do better attending the chamber pot about to be dumped on your head."

Ry leapt to the side of the street just as the arc of piss water came raining down into the gutter of the street.

"To get her out of the way. The risk of her disrupting our mission is too great."

Jamie did not admit this was because of himself. Himself, with her self. Her vivid, unforeseen, remarkable self.

"Not to protect her?"

Jamie snapped his gaze over, all traces of strained tolerance gone. "I do not protect."

"You protect the king."

"I guard the king, with an end in mind."

"And have you no intent for Eva?"

"I intend never to see her again."

"I see." Ry spoke again, but mercifully, it was not of Eva. "What did Cig want?"

"Much. Mouldin has returned to his old ways. He is auctioning off Peter of London to the highest bidder."

Ry whistled, long and low.

"I've shocked you."

"I'm reeling."

A group of merchants and servants passed, lanterns held high to ward off the encroaching darkness. Ry waited until they'd passed to speak again, his voice low. "Cig must have been sore relieved to hear you already *had* the d'Endshire heir in your keeping."

"I'm certain he would have been," Jamie agreed.

"But you did not tell him."

"No."

"Why not?"

"I do not like him. And I do not trust him."

Ry raised an eyebrow. "But you will tell the king?"

They stepped over a pile of refuse. "Why do you ask?"

"Because I wonder."

Jamie shook his head. "Ry, I am distressed by your lack of faith in me. Young Roger has more faith in me than you."

"He knows you less well."

"Ah. That is so. Why would I not tell the king?"

"One might as easily ask, 'Why would you?'"

Jamie glanced over. "I am bound suchly, am I not?"

Ry did not answer.

Their footsteps thudded out dully on the cobbles, and their capes blew out behind them as they climbed to the steep center of town. Revelry was breaking out within buildings, shouts and laughter and the tinkling of lutes and cymbals. The sky had darkened further during their walk, and everything was deep in shadow now, except where lanterns suspended outside building lit the cobbles in shifting puddles of light.

"And so now we go . . . ?" Ry said.

"To the doctor. To find the priest before Cig does."

They were drawing near the wooden gates that marked the

entrance to the Old Jewry. "I wonder what Cig will say to that if we meet at the negotiations."

Jamie swept out his cape as they stepped around a pack of dogs fighting over entrails. "Cig can kiss my arse. In any event," he added as they swept around another corner, "I beat him halfway to hell and left him in a tanner's ditch."

Ry's groan carried them all the way to the doctor's front door.

Forty-seven

The door to Jakob Doctor's office was slammed in their faces. They looked at it, then each other.

"That was impolite," Ry said.

"It makes me positively curious," Jamie replied, looking up at the second- and third-floor windows. It was idle appraisal; he had no intention of scaling the outer wall. Much easier to kick down the door. The wood was strong; the lock was not.

But only if absolutely necessary.

"Do you know anyone here, Ry?"

"Here, where?"

Jamie looked down from the face of the expensive brick building. "Here, Gracious Hill."

Ry gave him an even look. "Being raised a Jew should in no way imply that I know every Jew in England."

Jamie returned the level look. "You might know a few, seeing as your mother's family was from this town, and I happen to know you visited often as a child."

Ry shook his head and stalked off, down the clean, cobbled streets of the Old Jewry, although there was no "new" Jewry. But there were pogroms every so often, and kings who sold "their" Jews, then ejected them, and years later made them pay for the privilege of coming back and having it happen all over again, sometime later, at the whim of some future king.

But King John was particularly protective, and in one of those odd bedmatings, at a time when ordinary citizens and rich barons were being pushed to their limits by John's incursions into their rights and coffers, the Jews were safer under the oppressive lordship of King John than they'd been under any other English king.

Fifteen minutes later, Ry came striding out of the spring gloaming with a stoop-shouldered man wearing a skullcap. Ry looked grim, but the rabbi looked even more dour. He spent a long, silently scoldful minute examining Jamie, then turned back to Ry with a severe look.

"I dearly hope your mother knows what you're doing."

Ry's eyes narrowed at the effort of resisting some obviously powerful urge—Jamie could only guess which—but Ry replied in a respectful, if chilly, tone of voice, "Mama died, one of the times they burned the Jewry."

The rabbi shook his head, whether due to disgust or grief, and turned to the door. He rapped on it thrice.

After a moment, the door swung open. The same shaft of yellow light spilled out as had before. The same servant poked his head out as had before. But this time, the booming voice was given form as another, taller figure came up behind him, who in addition to looking distinguished, looked highly irritated. He also had a blackening eye.

"What is the meaning of this—," he began, then saw the rabbi. "Mecham, what are you doing here?"

Ry's scolding rabbi sighed and gestured. "Rebekka who married Yakov's son Josef, in London, this is her son. Hayyim. He needs our help."

"Ry," he corrected curtly.

Jakob the doctor looked at them for a long time, then,

shooing the servant aside, stepped back and silently waved them in. Mecham shook his head again, having mastered the same combination of guilt and grief Jamie recalled from Ry's mother. The rabbi leaned in to clasp hands briefly with the doctor, then hurried away, back into the darkness of the ghetto.

Jamie and Ry stepped inside warily, scanning the rooms as they shut the door, pulled in the latch string, and followed the doctor into a large chamber.

Jakob Doctor went immediately to a far wall, straightening ceramic pots. Ry stepped to the far side of the entry, and Jamie stood by the doorway. They looked at Jakob Doctor's profile. He had a black eye.

"'Tis late," the doctor said, not looking over. "I am weary. What do you want?"

"We are here with a simple inquiry, Doctor. Did you have any patients this day?"

He moved from shelving ceramic pots to shelving glass bottles. Mottled green, they looked like small, wet, misshapen frogs. "Every day, I have patients."

"New ones."

"New ones. Every day."

Ry said quietly, "A priest."

The doctor's busy hands stilled, resting on the table in front of him. Then he started picking up jars and moving them up onto shelves bolted to the walls behind the table.

"Aye, I saw a priest."

"He was here?"

"In this room."

"And now?"

"He is no longer in this room."

Jamie gave a faint smile. "Doctor, if you do not want us here—"

"Is it so obvious?"

"—you need but answer my questions, and we will be gone before anyone will know we were here. Asking questions."

Jakob looked at him blandly.

"I can ensure that"—Jamie pointed to Jakob's black eye—"will not happen again, if you talk to me."

The doctor lifted his brows slightly, and Jamie sighed. He gestured to Ry, then made for the stairs. "Search the back rooms."

Jamie made a quick search of the upper-level rooms, the long, narrow hall, the bedchamber separated behind a tapestry, and found nothing He could hear Ry downstairs, moving through the back rooms. A peek out the window a moment later showed Ry investigating the small outbuilding in the back that no doubt housed chickens and perhaps a small goat.

"This is why people slam the door in the faces of armed men who appear at their doors unannounced," Jakob Doctor said when they returned downstairs.

"No doubt. Had you told us what we wanted to know, it might have been avoided."

"No, it would not have been."

They looked at each other, then Jamie smiled faintly. "No, it would not."

The doctor sighed and leaned back against the table behind him, crossing his arms over his chest. His long, expensive tunic swayed around his ankles. He peered at Jamie for a long moment. "The priest was brought here with a cough. Sent by a midwife."

"Magda," Jamie said in a low voice.

Jakob Doctor's eyebrow formed a stern line across his wrinkled brow. "Magda is a skillful midwife. Her knowledge should not be maligned."

"I am hardly maligning her knowledge," Jamie demurred.

"I examined him, gave a healing poultice for his chest. He is a wise man, and we had a pleasant discussion. The priest reported that in the past, several Christian doctors have suggested the priest had a devil in his chest, and this was the cause of his rheumy cough." The doctor lifted his brows, as if awaiting an opinion on this piece of idiocy.

"I assume you did not agree about the devil," Jamie said drily.

Jakob moved his arms in a gesture of futile anger. "Fools."

"In what state was the priest when he left?"

"Coughing. Pleasant." Jakob paused. "Familiar."

Jamie nodded slowly. "You would do best to forget that last."

Jakob nodded, glancing at Ry. "I forget many things."

Ry's face rippled. "I forget nothing."

"And such men suffer."

Ry gave a bark of harsh laughter and turned to Jamie. "Are we done here?"

Jamie ran his fingertips over the papers on the table, touching them lightly. "Did he say anything else?"

The doctor turned back to his table and began laying strips of clean cotton into a wooden box. "About?"

Jamie looked at the papers for a while. About what, indeed. "About . . . anything. Anything at all. Anything you recall might be of use."

Jakob looked over his shoulder, pausing in putting the strips into their container. "I was told I might expect a visitor, and he would settle the bill. A Jamie Lost." Jamie felt Ry's gaze on the side of his face. "I do not know who that is," the doctor said. "I do not think I shall see payment, do you?" He regarded them with haughty, cold dignity.

Jamie looked up from the papers. "Why did you do it, then? Render service?"

"I am a Jew. I am a doctor. I render."

"Is there anything else?"

A small ripple disturbed the refined, composed face of the

best doctor west of London and south of Chester. "Robert fitzWalter is here."

"Robert FitzWalter is in town?" Jamie held himself motionless, but inside, his blood was heating, churning.

Ry muttered some curse.

The doctor turned back to his straightening. "You did not hear that here."

After that, it was a matter of another swift minute, a few more queries, and they were done. Ry turned and walked out. Jamie nodded his thanks and rapped his knuckles lightly on the desk. The doctor looked down and saw a small felt pouch resting under Jamie's curled fingers.

"What is that?"

Jamie turned for the door. "Payment. I am Jamie Lost."

They left not ten minutes after they'd arrived, silent as darkness.

IN a cellar below, an armed guard stood at the base of the stairs, his head tilted, his ear aimed at the dirt ceiling above.

He was waiting for a message from his commander, Mouldin, and then he would deliver the priest. Hoped he'd make it that long. He glanced over his shoulder. The priest was lying, sleeping lightly, on the ground.

A moment later a beam of light shot down, then widened as the door above was swung wide.

"Come up," said the doctor.

The guard carried the priest up; it was not difficult, as the old man was light as a feather. He felt a twinge of discomfort at treating a man of God in this manner, but consoled himself with the thought it would only be for a short time. Mouldin would sell the priest to someone who wanted him very much and would probably treat him well.

As the guard crested the stairs, the physic regarded him

coldly and pointed to the back room. "Lay him on the bed. Be gentle. And do not touch him again."

"If someone else comes—"

The doctor drew himself up. "You will move him again over my dead body."

The soldier felt uneasy, but for the moment it didn't matter. He was simply waiting for Mouldin's signal, and instructions on whom to deliver the priest to, the rebels or the king.

JAMIE and Ry entered the inn's enclosed stableyard, talking softly, making plans. Soft sounds of snuffling horses chomping hay eddied through the dark. "All I want is a drink," Jamie muttered. "To sit in a moment of silence, and think. With a drink."

Roger stepped out of the shadows. "I ordered your bath, sir, and . . ." He drew nearer, took one look between them, and said, "Where is Eva?"

Forty-eight

Eva turned to the Scotsman as the echo of Jamie's bootheels faded. She looked way up to his eyes, which were set above a wild, hedgerow-thick brush of beard. She cleared her throat.

"Sir?"

He glared at her. "Not me. I'm no' a knight."

She nodded agreeably. "This is a common condition in England, is it? I have been surrounded by many men who insist they are not knights."

His narrowed eyes narrowed slightly more.

"I think the fewer knights we have, the better. Do you not agree?"

"Aye," he agreed slowly. Keeping a confused and suspicious eye on her, he sat at the table and reached for a tankard sitting there.

"They are naught but intrigue and politics," she elaborated helpfully.

"Mucking things up," he muttered in agreement.

She nodded, feeling as she went for chinks in this man's no-doubt-impressive armor. He would not be swayed by tears, that was certain—not that she had any to give; Jamie was not worth the salt in them—nor would he be weakened by feminine wiles.

Not that she had any of those either, she reflected.

No, he was a straight-on sort of man, albeit one who'd been terribly hurt, and it had not yet healed. Now, what sort of thing cut so deep and healed so slowly?

Betrayal, of course.

He watched her suspiciously, but it was less suspiciously than before, and so she deemed it progress. In this way, one maintained hope in the face of great odds.

"I, for one, am done with knights," she said with finality.

"Aye, lass, I'm certain ye are."

"Oh, you think 'tis your dangerous Jamie I mean, but no."

He shrugged. "I don't much care for them either, girl."

"Nor are you overly fond of Jamie."

He gave her a long, considering look, then said simply, "No."

She sat forward. "Did he tie you up?"

His eyebrows flew high. "Who, Jamie?"

"Aye. Is this why you do not like him? Did he tie you up?"

He looked startled. "Nay. Did he tie *ye* up?"

She shook her head glumly and sat back. "He did, but then he untied me very quickly and decided to bring me instead. For this, I am sad."

Angus burst out laughing. "Then ye needed bringing, I'm certain. Jamie's not one for a baggage train. If yer with him, that's where yer meant to be."

She didn't know if she liked the sound of that. But it told her something: this one trusted Jamie, respected him, and was very, very angry with him. "I feel just so, as you've described it, like a baggage train. The foodstuffs, perhaps. Or the pigs scooted along at the end."

Angus took a sip of ale. "Were ye a servant, then?"

"Do I seem like a servant? A goose girl, no doubt."

He eyed her from over the rim of his huge tankard. "Nay. You seem like a waif."

She sighed. "Is it so clear?"

He shrugged. She glanced at his mug. He followed her gaze down, then passed her the huge tankard by its wooden handle. Her thumb and fingers barely met around its girth. She didn't particularly want it, but one did not escape from bondage by refusing gifts from one's captor, however stinky those gifts might be. But this, she admitted, was not so stinky. She put her nose over it and sniffed again, then sipped. Then smiled.

"That is quite good." And she was not lying, this time. Jamie would be proud. Not that such a thing mattered.

"Aye," he agreed comfortably. "It ought ta be. My mam's recipe. Spend years perfecting it, she did. Have's much as ye want."

She took another little sip, then slid it back to him. "Your mother was a brewer," she said, liking the notion. It wasn't often she had such simple connections with people.

"Aye. Afore she passed," he mumbled, and crossed himself. Eva did the same. They fell silent.

She looked down at her boots. The wooden soles had worn down terribly on the sides, and the leather was cracked, made wet, then dry, then wet again too often. The hem of her blue overtunic hung to the lace straps, entangled and torn in one spot. She fussed with it a moment. When had she last taken her shoes off? It felt like weeks. And her fingernails . . . it hardly bore thinking of. They were washed clear of any decoration, pale pink but for the the smiling half-moons.

"Have you any cherries?" she asked suddenly.

Angus looked up from his mug and eyed her in a vaguely suspicious, entirely confused way.

"If you have a cherry, or any sort of plum, I can do a remarkable thing."

He sat back and crossed his arms over his chest. It was suspicion no longer, but doubt, skepticism, along the lines of

How could this dirty little thread of a woman do something remarkable with a plum?

Yet she could. With cherries, plums, carrots, and ever so many other fruits and vegetables, and even the bark of apple trees. Everything but a human heart.

"Aye," he said warily. "My neighbor's got a few cherry trees."

Eva looked skeptical. "But we will not need to bother them?"

Angus might have actually blushed, under all his fur. "Nah, I just reach over the wall."

She laughed. "This is most good. And perhaps a carrot, in your garden? And an egg, or two, but if there is none, it is not a thing that will stop us."

"Good to know." Angus took another sip of ale. "It doesn't sound like anything my mam did for us. But then, she wasn't making many fruit pasties."

"This is not a pasty, Angus. How may 'us-es' were you?"

He rubbed his thick, calloused thumb over the edge of the table, then said quite proudly, "Eleven, all boys, and we all of us survived to manhood."

She fell back in her chair. "But this is terrible, this sort of hearty stock! Your poor mother must have been dismayed, her home filled with all your big dirt."

Angus laughed and stretched his tree-trunk legs out in front of him, crossing them at the ankles. His boots were scuffed and white-brown in all the grooves, like a dirty map showing all the work he'd done in them.

"There were days she fairly fainted from it, to be sure. But ye'd hardly have known. She was goodly. Never lost her temper. Well," he quickly amended when Eva frowned, "never without cause, and the good Lord knows we gave it to her."

"And this purveyor of hearty stock, what did she look like?"

Angus seemed taken aback. "Oh, well, she was"—he lifted his hand about level with his shoulder—"and somewhat, well . . ." He lifted his other hand and held the two apart in front of him, looking baffled as he tried to explain his mother using these imprecise physical dimensions. "I mean to say, there were days, o' course, but then . . ." His hands flailed helplessly.

"Hair?"

His eyes flew over. "Brown."

She shook her head in despair. "What *manner* of brown? Like the trunk of a tree you climbed and no doubt fell from some afternoon, frightening your poor mother half to her grave? Or brown like a shallow river after a storm?"

"Like this." He jabbed his blunt finger with great emphasis and certainty at the burl lines on the table beside him. Dark, but red tones, Eva assessed swiftly, expertly.

"Good. And her face?"

He stared at her blankly. "More like . . . the shallow river?"

She fell back in her seat a second time, laughing. Angus joined her, and for perhaps a half a minute, they laughed at the notion of Angus's mother's face having the hue of a shallow, muddy river, for Angus's trapped response that had prompted the assessment, and for a hundred other things that perhaps should have been laughed at over the years, but there'd simply been no time. Eva suspected this might be true for this hard-soft Scotsman as well. So this laughing, for a brief moment, was a simple and good thing.

"I will not draw her thusly," Eva said, still smiling, as she rose and walked to the fire grate.

"Draw her?"

Angus shot to his feet as she passed, torn no doubt between ensuring she did not escape and being the sort of host who would get things for a female guest. Surely his mother had instilled this.

Eva removed the necessity of worrying by kneeling in front of the fire pit and feeling around its cold edges.

"I was going to light us one, just got distracted," he explained gruffly.

"That would be nice." Eva touched what she wanted with her fingertips. "Soon the night will be chilled." She stood with a charred, half-burned chunk of wood in her hand. He looked at it blankly. "To draw. Might we steal a cherry from your neighbor now?"

His face cleared. "Ahh. The cherries."

"Ah, the cherries. Just a handful or three."

Quickly, she had a charred charcoal stick and some makeshift dyes, and with quick, deft strokes, she spoke to Angus about his mother and sketched her on his tabletop, making long, loose sweeps of charcoal and fruit paint across the six-foot span. She stood, moving around it at need, leaning over, her hair tucked down the back collar of her dress, her eyes on her work, her ears attuned for nuances of emotion and truth Angus would not even know he revealed. When she was done, his mother was five feet long, bumped where her likeness crossed the planks of wood, lying flat on his table, smiling up at him.

He'd long gone silent. His breathing was uneven, his hands fisted where they hung beside his thighs.

"'Tis just her," he muttered thickly.

She nodded as they looked down at it. "That is good."

They stood staring down at it in silence for a long time. After, he lit the fire, and they transferred their silence to the sitting sort. Somewhere outside, a dog barked. And farther out, Jamie had Gog, he might have Father Peter by now, and he was most certainly leaving her behind.

"You call him Jamie Lost," she said quietly.

Angus shifted in his seat and looked over. "He was lost. We were all lost, children on the streets. London. He found us."

"Why do you hate him?"

A twisted smile burned on his face. "Someone found him."

"And not you," she understood quietly.

He got to his feet slowly. "I'll put ye in yer room now."

She rose without argument. "How long do you keep me here?"

He just pointed toward a narrow ladder set in the back of the wide room. At the top was a small, windowless loft. She put her hands on the aged, gray wooden rungs. Draped over the edge of one were several ribbons, dusky, dark pinkish red, quite remarkable, really. A silent, deep, stunning shade. Silk.

She looked away and reached for the next rung.

"They're for yerself," Angus gruffed.

She stilled.

"The ribbons. Lost left 'em for ye."

She reached for them, clutched the delicate silks, crushing them, which was a terrible thing to do, of course, but she had no choice. Holding them to her chest, she started up the ladder. Then she paused and looked over her shoulder, down at Angus's bristly, damaged face and angry, sad eyes.

"Might I have a sip of wine, Angus? Or perhaps a drop of water?"

Forty-nine

Roger and Ry sat in the common room of the inn while Jamie went up to bathe. They were ready for their second servings of ale by the time he came down. The drinks were brought swifly, along with a plate of cheese and bread.

Roger picked up his mug and drank with such great gulping swallows, Ry and Jamie lowered theirs to watch. Eventually, Roger pulled it away, wiped the back of his hand over his lips, saw them staring, and grinned.

"Eva doesn't often let us stop at alehouses."

Jamie smiled. "No, I expect not."

He took another casual survey of the room. The tavern was loud but not overly crowded, and no one looked particularly interested in three men, only one bathed, who were drinking ale.

"Tell me, Roger, are you still in mind of hiding as you have all these years?"

Roger sat up straighter. "Nay, sir. Not at all."

"Know there has been merit in this course. Eva saved your life by it. Coming out of the shadows,"—Jamie met Roger's eyes—"'twill be a hard row."

Roger nodded gravely but looked undeterred.

"You have a choice to make, before all else," Jamie said, picking up his mug.

Roger looked uncomfortable. "Eva said you were King John's man."

Jamie looked over the rim of his mug. "You certainly should think of me that way."

"Then are you not bound to take me to the king?"

Jamie drank, then replied, "I am no man's conscience, Roger. You are not a cow being led to the field, and the battle has not yet been launched. I found you, that is all. Or," he amended, "you and Eva found me."

"And if you deliver me—"

"I would not deliver a sheep to his father's murderer."

Roger's face was taut and pale. "Eva told you about that night."

Jamie nodded. From the corner of his eye, he saw Ry take a visual sweep of the room. They'd spent their lives in constant surveillance. God knows, he was weary of it. Suddenly, crushingly weary.

"I still dream of that night, upon a time," Roger muttered

Jamie looked back. "As do I."

Roger started in surprise. "You, sir?"

"We have a great deal in common, Roger. My father was murdered too. I watched it."

Then ran. He'd stood ten feet away as they murdered his father, then he had run. And for that, he was already in hell.

"I didn't have to watch it, sir," Roger said, his voice as low-pitched as Jamie's. "Eva put herself in front of me."

They both stared down into their mugs.

Then Roger downed the rest of his tankard in two long swallows. Ry silently signaled for more. The maidservant brought them, weaving through the swaying bodies crowding the room. Roger sat back, leaned his shoulders against the wall, and muttered, "How to choose? The rebels or the king?"

"Some would say do what your conscience guides."

"Is that what you say, sir?"

Jamie hesitated slightly. "I say lay your money on the side that will win."

Roger sat forward. "Then you think John will prevail?"

Jamie said nothing.

"But if you had to choose, sir . . . ?"

Jamie wiped his hand over the top of his thigh, suddenly restless. Mayhap it was all Roger's eager, admiring energy, aimed at him. "I do choose, Roger. Every day. My choices are my own. Yours are your own."

Roger looked taken aback at the sudden sharpness in Jamie's voice.

Ry leaned forward into the tension, to deflect it, or perhaps absorb it. "Jamie. What is it?" he said quietly.

He shook his head. "I do not know."

And there was no time to wonder on it, for Angus's beefy, bearded visage suddenly appeared amid the shifting bodies at the far end of the room. He waded over and gave a great, heaving sigh when he reached their table. "'Tis sorry I am, Lost, but she escaped. Just like ye said."

THE hot rush of happiness stunned him, the simple, expanding experience of it. So this was happiness. Joy. It suffused him, filled him like drinking hot mead.

"I'm a rare sort of sorry, Jamie." Angus hung his head. "She did just as ye said."

"Which was?"

"I'm ashamed to say." Angus's next words were muffled. "She asked for wine."

Jamie nodded. The urge to smile was strong.

"And after we'd already been drinking my mam's ale," the Scotsman said in misery.

Gog sat forward with interest. "Eva drank ale?"

Angus tipped his shame-descended head up a bit and stared at Roger, whom he'd never seen before. "Aye," he admitted suspiciously.

"Did she like it?"

"Aye." Angus sounded indignant now. "'Twas my mam's brew." He turned to Jamie. "I've been guarding everything from sheep to soldiers for years now, as ye well know, and ne'er has someone slipped my net. I canna tell ye how . . . bleeding surprised I am. And sorry." He hung his head again.

Jamie watched the huge, angry Scotsman prostrate himself on the altar of Eva's escape. It was highly satisfying. In all these years of Angus refusing to do more than acknowledge the debt he owed Jamie for calling off King John's wrath years back, and incurring much suspicion and some good debt of his own as a result, Angus had never truly exhibited sorrow. Or remorse. Until now. Eva was giving gifts even when she was gone.

"But I'll tell ye, Lost, anyone would have been distracted by the lass."

"Is that so?"

"Ye should have seen what she did on my table," Angus said darkly.

"Your . . . table?"

Angus nodded grimly. "Aye. My mam."

Jamie nodded blankly. "Your mother."

Angus flung his hands around as if he were scattering seed. "Aye, my *mam*. On the table. Painted with fruits and the like. Fruit, Jamie. With her hands, and her"—he sputtered a bit—"her blessed mind, she drew the likeness of my dear mam right there, on the table."

"Ah. She's surprising," Jamie murmured. He wanted to smile. Smile large, and not in amusement. In . . . happiness?

Angus stared. "*Surprising?* That's like to calling her *charming*."

"Is she not?"

Angus fixed Jamie in a glare, then planted his palms on the table and bent down. "Ye're no' comprehending, Lost. She's no' *charming*, or *pleasin'* or whatever pale goods ye're flinging about. She's more'n all that. She's, she's . . ." He lifted a beefy palm to wave it about, as if pushing aside mists to find his word. Then he leaned close again, pinched his fingers an inch apart, and said, *"This close to being fycking magic."*

He straightened and gave a sharp tug down on the hem of his tunic, adding in grim tones, "You'd best take care, Lost."

"We are far past that," Jamie said, setting down his mug. "Go home, Angus. The debt is settled."

But the Scotsman shook his head. "Not on yer addled life. The debt is no' settled, and I'm weary of it hanging around my neck. I'm sticking till 'tis over."

"What if I do not want you?" But he did. Angus's sword arm would be an immeasurable boon. As would repairing the damage done to this old friendship.

Angus thrust out his chin. "I'm sticking, Lost. Like as not there's a whole host of men wanting to wring yer stubborn neck come morn"—Jamie and Ry exchanged another, more guilty glance—"and I can help. I'll start by finding the lass."

Jamie shook his head, rising. "I know where she is. Ry, hie me for the watch at matins. And get another room for the night."

And he went upstairs to wait for her.

Fifty

But she was already there. He knew it the moment he pushed open the door. Eva, waiting in the shadows, on the bench by the wall.

He scanned the rest of the darkness, then moved in and stood, arms crossed over his chest, shoulder against the wall. Eva remained sitting.

They looked at each other for a long minute.

"Allow me to be clear," she said in her low, throaty non sequitur way. "I have changed my mind."

He felt a smile begin deep inside. She spoke as if they were continuing some previous conversation. Perhaps they were, in her mind. Perhaps she'd been speaking to him ever since he left her. There was something debilitatingly potent about this.

He shifted his shoulder against the wall. "Changed your mind about what?"

"You."

He gave a soft laugh. "Now that I have turned you over to mine enemy, now that you have escaped, *now* you have altered your opinion of me? Keep your original one, woman." He shook his head.

"How many years have you served King John?" she asked quietly.

Ah, so they were to do this after all. "Fifteen."

"How did you come to that position in the king's household?"

"FitzWalter."

"He placed you there, to kill the king."

"Aye."

"You did not do it."

"Clearly."

"Why not?" She sounded confused. But he did not want to talk politics. He wanted to lay her out on the bed and undo her.

"We have spoken of this already, Eva; there is always something worse. Anything else?"

"But you do not esteem John," she insisted. "In your heart. This I can see."

He was quiet for a moment. "No. I do not."

"Why not?"

"He killed my parents." She gave a little gasping laugh, but he ploughed through the sad, shocked sound, churning up details. "My father was killed when John was but Regent. He was the first to return with news that King Richard was not dead, only imprisoned, and in need of a very large ransom. John had been hoping to keep that news from spreading; he was next in line for the throne. My mother was murdered years later, after John was crowned. I do not know why he killed her."

But you do, he thought.

She considered him through the dim light of a single candle stub and the brazier, and the moonlight spilling through the shutters. "How could this be, Jamie?"

"How could what be?" he said, surprised to hear his voice gone hoarse.

"How can you serve the man who murdered your parents?"

He gave a twisted smile. "Revenge."

She shook her head. "That makes no sense."

"I have not achieved it yet. Is there more? Or are we done?"

She inhaled, lifting her chin. "Why did you leave me with Angus?"

He shoved off the wall. "Eva, this serves no purpose. You have not been wrong about me. You should go."

"Why do they call you Jamie Lost?"

He reached for the pot of wine on the floor and poured a drink. He extended the cup. She glanced at it but did not reach.

"You came for Roger," he said, setting the cup down and turning away. "Go get him. I will not stop you, not from anything you wish to do."

"That is good." She unfolded to her feet, and he saw she was wrapped in furs from the bed. "For I did not come back for Roger."

Deep inside, in the dark pit of him, a small spark, which had been banked for many years, suddenly lit. Slowly she extended her hand, her pale arm moving through the firelit darkness like a dancer's. On her palm hung five dusky red ribbons.

"What are these?"

"Ribbons." He did not recognize his own voice.

"Why?"

"For your hair." It was choked, the words forced through his twisted throat.

She nodded. The furs slipped off her shoulders and draped down her back, held only by her elbows and forearms. In the darkness, her body shone.

She moved through the room toward him, slow, languid, her eyes never leaving his, her body sinuous, her hair down, damp. His bath. She'd been naked in his bath.

"I am what I am, Eva," he said hoarsely. "You have already seen the best of me, and 'tis not a high plain."

"We shall see, shall we not?"

"We shall see what?" he almost growled.

"Who the good man is," she said, and it was ridiculous, for it would never be him.

He felt a surge of . . . something with no name. Not anger, not arousal, not fury or vengeance or hate. He knew those things well, and it did not taste of them. It was not even desire. It was nothing he'd ever felt before, and it beat its hard, swooping wings in his head and chest, like a dragon taking wing. It hummed.

This was the thing that should not be loosed. All these years, holding it in, and now Eva was believing so boldly in something that was not within him. Instead, what *did* lie within, all the dammed ferocity, might come flying out, and never stop its rampage.

He held himself rigid, hands clenched at his sides. "Know this, Eva: you tread on dangerous earth. Do not be mistaken. I *will* take you, if you lay yourself out before me. But you are meant for something other. Better."

She kept moving toward him. "Know this, Jamie: you are wrong about me. From the moment of my birth, I have been meant for maneuverings and much coin, but I am whelped from witchy blood. I do not want the things I have been made for. I want you."

His blood was churning. She was only a step away now.

"You do not know what you are saying," he muttered, but he stretched out his arm and ran the tip of a finger into the valley between her breasts. She tipped her chin up to exhale, her eyes on his. His desire surged hot and thick. He unclenched one hand and, splaying his fingers, cupped the curve of her spine, pulling her roughly forward. Their bodies collided, belly to belly, chest to chest, their gazes locked.

She pushed up on her toes, put her lips gently on his, and he kissed the breath of her next words: "*I choose you, Jamie.*"

"Then know what you choose, Eva," he replied hoarsely. "I

am Everoot." And in that way, decades of secrets slipped out in a kiss.

He did not want to share them, but if desperate Eva was choosing, she should know what poison she drank.

"I am Everoot," he said again, harshly, "and I shall never claim it. But you, I will claim."

Silence and stillness, then she exhaled, a long, *realizing* breath. He wanted to kiss this breath too, but instead stood motionless, one hand splayed across her back, the other still hanging, fisted by his side.

Give her a moment, he thought, feeling dizzy. A moment to understand the implications: that the Everoot heir was not dead; that the home Eva had lived in for years was in fact *Jamie's* home; that the woman Eva had grown to love as a mother was *his* mother.

That Jamie had watched his father be murdered, then run and never returned. Never tried to return. Everything had been blanked out by the almost-blinding desire to wreak his vengeance on King John, only to be thwarted by the utter inability to follow through, because then the country truly *would* fall to wreck and ruin.

But at least King John would never have another Everoot pledge him fealty.

So let Eva see the blackness inside him, the charred emptiness of him. Then she could decide.

For a long moment, there was no response but for her breath touching his lips, her gray eyes thoughtful on his. Then she laid her palms on his cheeks and, smiling, whispered, "But of course. I see her in you. You look like your mother."

He felt as though he were falling backward.

"Do not fear this, Jamie." She kissed his chin. "I still choose you."

His head roared with silence. It rolled through him like

a flash flood coming down a mountain. *Now* it was time to unleash. To claim. Eva.

He cupped the back of her head and kissed down her neck, lips, tongue, teeth, nipping, devouring, inhaling. She pulled him back up, wanting to kiss him, and it was like a flame laid to wood; they ignited.

He assaulted her mouth, not tasting but taking, sinking into all the private places of her, laying claim to the hot, hidden recesses of her mouth. This is what he'd wanted, in the tavern, against the tree, every time she smiled, his whole life. Her. Eva. In his hands. His.

He backed her up to the bed, never stopping his kiss, while she tugged impatiently at the ties of his braies. He moved into action. Sword belt, tunic, everything was scattered behind him until her knees hit the back of the bed and she sat. Swathed in furs, she scooted back as he yanked off his boots and hose, then put a knee on the bed, hot satisfaction and a sense of destiny thudding inside.

His gaze raked her body. She was stretched out before him like a gift. Curved waist, high, small breasts, long, muscular legs, and the tangle of dark curls between her legs brought him dangerously close to the edge. He dragged a testing fingertip across her belly, raising throaty whimpers and an arched spine. Her face, always so pale, was flushed with color, her eyes dark and filled with passion—and trust—as she reached for him.

He kissed her hand, then propped himself up on an elbow and stretched out beside her. She made an impatient sound and tugged on his shoulder.

"What is this, this *stopping?*" she complained.

"This is not stopping," he disagreed, and slid a palm down the front of her, over her breasts, down her belly, down one shapely thigh, to her knee, a long, possessive swipe. She took a sharp inbreath. He looked up. "You see?" He slid his hand back up to cup her breast.

"I think I see," she whispered weakly.

"This is called *beginning*," he explained, and bent to her breast.

He took a slow, lapping journey across her chest as her body arched for him. When he heard a whimper drift from her lips, he expanded his caress, exploring every inch of the hot weight of her breasts, licking and nipping, until she was lying across the forearm of his bent arm, her fingers threading through his hair. She whispered something as he slid his hand down the silky length of her leg and slicked his finger between her thighs, into her folds, a slippery swipe.

The breath exploded out of her and their mouths met in a hot, messy kiss. He dipped into her again, teasing with hot, slow strokes of his finger. At first he was gentle, holding himself in check, but when she lifted her hips to his touch, her knees spread, when she held his face between her palms and kissed him as madly as he was kissing her, open-mouthed, panting, he pushed her harder, faster. Her body rocked beside him, her breath hitched on each inhale, then she gave a ragged cry of his name.

"This is somewhere near the middle," he murmured into her ear. "Of the first time."

"Jamie," she whispered brokenly, tugging on him. "You are not a kind man."

"No, I am not," he agreed, and slid a finger hard up inside her, a single swift thrust.

She dropped back to the bed with another sobbing cry. Head spinning, he pushed in a second finger, spreading her open. He worked her deep, pushing her with fast, hard strokes, her hot flesh around his fingers, his slippery thumb a constant assault from the outside, until her neck was arched, head pressed into the mattress, hair spilling in a dark circle around her tossing head. Her hands gripped the sheets in tight little fists as she inhaled in unsteady little gasps. Then her body tensed, her breath stopped.

"Look at me, Eva," he ordered.

She dragged her eyes open.

"I have waited for you and this moment for all my life. Do not make me wait anymore."

He pushed in again, hard and deep, curling his fingers, driving her relentlessly into climax, until she came apart, her body shuddering, her head tossing, fingers tugging in his hair, crying out his name. Perfect, beautiful woman. His. Time to claim her.

His head was roaring as he rose up and knelt between her thighs.

Fifty-one

Eva's body was humming. Radiant and humming as the velvety solid tip of him nudged through the wetness of her. She gripped his arm and whimpered. He paused and looked up.

"Again, you stop," she whispered, reaching up to his neck. Was her voice humming too, the way her body was?

Dark blue eyes locked on hers, filled with male arousal and the intensity of a hunter. She realized that she did not mind this look from Jamie whatsoever. He positioned himself between her hips and put his hand on her knee, pressing out. "I will be gentle," he grated.

"That will not do a'tall."

He hesitated. "How, then?"

She ran her hand by his cheek, and he ducked into it, ever so slightly. "As we ever have, Jamie. So there is no going back."

He turned his head to nip her palm at the same moment he thrust into her with a single, deep rocking penetration. They both flung their heads back and cried out, then stilled.

"Are you hurt?" he asked in a thick voice, looking at the ceiling.

"Aye," she whispered. "Do not stop."

"It will get better," he promised in a rasp, and one palm

planted by her head, the other holding her hip, dark hair falling forward past his cheekbones, he began moving in slow, rhythmic sweeps.

At first, Eva just held on, trusting the way his eyes never left hers, the way his body, so perfectly formed, sought hers, the way, after a few moments, a very small, very hot core started forming deep inside her, getting hotter each time Jamie rocked his hips into another slow penetration.

He knew it too. Her lips parted once and she blew out a breath. He smiled that little half smile, and she smiled back tentatively.

"Better?" he murmured.

"Aye, a little—oh, Jamie," she gasped as he shifted slightly, angled his hips just so, and pushed in. Something hot and wicked snaked down her back, like fat lightning hitting the earth inside her. She gasped and froze.

"A little better?" he asked wickedly.

"Aye," she whispered. "The smallest, little bit."

He did it again, that long, slow, perfect thrust. "Bigger now?" he whispered by her ear.

Cold-hot tremors ripped up her back and her belly, the shivering sensations so good and deep it was almost frightening.

His eyes gleamed as he gripped her hips and surged into her again and again, each time nudging her flesh apart to go deeper into some wild place high inside her that made her want to grip his hips with her knees and howl. So she did. She bent her knee and Jamie clamped it against his hip. She lifted the other and locked her ankles around his back, her arms around his shoulders.

"'Twas, perhaps, the tiniest bit better," she murmured as she hung beneath him, her hair falling to the bed. "But I've almost forgotten it now."

He laughed. An intimate, masculine, powerful-quiet laugh, and her heart turned a bend, so she could only see it from the back now, as it moved toward Jamie. Hurricane Jamie.

And now, given a choice, she knew she would always choose this, to swing over this pit with him. Jamie and his scarred heart, his noble, bad choices, his holding power. She would give up every choice that was to come, to have *this* choice, of turning toward Jamie.

He planted his hands on the bed and his thrusts grew deeper, faster. His harsh male breath was by her ear, and he was like a sun inside her, until the hot pulsing inside her become a shivering undulation through her body.

"Oh, Jamie, please," she whispered. "Do not stop."

He rolled them over suddenly, so Eva sat astride him.

"Now 'tis you who must not stop," he said, his hands on her hips, holding her in their reckless, sweaty rhythm. He fisted his hand around her hair and tugged her head back, so her body arched up for him, wanton and exposed. Back arched, head tossed, knees dangling over his sculpted body, Eva felt as if her soul were burning.

He pushed his head back onto the mattress, the cords of his neck revealing the taut power of him. He shoved his hips up into the air, so she was riding him, her knees dragging against the bed. She leaned over him, reaching for the bed, gasping hot, meaningless sounds, kissing his hot neck, their tongues meeting in hot, hungry swipes. She could not even form words, she could only sob and feel his body consuming hers. She was overcome.

He surged into her again and she shuddered over the edge. Her head jerked backward as her body exploded in thudding tremors that undulated along his shaft, and he lost himself too. Hard, hot spasms of orgasm surged through him as he erupted inside her. He propped himself on his elbows as she collapsed atop him, and their bodies pounded together for plunge after plunge of hot, wild thrusts, Eva calling out his name into his neck, sobbing.

There was no time after that, just long moments of slowing heartbeats, awareness of trembling muscles, panting kisses along jawlines and necks, and then there was Jamie, wrapping his arms around her back as if she were a gift and holding her to his chest until they both fell asleep.

Fifty-two

It was still dark when Jamie awoke. The moon slipped like water between the shutters, pooling in pale white spills around the dark and shadow-throwing things in the room: bed, small table, his boots. Eva was curled up beside him like a cat under the furs, her back to him, her feet against his thighs. He rolled to her. Her hair was a tangle of blackness. He ran his fingers through it gently, combing out the knots their sweaty lovemaking had created.

"You do that most well," her sleepy voice drifted up a while later. "I fear you must have practiced on many women."

"Scores," he teased.

She rolled onto her back and looked at him. "I must insist you break all their hearts at once. You will practice on me alone."

"My whole life has been practice for you, Eva." He bent to kiss her, then pulled back to peer at her hair again. "It does need a great deal of attention. All the knots."

She arched an eyebrow. "Stop gripping it so"—she held up her hands in little fists and shook them, growling a little—"and it might come away less so."

He laughed and ran the back of his hand down her cheek.

"Jamie—"

"No." She was filled with questions. He knew what they would be about. He did not want questions. "Not now."

Moonlight spilled over the edge of the furs, and she nodded. "No, you are right. All that is for later."

"I simply wished you . . . to know."

Wished someone to know. Wished the past were not the past, and, more often, his future were not his own. But right now, holding Eva, feeling her small ribs beneath his calloused palm, this was enough. Which was noteworthy in itself, for until this moment nothing had ever been enough.

"I will know this very fully, and very secretly," she promised. He ran his hand down the furs over her belly and the top of her thighs, and back up. She felt like a furred animal, her legs and arms under the silky pelt. "I am good at secrets."

"Yes, you are," he agreed drily.

"We shall speak of things other than secrets."

"And politics."

"And what has been."

"And what is to come."

She eyed him. "Perhaps we should speak of clothing."

He smiled as his gaze traveled over her face, now flushed with color. "Tell me about your river wine, Eva."

His rumble was low-pitched, the dusky shadows on his sculpted face deepened by his smile, making small lines curve beside his very capable mouth. Eva felt a ray of heat shoot through her, shivering-bright, a single beam up from the center of her heart. It was as if a little sun were rising inside of her. Best not to look directly into it.

She looked up at the ceiling and said lightly, "Ah, see, I am turning you to the wine already. Let me think." She thought a moment, then brought her gaze down and smiled at him. "It will be a small cottage, with a red roof and a little garden. Most certainly, there will be turnips and leeks in it. And garlic, of course, for you, having been raised here in England, will wither without it."

He gave a snort of laughter.

"And I will make us supper, and maybe a friend will be by to visit, but mostly, I think, not. After, you will hold your belly, you will have eaten so much. My cooking will be that good."

She lifted her eyebrows a little, daring him to disagree.

He propped himself up on his elbow and shook his head. "I can almost taste it now. Delicious."

She laughed.

"Turnips?"

She turned her head to him, and the small movement pushed arcs of black hair across the pillow. "They are quite good, mixed with bread and eggs."

"But, turnips? This is a fancy, Eva. It could be anything you might dream of."

"Turnips," she said firmly. "One does these wide-awake dreams about the things one has never known, but wants, is that not so?"

"That is so." He looked at her. "You have ne'er grown turnips?"

"Or leeks. Or kept sheep or chickens. Or had a home by a river."

He smiled. "Then these are the things to dream of."

She smiled and ran her hand over the back of his head, a smooth stroke. "I knew you would understand."

He tipped forward on his elbow to place a kiss on the sweaty side of her head, then moved down, a kiss for the neck. She tilted her head, granting him access, and continued her stories, while he continued kissing, both of them doing what they were good at.

"Then," she whispered, "while the fire burned behind us in its little grate, as the stars were coming out, we would sit by the little river, you with your ale, and me with my wine . . ."

She stopped then because words such as *you* and *your* were troublesome, in that they painted a picture that most certainly required Jamie. But he was an earl. What they were doing here was only for here, for now. Cottages and rivers and humble wine did not mark a great man. And then, of course, he served King John.

"Would you have me?"

She jerked her head around at the sound of his voice.

Dark eyes were waiting for her. He was waiting for her. His hand was resting on her belly. "If you would have me, Eva, I will come to your cottage, if that is what you want."

Eva felt heat. It was so pure and bright, raying up, it was like light, starting in her belly and expanding from within, the sun rising, eating up the cold darkness of her heart. It went to all corners of her body as if a torch had been lit inside her.

The brightness of all this made it hard to see; she had to view Jamie through the veil of shimmer. "Would you?" she asked.

"If you would have me."

She gave a little broken laugh. "*Have* you?"

He seemed to sense her tears—he was a hand's breadth away, so how could he not? And the broken sob . . . oh, he had ruined her. All her old vows—no tears, no heart, nothing to matter—were slipping away like sand.

He cupped her jaw, his eyes never leaving hers. "I will come. With you, I can do good."

The shimmer spilled over, just a bit. "Oh, yes, with me, you can do very good things."

He smiled and brushed his thumb down the track of wetness on her cheek.

"But, of course, I must tell you, it is far from here, and in grave need of repairs. It is in almost as sad a state as the little hut you have seen here in England. Clearly, these are the sorts of homes I am destined for."

He smiled. "Then we shall go and rebuild it."

"We will rebuild it." She touched his hair, brushing it back from his face, tucking it behind his ear. He did not push her away.

"And drink wine," he said, his voice low.

"Yes."

"And watch the sun set."

"Yes."

"You will make me supper." He bent to her mouth. The gentlest kiss, across her lips.

"Oh, yes," she whispered, and it was hardly a sound anymore.

"And I will repair the red, red roof."

"You will." A tear spilled over.

He curled his fingers slid beneath her chin, lifted her face when she would have lowered it. "And we will grow turnips, and leeks, and any number of other root vegetables." She gave a gasping, watery laugh. "This makes you cry?" he teased softly.

Really now, there was nothing but an array of light inside her. She felt as if she glowed. She nodded as the tears fell, over her cheeks, his hands, his lips, kissing her from ear to ear, his murmured words, "You are my mission now, Eva."

"I accept," she said, laughing.

"But there are some things you must know, Eva. I was going to kill the king." Jamie let her smile fade before he continued, "You heard this, in the tavern."

She shifted, but not away. She only turned a little, slid her hips closer, her shoulders back, so she could look at him more directly. "Yes. I heard."

He gave a clipped nod. Why was he saying this? Why was it leaking out now?

Because he'd been wrong.

Having thought himself a barren plain, Jamie realized now he was a reservoir. And he ached. Ached with shame for running, for want of going home. And he never could. Never did. Found every reason under the sun to induce John to send others to Everoot when judicial eyres brought the king's men up North, when civil unrest required royal forces, when itinerations rounded northward to occupy the empty castle at Everoot. Jamie had stayed away, ever away, ferociously, desperately away.

It was a shameful thing, these two little facts, one that had taken no more than a moment, the other that took the rest of his life: run from your father's murderers, and never go home again.

But now . . . now he wanted something. He wanted Eva.

His palm rested lightly on her chest, and he looked her in the eye as he revealed his shameful self.

"He killed my father. That is why I was willing to kill the king."

"I imagine it was a hot, driving thing," she said quietly.

He pressed onward. "And when John killed my father, I ran. I watched my father drop to his knees, and then I ran away."

There it was, the burning whole of him. Out in the open. He had to open his mouth to keep breathing.

Eva nodded slowly, thoughtfully. "Yes. I can see this. It would be the only sensible thing to do."

He felt unsteady at this validation.

"This is just what a person does when they are faced by men with swords who are much bigger than they. It is what I would do. I would venture to say it is what your father would have wanted you to do."

He could hear his father's voice even now, ordering him to run, even as he went down.

She looked over. "This is why you do not do the sensible thing now, Jamie, no? Ry worries that you are trying to get yourself killed. But you will not do that anymore, will you?" She put her hands on the sides of his face and pulled him down to her face, close. "I would much prefer you stay here. With me. We will go to my river and grow things."

He felt washed through, but managed a faint smile. "I have a question, Eva. Only you can answer it."

The braziers had burned down and only one candle burned now, guttering in its holder. The moon had risen, filling the room with silvery light. Eva considered him for a long moment, then propped herself on an elbow, facing him. Her hair spilled down over her arm.

"I am prepared," she said in a solemn voice.

"Why did John kill my mother?" He forced his voice level. "For years he'd been sending gifts north, as he often did to widows and wards."

She nodded. "Yes, John has a great deal of patience with those who cannot hurt him. He ought to have been a falconer. For years, he was most kind to the folk at Everoot."

"Then why?" He pulled his gaze away from hers and focused on the glimpse of a rounded white shoulder visible beneath her dark hair.

"Jamie, I cannot say whether or no John murdered your mother. I know for certes he killed d'Endshire, for I saw that myself. He claimed he was within his rights. I do not know if that is so or not. Was it treasonous for a vowed vassal to do what they did?" He heard her take a breath. "But your mother, the countess. . . . Jamie, I think she might have died of a broken heart. That was the second man she'd loved whom the king had slain."

He lifted his gaze. "Second?"

She nodded slowly. He let it lie a moment, then nodded too. "What treason did John claim was done at Everoot?"

She swallowed. He watched it move down her throat. "The treasures."

"Treasures," he echoed.

"There are treasures rumored to be in Everoot's cellars, Jamie. *Your* cellars."

"I know that," he said quietly. He'd known it since he could walk, since his father had led him down the steep, hidden stairwell behind the lord's chambers, taken him into a dusty vault filled with bright metals and gems and other things that Jamie had not understood and had never been explained.

When it's time, son, his father had said, *you will know. One day, you will be Everoot. Until then, I or another caretaker will hold the keys.*

But now his father was dead, and no caretaker had ever shown himself.

Eva was speaking quietly. "Your mother and Roger's father were trying to spirit these treasures away before John came for them. They feared the state he was in. He needed coin for his wars, he needed support against the papacy, he needed—" She shook her head impatiently. "To be thought well of. He needed inducements to make people love him, no? Your mother feared he would recall the forgotten treasures of Everoot. She was trying to get them away."

"And I left her to it," he said, his words devoid of emotion, no change in tone or tenor, just a single pitch, flat and cold.

Eva tipped her head to the side. "You were a child when your father was killed."

"Not when my mother was." Anger sawed at him, making him sharp with the one person in the world who did not deserve anything but gentleness. He took hold of her arm and said through a clenched jaw, "When my mother died, I was in France, serving the king. Preparing my vengeance. All those years, letting her live alone, thinking I was dead."

She tolerated his fierceness in the room, neither rejecting it nor joining in it. She just watched him. Slowly he loosened his hold. His hand fell back to the mattress.

Then she tipped in, so close her nose almost touched his.

"Your mother was not alone, Jamie. *I* was with her. And she loved you very much. She knew you were not dead. She told me this, many times."

"I have thought of her," he said thickly. "Every day, for twenty years."

"Perhaps she felt your regard, for she said it very often, very calmly, a thing she knew completely. *My son is not dead. He is too strong for John to kill, and too smart to come back.*"

He felt a roaring wash up the back of his skull, blowing white noise through his body. Was the bed shaking under him? The muscles in his arm, which had been propping him up, felt weak.

She kissed him, then sat up. "I would like to show you something."

He gave a ragged laugh and dropped back to the bed. "All right."

She started pushing the covers aside. "You have perhaps spoken with Angus, and he has perhaps told you what I did to his table?"

Jamie laughed. "I have and he did. I think you made a Christian out of him again, Eva, and that was a bone-hard task, for Angus has been past penance for many years now."

"He is hurting, that is all." She slipped her pale undertunic over her head and reached for his hand. It tingled, as if she were lightning touching him. She squeezed, then unfolded her graceful body and got out of the bed. "But he is quite angry with you. I encouraged him in this, of course."

He felt the smile rise up out of the wash of his head, bold and wide. "Of course."

"We are not fond of knights, he or I."

"Nay."

"But I very much like to paint." She smiled at him. "And I very much loved your mother."

"Did you?" he said, but it sounded dim to his own ears. The center of his chest suddenly went heavy and crushed, as if a steel punch had landed. Dense, as if packed with a hot ball of heat.

A heart, he thought dimly. *This is what it feels like to have a heart.*

She was wrecking him. Ruining him for ruin.

She walked to the brazier. "I have never met Angus's mother, but he thought it was a goodly recollection nonetheless. But, Jamie, I lived with your very good mother for *many* years, and I would like to paint her for you."

"I would like that," he rasped, and did not recognize his own voice. He pushed himself up to sit against the bedstead. He felt drunk. He felt sparkling. He felt as if a ghost had punched him in the head and gone right through him, so while there was no pain, he was reeling. Eva walked to the wall.

"Angus will not mind that I brought these little paints with me," she murmured, "but it is mostly with charcoal from the brazier."

Then, across the whole of the chamber wall, while she told him about his mother and the small things they'd shared during the years Eva had lived there, and how the countess had pined for Jamie on the ramparts each evening, willing her son to come home, believing when no one else did that he was yet alive, while Eva did all these heartrending things, she painted his mother across the wall of the room with her fingers and hands, until they were black and red and blue. For him.

When she was done, she stepped back and turned to face him, smiling, her arm flung out, gesturing to the wall, as if he had not been watching every motion of her generous, dancing body for the last half hour. He felt as if the freshest breeze were blowing. The moonlight spilled over his bare feet, sliding down his shins, and he sat, stunned.

"Is this her, Jamie?"

He felt as if he'd run up a mountainside. He felt as if he'd tumbled down a crevasse. He felt as if he *were* a mountain, pushed up out of the hard-rock past that was his life.

"That is her," he rasped, pushing to his feet.

The power washed back into his stunned limbs. The room felt smaller, he felt taller. He was the mountain. He took three steps to reach Eva's side and pulled her to him. He lowered his mouth over hers and paused just above her lips. She brought her painted hands down and rested them on his shoulders.

"For twenty years, I have been a man of one deed, Eva. But you are my mission now. You are wind and water and air, and you—"

He stopped short. There was no end to that sentence; it might go on for years, all the things Eva was, so he simply stopped talking and kissed her.

They stood in the moonlight, their arms resting on each other's hips, and softly, slowly, kissed each other for a long time.

"So you will not tie me to a tree and leave me for dead?" she murmured as he began to move his attention down her neck. She put her hands on his shoulders, trying to pull him up.

He resisted, but he did pause and throw her a glance. "I did not tie you to a tree."

"No, that is so. And yet, is it chivalrous of you to mark the distinction?"

He moved down her neck, every so often scraping the edge of his teeth against her hot skin, until he felt her body begin to press into him. "I will not leave you for dead," he said, his words muffled by her neck.

"But will you," Eva gasped as he nipped her earlobe, harder than she'd expected, "tie me up?"

He lifted his head from his ministrations. "Would you like me to?"

And, oh, as Jamie was naught but dangerous by any

measure, the danger of *this* notion, with his darkened blue eyes on her, his calloused palms cupping her naked chest, was almost dizzying.

He leaned close to her ear. "Shall I, Eva?" Even as his voice, soft and gentle in its rough-edged rumble, coaxed her to relax, his hand made a wonderful, snapping tension sizzle through her blood. He skimmed his hand up the side of her ribs, up to her arm. Then he grasped it loosely but indefinably trapped it behind her back.

"Shall I do that, Eva?" he said, keeping up his quiet, sensual demands that were making her dizzy. "I am yours. I will do as you wish."

Fire exploded in her body, already arched up to his. His fingers closed around her other wrist and he pressed them together.

"You see?" she gasped, as his eyes darkened even further. "I knew, in the end, you would be chivalrous with me."

"This isn't the end, Eva," he growled. "And I am not chivalrous. Stand against the wall."

Her mouth rounded, half between a gasp and a smile. "The wall? Why?"

He looked at her. "So you do not fall over when I make you come."

Her jaw dropped entirely as he cupped the nape of her neck and, holding her, walked her backward. When she hit the wall, he reached over to the bed and plucked up the ribbons that had been discarded, tangled amid their lovemaking.

"Turn around."

"Jamie," she whispered, cautionary.

Hands on her shoulders, he turned her to face the wall, then, in silence, raked his fingers through her hair, from her skull to the ends in his hand. Eva's head tipped back into the shockingly gentle caress. Slowly, inexpertly, he braided her hair with the wine-red ribbons. Each tug of his fingers sent shivering cascades of chill down her scalp and back. Her whole body trembled, as if she'd been caught in a rainfall.

"Look at me," he ordered in a low voice, and when she turned again, he bent to kiss her, first her mouth, then her neck; then he dropped to his knees before her, his mouth sliding down her body, kissing as he went.

The air rushed out of her lungs. "Jamie!" she cried.

Although it was the first evidence of true *exclamation* that he'd heard since he'd known her—he must try this activity more often—Jamie chose to ignore her. Or rather, overwhelm her. He began by affecting nonchalance. And great ignorance.

"What?" he murmured, testing the span of her ribs with his hands.

"What are you doing down there?" she asked worriedly.

He slid his palms up, resting his thumbs beneath the curve of her breasts. "I dropped something."

She laughed. It was an ineffable sensation, her body vibrating from enjoyment *he* had given her. To the extent it was in his power, he would give her everything her heart desired, except that she desired nothing but peace and leeks and a little cottage by a river. So he would give her those things. And this. He slid his mouth lower. As often as she wished. Should she evidence a desire for horses or castles or cabbage, he would see to those things as well.

He ran his mouth across her belly like he was measuring the space of a room, from one side to the other, marking her with slow, tender kisses. It was painful, holding himself to such gentle measures when she was making unsteady little sounds of desire, when her hips occasionally arched out from the wall, pushing against his collarbone in unbridled little thrusts.

When what he wished to do was spin her around, bend her

over, plant her palms on the wall, and thrust inside her so hard she'd throw back her head and howl.

But she might misunderstand the generosity of the gesture. So instead, on his knees, he kissed her slowly and wetly, with only the lightest, sweetest nips. She possibly didn't even notice his hand slipping up her inner thigh. The curls at the ends of her long hair and the silken shreds at the ends of the ribbons tickled his ears and nose. He pushed them out of the way.

His reward came a moment later, when her fingers fluttered down to rest lightly on the top of his head.

He slid more boldly up her thigh and pushed against her knee with his forearm, nudging it to the side. "Now, Eva," he murmured, "do not make this difficult."

Her fingers tensed in his hair. "Make what difficult?"

He bent to the dark curls and touched his tongue to the heated juncture below. Her hips whipped out from the wall on a shocked gasp, which only served to bring them closer together, so that his hands cupped her buttocks, his mouth pressed tightly to her hot, scented wetness.

"This," he answered thickly, and flicked his tongue up, hard on the slicked crest of her.

Her fingers clenched in his hair and her head dropped back against the wall on a long, low moan. No, she would not make this difficult.

With one hand, he exerted a small pressure on her leg, urging her to lift it. She did, bending her knee, and he draped it over his shoulder. This made her womanhood his entire world, the focus of his devotion, and he let her know it. He spread her apart with his thumb and licked her senseless. Her hips moved with reckless little pushes that forced his tongue and teeth against her harder. His head spun, his cock pounded, and his breath came as ragged and shallow as hers as he delved into her with his tongue, then slid back up to the swirling nub and sucked it into his mouth swiftly. She gave a strangled cry. He sucked again, teasing her, sliding his fingers around her slippery entrance, but not pushing in.

"Please, Jamie," she whispered.

He savagely pushed one up inside her. She gave a low, sobbing cry.

"Please what, Eva?"

Her knees were weakening, he felt it. She tilted her face down, making her hair fall in a dark curtain around him. "Please, find what you were looking for."

He gave a low laugh and knew, in that moment, the world meant nothing. All that mattered was right here, assuring Eva she'd done the right thing by giving herself over to him. Eva, his love. "I've found it."

Tongue, thumb, fingers, lips, he focused everything on her, glorying in her response as she exploded into a passionate, unbridled orgasm stretched between him and the wall, until her legs gave out entirely and she slowly, gracefully, collapsed to the floor.

"You fell even though the wall was there," he murmured, catching her.

"I am a weak woman. Floors are not for . . . this," she whispered, just barely, in his ear. Her arms were weakly draped around his shoulders.

"Floors are for anything I need them for." But notwithstanding such talk, he lifted her in his arms and dropped her onto the bed.

They did not sleep for a long time. They talked, languidly, in the rhythm of sated lovers: words, then silence, then more words, as they watched the moon unfurl its full light. They spoke of animals they might keep and the best angles for roofs and where Roger might wish to stay when he found a woman of his own. Neither of them pointed out that, of course, Roger would be staying in England now. He was the d'Endshire heir.

Neither spoke of Jamie's being Everoot's heir.

Nor did they speak of Father Peter or King John or anything farther off than the walls of this room and their hopes.

For the first time in her life, Eva felt safe. She was embracing this night of brightness, of Jamie and all his dark goodness. There was only one blemish on it all, and no matter how she turned her back or looked the other way, still it lay there, a shadow on her sun.

Jamie thought her an orphan. But she was not. One must have dead parents to be an orphan. Hers were not dead.

It was much worse than that.

"SOMETHING is wrong," the king muttered.

Brian de Lisle, his chief commander and right arm to Jamie's left, looked up from the papers he'd been delivering. He'd been headed to Windsor when an outrider had found him and detoured him here to this small, wooded encampment, a day's ride from Everoot. He had been quite surprised to learn the king was in the North, heading for Everoot in secret and in haste.

But then, John was known for his energetic and abrupt itinerations. And his paranoia. And his inability to tolerate even the smallest dissension amid his noble ranks.

Which is, of course, why he had so much dissension amid his noble ranks.

"My lord?" Brian said, laying down the papers. The king did not so much as glance at them. The wardrobe official did, but he quickly sat back again when John rose from his seat.

"Something has happened. Something is amiss." The king swung about, the hem of his robes rising, then settled back as he fixed his gaze on Brian.

He raised his eyebrows. "My lord?"

"Everoot and d'Endshire have been empty too long. They have plagued me too long."

There was nothing new here.

"I am going to ensure, once and for all, that they cease to be an albatross."

"How, my lord?"

John pulled the papers to him, glanced at them idly, then looked up. "I shall grant them. To the highest bidder."

Sell them, Brian thought, impressed. The king was going to sell the estates of the missing heirs.

"Everoot has been a thorn in my side for far too long. It is a curse, which is why I have ne'er tried to fill it," the king snapped. But Brian knew a better reason to explain John's reluctance to fill the Everoot earldom, even after the decades-long absence of the heir: fear.

If the powerful Everoot heir was out there somewhere, lurking . . . well, in short, the king was afraid.

Additionally, of course, for the king to seize yet another estate from another noble family would only hammer another nail into his political coffin. But in the end, John had not filled Everoot because of fear, fear the heir was out there, lurking. Fear of what he would do when he discovered the king had taken his birthright.

Perhaps retrieve those fabled treasures in the vaults and bring John's kingdom crumbling down?

"How much loyalty do you think Everoot could buy me, de Lisle?"

"A great deal, my lord," he said slowly.

The richest honor in the realm, the earldom of Everoot. The powerful barony of d'Endshire all along its eastern borders. How often did such glittering riches come up on the auction block?

Once in a lifetime.

God's bones, de Lisle might just bid on it himself.

The king gave a clipped nod. "Deliver the news to these few select men." He rattled off a few names. "Keep it secret; no one else shall know until the deal is struck. Then they all shall find out together: the rebels, Langton, the French king. The country shall fall, shire by shire, and there will be no need for any charter a'tall."

Fifty-three

They stood in the stables early the next morning, checking weapons and speaking in low murmurs by the light of torches that burned against the foggy air with a ruddy glow.

"There should be a back entryway to the vintners' hall," Jamie said in a hushed voice as he rechecked the buckle of his sword belt. Roger handed him another small, thin blade. He bent and tucked it in his boot. "It may be guarded, but you can manage that, can you not? You and Roger?"

Roger snapped a nod. "Aye, sir."

Ry looked equally grim and far less enthused. "Aye."

Jamie paused in sliding a dagger back into its sheath on his leg and tipped his head up. Dark hair fell forward to his jaw. Eva resisted the urge to push it back. She was always resisting hair-pushing urges for the men she loved. Instead, she listened to him address Ry's unspoken but loud concern.

"Have you something to say, Ry?"

Ry's regard was close and level. "You need to have a better plan than 'I go in and come out with the priest.'"

Jamie paused. "It sounds like a goodly one to me."

"Aye," Roger whispered.

Ry and Eva exchanged glances of the long-suffering sort. "I

believe Ry speaks to the 'how,'" Eva explained kindly, to ease their way through this complicated idea.

Jamie shoved his last blade in and Roger turned to her. They both shoved hair behind their ears. She sighed quietly.

"I shall go in however needs must, Ry, but only if it comes to it will I draw a sword. We'll be in and out before they can gather their wits."

"That takes care of coming *out* the door, Jamie," Ry pointed out. "First you must get in."

"How about if I break down the door?"

"And then? When they all jump you and grab you?"

"You'll come crashing in?" Jamie said hopefully, but with a hardness to his voice. Eva saw an equally hard look on Ry's face, perhaps because, in this, he realized Jamie might at last accomplish his purpose of discovering the danger that was too much. Ry did not know Jamie had made her a promise to no longer do such things.

"I can only do so much," Ry insisted.

"It will have to be enough. I have nothing more."

"You have me," Roger said into the tension. Jamie and Ry turned. Roger looked pale, but he repeated himself. "You'll have my arm."

Jamie clapped him on the arm and nodded.

"And as for me," Eva chimed in.

They all turned and looked at her.

"You," Jamie said coldly, "will wait here with the horses. Right here." He pointed at a particular spot. Eva moved an inch to the left to occupy it. He was not amused.

"Precisely. Right there."

The curt order belied the emotion she now knew underlay it. His face was set in hardness, his jaw tight, his eyes shadowed by dim torchlight and banked emotion. He needed focus and single-mindedness now, not worry or strong emotions. As she had no intention of doing anything *but* waiting here with the horses, very docilely, she gave a tranquil nod.

"This will make the horses happy. They like me. Yours especially. I am fairly certain he likes me more than you."

His gaze stayed on her a moment more, then the men went back to finalizing their plans, which seemed to consist of "I hit . . . then you slash . . . and we run . . ."

Suddenly Angus poked his head in from where he'd been keeping watch out front. "Sun's rising," was all he said.

Jamie turned and, without any explanation to Ry or Roger, although surely they did not need one, took her by the waist, lifted her up on her toes, and delivered a single swift, hard kiss, which made her heart hammer. He set her down and turned away without a word.

The three of them strode off into the misty predawn to see the slave trader Mouldin and ransom back the priest.

THEY strode through the wakening world. The gates were open, and early fairgoers and traveling merchants and the entertainment—tumblers, tricksters, the men who ran the dogfights—flowed into the town and spread out through the streets inside.

The old vintners' guild hall occupied a corner lot and was abutted on either side by shops. Across the way was a tavern. But inside, it would be deserted.

Smart choice. Enough people passing by just outside to keep people in line, but still deserted, with sufficient shadowy corners and upper balconies to make the others worry on where Mouldin had placed all his men.

Jamie, of course, knew precisely where they were: where he and Ry had left them after dragging them into the woods five days ago.

Some people were around, early shoppers. Roger and Ry and Angus went up the back alley and Jamie strode boldly up to the door. As anticipated, no one even approached.

He paused, closed his eyes to help quicken their adjustment to the darkness he knew he would find inside, and flexed his hand around his sword hilt. How many times had he stood thusly, about to go in and report to fitzWalter, his old mentor and trainer in assassination? To the king? Always to men he had no respect for but was nonetheless bound to?

No longer, though.

He was done with it. He'd told Eva true. He wanted very much to see her cottage, to repair her roof, revel in her body, make her feel safe. He would take Eva, and everything else could go to hell.

He unslung his sword. Keeping his eyes shut, he kicked the door open and leapt to the side, out of the doorway, out of the light. A sigh of coldness extruded from the cavernous interior as if it had substance. It smelled of old wood and cobwebs.

He opened his eyes.

A moment passed in silence, then a voice said quietly, "Enter."

Two torches were burning, illuminating a few other figures in shadowy blotches. Sunlight leaked weakly in through the line of shuttered windows on the upper floors.

He heard someone shift.

"God's teeth," the person hissed. FitzWalter. Good, he was here. "You always were one for sneaking up, Lost."

"Aye. You trained us well."

Silence for a moment. Jamie's eyes searched the interior. There was fitzWalter, standing in a wash of pale light. He was smiling faintly.

"Ah, yes. I heard you saw Chance."

"It was fleeting."

Another small grin lifted Baynard's glossy beard. "She was hog-tied and had a rag stuffed in her mouth, her hands this close to being broken."

"What I meant was, it did not take long."

Baynard gave a bark of coarse laughter.

"Jamie Lost."

Mouldin's gravelly voice was recognizable anywhere, even to Jamie, who'd only heard it once, on the streets of London. Jamie turned toward it.

"I am honored," Mouldin said. "In a hundred years, I never expected you to show up here. But I am pleased to have two such esteemed emissaries from King John." Mouldin turned and indicated the other shadowy figure in the room, standing against the far wall. Cig. Damn. "How sad for you all that you cannot kill me."

Jamie met Cig's eyes.

"You bastard," Cig said in a low voice.

From the corner of his eye, Jamie saw fitzWalter grin.

Mouldin spoke, amusement in his voice. "Tell me, Jamie, are there two parties bargaining, or are you making a separate offer? In other words, where do your loyalties lie?"

Jamie held Mouldin's gaze for a long, silent moment. "Have you hurt the priest in any way?"

Mouldin grinned. "Lessened his value? Not whatsoever. He can speak and think and excite you with his wit. Has a bit of a rheumy cough, but naught a physic could not remedy, one hopes, as so many hopes are pinned on him. Particularly yours, Lost."

Cig's gaze burned through the flickering shadows. "You're a dead man, Jamie."

Mouldin gave a short bark of laughter. "And the deterioration continues before mine eyes. I admit, I cannot fathom a better ally to have in one's camp than Lost, but then, maybe we do not know who claims his allegiance?"

Cig and Mouldin looked at fitzWalter.

"I am not his," Jamie said simply.

Mouldin might have clapped his hands, he appeared so pleased by this. "So you *are* an independent agent, Lost. This is tremendously gratifying." The mocking amusement vanished as he turned to fitzWalter and ordered curtly, "Your men, outside." He turned to Cig. "Yours as well. Four blocks down the hill or the negotiations are canceled."

Neither man moved.

Mouldin's voice hardened. "Should you think to trifle with me on this, I have my own guards already placed. More importantly, there are other parties equally eager to have a go at placing a bid for Peter of London. 'Twas professional courtesy to offer him to the rebels and the king firstly. But the King of France showed marked interest when the possibility was put to him, so I say again: your men down the hill. And your swords here." He pointed to his side.

FitzWalter's soldiers tromped out sullenly. Surely no one believed they were going to position themselves a full four blocks off, but then, no one believed Mouldin could be here alone, without his own men scattered all about, in the tavern next door, in the streets outside.

But for the moment, Jamie was strangely allied with Mouldin. Telling Fitz that Mouldin had no men would only mean he'd attack, hard and fast, and Jamie would lose his chance of ever regaining Peter of London.

Mouldin seemed to realize the irony as well. Or perhaps it was pure malevolent enjoyment at the proceedings. In any event, while everyone was ordering his men out and away, Mouldin turned and smiled at Jamie.

FitzWalter and Cig laid their blades down, making a steely pile. Mouldin gestured to Jamie. "All of them, Lost."

When the bidders were as disarmed as they were ever going to be, the negotiations began.

"Shall we commence?" Mouldin stood by the back wall, nearest to the other door. He toed the underside of a short bench and dragged it out. He rested his boot on it, leaning forward to rest an elbow.

Silence.

"Come, I brought you all together for a purpose. To out*bid* one another. You do know what you are bargaining for? The king has offered a thousand livres. And the rebels?" He looked at fitzWalter.

"Two. And transport across the Channel to Normandy, for you will surely need it after this."

Mouldin laughed. "How kind, seeing as you all are planning to murder me once the transfer is done. And for this reason, I do not know why you don't offer me the crown jewels, Cigogné. And why the rebels do not offer me more yet."

"Then I ought kill you now," snapped fitzWalter.

Mouldin smiled. "Father Peter is not here. If I die, so does he. What a loss. Come, you cannot think these offers meet the mark of Peter of London's merit."

"He's old and sick," snapped Cig.

"You are not in pursuit of a hale warrior. You want his mind. And his pen, and the incriminating things he draws with them."

FitzWalter took a step forward. "Have you brought no proof of your claims? Not even the finger of the priest or one of his sketches?"

Mouldin smiled. "How interested would you be in a full-color scene of King John murdering the earl of Everoot?"

In the quiet room, with only the echoes of boots and

laughter from outside, the sound of Cig sucking in a breath was harsh. Jamie flexed his fingers around an empty sheath.

"'Tis quite an impressive sketch," Mouldin said. "I was there that day with the king. I know how accurate Peter of London's depiction is." He looked over and pinned his hard gaze on Jamie. "Knowing this, have you an offer?"

Jamie appraised the distance to the stairs behind him. Four running steps.

Fitz shifted impatiently. "Did Peter give you no news of the heirs?"

"Oh, 'tis more than *news* of the heirs. The heirs are here in England, are they not, Jamie? All of them. Father Peter is the magnet. 'Whither goest the priest, so goeth the heirs.' All of them."

Fitz stepped forward. "She?"

The hair on the back of Jamie's neck started rising. "Who?"

FitzWalter made an impatient gesture. "Father Peter is not the crucible. It is she. The one who took the heir d'Endshire. His 'nurse.' She is no nurse."

A cascade of coldness moved through Jamie, from his chest to his arms to his hands and down to his legs. "What is she?"

FitzWalter gave a bark of laughter, so it was Mouldin who replied in a low, cunning voice.

"A princess."

Fifty~four

Eva stood in the stables and looked at the horses. It was warm and quiet and comforting in the stables, with the crunchy hay and the furry, softly snuffling beasts.

She was not reckless or stupid. She was well aware that since this matter involved men, it would almost certainly also involve fighting. She was further aware that she could do little in a fight but get killed. She was not interested in this whatsoever.

But she was *most* interested in getting everyone she loved out of England alive. And not tortured on her behalf.

Jamie seemed confident that people did and said things when they had blades held at their throats, and this was often true. But other times, when they wanted something dearly, they resisted revealing things even to their last breath.

If Jamie did not yet know who she was, he would soon figure it out. And right now, it did not matter if he knew *who* she was; he knew *where* she was. Roger knew. Father Peter knew.

Even if she ran, right now, started running and never stopped, people would question Jamie and Roger and Father Peter about her and her whereabouts. And Jamie, like Father Peter and Roger, would reveal nothing.

Then they would be hurt. Perhaps terribly. Protecting her.

Eva had no qualms about hiding. She'd done so with great

success and vigor her entire life. But now everything was unraveling, and it was wrong to allow others to be stuck with swords on her account.

This could not be.

She patted the horse on the nose and, in a dim, faraway way, saw her hand was trembling. She turned and walked out the door.

She told herself she had no intention of being taken. She was no martyr. She had infinite faith in Jamie's ability to rescue her from a castle tower if need be; this was not in question. But he needed not to be hanging upside down from a rack in order to do so.

So, she told herself, this was a matter of self-preservation. The thought made her feel better.

She looked down. Her other hand was shaking now too. Her knees were made of broth. Her lips felt cold and tingly.

She stayed to the shadows and kept walking.

THE shock of Mouldin's words moved through Jamie in waves.

"She is the daughter from John's first marriage. The king hid her the moment she was born, and few know of her existence. But John always had his eye on the throne, and his first wife, Isabella of Gloucester, was neither so richly endowed nor so noble nor so nubile as Isabella of Angoulême."

Jamie shook his head. "That marriage was annulled," he said, fighting off the stubborn wet heaviness that was entering his limbs, making him want to sit down. "She has no significance in this; the king has many bastards."

Eva, of royal blood. Eva, on the run, hunted by the great and powerful, a threat to the crown. Eva in danger.

"Lowborn, wenches, mistresses," fitzWalter said dismissively. "He has children by such women as these. This one, she is born of a countess."

"She is not legal," Jamie said dully.

FitzWalter gave one of his gravelly barks of laughter. "What matters that? The king of France just had his illegitimate children legitimatized. How hard would it be for us to do?"

This ephemeral cloud of aggressive hope fitzWalter was spewing had substance. For hundreds of years, the lines of inheritance and rule had been more about a powerful sword than legitimacy. It was not so far back in time that England had been conquered and ruled by a bastard. Sooth, King John had murdered his own nephew Prince Arthur to silence the opposition to his own ascendancy, for even twenty years ago the question of rightful inheritance ran hot and sticky. The answers were hardening, but not yet solid.

In these dark days, people were looking for any good cause, anything binding upon which they could hang their homage. An illegitimate daughter was not such a peg. But a royal-born daughter married to a powerful, ambitious baron?

It could bring down a kingship.

"So, is she here?" Fitz demanded.

Mouldin answered, but he was looking directly at Jamie as he did. "Aye, she is here."

Things had just rounded the bend. The only way to come out of this was to push it further, faster, than anyone expected. It was all going to hell. Swords would be drawn, people would die, and the only way to come out the victor was to be the instigator. Set the terms.

Everyone was readying himself, but "readying" was not "ready" and Jamie made his move. He reached down and yanked the small blade out of his boot.

"Enough!" he roared, throwing up his hands, stepping forward. Mouldin immediately stepped back and swept up his blade. His one remaining soldier stepped up to flank him. "You fools," Jamie shouted, circling. "A priest? We stand here fighting over the entrails of a *priest*? Keep him." He was shouting. "I want the heirs."

"Nay," Cig shouted, leaping forward, scrambling for the pile of swords. "He does not represent the king anymore. Jésu, Jamie—"

"Not on my life will you have even one of the heirs," roared fitzWalter, knocking Cig aside.

The door burst open and men came pouring in, and amid them Jamie saw Chance's blond head. Jamie lunged forward, crashing into Mouldin's henchman, knocking him out of the way. Then he rolled to his feet and grabbed Mouldin before he could run, wrenched his arm up and behind his back, almost to breaking, and put his blade at his throat. The room froze.

"Now, Hunter," Jamie said, his voice low, his gaze on the frozen figures of fitzWalter and Cig, "you will tell me where Peter of London is, and you will live to see another day."

Mouldin was breathing heavily, his eyes angry but calm. "The priest spoke of you, Jamie. I know who you are."

Jamie jerked him. "He did not tell you that."

"He did not have to."

"Where is he?"

Mouldin shook his head. "You will never find him. And she will never tell."

Heat flowed into Jamie's limbs. Confidence. "Do you mean Magda?"

Mouldin froze, then roared in anger and threw up his arms, a powerful move from a powerful man. It released the frozen room, and fighting exploded. Jamie let the move throw him backward, twisting to dive for his sword.

"Get the priest," shouted fitzWalter.

"Bring me Lost!" Cig roared.

Jamie's hand closed around the hilt of his blade and a

measure of calm suffused his body. He bounded to his feet, and the room turned into a vine garden of slashing steel. Jamie held his own, allowing himself to be backed up to a wall. When he was close enough, he leaned to the side and shouted out the window, "Now would be a ripe time!"

He needn't have bothered because Roger and Ry and Angus had just burst through the door.

And at the edge of his vision, Jamie saw Chance disappear out the back.

Fifty-five

Eva crept up the back alley. She was skilled with alleys after her time in England. She hurried up, soft as a mouse, a minute behind Ry and Roger.

But there was also no need to be stealthy like a mouse, she realized as she drew near. It sounded like a shipwreck inside, with waves and wood cracking and men being tossed overboard. She withdrew her blade and took a deep breath, just outside the door.

She froze when she caught sight of someone coming out. Pressing herself to the wall, she watched the willowy figure. Was that not the woman she had seen with Jamie?

The woman saw her and stilled, paused as if in indecision, then turned the other way. The woman glanced back over her shoulder and whispered, "You can have him. I will take the rest. But the king is coming for him. He is doomed."

Long, glossy hair swished around the corner of the doorway.

Another loud crash came from inside, and Eva turned for the door.

Right now she had to take care of Jamie. She could not worry on Jamie's women.

The battle was fierce. Men were scattered about, groaning or bleeding or dying or all three, but a few men fought on.

Unfortunately, fitzWalter was one of them, and he was facing Jamie, standing near an overturned table, sword in hand. From the edge of his vision, Jamie saw Roger engaged with one of the soldiers, holding his own but clearly outmatched by the powerful, seasoned fighter. Ry was fighting Cigogné, while Angus appeared to be holding back two men.

"Jamie," fitzWalter said, holding out his hand, up slightly. "This will not go well for you." He took a breath. "But it need not end this way."

"How do you see it ending?"

FitzWalter took a step forward. "You could join me yet. I can give you land, Jamie. I know Softsword has balked on that. He has the acumen of a goat." FitzWalter lowered his hand slightly. "John has no chance anymore, Jamie. You know that. When the heirs are exposed, everything will be tainted. *Everything.* And, Jamie, I am telling you, all we need is a taint. The whiff of something odious enough to sway the countryside. There are enough people who wish it tainted. John cannot stand against it.

"The king's son is seven years old. I could run him over with my pony cart. But the daughter?" fitzWalter said, stepping closer. "She is a princess, and in these ravaged times, it only takes a man with ambition and an army to wed her and claim England as his. He'd have to be willing to fight for it. Which hardly qualifies as an obstacle."

"You have someone in mind," Jamie said coldly.

"Several."

"She is not for sale."

FitzWalter stilled. "Jamie. You and the king's daughter?" He barked in laughter, then met Jamie's eye. "If you want her, mayhap you could be the one. Nothing is decided. I can still use you, raise you up." He took a step closer, his voice lower. "Something in you wants greatness, Jamie. I can give it to you."

"Something in you wants to die," Jamie retorted, pushing the overturned table out of the way with his boot.

FitzWalter raised his sword, grinning as blood ran down into his beard from a split lip. "You're making a mistake. We can end this war right now."

"You revel in war," Jamie said coldly.

"It serves me not to rule scorched earth," fitzWalter said in a low tone. "If you join with me, if we have the daughter, the king will go away. Ignobly away, but away."

"Never," said Jamie. "Never again."

FitzWalter's coaxing smile turned to a sneer. "You think you are too good for *me?* You're a goddamned mercenary."

"You're a goddamned traitor."

"This is as good as it gets for the likes of you, Lost. You cannot think the king will let you have her. His *daughter?* To a common soldier? If you want her, Jamie, I am the way."

FitzWalter took another step forward, his hand up in a placating gesture. Then, swift as a whip, he snapped his hand down over Jamie's hand and hilt, gripping tight. Jamie ripped his arm up, but fitzWalter's hold stiffened. Their faces were inches apart, their arms trembling from the pressure.

"Change your mind before I have to kill you, Lost," he hissed.

"Everoot," Jamie corrected, and ripped the sword free with a mighty jerk. "And I have ne'er been lost."

FitzWalter went stumbling backward, his sword flying. It skittered across the floor, out of reach. His face was confused and shocked as he backed up. Then it cleared into comprehension. "God's bones, I see it now. You *are* Everoot."

Jamie advanced, forcing fitzWalter back until he tripped and fell. Then he stepped forward and put his sword tip to Fitz's throat. There was no rush of satisfaction, no elation at besting this old enemy. There was only the desire to be done.

"Why?" FitzWalter's voice dropped into a hoarse sound. "I could have made you great. Why did you not tell me who you were? *Why did you betray me?*"

Jamie chose his words slowly, methodically. "Because John is anointed and you are not. Because he is the king and you are not. Because, upon a time, all you had to do was present a single man, one decent man, and I would have supported you to the end days. But you could not do even so much as that."

"I will now," he said, grabbing Jamie's wrist in a weak fist. "I will take counsel with you. We already have London, and the French king sails for England—"

"So England shall heel for Philip now?"

"But if you think otherwise, I shall listen. We shall all listen. Come, Jamie. Reconsider. It can all be yours. Everoot, all her lands, her castles. They stretch from Scotland to Wales."

"I will claim Everoot neither for king nor for rebelmen. If there are no other choices, it shall go unclaimed."

FitzWalter seemed to snarl. His hand tightened on Jamie's wrist. "Then you had best slay me now, Lost, for I am surely going to kill you."

Jamie leaned in close and made a flat-palmed swipe against his own throat. "I am full to here of killing," he said harshly. "I am awash in blood. I am sick to death of it."

"I am not."

"Then I suppose I will see you in Hell." He cracked Fitz's head against the ground with a thud, his eyes rolling back in his head. Jamie stared down at him. Something had just ended. Something dirty and half done was now . . . done.

Ry had his boot on Cig's shoulder, giving a final yank to the rope that bound him to his mate, his feet to his neck. He dropped the rope and Jamie strode over and clapped him on the shoulder.

"My thanks," Jamie said roughly.

Angus had finally taken Mouldin down. Dead, an inglorious end to an ignominious life, but even Mouldin had someone to mourn him: Magda. Who knew where Peter of London was.

Roger stood above another soldier, who was flat on his back and . . . Eva crouched beside him, her little knife tipping against a vein in his throat.

"Ah, but you see, it could be an accident," she was saying in a friendly voice. "I have it just so, against a very important part of you. The tip slips, just so, and that is as good as intent."

Jamie stepped up behind her and touched her on her back. She got to her feet and backed away. Roger's eyes were fixed on his prey, and Jamie reached out and slowly pushed on Roger's hilt, moving the blade away from the man's neck.

"You did fine, Roger. We don't kill them unless we have to. Get good with ropes." Jamie gripped his shoulder. "Once again, you've my thanks."

"And you've my sword, sir."

Eva stood near the door, in the shadows, as was her wont. Jamie strode to her while Ry and Angus hauled the man to his feet. He spun her, pulling her into his chest.

"Why did you come?" he demanded, burying his face in her neck.

"I have spent my life hiding in shadows, Jamie. Occasionally, one must step out. Particularly when one's loved ones are in danger."

He lifted his head. "What did you think you could do to help?"

She put her hands on his arms. "I have not been entirely honest with you."

He gave a small laugh. "I have been educated about who you are."

"I ought to have told you. It changes nothing for me," she said swiftly, then looked away. "But perhaps, for y—"

He cupped her jaw, trapping strands of her hair under his gauntleted hands and pulled her up to her toes, close to his face. "I will get you out of here," he whispered. "We will go to your cottage. And as you do not wish it, I swear that John will never find you. I vow on my life."

She nodded, her eyes bright and wet. "Let us hope it will not come to that. We shall retrieve *mon père*, and go be irretrievable."

He kissed her one last time and turned to the others.

"Let's go get him."

Fifty-six

Eva found him.

"He'll be with Magda," Jamie said as they hurried out into the bright spring day. The sky was screaming blue, the sun blinding. Even the cobbles seemed reflective.

Fairgoers moved everywhere, making crowds in front of shops. Criers were out, announcing new wine and ale, selling pasties. Animals were being herded through the chaos, goats and ewes and a pony, heading for the horse market outside the gates. Children and dogs ran in and out of the bright skirts and booted legs of adults out for a day at the fair. There was noise and light and brightness. It felt like another world.

Jamie kept Eva and Roger in front of him, Ry at his side. Angus tromped behind, a sort of one-man rearguard. They moved as swiftly as they could, dodging people and animals, as Jamie explained, "Mouldin said, 'She will never tell you.' He meant Magda."

"I am certain he did," Eva agreed. "But Father Peter is with the doctor."

Jamie looked down at her sharply. "Magda and the physic are on opposite ends of the town. We must choose right. Why do you say the doctor?"

"Because Magda is a caretaker."

"And so she'd have kept the priest with her."

Eva shook her head and pointed to the street that lead to Jakob Doctor's. "That is not what caretakers do, Jamie. They make sure the vulnerable ones are with whoever can take care of them best. Father will be with the best physic in the west country. I am certain." She met his eye. "It is what I would have done."

Jamie grabbed her hand. "Ry, you and Roger go get the horses. Angus, come with me. We're going to Jakob Doctor's."

EVEN as they drew near, they could see it had been wrecked. The front door was flung open. Inside, tables were knocked over, glass phials and cups shattered, sprayed all across the floor. Unguents and various liquids dripped down the edges of the wood tables. An odor of spoilage and floral filled the air, an acrid, cloying scent. Papers ruffled in the faint morning breeze. All was silent.

No one was in sight. This was odd. People gathered to stand like children at a puppet show simply to watch a miller break apart a beaver dam. They would surely be standing about this scene.

Unless they knew something. Something that would keep them away.

"Jamie," Eva whispered. "Hurry."

Jamie slid his sword out, holding his hand out, keeping her back. He directed Angus to stand watch, then stepped inside and listened. As eerie as it was, as silent and gravelike in the bright spring morning, the place had no feeling of impending danger or poised attack.

He gestured Eva inside.

She went at once to the stairs and, gesturing her intent silently, went up, silent as a cat. He turned for the back room and swung open the door.

Jakob Doctor. Sitting on a bed beside . . . Peter of London.

Jamie lowered his sword. Jakob turned slowly, his shoulders moving with his head, as if his neck had stiffened overnight and would not swivel smoothly.

"I thought you would return" was all he said.

"What happened?"

Jakob glanced at Father Peter. "He asked for you." He touched Peter of London's shoulder as Jamie came forward. Peter's eyes flickered open.

Jamie knelt beside the bed. "It has been a long time, old friend."

Father Peter smiled faintly. "Ah, Jamie. You have come."

Jamie took the pale, elderly hand and squeezed lightly. "I would have come the moment I heard your name, Father, but you should know this: John sent me for you."

Peter of London painfully lifted a hand and moved it to rest on Jamie's arm. "I know. I have ne'er faulted you for serving faithfully, Jamie."

Jamie shook his head. "'Twas not always faithfully done."

"'Tis now, and that is all that matters."

"Who did this to you?" Jamie looked at Peter's face, taken aback by the violence. The bedsheets were stained red.

"The king."

Jamie recoiled. "Cig did this?"

"A woman."

"*What?*"

Peter met his eyes. "She was blond." Chance. Oh, the deadly irony. Chance, a hidden agent for the king.

Peter waved his hand. "This is hardly the issue now, Jamie. The time has come. I have your father's things for you." He reached for a small bag at his side, a little larger than the usual packet that hung around travelers' necks containing traveling papers, safe conducts, maps, letters of introduction, and even coin if one was foolish. But what Peter of London, old confidant and friend of his father's, handed over now were the heirlooms of Everoot.

His father's thick signet ring with the famed Everoot seal, a twice-blooming rose roped around in thick cords of gold and silver, a glowing green gem right in the center like a dragon's eye. The small, tricolor key. An Everoot surcoat, carefully folded. And last, a small gold locket, and inside a lock of hair. His mother's.

Father Peter watched Jamie sift through the offerings. "I offer my profound apologies for taking so long. I should have brought these to you many years ago."

"I do not think I would have accepted them before now."

"There are sketches as well, Jamie, and documentation." Peter nodded to the bag. "Look inside."

The air seemed to grow thinner as Jamie reached in. He took out several pieces of parchment, scrolled and tied. He unlaced them and rolled them open.

First to hit him was the image of him and his father, the strong towers of Everoot in the background. Then another, of Jamie as a child of six, in the forest, whittling wood.

Yes. He recalled that day. Father Peter, a much younger man, had been visiting his friend, the earl of Everoot. That was the day Papa had given him a little knife. The day he'd taken Jamie down to the vaults, to the room of treasures.

Next was the scene he'd been seeing in his mind for the past twenty years: his father's murder. King John, striking down his father, a few great men leaping forward on the grimy cobbled streets, trying to hold back the king.

"I was there." Father Peter's voice seemed to come in from a great distance. "I was with the king that day, when your father returned with news that King Richard was not dead, as John had been claiming."

Jamie nodded silently. What was there to say? He'd been there too, and run.

"I tried to find you," Peter said quietly, but it felt like a shout. "I could not."

"You were not intended to," he replied thickly.

Peter nodded toward the drawing. "John knows I sketched that, and knows its danger. It will serve you well, should you need it. Everyone in that drawing is a witness."

Next was a document. A writ of some sort. No. Scrawled words on a page. Signatures. A record of his baptism.

"These cannot be pleasant for you," Peter said gravely. "But they will be proof, my lord."

Jamie looked up sharply. "Do not call me that."

"I *am* calling you that. You must claim what is yours."

Jamie sat back on his heels. "No."

Peter looked at him sharply. "You must. You must claim Everoot."

"No, *curé*. I will not. I am leaving. I go with Eva, if she will have me. I am done."

"You do not have that luxury, Jamie of Everoot. You cannot decline."

"Watch me."

Peter's gaze grew stern. "Everoot is not a gift, Jamie. 'Tis an obligation."

Jamie gave a faint smile. "Now you sound like a proper churchman." He looked down at his father's surcoat in his hands, let it drop into the bag, and sat back on his heels. "Is this why you came back?"

Peter raised his eyebrows, and Jamie touched the bag. "For this?"

"Yes, that," Peter replied crankily. "That, and the thing I have spent the last year of my life in pursuit of. The one thing that may rescue this land from incessant warfare. The charter."

His regard of Jamie grew harder and more intent, which, coming from a man well into his sixth decade, was quite hard and intent indeed. "A charter you are going to help bring to fruition, Jamie, when you claim Everoot."

He shook his head. "You have been too long among books and monks, priest. A piece of paper will not stop either the rebels or the king. It will never hold."

Peter's eyes fairly snapped fire. "Either you are very stupid, or you think I am." Jamie laughed. "Of course it will not hold on its own," Peter said firmly. "'Tis *parchment*. But neither can a castle wall do much good if it is unmanned. It takes *men* to make it hold. It will take men, powerful, influential men, to make this charter hold. Men with the internal resources to see it through. Men with castles and vassals and money. Men with courage."

Their eyes met and held.

"I am not that man, *curé*," Jamie said quietly. "I am sorry to disappoint. I am nothing like my father."

Peter dropped back on the pillows with a grunt of disgust. "You are like him in your complete and utter stubbornness. If only your mother were here."

"If only," Jamie echoed, getting to his feet.

"You and Eva shall make a fine pair," he added bitterly. "She is as hard-headed as you."

"You are both very stubborn men," said a quiet voice from the doorway. "But I am glad to see you and your very hard head."

Jamie felt Peter's heaviness lighten. "Ah, Jamie, you brought me Eva. That was well done," he said quietly, then turned his head to the door.

She came into the room, her gaze touching on everything, Jamie sitting at the bedside, the faint red smear on one side of the linen sheets tucked in around the priest.

Then she was hugging him, talking softly, saying nothing of the sheets or that he was dying, for Eva was wise enough not to waste time on the things that could not be changed. Jamie sat back and watched them a moment, these old friends, Eva tucking and fussing and chatting, Peter waving her off, shaking his head.

"Stay with Jamie, now, Eva," Peter said after a few minutes, his eyes closing.

She stood beside the bed, her fingertips resting lightly on the sheet above his chest. "But of course."

"And Roger?" he asked, his voice fainter even than a moment ago.

Eva didn't reply. Jamie looked up and saw her face was fixed as rigidly as iron, her jaw tight, her eyes staring, as little shivers trembled her head all the way down to the ends of her hair.

"Is safe," Jamie answered for her. "And brave. He will be a boon to whomever he serves. You and Eva raised him well."

Father Peter's lips pursed slightly, his eyes still closed. "'Twas all the hardheaded woman's doing. I said he was a lost thing. She insisted no and brought him back."

Eva's emotions spilled over in two tears, down her face. But she smiled and said, "I sketched a picture for someone last night. Of his mother. He said it was well-done."

Father Peter patted her hand once, faintly. "All you do is well-done, Eva. I am proud."

He was quiet after that. Jamie stood beside Eva, his hand on her shoulder, and they waited in silence. It didn't take long for Peter to die.

"I think it made his passing right, to have you here," Jamie said.

She reached up for his hand. He took it, and they both said their prayers for Peter of London.

Ry burst through the front doorway, breathing hard, clutching the doorframe. Blood poured from his split lip. One eye was pulsing red, swelling shut.

"They took him," he gasped.

Jamie was already striding out the door by the time Ry said, "You must come now." Eva was fast on their heels. They took off running down the street, pushing people out of their way.

"The rebels?" Jamie shouted.

"No. The king."

Everything Eva did from that moment on was as if it took place underwater, as the decision took shape inside her. Took more effort, felt slowed and wavery and as if she were swimming against a great force.

Although it wasn't so much a decision, she realized through the water haze. It was more like uncovering something put in the ground a long time ago, something buried, like roots of your garden, or bones of your loved ones. In this way, the uncovering was not so much a revelation as a reminder: *You forgot about me, but I did not forget about you.*

The seed had sprouted. Roger was in danger, Jamie was in danger, Father Peter had been murdered, and the binding cord of her promise was cleaved.

She was going to kill the king.

Fifty-seven

hey fought their way out the town gates as everyone else was pushing in, but they were too late. Far too late. They stood on the hilltop, Ry with his bashed and bleeding face, Angus looking grim, staring at the road below.

Eva backed up a few unsteady steps until she sat, abruptly, on the grass. The world was rocking like a little boat under her feet, and she could catch neither her breath nor her footing. She stared straight ahead. The green grass hurt her eyes.

JAMIE stared ahead into the distance, the way the king's men had ridden. A day's ride to Everoot. Whose horses were faster? His or the double agent Chance's? They'd have to see.

"I must go after," Eva said calmly, as if she were reporting the need to gather herbs.

"Aye, we will go."

Ry's hand fell on his shoulder. "You cannot, Jamie."

"Cannot what?"

Ry's face was hard. "Are you going in as Everoot?"

Jamie said nothing.

"Jamie if you go to the king, you must go as *you*. As Everoot. If you go as Jamie Lost, the king's knight, you will never make it through the gates alive."

Jamie looked down the hill.

Ry's voice hardened. "King John will kill you. Do you see what they did to me? Be assured, I was released only as a message to you. This"—Ry gestured to his bashed and battered face—"is the message. John will eviscerate you."

Eva stepped forward. "That is what the blond woman said to me, also. She said John would be hunting you."

"Someone is always hunting me," Jamie said shortly.

Ry's eyes narrowed. "Had you ever a doubt in your mind as to the king's plans for you, Jamie, you can no more. He no longer trusts you." Ry's bloodshot eyes bored into Jamie's. "You cannot go in without the protection of Everoot upon you. Claim it now, Jamie. 'Tis time. Or they will kill you."

"They will try."

"God's *mercy*." Ry grabbed a handful of Jamie's tunic, shouting, "I cannot protect you in there!"

They stared at each other for a long moment, then Ry stepped back. "You will not claim it even now, will you, not even when so much is at stake?" Cold, hard fury filled his words like a glass ball. "You neither claim nor let it go, Jamie. That is wrong."

"That is right," Jamie said, his voice lethally low. "I do neither. I have claimed Eva."

"That is not good enough."

"I do not care. You dare speak to me of claiming? You, who have a father and a family, a *heritage*, yet have renounced it all. You, who have seen me at my worst—"

"You were eight years old!"

"—you with a woman waiting, should you only choose to reach for her—do not think I forget Lucia—and yet you renounce all those things. Instead, you are here, with me." Jamie jabbed the tips of his fingers into his own chest. *"Me."*

If all the timbres of shame could have been rounded up like

ponies and herded into a syllable, they would have been penned inside this one of Jamie's.

Then, sitting on the grass, Eva understood. Jamie could not fathom why someone would choose him. Why Ry chose him. Why she chose him. Because he had not yet chosen.

Silence echoed on the hill.

"I do not know why you stick," Jamie said coldly. "Go protect the family you abandoned."

"I cannot—" Ry's voice cracked. "Save them."

Jamie stepped forward, moving in so close their chests touched. *"I am not to be saved!"*

Ry took a step back, then another. He turned away, head down, and for a long moment it was silent. Then they heard the hiss of a blade sliding past metal, and Ry turned back and lifted his sword to Jamie's neck, flat side out. A twist of the wrist would turn the cutting edge against his vein.

"I ought to do it now," Ry said quietly, his red-rimmed, exhausted eyes holding Jamie's. "What you've been trying to do for years, I should just do it for you now."

Lightning energy crackled through the air on the hill. Neither man moved, their gazes locked.

"Do it, then," said Jamie.

Eva got to her feet and walked over, placed the tips of her fingers on the cold blade, and pushed it away.

"Swords are sharp," she murmured. "Let us use them only if small children will die should you refrain. Since you are both very angry, and there are no small children about, we will stop and breathe, rather than kill each other and give our enemies great joy."

Ry let her push the blade down. Its tip raised a miniature puff of dust as it hit a bare spot on the earth. Angus cleared his throat.

For a moment nothing happened except the blowing breeze. Then Ry resheathed his blade and walked away, down the hill. He did not look back.

They watched him go. Eva felt stunned. She turned to Jamie. "Is he—?"

"Not coming back," Jamie said grimly. "I know where they are going," he said, almost to himself. "Everoot." He looked down at her.

She nodded. "Then we had best leave at once."

"Angus, stick with Ry," Jamie said as he turned and strode down the hill. "God knows what he'll do just now."

They separated at the bottom, Angus to find Ry, Eva and Jamie for Everoot.

Fifty-eight

A day and a half later, they drew rein just to the south of the Nest, the impregnable, indominable *caput* of the vast Everoot earldom.

Its stony towers thrust like fists out of the earth into the bright blue sky, towering over the valley and village below. No pennants snapped along the ramparts; the king was not announcing his residence. He would hardly wish to announce he'd fled Windsor. Eva assumed few knew he was here. This would be to her benefit.

Nonetheless, a stream of people came and went through the heavily guarded gates, on foot and horse, some with carts. It was impossible to keep the king a secret long.

Jamie's gaze stayed unmoving on the towering gray spire of the main keep. It was a twisted homecoming for Eva, but she could not begin to imagine what Jamie must be feeling.

"I should leave you here," he murmured.

She nodded. "Of course, but this will not occur. You are headstrong, and do not always do as you should."

The faintest smile lightened his visage as he looked down. "You do as I say, every step, Eva. Do you hear me?"

"Very loudly," she said, nodding. That did not mean she would obey, but that was for later.

Even from here they could see a line of people who did not seem to be dressed in armor walking the baileys.

"The place is busy," Eva noted. "This is to our benefit."

Jamie, fully armored, mail hood lying in a pile of crumbled mesh links at the back of his neck, sat in his saddle, saying nothing. One arm was bent slightly, so his palm could grasp the hilt of his sword with its swirling silver lines. His other hand was loose on the reins, his gaze locked on the castle. His horse's proud head hung tired and low. His clothes were dark and nondescript, his cheeks and jaw darkened with hair. He looked like a weather-beaten warrior after a campaign, alone with his horse and the wind.

"Let's go."

THE porters, who knew Jamie well, had apparently not yet been alerted that Jamie was now an enemy of the king's.

They quickly opened the small door in the north tower of the barbican to let him and Eva pass through. The tower soared up sixty feet, and they stepped into its cold shadow with a wary exchange of glances.

"Where is the king?" Jamie asked.

"Not yet arrived, sir."

Jamie nodded. "Good," he said, then whispered in Eva's ear, "We have time." They hurried through the outer bailey. "This is when things get dangerous," he said, guiding her to the edges of the vast inner ward.

Despite the king's coming in secret, people moved everywhere through the baileys, servants and squires and merchants. But even when John's resplendent entourage of servants and courtiers was added to the mix, it would not have filled up the wide sweep of Everoot's vast baileys.

They had made it halfway across the bailey before Jamie detected something amiss. A discordant note in the bustle of a castle with people in residence.

The king might not be hanging his banners to alert that he would be in residence, but someone knew he was here, for . . . was that not the livery of Geoffrey de Mandeville upon the squire trotting by? And . . . Essex. Hereford. Norfolk.

Every noble or noble-aspiring man seemed to be here, or have sent a representative.

What the hell was going on?

Jamie moved them to the shadows, keeping Eva on his inner side, and almost bumped into Brian de Lisle coming down the covered stairwell.

He stopped short. "Jamie!" He clattered down the last steps, reaching out for his arm.

Jamie wanted to shove Eva into yet another alley, but there was none to be had. He needn't have worried. When his step slowed, Eva simply sailed past him, fumbling among her skirts, muttering to herself, as if she were on an important errand.

De Lisle glanced at her—it was impossible not to—but then grabbed Jamie's forearm in a tight grip. "Jamie Lost, you are past mad, coming here. 'Tis most good to see you."

"And you, Brian," Jamie replied, returning the gesture, steeling himself for things to go badly. Again. Brian was one of John's most trusted and highly rewarded captains, smart, savvy, and, fortunately, independent-minded. He was also lethal. He would also know what the hell was going on.

"You just arrived?" Brian said.

"Aye. I was on a job."

"I heard." Brian's eyes searched Jamie's as they released one other. "You are a wanted man, Jamie. What the hell are you doing here?"

Jamie met his gazes. "Are you equally intent on me?"

Brian hesitated, then shook his head. "No reason to hate you yet, Jamie. I have yet to see you do a thing without cause." Brian eyed him. "Want to share it?"

Jamie felt cold relief. He had not wanted to strike down Brian de Lisle. It would make things to come more difficult. "Soon. Are you willing to give me a few hours?"

Brian signaled to one of the glinting helms up on the ramparts. The guard nodded and hurried toward the stairwell. Brian looked back down. "You have less than an hour of liberty, I'd estimate, before the king arrives. You do not have the priest?"

Jamie shook his head. "He has passed on. What the devil is going on?" He gestured to the de Mandeville squire, who was just disappearing into the stables.

Brian de Lisle shook his head, but was grinning. "The king is beyond reason, Jamie, but in this, he might have had his one brilliant idea."

"Which is?"

"Selling off the estates."

Jamie's heart slowed. "Which estates?"

"The d'Endshire barony was offered to sweeten the pot, but it's a dicier issue now, as the boy was brought back last night."

Jamie gripped his arm. "Is he here?"

Brian glanced down in surprise.

"You've seen him?" Jamie pressed. "D'Endshire?"

"Aye, I have seen him. I hear you did as well. Ten years a'missing, and you found him within a week." Brian shook his head with a faint smile. "I am impressed."

"And the king . . . ?"

Brian shrugged. "Maybe less so. Still, d'Endshire seems a loyal sort, and I expect the king will accept him. In this, a rightful heir is likely better than a bought one."

Jamie nodded and inhaled. The news felt like a small window of reprieve. "Where is he?"

Brian's mouth curved up in a smile. "Not on your life, Jamie.

Which it may well be, I am beginning to think." He eyed Jamie, then someone shouted for de Lisle. Brian glanced over, waved, and turned back. "Everoot is up for sale too."

The words echoed inside Jamie's head. "What?"

"The king is selling Everoot to the highest bidder. Very quietly. Very quickly."

Jamie felt it as if he'd been punched.

"De Mandeville, Essex, they all have sent emissaries. 'Tis astonishing how quickly these men can move when properly spurred," Brian said, blithely unaware Jamie was hearing only one word in three as the blood was roaring through his head. "The king is making his move."

"He is making a mistake," Jamie said coldly.

Brian shrugged. "Who knows? The king might have just found a way to avert the charter and win the war, in one fell swoop." Brian glanced over Jamie's shoulder. "I must go."

He gestured to the top of the stairs and one of the king's chamberlains hurried down. "Take Sir Jamie to a room. Assuming you are still alive come sundown, we shall drink hard this night, you and I. There is much to discuss, and mayhap to celebrate."

Brian strode off. The chamberlain looked at Jamie. Jamie smiled. "Prepare my room as Lord Brian commanded."

"Sir—"

"I will join you there directly."

Jamie turned and headed for the keep, the way Eva had gone, moving around the people coming down the steps of the gray-stone castle that used to be his home, that the king was selling off to the highest bidder.

LATE in the day, after Jamie had ridden off, after a string of long and bitter drinks, Ry made it to the stables and began saddling his horse. A monstrous shadow loomed across the beams overhead, then stilled. Ry turned around slowly.

"God's love, Angus," he muttered, and turned back to saddling.

Angus took a step into the stall. "You were wrong."

"I'm certain that is so."

"Do you know what he's doing up there, at Everoot?"

"Jamie? Getting himself killed."

"Aye, well, I can no' let that happen, see? I'm going tae settle this debt if it kills me."

"Not if he kills himself first." Ry dropped the flap on his saddle and patted his horse's neck. He took up the reins and led him from the stall. Angus stood in the way, arms crossed, frowning. Ry frowned back.

"Ye look like hell," Angus said bluntly.

"Aye, well, that's what happens when you try to protect Jamie."

Ry started to move past him. Angus didn't budge. He stopped, and Angus's gaze bored into him. "I don't understand why ye left him."

Ry shrugged. Because one could only save a man bent on self-destruction for so long. Ry had adequate experience with lost causes, and he finally had to admit Jamie was one. "Bored," he said shortly.

"What the hell does that mean?"

Ry took a hard step forward and this time, the Scotsman stepped out of his way. "It means 'tis always the same thing with Jamie. Almost getting killed, almost, almost, until one day, he finally will. I don't want to be standing there watching when it happens."

Angus threw up his hands. "Bloody bones, Ry, that's wholly the reason ye're with him. We all knew, back then: Jamie'll get himself killed, and Ry'll bring him back again."

"Not anymore."

"Why not?"

Ry glared. "Because I'm done."

Angus glared back. "Ye always said Lost was stubborn, Ry, but no one ever beat yerself. And now?"

Ry pushed past him with a shove. "Now I'm going to clean up our mess."

Angus turned, clinking and creaking with leather and weapons. "I'm coming with ye."

"I mean in truth. I am picking up wardrobes and broken crockery at Jakob Doctor's."

"I'm coming. Jamie told me to."

Ry stopped so short the hilt of Angus's sword poked into his back. "What?"

"He didna want ye to do anything. . . ." The Scotsman pondered his next word for a long time. "Rash."

Ry turned coldly. "Rash? *Rash?* Me, rash?"

Angus backed up a pace, palm in the air. "I'm just saying what Jamie said."

Ry stared at him a moment. "Why did you leave us, all those years ago?"

Angus's cheeks flushed. "I couldn't take owing Jamie so much, not being able to repay him. And he never let me forget it, either."

Ry turned on his heel and started for the door. "You do not understand Jamie. He never let you forget because he never forgot. He will never forget, and never forgive. *Himself.* There is naught I can do about it."

"Ye're not supposed to do anything about it, dammit," Angus muttered. "Ye're just his friend. Ye pledged to him."

Ry stopped at the doorway. Spring sunshine made a threshold of light just outside the stable. "And what of me?"

Silence, then Angus said, "I s'ppse ye're to do what ye think is right. I just don't see how leaving him to die is the right thing here. And what of the lass?"

Ry took a deep breath.

"I don't know what he'll do without ye, Ry."

"So I'm supposed to just watch him die?"

He heard Angus shift his bulk. "Well, now, Ry, I don't know about ye, but I don't aim to let him die. No matter how set on it he is."

For a moment they were quiet. Then Ry turned to him. "Everoot is two days' ride."

"Less with fresh horses."

"First the doctor's. He deserves that much."

"Quickly then, Ry," Angus said as they started out of the stable. "Jamie looked awful determined, and I heard the king's selling off estates."

JAMIE got Eva into an unused bedchamber—there were many, as the castle was hardly full. Chambers lined the walls and several of the guard towers. He simply opened the door to one of most distant, then directed two wide-eyed servants to bring bedstuffs and clothes and a brazier to the room of the widowed countess of Misselthwaite, who'd just lost everything when her baggage train was caught in the rushing tides of The Wash, and why in the king's name had it not been done *before*?

They stared wide-eyed at this unknown, irate nobleman shouting at them about something they should clearly have known. Then they bolted down the hall and, very soon, were back with all the ordered items as well as a few additional ones, such as candles and a plate of food and a polished metal mirror.

Eva held the mirror to her face as the maidservant scurried about under Jamie's scowl, preparing the bath with scented herbs, then hurried out. Eva poked at her cheek, still looking in the mirror. She tilted her face to the side and peered at her profile. Pale, skinny, resolute. These were the things she could see in her face. She could not look at Jamie too closely, else he'd see that last as well.

She set the mirror down. "You have made this all very nice," she said placidly, circling the room.

"You're going to be here for a while."

She touched the bedstead. "That sounds like a threat."

"'Tis an order, Eva."

She ran her hand across the bed hangings hurriedly looped.

"You will wait here. I will manage this."

She glanced out the window; it looked down on the inner bailey. She pulled her head inside and turned. "Misselthwaite?"

He shook his head with a weary smile.

"I think it is a very good-sounding name. Perhaps our cottage is a Misselthwaite."

He reached for her hand, then pulled her to him. "Roger will be fine," he murmured against her lips. "I shall see to it."

She did not respond, as Jamie could not see to such a thing. He would try, of course, with his noble heart, and be dead soon afterward. Since he had an earldom to claim, clearly this was not conscionable. Sacrifices must be made, but they would not be Jamie's. Nor Roger's.

They would be Eva's.

Jamie had his arms around her. It was not something she could describe, the awareness that this good man wanted her, so she didn't try. She pressed her cheek to his chest and they held each other, breathing together. She realized her heart was expanding. She could feel it, filling up her chest, down through her groin. Filling her with Jamie. She felt as if she were all one beating heart.

That was a much better way to go out than any she'd ever imagined. And in ten years, one had time to imagine a great many unpleasant ways to go.

They both heard it, the arrival of the king and his entourage. The clatter of hooves on the cobbles in the bailey, the shouts of men and grooms, barking dogs, servants scurrying about. Then doors slamming, hooves fading as the horses were led away. Bootsteps loud, then quieter, as the men circled the keep and entered.

Neither of them moved.

Hot, bulbous tears filled Eva's eyes. It was unimaginable, all this crying since she'd met Jamie. She closed them and squeezed him tighter.

He shifted, but only to bend his head and rest it on top of hers. The bones of his forehead pressed on her. His breath, low and even, warmed her ear. The powerful strength of him was, for a moment, in repose. He was readying, preparing. He was weary.

Eva unlaced her fingers and slid them up his back and began rubbing his shoulders.

He made a low rumbling sound, like a groan. "I must go," he mumbled, not moving.

"Yes," she agreed, pressing her fingers down harder, kneading in deep circles. She felt his arms droop. "In a moment. But he is already here. There is naught to prepare for, no way to position yourself where he will come before he is there himself. So, you will take this moment and receive me."

He put his fingers under her chin and tilted her face up, smiling faintly. "I will receive you tonight, Eva."

"Perhaps a little, now?"

"There is no time now." But he was kissing her as he said it, so she knew there was perhaps a bit of time. He backed up, bringing her forward with him, until he sat on the edge of the bed. He pulled her onto his lap, facing him, her legs on either side. His long-lashed eyes were swept closed as he trailed a line of kisses down her throat, leaving hot, red places that throbbed when he moved away, sliding lower, his touch desperate and fierce and all about her.

She could feel his desire in the thick rod of flesh pressing between her skirts, his fierce kisses, his ever-searching hands, and, most of all, in the almost inaudible murmurs spoken against her skin. What was he saying?

She cupped the sides of his face and kissed. "Whatever it is, aye, I will," she whispered, pulling at her skirts, tugging them recklessly up. He took over, wrenching them to her knees. He unlaced his hose swiftly and, without warning, lifted her up and lowered her down on him.

"I said, do not ever leave me," he rasped, his eyes on her.

She threw her head back as he entered her. It was a swift, hard, messy coupling. They were like mad things for each other, teeth bumping, hands gripping, squeezing, hard, deep movements designed to emblazon and possess. It was as if even Jamie, whatever he would admit aloud, knew that perhaps this was the last time they would touch.

He yanked at the ties of her tunic, unlacing them at the sides, and yanked down on her collar until he could close his hot mouth around her breast. He suckled as he pumped into her, lifting her on each surge of his hips, entering her deeper, his hands gripping her hips. In moments, she shuddered over the edge. Her head jerked backward as her body exploded, and she felt him clench her hard as hard, hot spasms of his essence pumped into her as she whispered his name into his neck, holding as tight as she could.

He fell back on the bed, Eva sprawled atop him, still kissing, and he did not seem to notice that she was tying his wrists to the bedpost until it was too late.

Fifty-nine

va?" he mumbled, suddenly aware of a rope tugging on his wrist. No, both wrists.

"Jamie," she whispered, sliding off him, rustling her skirts back into place, standing a safe distance away. She ran her fingers down his bare belly, then . . . turned away.

He bolted upright. The ropes jerked him back down. "What the hell is going on?" he demanded, yanking on the ropes. They were firm and tight. He looked up at Eva. She was at the door.

She was leaving him.

"Jamie, whatever you may say, Roger is not safe. The king is mad. He must be stopped."

His heart hammered. "Eva," he said darkly, slowly. "What are you doing?"

She continued as if he'd not spoken. She had clearly rehearsed the lines. "How useful can John find one fifteen-year-old man whose only riches come from the land the king himself already holds? Compared to the great and rich men who will no doubt be putting their petitions forward, Roger rates as notably as a gnat. And you?" She shook her head. "He will see you hang."

He yanked again on the ropes, struggling to sit up. "Eva.

What you say has merit. We will talk, I will listen, but, Eva—"

"That is because you are a good man. The king is not. I know this. He is my father."

"Eva, *do not do this.*"

She put her hand on the door as he struggled against the ropes. "I hear your warning, Jamie. My whole life has been warnings. And do you know what is to come after? More of the same. All due King John. More more running, more darkness—"

"You cannot show yourself to the king until I—"

"—and it will be this way forever."

"—marry you!" he shouted.

She stopped talking for a brief moment. "And how is our marriage of value to King John?"

His heart thundered in his chest. "I will claim Everoot," he said, and it felt as if he'd meant to say the words forever. "I will claim it, and you, and *that* has value."

His declaration did not seem to impress Eva. "And then you will be naught but a bigger threat. A powerful lord, wed to the daughter of a king? And after what he has no doubt been told by your Cigogné? After he learns that you intended, for a while, to kill him." She shook her head and opened the door. "Nay, Jamie. There is but one way to settle this."

He stilled. "What does that mean? What are you going to do?"

"This not killing the king, Jamie, this was not so good a thing. And now all the good men are dead or soon to be. I will take care of this, since no one else has."

"Jésu, Eva, you are mad." He had a sudden, crushing vision of how Ry must feel toward him. "You have no idea what murder does to a person."

"You have killed," she said placidly. She had no idea the enormity of her actions. "And you are a good man."

"Aye, I have killed, and I am a dying thing inside. I *was* dead until you, Eva."

"But for cause," she whispered, her hand on the door. "For good cause? Surely this matters."

"It matters. For a while."

"I have only one deed to do."

"You do not comprehend me Eva: *one is all it will take for you.*"

"That is all I have in me, Jamie. One."

He gave a roar, and fisting one hand atop the other, he yanked on the ropes with a vicious jerk. The wood post gave a thin, loud crack. Eva started; her face paled. "I swear, I will kill you myself," he growled.

He yanked again. Another crack of the wood. She stepped through the doorway.

"I have lived in darkness too long, Jamie," she whispered, looking over her shoulder. "I cannot do it anymore. Neither shall Roger. Neither shall you." She pulled the door shut behind her, but not before she whispered, "I love you."

Then she was gone.

He put his head down and renewed his assault on the bedposts. At this rate, it would take half an hour.

EVA walked down the familiar corridor to the lord's tower. White rushes of sound swept through her skull like wind as she counted the stones under her boots. The world she'd lived in was receding like land from a boat, as you slipped out to sea on powerful but invisible currents. She felt as though she had just given the oars a little push, and they had slid over the sides and into the water. There could be no changes in direction now. She was aimed like an arrow and would travel on, unstoppable.

It was impossible to contemplate that she would never see Roger again, so she did not. It was impossible to imagine she would never see Jamie again, so she did not. Never have Jamie mark her like a target with his smile, never have his thumb caress her neck, so much power, so restrained, on her. Never hear wolves. Breathe air. Feel her hard, ugly boots hit the hard, beautiful earth again.

The things she could not think of grew and grew, until she was a tiny prick of darkness in all the bright things she could not imagine in the world.

She slipped into the king's outer chamber. It was not difficult; Eva knew how to make herself invisible. She sat on a small bench against the wall, staring at nothing, until she heard a sound, a scrape of a boot on the stone outside.

She got to her feet and pulled her cape closer around herself, so she could go unseen as long as possible, and kill her father the king before he destroyed anyone else she loved.

Sixty

Jamie jerked his arms again. No crack of wood. He clenched his fists and jerked repeatedly, until his arms and belly burned, then stopped to catch his breath. He stared up at the ceiling.

Eva had been right. Ry as well. Ry mostly. Jamie had lived in a netherworld for years, neither reaching out nor moving away. Indecision had marked his life, for all that his actions were unwavering.

But now came the convergence. If he did not claim Everoot, others would. This had lit a fire inside him, although he'd ignored it. When presented with the possibility that someone else might rule Everoot, it had simply taken his breath away.

Needing to claim it to save Eva gave it back. He could do this thing. Would do it. A sense of power and destiny snapped through him a hot whip of intent.

Enough of sawing on the bit; 'twas time to come unleashed.

Lying here naked, strapped to a bed, did give one cause to reflect on one's past errors. For instance, he would have to be sure to impress upon Eva how very much he did not approve of her method of solving problems.

He renewed his assault on the bedpost.

R<small>Y</small> and Angus got into Everoot by blending with a wagon train of merchants and whores. They went looking for Lucia, the dark-skinned, hot-blooded Italian lass who'd worked years ago at Baynard Castle, who had left when Ry had. *Because* he had. She cared not that he was Jewish, nor that he lived most of his days in mortal danger, nor that he could barely keep his hands off her whenever they were close. In fact, she seemed to like that a great deal. She cared only that he smiled at her, looked at no other woman, and would commit to spend the rest of his life with her.

This had become a bone of contention: Ry's life was about saving Jamie's, since he could not save his family's, and he had not been able to leave off it. Not even for Lucia.

So she'd finally tossed him aside with an airy flip of her thick, dark hair, and said she wished never to see him again.

Ry hoped that was not true. She had not married another, and she had not left the king's service, which surely she could have, got a place in any noble household. If she truly wished never to see him again, that is what she would have done. Correct?

He and Angus hunted her down through the endless corners of Everoot's castle and battlement walls. Ry planned the reunion in his mind. He would kiss her, ask her to marry him, demand to know where Roger and Jamie were. In that order.

J<small>AMIE</small> clenched his jaw for yet another mighty pull as the door flung open. He jerked his head up and stared. Roger and Ry and Angus stood in the doorway.

They took in his naked body, lashed to the bedpost, and their jaws dropped. "Jésu, Jamie," Ry muttered. "What happened?"

"Eva happened," Roger interjected with the sort of grim certitude Jamie would expect from someone who knew Eva's tricks. Jamie would have to take counsel with him. Perhaps while Eva was tied to a tree nearby.

"I have no idea how you have come here, but I have ne'er been so glad to have three men ogle my naked body. Untie me."

Angus took door watch, while Ry and Roger hurried over. Each took an arm, as Jamie flung his head to swing the hair off his face. "I owe you," he said with feeling.

"Again," Ry grunted, head down, focused on the ropes.

"Why did you come?"

"I like the idea of you being indebted to me. And I was wrong," Ry added. "I am sorry."

Jamie shook his head. "No. You were absolutely right. About everything."

"I feel as though I should commemorate this moment somehow," Ry muttered, sawing at the ropes. "I wonder if an engraved plate would do."

"How about me owing you my life?"

Ry smiled faintly. "My mission is done."

"I will repay you."

Ry shrugged as he shifted how he cut at the rope. "I manage all your accounts and coin, Jamie. You are a rich man. I will just steal what I want."

The ropes fell away and Jamie swung up, clapped Ry on the shoulder, then Roger, then shot off the bed and reached for the small pack Peter of London had given him. He pulled out the Everoot surcoat and pulled it over his head. "How did you find Roger?" Jamie's voice was muffled by the silk.

"Lucia." Ry reached over and pulled the surcoat down. Jamie's head popped out. He looked surprised. Ry grinned. "She does indeed *pine*."

"That is good. I am glad." He put on the ring. It felt heavy, more heavy than the metals constructing it. It must be the weight of destiny, settling down on him. "How did you find me?"

Roger was bouncing on the balls of his feet, his big, young energy almost bursting him out of his skin. "I did that, sir. I heard the servants talking about the countess of Misselthwaite, absent all her belongings and escorted by a very demanding courtier. I knew it must be you."

"Roger, you have a future as a judge if you wish for it." Ry grabbed Jamie's other sword belt and carried it over.

Jamie took it, and looked at him. "And you?" he asked quietly. "Where did you go?"

Ry's smile faded. "Nowhere. I drank. I helped Jakob Doctor repair his home. Angus told me I was a fool. But what news, that?" He got up and strode to the door. "Where is Eva?"

Jamie put a hand on his shoulder as he passed. Ry stopped but didn't look over. "You have long been after me to put the money to good use. Your family is good use. Get them out of London. Buy land. Take them there, where they will be safe."

"Where, Jamie? Where shall I buy 'safe land'? In all of Christendom, there is no safe place. They would have to declaim what they are, and that, they will not do."

What was there to say? The enormity of the thing was towering, like a black cloud stretched across the horizon. You knew it was going to bring destruction, and you could do nothing about it.

Jamie clamped tighter on the hand he'd placed on Ry's shoulder. "We can still do good."

Ry lifted a brow. "Only if you are claiming. If not, then we shall simply die."

"Why did you come, then?"

Ry put his hand atop Jamie's. "Because I am your friend."

Jamie grinned. "That matters more than all the rest." He reached for his cape and pinned it with the Everoot brooch at his shoulder. Its green eye glinted, as did the gem on the signet ring. They would not be missed. "I am claiming, Ry. I am Jamie of Everoot."

Roger stepped forward to their sides. "And I am Roger d'Endshire."

Angus poked his head in. "Ye're all a lot of fools. What are we waiting for? A whole herd of nobles just went into the keep, Jamie. Like for an audience or council."

Jamie flung the door wide and they strode out into the danger as their fathers had done.

"Let us go make them sorry."

THEY went to the main keep along the battlement walls, not even attempting to hide. Up here, the winds blew briskly and the sun burned hot. It seemed the news had spread now that Jamie Lost was a wanted man. They could hear the shouts, word traveling. The king was here, and he wanted Jamie.

They sized up the best direction to circle around. "I was young, my lord, I do not recall which way will get us there the quickest," Roger said quietly.

"I do," Jamie replied gravely. His head was up, his cape blown back, the ring on his finger gleamed, and the cobalt of Everoot's colors burned in the sun.

Then Roger realized the Nest had once been Jamie's home. Although he'd been gone from it since he was very young, it must be mapped on the inside of his brain. There was no hesitation, no falter in his step.

Just how Eva moved. How she'd moved that night when she shoved Roger into a crevice of the battlement wall so hard his cheeks scratched on the knobbly stone, then crouched in front of him, blocking him from witnessing his father's murder.

Jamie and Eva belonged together. Roger knew this with a certainty that made his heart beat stronger. That was a good thing. He could do almost anything, knowing that.

"My lord, have you never been home before?"

Jamie started off for the tower of the Nest. "I am home now."

THEY strode in a single, determined line around the ramparts to the passageway that connected the battlement walls to the lord's tower. Jamie ripped the door open and a gust of cold, musty air puffed out over them like a dead dragon coming to life.

"*Now* we hurry," he said. "Third level."

They took off running down the stairs. Jamie leaped down the last few steps onto the landing outside the lord's chambers. Ten of the king's crossbowmen stood there. Their faces registered first recognition, then respect, then shock as they recalled their new mission. They fumbled for their weapons.

Jamie drew his sword. "I must see the king."

Sixty-one

Eva was sitting in the outer chamber when one of the king's soldiers came rushing in. He saw her and stopped short. Then he stepped forward, the slitted sides of his surcoat ruffling in the breeze his swiftness created.

"Mistress," he said, taking her arm. "I'm sorry to say you cannot be in here."

Eva lifted her face. He was young, his face unlined, but he seemed purposeful of good intent. This was not helpful. She required much more corruptible men right now. She gave one of her large, winsome smiles.

His eyebrows rumpled, then, slowly, he smiled back.

"I am most sorrowful, young sir," she said softly. "His Grace asked me to come to him, and I thought . . . I do only as he bid."

"Oh, well," the soldier said, patting her arm in a comforting way, "that is the way to do it. But you cannot wait in his room. I'll take you down to him."

He turned her to the door of the outer chamber. A soldier armed with a small crossbow appeared next and stopped short. King John had far too many men working in his bedchamber.

The crossbowman looked between Eva and her escort. His fingers flexed a minuscule amount on the wood of his weapon. She recalled Jamie saying something about how the king kept a personal guard of crossbowmen with him. This must be one of that happy bunch.

"Who is she?" the crossbowman demanded.

"The king's doxy," the soldier explained happily.

She smiled.

"I was taking her down to the hall."

The much more suspicious crossbowman encouraged this. "Aye. We'll take her to His Grace," he said in a most unpleasant way. But this did not matter at all, for it was just what she wanted.

The young one had her by an arm, the crossbowman behind. They turned her for the stairs.

They all heard the crunch of pebbles on stone at the same time. Boots, coming up the stairs. A head appeared, then the whole person emerged at the top of the stairs.

King John.

"Release me," Eva commanded quietly, and the young guard did.

She pushed away all thought of the people she loved and what they had and had not wanted for her, feeling only the comforting length of the sharp misericord tucked deep within her skirts.

"Your Grace," she said.

King John paused for a long moment. Then he turned to the shadows, almost as if he knew.

Another crossbowman stood behind the king. He glanced at Eva and hefted his arbalest up in his arms, spreading his boots. Surely the crossbowman behind her was doing the same.

The king said, in a gentle voice, "Eva."

She took another step out into the landing. Sunlight poured through the tall, narrow window, but inside, the icy coldness was a solid pushing thing. It rose up within, miles above her head, stretching her into something frozen and white, so she felt fused into a single block of ice.

She and the king stared at each other. Oddly, Eva's first thought was to wonder if she looked like him. She did not often see her own face, and it had been ten years since she'd seen her father's.

He was fatter than he had been ten years ago. Significantly so.

"I had gifts for you," he said out of nowhere.

They were having the most peculiar first thoughts upon encountering each other.

His was so unexpected, it almost threw her off trajectory.

"Dresses," he said, and took a step closer, looking at her, half in the shadows, half lit by the sun. "A pony. Gifts. For you. But you ran."

"I have dresses." She plucked at her skirts.

"Why did you run?" He sounded truly baffled. She must be gentle with him in this, then, for his mind was clearly gone.

"It was the killing, you understand," she said quietly, and took a step nearer.

He waved a hand at the crossbowman, who had his weapon cocked and aimed at Eva's chest. "Leave us."

"Your Grace," the soldier said in quiet dissent.

"Go."

The soldier slowly turned and descended the stairs.

The king never turned his gaze from her. "Why have you come?"

In her mind, John was a demon. His voice always bellowing in her memory with a rasping, frantic horror-shout. But, yes, there had been this quieter voice as well. He had used this one when he'd come to visit her hidden self, away at the Nest. People marveled at how frequently King John itinerated northward, more than any previous king. But Eva knew why; he'd come to see her. He'd concealed her from the world, but he'd still come north to visit throughout her childhood.

She tightened her fingers around the blade hidden in the skirts of her tunic. The king's gaze dropped to her wrist. "Father Peter is dead."

He looked up swiftly. "What happened?"

"Your men."

His face paled above his black beard. Careworn eyes squinted as if he'd taken a blow. He seemed truly shocked. "I did not call for that, Eva, I swear to you."

She smiled a bit. "Did you need to? Might you not have just let them know how pleased you would be—"

"I am not pleased. I needed Peter, with me, not with the barons, not with Langton, *with me*, so I could speak to him, remake this blasted charter."

John was sorely mistaken if he thought he could talk the *curé* out of so much as an afternoon repast. But Father Peter, he might have talked John into any number of things. Of course, he would not be talking anymore. Eva was, though.

"It is not ridiculous," she said formally. "A very great man thought it had merit. Now he is dead."

"I did not order that. I swear to you. Come in, Eva." He stepped back to let her pass into his chambers. "We will talk. About anything you wish."

She thought about this for a long time. She thought about the people her father had destroyed and the ones he had lifted up. She recalled, quite unwillingly, how John had shown great kindness for many vulnerable people and been horrifying to a great many others. He was thesis and antithesis, all folded in on himself. It must be quite painful.

She thought about Jamie and the other great men who served the king because of an oath. Because of honor. She thought of her beloved, irritable *curé* and the things he'd devoted his life to: a charter to ensure some restraint, and people who needed protecting. It might be a foolish wish, but Father Peter had believed such a charter was possible. That is, he'd believed it was possible if men like Jamie hung it on their pennants.

But if Jamie left England, of course, that would not happen.

And yet, Eva could never leave without Jamie. One did not stumble across one's heart's desire, then walk away from it. That was impossible. But neither did one go about killing the lord one's heart's desire served.

She thought and she thought, and John did not say a word, did not hurry her in the least.

"Are you frightened by me?" she asked suddenly.

"Greatly," came his reply.

And that is when she thought, *Why, perhaps there is something here to work with after all.*

Penance, she'd heard from a hard-headed source, was ofttimes a thing that could heal the soul. Perhaps an extremely painful one would assist in the king's salvation.

In death, *le curé* had turned her into an instrument of God. *How like him,* she thought, smiling faintly.

The king's arm was still swept out, inviting her into his chambers.

"If you will speak to me of this charter, then yes, I think we can have a little talk, you and I. A very good friend thought it mattered."

"Come inside," the king murmured.

She slid her hand out of her skirts and left the blade behind.

Sixty-two

"I must see the king," Jamie said again in a low voice.

Ten armed men faced him down. One crossbowman—*his name is Gilbert*, Jamie recalled—stepped to the center of the landing.

"How the hell did you get in here, Jamie?"

"I must see the king."

Gilbert gave a brittle laugh. "Jamie, you are past mad. You and I, we go back. I know you well. And I am asking, for once, do not make this go more bloody than it must. Don't be a *berserker*."

"I must see the king."

The men lifted their weapons, shifting nervously. The space was too small, the stakes too high. This was going to end quickly, one way or the other.

"I am for the king as well," Roger said loudly, stepping forward. All the crossbows swooped his way with a rush of air and clinking metal.

Gilbert looked at him coldly. "Who the hell are you, and what business have you here?"

Roger met his gaze dead on. "I am Roger, the heir d'Endshire, and have come to claim my inheritance and pledge fealty to the king."

The other crossbowmen kept their sights trained on Roger, but Gilbert looked back at Jamie. "What the hell is going on?"

Jamie never shifted his gaze, and he never lowered his blade.

"Jésu, Jamie." Gilbert sounded almost pleading. "There's a roomful of nobles inside. *Rebels.* The king's called them here. I can't just let you . . ." His voice trailed off, as if he realized futility.

"I must see the king."

This was the fourth time he'd repeated the words, and this time, they stepped aside. Jamie strode to the door and for the second time in less than a sennight, he flung open the door to confront a man he'd once betrayed and who now wanted to see him dead.

Surely he needed less monotony in his life.

He twisted the latch and swung the door open. The king looked over. He was standing by the window. Alive. And Eva . . . Eva was at his side.

Jamie felt such great rushing relief he didn't know what to do with it. Their gazes locked for one swift, powerful moment, then Jamie looked to the table in the center of the chamber. Around it sat half a dozen nobles and their agents, staring at him with hard eyes.

"Lost," said a few, nodding in respect, but others kept silent, their fierce gazes pinned on the king's most feared lieutenant.

The king pushed away from the wall and drew his sword. Eva stood rigidly a few paces back, hands clenched at her sides.

Moving slowly, Jamie laid his sword on the floor. The king stilled, his own sword half-drawn from its sheath. He took a quick glance at the doorway, where Roger and Angus and Ry stood, perhaps with crossbow quarrels aimed at their hearts. The king looked back at Jamie.

"I have heard of your treachery."

Jamie straightened. "Cig lies."

"Not Cigogné." The king took a step closer. "Robert fitzWalter. Your *mentor*."

Jamie said nothing.

"Does fitzWalter lie? Tell me it is a lie. Tell me you were not his man when you came to serve me."

Jamie shook his head, jaw tight. "I cannot, my lord. It is true."

John threw his head back with a shout of anger. Men around the table shot to their feet.

"I will make of you a warning to all traitors, Jamie Lost," the king snarled. "Drawn, quartered, hung whilst alive, it hardly touches your crime. *How could you?*"

Jamie said quietly, "Serve you, my lord? 'Twas not easy. But I did it, every day."

John face flooded red. "You betrayed me."

"I betrayed Robert fitzWalter, sire. I did not betray you."

"You pledged *fealty* when you joined my service!" the king shouted. "Then you *turned*."

And that is what John feared the most. It was what he'd spent his life trying to stamp out with his mad, paranoid plotting: that his closest allies and trusted confidants would prove to be untrustworthy, plotting fiends.

Jamie was John's worst nightmare come to life.

"When the moment was at hand, sir, I chose you," Jamie said quietly.

For a moment, John stared at him, breathing heavily. "I have killed men for less than that."

"I know."

Something dark was in Jamie's words. Everyone heard it. It gave the king pause; then he leaned in until his face and bobbed black hair was an inch away from Jamie's.

"I will cut you where you stand, Lost."

"As you did my father?"

John drew back. His eyes narrowed, then widened. His face paled, his jaw dropped. It was as if he saw everything—the surcoat, the ring, the resemblance—in one fell blow. Wonder and incredulity shouldered aside rage and the king took a step back, then another, reeling slowly across the floor.

"Holy God," he whispered. "You are Everoot."

In the subsequent roaring silence, his whisper bounced off the stone walls.

"Christ on the Cross," muttered one of the men around the table. They all got to their feet, shifting in amazement and tension. After twenty years, the missing heir had finally shown himself, and he'd been amongst them all along? It was almost too much to take in. Particularly as some of these men had been here to bid on Everoot themselves.

"How could I not have known?" John's voice was hushed. He searched Jamie's face. "But then, it has been so many years. So many years since your father died."

"Was murdered." Jamie leaned forward, so that only the king could hear his guttural rasp, "You forget, my lord: *I was there.*"

John jerked as if struck.

"Should you require a reminder, I have one."

Jamie drew Peter's drawing from the bag and unfurled it under the king's nose. John froze. The implications lay there, splayed out like dominoes: John had murdered Jamie's father. Jamie had witnessed it. Jamie could bring John's kingship crumbling down with a few spoken words. At this distance, with a dagger thrust.

Fear raced back onto the king's face. Fear made him unstable, like a bridge on sandy shores. Fear made him attack.

Then from Jamie's side came an unexpected thing. "Sire," said a feminine voice, quietly, as though speaking to a panicked animal. "Jamie displayed naught but fealty in Gracious Hill. And before."

It was Chance.

Jamie was so battle-ready, so primed for death, he could not feel anything about the startling development of Chance defending him. Except perhaps the desire to hurt her, for seeing to Father Peter's death. But all that had to wait. Everything had to wait, to see how the king would choose to settle this matter of one of his greatest nobles coming back from the dead.

"I should kill you," the king whispered hoarsely.

Someone stepped forward from behind. "No, you should not." Brian de Lisle strode to stand beside Jamie. His hand was on the hilt of his sword, not yet drawn. "We need Jamie, and we need Everoot. The rightful one."

Brian did not look at Jamie, and Jamie did not look at him. But surely his two greatest lieutenants, standing shoulder to shoulder, one of them now revealed as rightful lord of one of the greatest earldoms in the realm, had a moderating effect on the king's rage.

Perhaps the roomful of witnesses helped as well.

Slowly Jamie drew out the other documents Peter had given him and tossed them on the floor. They rolled a little, back and forth, then lay there, curled at the edges. The king stared.

Silence expanded. It pushed into the corners of the room.

"I can never trust you again, Jamie," John said, looking up.

Jamie crossed his arms and almost smiled. "My lord, I am the only one you *can* trust. I have had your life in my hands a thousand times. If I wanted you dead, dead you would be." From the table came grunts of shock, shifting boots. John's jaw tightened, but he did not interrupt. "That makes me the safest person in the world for you, sire."

The king glanced at the table of nobles, then back to Jamie. "If I invest you with Everoot, you will ally with me in good faith?" he said cautiously.

Jamie uncrossed his arms. "If you give me what I want."

John looked confused. "I am giving you Everoot."

Jamie bent his head slightly, a nod to his king, an admission of authority. But his next words answered any questions about whether Jamie was making requests, or stating terms.

"I am *claiming* Everoot, my lord. I require only one thing in return."

"What?"

"Eva."

John inhaled sharply, then slowly gave an unamused smile. Jamie could see him reckoning with the Exchequer of his heart, accounting the cost and benefits of giving Eva to the heir of Everoot. Great lord wed to a princess bride, striated history of loyalty, deadly. It had to be a difficult decision.

The king looked at Eva. So did Jamie. So did everyone else in the room, and he had to assume they saw what he did: a slim, pale woman with flowing dark hair in a blue tunic, whose eyes never left his as she held out her hand to him.

"You will serve me?" the king said quietly. "Faithfully?"

"I have always served you faithfully, my lord," Jamie said, already striding across the room. He did not ask leave and he did not look back. He reached for Eva, who was walking toward him, and pulled her to him. He was fairly certain people were speaking to him, but it was all dim beneath the brightness of Eva's being here, in his arms. He cupped the back of her head and kissed her. It was only one kiss, but it was thorough, her arms around him, his fingers in her hair. He tipped her face up. "Can you be content with a castle instead of a cottage, Eva?"

"But of course," she whispered. "If you are able to resist the urge to lock me up—"

He drew back. *"Me?"*

"—then yes."

He looped his hands together behind her back and eyed her. "Fine, yes. I will take that."

"But this putting me with one-eyed Scotsmen for my own protection, it will not do. While I am most gratified to see how deeply you care, I am not the sort to appreciate such unexpected protections. I prefer to choose them myself. Such as when I am bathing in a river and do not wish to be accosted by men or otters, this would be helpful protection."

"Ah. The otters. I shall recall that to mind."

"And if knives are being poked at me, I would like to be protected at such times."

"One would assume."

She adopted a stern look. "But, Jamie, you cannot put me in places and walk away. For one, I will leave. For two, I will follow. For three, I do not like someone else deciding on the matter of where my bones are. It is only that for so long, I have made those decisions myself. Do you see?"

He nodded. He thought he heard someone distantly saying his name. "I see."

"I realize this is not to be borne. Yet I ask you to bear it. Will you?"

"I will. For you. Now, for my terms."

She brightened. She hadn't realized they were discussing terms. She settled her hands on his shoulders and nodded encouragingly. "I am prepared."

"One." He brushed the curve of her jaw with his hand. "You will share with me your thoughts."

She affected a sigh. "You drive a difficult bargain, sir, but I accept."

"You will share with me your body."

"This I have been doing since the moment you dragged me into a tavern."

"You will additionally stay away from docks, roosters, alehouses, and anywhere that men are fighting. And you are *never* to handle a rope again."

She pushed up on her toes. "I have scared you," she whispered. "Jamie the fearless knight is frightened."

"Terrified." He ducked his head, brushing his cheek against hers. "I promise, I will get you your cottage one day, Eva."

"This is not a thing to worry on, Jamie."

He entwined their fingers. Someone was most certainly calling to him now. "Everoot does not have a red roof, but you can grow turnips in its soil."

"See, you are so clever, to seduce me with vegetables." She smiled up at him. "A man with a sword who is willing to repair roofs, and a place to grow my turnips. How could I not be very happy?" Her eyes were shimmering at him.

"What more could a princess want?" he murmured as he turned her to face the others, to begin living the life he'd held at bay all these years.

"Only you, Jamie. Nothing but you."

Epilogue

Eva was in the orchard of the outer bailey, rescuing wrinkled apples from the late bite of autumn. It had been a glorious harvest, enough to soften up many of the hard edges of her heart in regard to England.

She was happy. Everoot was a strong home, and Roger was only a half day's ride away at Endshire, wrestling with the tasks of running an English estate. It was quite different from running through French forests, so Ry was often there, helping unwind the mess ten years of absentee lordship had wrought. Angus was sent back and forth between the two estates, muttering that the English were a lot of fools, and he'd be better off in Scotland, but he never went. Eva plied him with a plethora of meat pasties and very good ale, and in the end, he stayed.

"Only 'cause I'm not sure the debt's settled," he'd mutter.

"Oh, it is not," she'd assure him, patting his arm, and this made them both happy. Jamie rolled his eyes.

Everoot was filled with knights and retainers who were turning out to be fiercely loyal and rather too admiring of their rediscovered lord. Eva worried all the adulation would go to

Jamie's head, after all the years of loathing and wariness aimed his way. It hadn't happened yet, but one never knew. Eva kept him in check by engaging him in the most mundane of tasks with great regularity, claiming incapacitation. A child on the way gave her the right. Jamie *doted*.

No one knew her true identity—she and Jamie and the king had agreed to this—and Eva did not wish it any other way. She was Jamie's wife and wanted nothing more.

She gently poured the little apples she'd been holding in her skirts into a basket, and saw Jamie striding toward her, coming from the exercise yard where he trained with his men.

His long legs swung with his confident stride. He threaded his fingers impatiently through his hair, pushing it off his face. His face was scraped as clean as Eva could get it, but she secretly did not mind when they missed a few days. She enjoyed the dangerous way he looked and the gentle way he touched her.

Well, sometimes gentle.

She was fortunate that he was home, for civil war had broken out. The charter hadn't held. Barely three months after it had been signed by all the great barons save Jamie—"It will not hold," he'd said when they'd asked him to sign. "I will serve, but I will not sign"—war had broken out again.

The Nest remained a refuge, though. Couriers and messengers and barons used the Nest as a base for the ongoing negotiations, a place of calm amid the madness.

Jamie reached her side. He took her hand and kissed it absently as he peered into the basket of apples. He picked one up. "Apples?" he asked as he bit into it.

She shook her head. "Berries."

He grinned as apple juice trailed down his chin. She leaned up to kiss it away. That's when they heard the rider, coming up the hill to Everoot.

"The king is dead!" he shouted from dozens of yards away. "King John has died!"

The news spread quickly. King John had died from a surfeit of lamprey eels. Nine-year-old Henry would be crowned in Westminster. William the Marshal had vowed to carry the boy on his shoulders from sea to sea, if need be, to make the country pledge. The most powerful men were forming a regency government to advise the young king. Jamie's presence was called for. They planned to re-issue *Magna Carta*. The rebels would heel. The war would end.

Everyone gathered in the bailey. Villagers, knights, merchants on delivery. It had become the scene of celebration. Jamie gave a quick order to bring drink, in honor of a kingship begun. When the first barrel of ale was rolled out, a great cheer went up. More people poured in. Children were sent scurrying home to gather cups. The revelry reached new heights, with frequent cries of "Long live the king!" and "Long live Everoot!"

"Eels," Jamie mused and looked down at Eva. "Did we not recently send a shipment of eels to the court?"

"Did we?" she replied vaguely, slipping her arm through his. "I cannot recall such a small matter."

She felt him staring at the side of her head. "You recall where the wash buckets are stored, and the anniversary of Cook's mother's passing. Nothing escapes your attention."

She tapped her rounded belly. "It is your son. He muddles my head."

This distracted him. He looked at her belly. "*He* might be a *she.*"

Her smile grew slowly, but it grew so large it hurt her cheekbones. "Yes. She might."

The celebration continued apace. A lute was produced. Children and adults danced. Dogs barked. Someone overturned a bucket and drumbeats were heard. From the ramparts above, cheers drifted down from the soldiers on the walls.

"Your father is dead," Jamie said quietly, looking down.

She nodded, then quickly shook her head. "I suppose that is so, but it does not feel that way. What mourning had to be done was done a long time ago. Now, the war will end, the harrying will cease, the winter will be easier. I feel no grief for these things."

"Have you grief for other things? Such as spending a cold winter in the north of England?"

She waved her hand. "Parts of France are very cold indeed, both the places and the people. I am happy here, with you."

He slung his arm around her shoulder. "And I with you."

She smiled. "My only sadness is that it will be months until the babe is born."

"Aye, well, I did the best I could." He tipped forward and kissed her belly. The sight of their lord kissing the heir-bearing belly of their lady occasioned an outpouring of cheers. He tilted his head to the side and grinned up at her. "They like when I kiss you."

"They have very good sense, these people of yours. They like when you make me have babies."

He laughed and straightened. "As do I."

Eva reached for his hand. "Come, remind me why I want to have many children with you."

"We cannot make any more just yet, Eva."

"I think of it more as practice," she assured him.

He laughed and grabbed for her hand. The slanting rays of autumn evening sunlight shone down on the celebration as Jamie took her inside to practice for the only thing she'd ever wanted: a family of her own, with Jamie at her side.

Author's Note

The Assassination Attempt on
King John's Life and Simon de Montfort

There actually was an assassination plot against King John in 1212. Robert fitzWalter and other baronial rebels really did flee for their lives, and were let back only after John patched things up with the Church, as a condition of lifting the excommunication.

The Simon de Montfort most people know about lived some fifty years after this story is set. He was in conflict with King John's son, Henry III, a struggle which helped, as did the *Magna Carta*, in forming the beginning of parliamentary rule. The de Montfort referenced in *Defiant* is the father. He was acknowledged, even by his contemporaries, to be exactly as Jamie described him: brutal, acquisitive, and a master military man. He led the Crusade against heretical Christian sects in the south of France (which resumed with much bloodshed a few decades later).

I fudged the history a bit and collapsed the time line. It's possible that scions of the disaffected baronial forces did indeed offer the crown to de Montfort in 1210, but the foiled assassination attempt did not occur until 1212, two years later.

I could find no indication of whom the plotters thought to put forward as a candidate this time (even fitzWalter, pompous and a bully, was not so arrogant as to consider himself an acceptable candidate). I thought it plausible to guess they might offer it to the same man as before: Simon de Montfort.

What is more likely is that if they offered it to anyone, it was King Philip of France. Philip was occupied with other campaigns in 1212, but by 1215 and 1216, he'd become quite enchanted with the idea of invading England.

The Character Of Mouldin

There has never been a "Keeper of the Heirs." But wards and heiresses and minor heirs used to be one of the Crown's greatest resources. King John did not generally hold on to them; he sold the rights to them, as did all his contemporaries, as part of the complex and shifting network of patronage, fealty, and cold-hard business dealings.

But there *were* Keepers of many other things: of the (king's) Body; of the Privy Seal; and by far the most important, Keeper of the Wardrobe. Keepers were vital positions in the king's government. I thought to plug what was clearly a hole in the administrative functioning of medieval kings, and give John a Keeper of the Heirs.

On John's Methods of Subduing Opposition: *Starvation and Murder*

John is accused of having murdered his noble nephew, Prince Arthur of Brittany. There is no proof, but a great many people, contemporaries and historians, believe it to be true. John had his father's eruptive Angevin temper, and people had learned to be wary of it.

The idea of starving Mouldin's family was modeled on the events surrounding William de Briouze (de Braose). De Briouze was an up-and-coming household knight who served King John in many roles, one of which was gaoler. Some said de Briouze saw John murder Prince Arthur of Brittany. Apparently, his wife talked about it.

This was unfortunate. Citing unpaid debts to the Crown, King John chased de Briouze across the length of England and all the way to Ireland, then to the Continent, and when he couldn't capture de Briouze, he turned on the wife and son, and held them prisoner and starved them to death.

The War Following the Charter and Jamie's Loyalty to the King

The peace of *Magna Carta* lasted approximately three months. There was double-dealing and a lack of will on both sides from the start, and the war was in full swing by the time the harvest ended. Throughout the winter, the rebels besieged, the king marched, sent his *routiers* harrying the countryside, and soon enough, Philip of France came sailing over. England was ripe for conquest.

But some stayed true to their oaths to the king. W. L. Warren describes it in *King John*. I love his account of the outbreak of war and arrival of the French king, while a few men held to their oaths to the king, when they had every reason to turn on him.

"Up and down the country castles were held for him by determined men who owed everything to John. Engelard de Cigogné hurled defiance at rebel besiegers from the walls of Windsor. Hugh Balliol held out at Barnard Castle against the Scots, and Phillip Oldcoates in Durham. Hubert de Burgh, now justiciar, sat tight in Dover against all that Louis [my note: King Philip of France's son] could do against him from July to October. Odd sparks of loyalty fired local resistance movements: the citizens of the Cinque Ports had been obliged to take an oath to Louis, but their vessels harried French shipping; William of Kensham, operating under the name of 'Willikin of the Weald', organized a band of loyalists that preyed on Frenchmen in Suffolk and Kent. The west midlands were held securely for the king . . . by the vassals of two elder statesmen, William Marshal and Ranulph of Chester. They had served his father, and despite the insults they had suffered, would not desert the son." (W. L. Warren, *King John* [University of California Press, 1961, 1978], pp. 252–53.)

I placed Jamie among these men: loyal when it was inconvenient; steadfast when everything sensible counseled flight; fundamentally bound by deeper ties of oath and fealty when the world was unraveling around them.

In the end, though, it was not loyalty so much that saved England but death. King John died in the spring. His son Henry was crowned ten days later, and ruled for fifty-six years, an impressive run for any monarch. He tried and failed to reclaim any French lands, suffered through another civil war, and (begrudgingly) called the first official Parliament. He was an extravagant king who loved architecture and blew with the winds of varied counsel and perhaps was not suited to being a king. His son was Edward I, a man suited to be a medieval king in no uncertain terms.

On Misselthwaite

Yes, I know. It's my little homage to *The Secret Garden* by Frances Hodgson Burnett. I love Misselthwaite Manor, and I imagine the cold, unfriendly castle as precisely the sort of place Eva could have transformed. The secret garden would have been her refuge. And whether he loved it or not (which he would have), Jamie would have been happy there, too, as long as he had Eva.

Look for

Kris Kennedy's

next sexy medieval romance,

coming from Pocket Books in Spring 2012.